FIRES IN SMITHFIELD

A Novel of Mary Tudor's Reign

This is one of the rare historical novels for which it may justly be claimed that it is as good a novel as it is sound history. The period is 1558, the last year of Mary Tudor's reign, and one of great stress and change which saw the climax of religious fanaticism in England and the break into the Elizabethan age, when modern England begins. The story is that of two citizen-families of London, their clashes, loves and hatreds, and the furious divisions brought about by the cleavage of creeds. It is a story filled with movement and drama; but no less living than the characters are the time and place, the epoch and the town. The book conveys to an extraordinary degree the colour and feeling of life in London in that dramatic year.

FIRES
IN
SMITHFIELD

A Novel of Mary Tudor's Reign

Jack Lindsay

CEDRIC CHIVERS LTD
PORTWAY
BATH

First published 1950
by
The Bodley Head
This edition published
by
Cedric Chivers Ltd
by arrangement with the copyright holder
at the request of
The London & Home Counties Branch
of
The Library Association
1972

SBN 85594 772 1

100184

Printed in Great Britain by
Redwood Press Limited, Trowbridge, Wiltshire
Bound by Cedric Chivers Ltd, Bath

CONTENTS

For my brother Philip
to make amends for
trespassing on his fields

NOTE

THERE ARE MANY reasons why I have chosen this year 1558 for a novel—reasons which should be apparent from the work itself. I should like, in passing, to warn the reader that where he may think he finds anachronisms of phrase he is probably wrong. Terms like *hot gospeller* and *desperate dicks* are common in the period; and I can give a full contemporary reference for every religious, social, or economic statement made by any of my characters and for the terms in which it is made. For instance, Daunce's religious attitude (VII, iii) may seem airily modern: but it will be found in Foxe's *Acts and Monuments* (edited by J. Pratt, VIII, 108) in the mouth of a martyr of the year 1556. (Daunce himself, like practically everyone except the members of my two families, is an historical person.)

I have interspersed my narrative with short passages (*printed in italics*) which are taken directly from Foxe or other narratives of the time. I felt that these would serve as a kind of choric voice, broadening the individual perspective and giving a sense of the historical pressures environing my people—until at last those pressures (I trust) are fully absorbed by the people and the story's perspective itself becomes that of history in its fullness.

These passages can be found as follows (F: Foxe's *Acts* VIII, and N: *Narratives of the Days of the Reformation*, edited by J. G. Nichols, 1848):

II, ii: F 450. v: F 497. viii: F 730.

III, i: *Machyn's Diary*, 59. iv: N 40. ix: N 29. xii: F 415. xv: 408.

IV, ii: F 220. vi: F 537. viii: F 217. xix: F 429.

The year is 1558.

THE TWO FAMILIES

OLD FABYAN RIGELEY
WILLIAM, his eldest son, a Merchant Taylor
NEST, William's wife
MERRIC, their elder son (who has been apprentice of Hawes)
STEPHEN, their second son (apprenticed to his uncle Hugh)
AGNES, their daughter
 CHRISTOPHER JONES, brother of Nest
 SANCHIA COYNE, servant
 YBEL ARMSTRONG, apprentice
 GLADUS SYNCLER, cook
 EDGAR LUNKS, servant of Old Fabyan
HUGH RIGELEY, second son of Fabyan, Merchant Taylor
MARY, his daughter
 ROSBEL, servant
 JON FLOYD, apprentice
BLAISE RIGELEY, third son of Fabyan, Clerk of Exchequer
DOUSABEL, his wife
 TABITHA PLOTTE, servant

GREGORY HAWES, Clothworker
GERTRUDE HEYGATE, his sister-in-law
RAFE HEYGATE, scholar, his brother-in-law
MARTIN, Hawe's son
JACINT, his daughter
MRS. PERNEL WICKE, a widow, whom Hawes marries
 TACE KEMPE, servant
 LETTICE, servant

CHAPTER ONE

Turn of Winter

I

ONLY WILLIAM RIGELEY heard the knocking on the door. He looked intently round at the others. Blaise caught the look and returned one of his sharp screwed-up grimaces. William cleared his throat. 'I'm going down to the cellar,' he said in even tones to his other brother Hugh, and Hugh nodded without looking up. Mistress Nest went on with her discourse, laying down an opinion with a slight Welsh lilt of defiance in her voice, 'I can only call such a one, in my vain judgment, as wise as Saunders' calf that ran nine miles to suck a bull.' No one contradicted her, and William went quickly and quietly to the door. As he turned to pass through, he sent a half-glance over the company. Most of all he looked to see if Blaise was still watching him with that tense wrinkling of the nose, that sidelong and upward glinting out of hunched shoulders. But he saw everyone except Blaise. Hugh sitting with closed eyes before the hearth of sturdily burning oakwood and seacoal; and Stephen behind him, rubbing his long chin, not so much like William's own son as Hugh's ungainly reflection in water. Nest still caught up in one of her babble-moments, with her nose whetted on the whirl of her angry words and her dark eyes catching the sparks thrown up; her right hand disconsolately turning in the air—though she was speaking of nothing more than a kitchen-receipt. 'So let them seethe together by the space of two hours, to gain an excellent colour and consistency without any superfluous tartness or the like.' And nearer the mantel, with slanted eyes veiled in the shadow of her hair, Agnes their daughter, as high-cheeked as

11

her mother but full of mouth, her body drawn up in a silence, with narrow shoulder-bones; while, behind her, in the corner, sat her grandfather Fabyan, mercifully dozing in his scarlet cap. And then Blaise on the edge, unglimpsed except for the bony hands knotted on the table beside the crust of venison as the whip of the light flickered.

The shadows on the walls rose up in a gust of reddening fire-glow, swirled as though about to leap and come down over the people in the room; and then the door closed. He paused in the sudden gloom, then went down the stairs, quick and quiet for all his bulk.

'Edgar,' he said, halting by the candle in the wall-niche. A slight form emerged from the darkness of the cellar-head. At that moment the knock came again, clear but not over-loud. 'Go to the door. I'll see to the malmsey.'

'I was going, master.'

'Never answer the door after dusk without being told,' said William with impatient lowered voice. 'But go now, at once.' He stood back into the shadow.

The boy Edgar went to the door and drew the bolt, 'Who is there?' he asked in a voice which quavered, not out of fear, but because it always got out of control the moment he grew aware of it. He opened the door an inch.

'Christopher Jones, your master's kinsman.'

The panted whisper, like an urgent and rusty echo of Nest's voice from the room above, reached William's ears, and he stepped forward. 'Let him in.'

Edgar unslipped the chain and opened the door wide enough for a tall lean man to push through. 'You're a good boy, a very good boy,' said Jones, patting Edgar on his tousled head, and then stood leaning against the wall as he unknotted the cloak at his throat. 'My dear and notable brother, so you are there too. Ah, a wet night, a very wet night it is.' He was trying to hide his lack of breath; he coughed. 'Ah, yes, a bad night indeed.' His words ended in a wheeze, and his chest rose and fell as he coughed, bending forward and trying to stifle the noise. His tongue stuck out and he pressed his shoulders up under his ears.

'Take the wine upstairs, Edgar,' said William, 'and say only that I am looking for some claret.'

'Ah, yes, claret, claret . . .', said Jones, and twisted up in an effort to smother another coughing-fit.

William waited till Edgar had fetched the tray of jugs from the cellarhead and gone up the stairs out of earshot; then he turned and looked hard at Jones. Jones had almost regained his breath. He managed to get his cloak undone, and, to win time, squeezed some of the water out of the cheap trimming of shagg-plush. Then he hung the cloak on a peg, dashed the rain from his cap, and passed a hand over his close-cropt head. His small eyes glittered darkly, and raindrops ran down his pointed beard.

'I thought you were in Hull.'

'Hell, Hull, and Halifax,' replied Jones with a grin that pulled up one side of his face. 'There are worse places, brother, worse places by far. Now I am in London.'

'A worse place for some persons.'

'For those who lack money.' Jones winked. 'Eh, we are not all of us such secure citizens as Master William Rigeley.'

William scrutinised his face. 'You did not come in the stealth of night at the turn of winter to tell me such a matter.'

'No.' Jones put a hand up to his throat as if the knot of string were still there, pressing in against his gullet. 'You have company,' he pointed up the stairs, 'worthy of your best wine.'

'No, my brothers.'

'Both Hugh and Blaise?'

'Both of them.'

There came a pause, and then Jones said, with a quick tug at the tip of his nose, 'I should rather see you alone.'

Without a word William took the candlestick from the niche, opened a door at the side, and led the way into his counting room. Then he turned abruptly and confronted Jones. 'What do you want? Why have you come at such an hour and in such a way?' He lifted the candle to throw its yellow light full on Jones's unblinking face. 'I have no money for your borrowing until you repay me what you owe.'

'I trust that my dear good sister Nest is well favoured in health,' said Jones, smiling evasively and staring straight at William, raising his left eyebrow. 'She is given to rheumatic pains in the dark of the year.'

'She is well, thank the Lord,' said William grudgingly.

'Not even a rheum?' insisted Jones. 'That is indeed most unusual. She is much given to wintry rheums, and this house of yours has a special dampness. You have told me yourself that you think there must be a spring under the cellar. I have often feared for her health.'

'The house is no damper than others,' replied William, yielding at last before Jones's hard stare. He put the candle down on the table and indicated a high stool. 'But to what purpose is all this? For two years you have not concerned yourself with the health of your sister nor the debts you owe to her husband.'

'I have been busy merchandising at Hull,' said Jones with a pert tilt of his head. 'Had it turned out as I hoped, it would have gone to her profit and thereby yours as well, brother.'

William frowned slightly as if in repudiation of the kinship. 'I need not press you with close questions. You have come with no pockets of gold to empty into her lap, as I can see. You have come instead to ask something of me; and before you ask, I know that I can guess at my own answer.'

'I want no money this time.'

William was still standing, swaying a little to and fro with bent head and lips compressed in deliberation. His square fleshy face was half in shadow. 'Why then have you come?' he asked at length.

'I might say I came to join the others of our family at a holiday supper, but you would not believe me, and indeed I did not know of their meeting.'

'You came running to the door, yet knocked without clamour.'

'I thought I saw thievish eyes in the doorway darkness of the tall house at the corner. Therefore I hurried down the street.'

'Well, what have you come for?' William again asked reluctantly.

Jones twirled his thin pointed beard and looked at his brother-in-law with a wry smile, lifting his left eyebrow. 'Your poor opinion of me, which I do not wholly deserve, makes it difficult for me to find a starting-point.' Then, as he got no reply, he went on. 'It is a matter in which you stand to make manifold gains on a small outlay.' William smiled scornfully, and Jones went hastily on. 'Indeed I desire no advances of money. I want only your roof and your advice for a few days.'

'You want to hide.' William's face was heavy and morose as he bit at his underlip. 'You were running from more than gutter-thieves or a harlot-rustle of the night. Tell me what you were running from, Master Jones, and I shall answer your request.'

Jones wriggled a moment on his stool and cracked his finger-joints. 'It is a long story, brother,' he said at last, 'but I have no wish to withold a jot of it from you. I desire only time and a convenient place to unmask the whole matter. Indeed I must tell you all if I am to gain your aid as I hope and pray.'

'Inform me of your purpose,' said William sternly, 'or I'll turn you out into the street at once. I shelter no felon at the risk of my own neck, most of all when his only claim on me is that he has cheated me once too often.'

'My purposes are honourable and golden.' Jones drew his legs up and twined them round the legs of the stool. 'For although I have wealth almost within my grasp, I seek it to relieve your needs more than my own.'

'What are these needs of mine?' William harshly interrupted.

'Nothing is muttered abroad,' said Jones with a grin. 'Have no fear, brother. I have my secret birds to sing me a tune in such matters.'

'God's blood!' shouted William, with darkly-flushing face, 'if I get my hands on those birds of yours, I'll wring their villainous necks, even though I pluck them out of my own bosom.'

'Now then,' said Jones in assured soothing tones, 'if you suspect my poor Nest, you are a blind man blundering in a night of storms. She is as innocent of such blabbery as a babe born last Tuesday. Indeed I have exchanged no words with her since I left London with your hasty curse on my head. But all this is far from the point of our discourse. I shall be brief, I promise you. Listen. I have the means whereby to lay my hands on a weight of treasure.'

'So say all thieves and enviers.'

'No, but this is different, for there is no trespass of the law in it, and no idle coveting. Only a skill of caution is required, since there are always many liars who lay claims unregulated

by justice.' Then, seeing that William was about to say something heated, he went hurriedly on. 'It is not a matter in which
outlay is needed. It is no trading venture, it is no bargain with
a false bottom, neither is it a throw at hazard. Simply, it lies
thus. There is gold in a chest, and I know where it waits—'

They both turned with set faces and looked at the door,
where Blaise was standing. For a moment nothing was said.
Then, with a quivering smirk, Blaise threw out his hands and
spoke.

'Pardon me if I intrude on a privy matter. I did not know
that Master Christopher Jones was here. I last heard of you,
Master Jones, from a clothier of Halifax.' He touched his
brow. 'But I think you had trouble there with a small matter
of cognisances.'

Jones had lost the air of assurance he gradually built up
during his conversation with William. He sat slumped on the
stool, fingering his beard. William took charge. He thrust out
his petulant lowerlip. 'Come on in, Blaise, since you are here.'

'We feared you had set your face under the claret-bung and
fallen into a sleep of Bacchus, that Thracian god,' said Blaise,
slipping eagerly in. He sat down in the leather-cushioned chair
by the chest, and remarked negligently, 'Gold, who speaks
of gold?'

Jones gave William a quick glance, then answered, 'I spoke
of it, in a way of speaking, as one who declares that he has
found a spring of life in a desert place or has come upon
unexpected succour in the midst of a difficult darkness. By
way of rhetoric, and in a figure of similitudes, gold representing the quintessential spirit or paradisiac milk.'

Blaise smiled and wrinkled up his nose. 'And in what
lurking-hole of the earth is this allegoric chest of yours
buried?'

William turned away, passing his hand over his face, and
trimmed the candle of its smut. When he straightened his
back again, he said in a low voice, 'Tell him what you told me.'

'But so far I have told you nothing,' said Jones, 'except that
I have a chance of digging up some minted gold from the
womb of our common mother the earth.'

'Have you been scrying?' asked Blaise. 'Or have you dug
up a dead man in a midnight churchyard?'

'Tell us all or nothing,' said William, 'and then we shall decide together whether we lend you our countenance.'

'It is an old matter,' said Jones, sitting back with his hands claspt round his left knee. 'Going back to the days when I worked as Commissioner in the breaking-up of the Abbeys. Going back, in truth, to a certain Friday in October, as I well remember, being a cold bright day when I rode with Dr. Layton to make an inventory at Folkestone, and thereafter to Langden. Where, descending from my horse, I was despatched with seven others to circumvent the Abbey and surely to keep all backdoors and starting-holes. I myself came to the abbot's lodge that joined upon fields and woods like a very coney-clapper full of vents, and I stood there a good space knocking. But nothing answered except a little dog that yelped fiercely from behind the lockt door. Then I found a poleaxe standing beside the pillar, and with it I dashed the abbot's door in pieces without delay. So I set the man with me to keep that door while I ran with the poleaxe round the house, having in thought that the abbot was a dangerous desperate man. But for conclusion his whore, alias his gentlewoman, came with slapping slippers and girded skirts towards her bolthole, and I caught her by the arm till she screeched.'

'What story is this?' asked William, 'and how does it concern our present case?'

'Listen,' said Jones. 'I sent her to Dover for the Mayor to clap in a cage, and that is truly the end of her, except for a paper I found thrust into her fat bosom among the laces, which I showed to no one. For on it were listed many things that the abbot never surrendered to the King, and I meant to make a private examination of him when he came out of Christchurch prison. But I had notice of the wrong day, and he slipped off by mischance to Southampton, whence he sailed to France on a day windy beyond belief. And though I digged in many places according to the brief and broken words on the paper, I found nothing except the tunnels of moles and the roots of trees. Yet I was assured in my heart that the treasure existed and had been set aside by the crafty abbot to his own lewd enrichment or the King's deception.'

'Why did you fail to seek out his harlot for further news?' asked Blaise, twitching his nose.

Jones nodded approvingly, 'No sooner did I lose the abbot than I sought his Jezebel. But she was dead of jailfever and lay stinking in the charnel-house, which I proved true with my own eyes and nose. So there was no further help in her fatted body.'

'And how is it that this ancient story has sent you panting with a panic fear on to my doorstep this night of nights?' asked William.

'Because I met the abbot in Southwark and had words with him. Angry words, as you may well guess.' Jones dropped his jaw in a hangdog leer. The candle fluttered and sent the shadows of the three men bobbing at the low plastered ceiling. A faint scratching was heard, and Jones gave a long, shuddering sigh, which was ended by a rap on the door.

'Who is there?' cried William.

The door opened and Hugh looked mildly in. 'Your wife wished to know why you lingered so long, Will.' He blinked round. 'Who is that? Ah, Kit Jones . . . Shall I tell Nest that you are here?'

'Come in and close the door,' said William. He stared round at the others. 'So be it then. We shall have a family council and consider the proposition in all its merits. Hugh, Master Jones tells us that he has wooed a noisy abbot into confessing where a hidden abbey-treasure lies. He makes us this offer: that in return for a share in his ghostly treasure he will accept present money from our purses.'

'I have asked no one for money yet.' Jones rose and stood back against the wall. 'Neither did I say that I had wooed an abbot for such informations. Rather, I first knocked him to the ground with a ragged stone and then set a dagger to his eyes.'

'Say that you had him under your dagger,' argued Blaise. 'Why should he not tell you lies to save his life?'

'I think not. For he swore on the cross and gave me a paper out of his wallet. He was too afraid to deceive me.'

'You did wrong,' said Hugh quietly.

'I hold such sodomitical devils to lie beyond the laws of God or man,' said Jones, twisting his face up on one side.

'Where then is the gold?'

Jones tapped his brow. 'I shall tell you in due time.'

'And the paper?'

'I held it so close against the pommel of my dagger that I pressed it into a sweaty rag. But not before I had learned its words beyond forgetting. Still, even if I had it, I should show it only to those who had sworn to help me.'

'The abbot will run bellowing to the sheriffs,' said William, 'and will remove his treasure to another place. That is, if there be any abbot and any treasure, which I am far from thinking.'

Jones hunched up his shoulders. 'He has gone into the river with bloody teeth and will say nothing more to man or devil.'

'Till the day of judgment,' said Hugh quietly.

'Then I shall have matter to fling back in his filthy face,' retorted Jones, with a violent gesture.

'No man shall judge his own case,' said Hugh.

There was a pause, in which the various thoughts of the men sounded like a dry scrabbling of mice behind the printed leatherwork on the wall. Then William asked, 'What then?'

'Give me shelter,' said Jones, 'till I make sure that no man raises a hue-and-cry against me. And then your aid in procuring the treasure from its hole.'

'Grant for the moment that we assent,' said Blaise. 'How then are we to share that which we gain?'

'I ask a half for myself. The other half you may divide among yourselves as seems best. Those are generous terms, which I should give only to kinsmen.' He licked his lips. 'Seeing that I have waited so long and taken so much upon my soul in this matter.'

'I want nothing of it,' said Hugh, and turned to go.

Jones slipped between him and the door. 'Swear that you will betray nothing of what you have heard,' he said, lifting up a crucifix that hung on a thread round his neck.

'I shall tell no one,' said Hugh calmly, 'but I will swear no mummeries.' He went out.

Jones looked at William, who said, 'He will tell no one. But what is your answer, Blaise?' His voice weakened for a moment, and he put his hand over his mouth, forcing a cough.

Blaise was staring at Jones with narrowed brows and plucking at his heavy underlip. 'Grant for a moment that an abbot has been killed. His body will be found . . .'

'It will wash down to the sea or sink in the marshes,' said Jones persuasively. 'It will be eaten of fishes and eels. It will rot in the mud. Why was the villain delivered up into my hands, unless I was meant to gain my long-witheld profit?'

'All things are possible,' said Blaise. 'Even that you are telling us the truth.' He and William exchanged a long glance.

'You may stay here for a while,' said William to Jones. 'At least till we sort this matter further. But in order that a fair seeming may be put on your lodgement, I think you had better feign a sickness or at least some such misadventure as a broken ankle.'

'I shall break it on your stairs after the morrow's breakfast,' said Jones, 'and my loving sister Nest shall care for me till I am a whole man again.'

'You agree?' said William to Blaise. 'I take this course only if you are of a single mind with me in it.'

'Let him stay,' said Blaise, 'but it would be best if you were to throw him down the stairs with your own hands and in very truth break his ankle or ribs.'

'Mainly I rejoice in this matter,' said Jones, throwing his head back, 'because it gives me a chance to make you both think more kindly of my intentions. I feel that God has put this business in my hands for such an end, to establish our family on weighty foundations and to wipe off many imputations from my character.'

'I am sorry that Hugh is not here to say Amen,' said Blaise, smirking. 'Let us now go up to the others and prevent their conjectures. Brother Christopher, I still think you should have lodged with the abbot's ladybird in her Dover prison till she had vomited out her full soul of wickedness into your lap.'

'I was young then,' Jones closed one eye and pursed his lips. 'I was ignorant in deceptions and easily confused.' He drew aside to let Blaise pass, and the eyelid of his closed eye began to tremble. But Blaise took him by the arm and pushed him out first. 'Hasten on upstairs to your sister, or she will hear of your presence from Hugh.' Then, hanging back, he muttered aside to William, 'This is a deep matter. Deeper even than it sounds, I dare wager.'

'Do you wish to withdraw?' said William, listening for Jones's steps on the stairs.

'I think not. At least not before I sift it further.'

They went out. Jones had paused halfway up the stairs. 'It is a windy and foul night,' he said.

II

The edges of the greasy woollen curtain over the tavern-window kept lifting with the draught. The crab-apple in the heated beer knocked against the tip of Merric Rigeley's nose as he drank, and the fumes tickled his nostrils. 'A thrice damnable night,' he remarked condescendingly to his father's apprentice Ybel. Then, as Ybel stared stupidly back at him without a word, he grew annoyed. 'Tell me, is it, or isn't it?'

'What?' asked Ybel gloomily, and scratched his untameable sandy hair.

'The night.'

'Ah, yes, the night,' said Ybel, and licked his crackt lips. Then he yawned, drawing down the skin of his short nosetip till it shone in the stinking lamplight. The many freckles of his face suddenly stood out. Someone was singing in a rumbling ale-voice:

Bring us in no bacon for that is passing fat,
But bring us in good ale, and give us enough of that,
And bring us in good ale.

But Merric had forgotten. 'I still don't know what to do,' he said, and took another drink. 'Say what you like, Ybel, my father doesn't treat me fairly. Why won't he put down the money to give me a good start as a master?' He kicked at the decaying rushes and herbs on the floor, where muddy boots had trampled-in the spittle and slops of beer. 'Some day I'll make him regret it.'

Ybel took the apple out of his leathern jack and began munching. 'He's paid the fee of your freedom, and that's more than anyone will do for me. What's the use of serving out my full turn when I'll never be able to afford ten shillings to become free of the craft? But I don't care. Nowadays apprentices trade without becoming masters.'

'In a small way,' grumbled Merric, 'with the fear of the law always before their eyes. That might suit you, but not me.' He stared at Ybel, and for a moment forgot his own angers. 'That uncle of yours still refuses to help you. I'll ask father to try him again.'

'I wouldn't do that,' said Ybel, and was about to say something more. But he put his hand over his mouth and pretended to wipe it. 'Ah, what clapper-tongues we've all got, ringing peals of scandal when once there's liquor to pull the ropes.'

'What's that you're saying?' demanded Merric. 'I offered you my help, and you go hinting things. I'm sorry I asked you out for a drink tonight. One more foul word from you, and I'll send you home squealing with your tail between your legs.'

'I didn't mean it,' said Ybel so disconsolately that Merric became complaisant again.

'After all, my father has treated you better than you deserve, and I won't have anything said to his discredit, do you hear? Maybe I speak a grudging word now and then, but I don't do it often, and even if I did I've got the right to do it. He's my own father, isn't he? Maybe there's times when he forgets it himself, and then I've got to stick up for myself or I'd soon be laid on my back in the ditch. But he doesn't do it often, and even if he did it's between him and me, and I can say what's needed in my own defence. The fact is, he's got a burden on his shoulders, enough to break anyone else, but it won't break him, you see. Anyhow, what's it all got to do with you? He does his duty and never tries to set you working on holidays. If I find you maligning him, I'll make you swallow your words on your knees.'

The three men arguing beside them burst into high furious words, and one struck another in the chest. The stricken man staggered against Merric, who turned and gave him a violent shove in the opposite direction. Ybel drew away, afraid that the quarellers would now turn on Merric; but luckily they were too engrossed in their own dispute. 'A slice of salt butter!' the tall man was yelling, as he tried to pull the second man's doublet up over his head. 'Do you still say so, you Shoreditch starveling?' The third man was looking round for something to use as a weapon; but by this time the rest of the drinkers had gathered round, and he couldn't break through to snatch up a bottle or chair. Then the tall man fell

over on top of the man from Shoreditch, and they both lay
helpless. The third, giving up the weapon-search, leant over
them and collapsed in turn. The onlookers shouted in derision,
and parted to let the tapster drag the sodden fighters over
towards the door. 'Call yourselves men!" contemptuously
remarked the broadfaced serving-girl, who had come in with
a pan of fuel for the charcoal-brazier by the chimneypiece.
'In the place I come from, they give the likes of you away
with a bushel of sprats in the late market.'

'What was I saying?' grumbled Merric to Ybel. 'It doesn't
matter. Don't look so miserable. What's on your mind? I
didn't bring you out to mope all night. I asked you for
company.'

'I'm not miserable,' mumbled Ybel with tremulous underlip. 'I . . .' He put the empty jack to his lips and tilted it up
to find if a trickle remained.

'Sanchia cruel to you again?' jeered Merric.

'She's never anything else,' said Ybel indignantly.

'You mustn't let women treat you like that. Wait for her in
a dark corner, or turn your back and find someone else, making
sure she hears all about it. She's an obstinate flighty thing,
Sanchia is. I've a good mind to teach her a lesson myself.'

'O no, please,' begged Ybel. 'I'm not complaining because
she sets a high price on her flesh. Only . . .'

'That's the way with us all. We want women to be stiff
virgins to all other men, but the kindest of whores to ourselves. And it doesn't work out that way. Fie, man, creep upon
her one night while Gladus is still at her kitchen chores, and
slip under the sheet with your green-eyed maiden. She won't
scream louder than an angry mouse.'

'I want her in honourable sort,' protested Ybel.

'No wonder she laughs in your face,' said Merric with a jeer.
Then he thought he saw a glint of mockery in Ybel's eyes.
'Are you throwing my own words back in my face? I tell you
that I don't care any longer for that bitch Jacint. I told her so.
I wrote her a long letter—though, to tell truth, I tore it up
because I knew she'd show it to her friends and they'd laugh
together over it, pretending that I was hurt because I said
what I thought of her. Still, letter or no letter, I put her in
her place. She thought she could play about with me at her

will, and I let her know that she'd been mistaken. That's the
very thing I was telling you to do. Stand up for yourself. If
you don't look out, I'll take this Sanchia of yours myself, to
prove what I say.'

'O please, don't,' cried Ybel, obviously certain that she
couldn't resist such a suitor.

Merric was mollified. 'Be careful then. As a matter of fact,
I don't want her, but I won't be laughed at.'

'I wasn't laughing at you,' gasped Ybel, 'I swear it by Saint
George and the Holy Virgin. I couldn't.'

'Right. Then let's go to the Three Cranes. I can't bear this
place any longer. I came out to enjoy myself. If you want to
be wretched, go home and say your prayers to Sanchia's
placket.'

They went out into the brisk air. Here and there, creaking
lanterns, hung out by householders from windows or over
doors, guttered with their dim lights through panes of horn,
Merric rubbed his hands together and looked up at the crackling stars. 'I pity the street wenches on a night like this. It'd
be a charity to take one—' Noticing Ybel's face, he roared
with laughter. 'And give her a drink, I meant. What are you
frightened of?'

'Nothing.' Ybel gulped. 'But after what happened to Rob
Perkins I don't want to be tempted.'

'Not by Sanchia?'

'That's different.'

'Don't be so sure.' Merric blew on his hands. They skirted
a heap of rubbish and almost fell into a foot-deep hole in the
paving. Round the corner came the watch, straggling with
bills and lanterns. 'Where have you been so late?' shouted one
of the watchmen.

The lads dodged off down a side street, and Ybel tripped
over a post which was propping a house up. When he caught
up with Merric, they halted by a stall against which a woman
was sitting on a block of wood. Ybel plucked at Merric's
sleeve, but Merric, to frighten him, called out, 'Hullo,
sweeting, want a drink?' The woman didn't answer. Merric,
driven to complete his gesture by Ybel's timid sleeve-plucking,
went over and took her by the shoulder. 'Wake up.' She fell
heavily off the block, and her cloak came open, showing a

swaddled baby. She lay rigid on the ground, bent still in her sitting posture. 'Come on, you fool,' cried Merric, and they ran on.

'Was she dead?' asked Ybel as they paused for a moment before the tavern door.

'Go back and ask her,' said Merric.

As soon as they entered, Ybel saw Merric frown and turn aside. Cautiously he looked across the room to see what had annoyed him. There stood Martin Hawes, Jacint's brother, a big fellow with a square cleft chin you couldn't mistake. Merric was moving back to the door; but when he caught Ybel's eye on Martin, he changed his mind and moved into the room again.

'Yes, it's Martin,' he said, 'and I'm not going to let him tell Jacint he drove me out of a house where I've as much right as he has.' He called to the bald tapster. 'Two pints of spiced ale!' But Martin didn't hear; he was talking earnestly to a small fellow with a gnawed-off ear. 'I'll pay,' said Merric to Ybel. 'I'm not going to let that stinkard say we were drinking small-beer out of a gill-stroup.' They stood there waiting, Ybel dejected and Merric with a defiant pout, watching Martin with sidelong glances. 'Because he was three years older, he tried to knuckle me down all the while I was apprentice to his father—though I will say it for Gregory Hawes, that when he found out his son's tricks, he took a hand in the game. He's a just man, even if he's got a face like a wormeaten lump of figwood. As for Martin, he's inherited his father's face but not his righteousness.'

At that moment the tapster came back with jugs and mug on a tray, and Martin, looking round, saw Merric staring at him and saying something. He turned away, turned back, scowled, and taking the small man by the arm came over. 'Did you stare at me, jackanapes?' he shouted.

'Yes,' said Merric, 'but it's all your own fault.'

'How's that?'

'Every time I see you, I'm surprised you're even uglier than I remembered.'

The small man sniggered, and Martin pushed him aside. 'You are still as black in your bile,' he said to Merric in his deep voice, 'and as little suited for honest communications.'

Then with a sudden lunge he clasped Merric round, pinioning his arms, and with a wrench lifted him off his feet. 'There's only one place for such as you. Out in the noisome street.' He swung Merric over towards the door.

'Let me go,' yelled Merric, 'let me go and I'll tear your ears off.' But he couldn't break Martin's grip.

Ybel moved away. The small man drew a dagger from a sheath at the back of his belt, and Ybel ran out. Behind him he heard the curses and raucous breathing of Martin and Merric, then a crash as Merric was pushed through the door and slid to a fall on the spiky ground. 'Farewell, frost!' Martin shouted and closed the door. Ybel bent over his friend.

'Are you dead? Please don't die, Merric . . . I'll kill him if you do.'

Merric grunted and sat up, fighting weakly for breath. 'I'll carve his eyes for crows . . . Help me up . . .' After a while Ybel managed to set him on his feet. 'He took me by surprise . . . off my guard . . . the skulker . . . I'd have beaten him in fair fight.'

'Of course you would,' said Ybel anxiously.

'I'd have beaten him in fair fight,' Merric repeated, muttering and throwing his hair back out of his eyes. 'O . . .' But he showed no sign of going back into the tavern. Instead, he looked round for a missile, and at last found a loose cobble as big as a goose's egg. He threw it against the door and ran heavily off, groaning. 'He put his knee into my belly, the cheat. But I'll get my own back. If ever I get the chance, I'll tread that sister of his. She's as bad as he is. To think I could have done it once, when by a mistake we were left alone in the house and nobody came back till after evensong. But she smiled at me and stroked my face, and in the end I went out so that nothing might mar her reputation.'

'Let's go home,' suggested Ybel hopefully.

But Merric didn't hear. He went on abusing the Hawes family, and this time he included Gregory Hawes in the attack. 'A vain and violent man who meddles with his servant Tace and thereby sets a bad example of appetite to the whole household. I was a fool to let his Jacint go free when we sat alone for a whole afternoon. And you're a fool too, Ybel, whining at a wench's bodice-strings. Admit it.'

'Yes, yes,' said Ybel, 'I promise not to do it again. Let's go home.'

'I'll have my revenge on the nest of serpents . . .'

Then as they turned the corner they came on the Lord of Misrule and his rout. The Lord was strutting gorgeously along with a peacock's feather in his cap and a gilt stick in his hand, from which dangled a painted wooden crown and a hare's tail. Before him went a drunken trumpeter who made spluttering and unruly blasts, while a rawboned fellow with ruddled cheeks was dressed in a woman's smock and rode astride an ass, giving dainty screeches. The fat man with chitterlings hanging from his split coat went beside an antic death, who juggled with a pair of skulls; and a wildman, wound with holly-leaves, spoke in unknown tongues and ate a monstrous piece of bacon. After them, and round them, with staggering feet and bawdy songs came the generality of the misruled, lugging flagons and wine-tankards, and then a horse piled with three drunkards who snored. Merric and Ybel stood on a doorstep to watch the revel by. But the Lord saw them and cried out.

'Strike up the drums! Here are fresh recruits for my flock of follies, or I don't know the colours of a good fellow's nose. Join with us, pretty boys, and I promise you a bad end in all jolly ways and a stinkified memory. Bind them with a badge of bawdery and give them a bladder of bilberries. Come on, good friends, for we go to attack the Compter and liberate our liege servants therein lying through the contention of cruel constables.'

The revellers surrounded the pair on the doorstep, leaping and laughing. A man with a beaked nose jumped on to the rump of the ass and made crowing noises. The Bessy screeched, 'This courageous cockerel has laid an illicit egg on the backside of my reputation. Addle his wits with a club.' So the wildman in his doublet of leaves came roaring over with a pole and knocked the crower from the ass, after which the Bessy clasped him round the neck, declaring him boisterously the Bird of her Bush. But the Giant came up from the rear, with his great wooden sword painted in red and yellow, and cried that killing came before copulation, therefore let the Dungeon be devastated and the tyrants trodden underfoot.

Then another, who brandished bones, said that it would be better work to slit the throats of a few Spaniards; and many agreed. And so the revel moved on down the street, arguing whether it was a more politic matter to attack the jail or the Spaniards; and Merric and Ybel went with a score of belching hellboys who sang the song of Jolly Jenkin, above the rattling of the drums and the squealing of the fifes. But as they neared the Compter, the cry against the Spaniards grew louder, and the Lord of Misrule climbed into a scaffolding to speak.

'We go through a sea of sack,' he cried, 'into the Golden Age. To wit, the Age where Gold was unknown except in the tresses of a lady and the ears of the corn. And this we assert is our heritage made indisputable by woodcock pie and Rhenish wine—'

But now a posse of constables, watchmen, and bailiffs broke out of a side alley and scattered the host. They overthrew the Giant on his stilts and arrested Death in the name of the Queen. The Bessy raised up her skirts and swore that she was ready for all of them, but a constable pushed her in the belly with his staff and the ass ran away. The Lord of Misrule was dragged down by his heels from the scaffolding.

Merric and Ybel, being among the most sober, had no difficulty in getting off the way they had come. 'Let's go home,' sobbed Ybel as they ran.

III

When Nest saw her brother come up into the solar, she threw her hands in the air and asked him if he had brought her the tinsel scarf he had promised when he went off to Hull. 'But that was two years ago,' he said.

'Two years too late then,' she answered. 'All the more reason for you to bring it now. Nevertheless I forgive you.' And she gave him a sounding kiss.

Old Fabyan woke up at last, looked testily round, and exclaimed, 'What, what, that coystrel scum is back again. String him up,' and closed his eyes with a long sigh.

Stephen rose and stood back, behind the chair of his uncle Hugh, smiling with his rueful shy smile; and Hugh leaned his

hand on his chin, regarding the fire. Agnes gave a slant look
at the newcomer, and then returned to her book.

'You shall have a thousand scarves of tinsel and shot silk
before the year is out,' Jones was saying to his sister, 'or call
me the worst liar out of Monmouthshire.'

'Ah, but I call you that already,' she said, and he kissed her
again. Then he turned and took Agnes by the chin, forcing her
to look up and remarking on her sweet likeness to her mother.

'What household book is this?' he asked, and took the book
up, finding it an Englished version of Erasmus's *Apophthegms*.
'Give it to the old man,' he said, 'and let him learn wisdom.'

Then old Fabyan woke again, and cried out, 'Is that fellow
still here? Let him be sent about his business.' And closed his
eyes again.

So Jones affably complimented Agnes a second time on her
likeness to her mother; and Agnes bade him keep his honey-
words for those who owned a sweet tooth. Then he tried to
get from her another courtesy-kiss, but she kept her face away
and Nest remarked that he had come back no better than he
went, yet since we were all God's creatures there was hope
of reformation for even the most wayward. And, as William
and Blaise came in, she called them to witness how peaked and
worn her Kit had become. 'Some folk never know where their
advantage lies,' she added, 'and they go seeking a treasure in
foreign lands when it waits under their doorstep.' Hugh gave
one of his uncontrollable shudders and muttered something to
himself.

At that Fabyan woke again, and again saw Jones. 'Where
did that man come from?' he testily inquired. 'I know him for
a very jack-in-the-box of trickery, as guile-crammed as a pox-
mountebank with a gawdy monkey. Yet fraud and frost come
to foul ends.'

'Return to the sleep of your age, old father,' said Jones,
baring his teeth in a dog-grin at the others. 'And become wise
in your silence. For it is sad to see a gaffer with a slipshod
tongue, earning a jest instead of respect from his posterity.
Thus the world falls apart in our days, and no man knows
what the morrow will whelp.'

'I leave you nothing in my will, not a jet ring or a black
ribbon,' said Fabyan. 'Therefore you see no reason to snare

me in your smiles or put on any face save that which God and
the devil between them have given you.'

'I spoke in all gravity,' replied Jones, bowing, "since I count
you indeed my father by right of Nest's devotion to your grey
hairs; and in proof I have brought you a gilt button cut by an
Italian.'

'Ah, you chop and you change,' said the old man, eagerly
taking the button. 'I maintain my opinion of you, but in this
matter of the button you have shown yourself dutiful, and
others might well learn their behaviour from you.' He considered the button. 'I shall ask my Agnes to sew it in my cap
for Sunday.'

Jones gave a sharp look over at William and Blaise, who
stood talking in low voices near Agnes. 'Where is your beauti-
fied wife, Mistress Dowsabel?' he asked Blaise. 'On such a
night she should have come to make complete the gathering of
our faces.'

'She had a vomiting fit at noon,' said Blaise quickly, 'and I
left her abed with a warm compress for comfort of her belly.
But it is nothing, it will pass.'

'Tell her how sadly I mourned at her absence,' said Jones.
Then he looked at William. 'Since I am making a beadroll of
the family: I see here your discreet son, Stephen, but where is
Merric roving?'

'Making his noise elsewhere.' William contracted his brows
and then spoke easily, with a broad gesture of benevolence.
'But he can look after himself by night as by day, and will be
none the worse for taking the bit between his teeth for a
while.'

'He has carried off Ybel with him,' complained Nest. Hugh
again made one of his sudden shudderings and clenched his
fists, averting his face from the others.

'I said they could go together,' said William heavily.

Agnes put her book gently down and went over to the
window. She plucked at the buckram curtain and peered for a
moment through the glass in the leaden jalousies, seeing
nothing of the night that whined and rattled outside. A finger
of cold caressed her cheek. But old Fabyan roused himself
from a dim contemplation of the button to hear half of what
had been said. 'Where is the boy?' he demanded querulously.

'You have sent him on an errand without my permission. Must I repeat every day that I have it all set down in writing, signed and sealed in undeniable fashion, enjoining upon you to keep me in a state befitting the fortune I have delivered up. Namely, attended by a nimble and assiduous boy, owning all the faculties of his limbs, at such hours as I solely determine, and having his wages promptly paid by you yourself? Where is my copy of the paper?' He began feeling about in the chair behind him and under the cushion. 'Where is it? Have you stolen it? Remember that the master-copy lies in the hands of the Master of the Company . . .' Agnes tried to help him, but he pushed her away, and she went back to her seat near the painted chest.

'Edgar is here all the while,' said William. 'It is Ybel who strays abroad.' He went to the door. 'What do you want him to do?'

'Only to see him,' said Fabyan in an exhausted voice. 'Only to make sure that you aren't cheating me of my rights. Let me see his face, I tell you.'

Edgar came a step into the room. 'Here I am, master.'

'That's all right then,' said Fabyan. 'Only, don't let them make uses of you other than those I authorise, that's all.'

'Isn't it time that the wine was poured out?' asked Jones, moving to the table and fingering the jugs. 'A sweet smell indeed.' The wind screeched in the chimney. 'All the sweeter when the elements batter on our doors. But it's a sad night for the creatures out in it with no roof against the bitter skies.'

Nest stood up trembling. 'You're not going out in it again, Kit, are you? Say that you're not.'

'I say it,' he said in very tender tones. 'Your spouse has bidden me stay for the night, as a loving kinsman should.'

She put her hand over her breast. 'That's truly as it should be. I wouldn't have you go out again into that hurly-burly for all the gold in hell.' She looked round and saw that Agnes was sharply watching her. She put her hand over her eyes. 'O Mother Mary,' she said in a slow voice, 'O Mother Mary, what's going to become of us all?'

'It's a beautiful button,' cried old Fabyan with a sudden return of strength. 'I shall wear it on my cap of Sunday.'

'And now let us all drink to a year of friendly warmth,'

said Jones cheerily. 'For love unites our hearts. May the months between us and the next Christmastide bring wealth and a goodly harmony.'

Hugh rose. 'I must go now. God be with you all.' He went straight out of the room, without another word of farewell; and Stephen after bowing hastily to his father and mother, went out close behind him.

'Wrap yourself up well, my son,' Nest called; but he merely inclined his head without looking at her a second time.

There was a pause, after the door closed. 'Let him go then,' said Jones, 'but he might have chosen a more comfortable moment.'

'It's nothing,' said William irritably. 'Hugh is like that. He sits quiet for a while, and then he goes away all of a sudden, sometimes without saying a word. I have thought of asking him to release Stephen from his bond; for I fear that his melancholy may infect the lad—'

'No, no,' said Nest in a high voice. 'They are best together.' She turned and again looked at Agnes, who was staring at her. She went with her hurrying sliding way of movement over to the table, and put her hand on her brother's arm. 'Pour out the wine for us, my dear,' she said in a soft wheedling voice.

Jones began pouring out, but his mind was still on Hugh and Stephen. 'A sad and godly pair beyond all question.'

Nest crossed herself. 'A man may be sad nowadays, yet escape hanging, and godly yet go unnoticed; but if he be both sad and godly, he is likely to be marked out for the burning.'

' Mother,' cried Agnes in tones of reproachful grief, letting the book slip from her lap, 'how can you say such an ill-omened thing about your own son?'

Nest put her hand over her mouth then recovered herself. 'It was but a manner of speech,' she said angrily, 'which it would be ill for anyone to twist against me and mine. For what I say and do in my own household-nook is said and done away from the world, and only an enemy would hold it against me or repeat it in the envious streets.' Her eyes flashed and she beat herself on the bosom. 'Who is it then that accuses me? It is you, William, my husband, or you, Kit my own dear brother risen up out of the night as from a tomb to gladden my eyes? Is it you Blaise, with your accounting eyes and your legal fingers? or is it you, honoured father? Tell me, tell me.'

'No one is accusing you,' began William, scowling; but he was interrupted by his father, who woke up with a jerk from his doze.

'What is the woman at now?' demanded Fabyan. He glared round and nobody answered him. 'Yes, I'll take a little white wine mixed with citronwater. I find it good for my wind. Another cushion please for my back.'

Agnes brought the cushion from the chest. The flames flickered, and the red roses painted on the wainscotting leaped richly out. The gilt button fell and skipped across the floor. 'Are we ever going to drink to our fortunate year?' complained Jones, lifting his cup.

'My button? where's my button?' wailed the old man.

IV

Merric and Ybel stood outside the Rigeley house in Finkes Lane, and Merric gave five little taps. Ybel leaned against the shutters at the side, yawning. A breath of wind brushed up the flames of the stars, and down the lane a tile slid off a roof. Almost at once the door slowly opened. 'You see,' said Merric to Ybel with a note of pride; and Ybel, pressing his cloak against his ears, muttered something. Faint lines of wavy clouds were covering up the gusty stars on the east; a muffled dog-bark sounded from a near yard. The door opened about a foot, and the lads slipped in.

Agnes stood there in her smock with a cloak pulled over, shivering. On her unflinching hand the candle ran in hot grease. 'Get to your pallet, Ybel,' she said, without looking at him, and he stopped gaping at her; he went into the shop-room on the right, where he had his bed made under the counter. Agnes turned and went straight up the stairs, followed by Merric with long careful steps. They paused in the solar which was still warm from the dying fire, though draughts were coming up more strongly from between the boards. 'Where have you been?' Her hair fell all round her face, combed forwards, and the faint rosy light picked out only the tip of her upturned nose.

'Drinking.' His voice mingled annoyance and pride. 'Drinking of course. All along the riverside, then at the Three Cranes.' He clenched his fists, and his breath came heavily. 'I'll break that Martin yet. You'll see . . . afterward the Lord of Misrule came along, and we went to attack the Compter, or the Spaniards in Holborn, nobody seemed to know which it was; and a man with morris-bells gave us a flagon of frontignac.'

'You might have been shut out.'

'I could have got lodging in Newgate Jail for fourpence, in clean straw. That's where the thieves go to escape the watch.'

'Listen.' She came closer, so that her hair caressed his face and he blinked. 'Uncle Kit is here.'

He stared at her a moment. 'O yes, is he? what's he doing? Father thought he'd fled to Holland. What's he doing?'

'I'm not quite sure . . .'

'You don't mean to say that father let him come in and stay here?' Merric, at last grasping the news, gave a low whistle.

'Listen. I heard father and uncle Blaise whispering together. Do you believe about the gold? asked father. Maybe, said Blaise, but the tale of the abbot has a counterfeit ring about it. Yet he admitted a killing, said father. Maybe, said Blaise, but some people admit things they have never done to cloak yet more dangerous crimes.'

Merric shook his head from side to side, blinking. 'Is that all?'

'Yes, and it seems enough to me.'

'I'll find the whole matter out,' said Merric with confidence, 'but you're a sweet sister for telling me.'

'I ask in return only that you tell me anything further you find of their stratagems.'

'I'll tell you, I swear it. You're not like other women.' He took her hand and fondled it. 'You can keep a secret.'

'I'm sure that mother is in it with him,' she said fiercely. 'She's always hiding something. She whispered to him, but I couldn't catch the words.' She stared into Merric's eyes as if trying to read them there.

'O, you're always suspecting her of something. What is it?'

'How do I know? That's the very thing which torments me.

Promise that you'll tell me all you find out, whatever it is.'

He nodded and changed the subject, still holding her hand. 'Have you seen Jacint Hawes of late?'

'You know we never meet since our fathers quarrelled. Besides, I never liked her. Does she still stick in your gullet?'

'No, I hate her. But I want to get a revenge on the Hawes. Martin insulted me tonight. I struck him back, but it still rankles. If I could bring her down, it would humble them all.'

'I wouldn't help you to that.' She drew her hand away. 'I thought you sweated with love of her body.'

'I did once . . . O, I don't know.'

She softly touched his hair and brow. 'You still desire her, Merric. What a sad family we are. See, you're weeping.' She pressed her palms over his eyes and kissed him.

'I'm tired,' he muttered. 'Godsbones, I'd better go to bed.' He drew away, sickly swaying. 'Tell me again in the morning . . . Snares all round us, Agnes . . . snares . . . we've got to walk carefully . . . I can't trust anyone but you . . . I hate them all.'

She put her arm round him and helped him out of the room, up the attic-stairs, to his narrow bed. The house creaked in a buffet of wind, and outside, in the street, a long-drawn voice rose and fell in snatches. 'Twelve o'clock. Look well to your lock. Your fire and your light. And so goodnight.'

CHAPTER TWO

January

I

WILLIAM RIGELEY WAS sitting in the solar on a carved joint-stool, with the light of early morning glistening in a chilly pallor through the windows. He opened a small square and looked down on the backyard where old Gladus was slowly picking her way through the frozen mud, muttering to herself on the way back from the privy. Over on the right the house-tops showed furry with a moss of silver light, and a crow came cawing across. A horse stamped and whinnied. William smiled and shut the square.

The carpet was gone from the table, and Sanchia was putting the earthen plates on trenchers of stale bread. The room was thick with the smell of boiled stockfish. William poured out some thin beer and drank. Nest bustled silently in for a moment, peered under a cushion, gave a flurried look round, and went out again. 'Has Master Jones been woken?' William asked Sanchia, who kept her small chin tucked close against her chest as she worked. She looked up with a wing-flash of her green eyes, not a single hair of her head showing under the tightly drawn clout of pale blue.

'I think the mistress tapped at his door and spoke to him,' she answered tentatively in a wondering voice, as if everything she said always mystified her. 'Shall I see?'

'No, let him be.'

Down below in the yard, Merric came out of the workshop, still rubbing his teeth with a piece of soft wood. He shouted to Ybel, who was looking wanly out through the open wooden shutters of the workroom. William, who had gone to the

36

window again, stiffened, ceased wiping the glass with his sleeve, and went back to the table. Then old Fabyan came stumping in, with Edgar at his side holding a spectacle-case and a red cloth. He began grumbling at once, smoothing down his bushy eyebrows and picking his nose.

'Gladus made Edgar blow the bellows this morning when I needed him to help me on with my breeches. I'll have the law on you, William, sure as I'm your father. It's as well for me that I had the master-copy of our agreement deposited with the Master and Wardens of our Company, or you'd thieve it from me and tear it up behind my back. But too many worshipful traders have seen it now for you to forswear yourself, much as you'd like to get rid of your obligations to me, your old father who sweated his guts out in days gone by when a man had to work for his money. You'd like to set a parcel of rats on me to gnaw the paper up and eat my heart out. But I'm not going to die yet, and you know it, you ungrateful dog.'

'You must complain to Gladus yourself, father.' William drank some more beer and began on the stockfish with his knife. 'I've told her often enough that you have first call on Edgar. You've heard me do it. But she can't understand why she shouldn't make him work when she sees him doing nothing.'

'Take care, William,' grunted Fabyan, motioning to Edgar for some beer. 'I've waived most of my rights; but if I find you failing in respect, I shall demand yet another boy to accompany me to church and elsewhere, as by the paper I am entitled.'

Merric came in, with a dull frown on his face, his wet fair hair combed back. Ybel dodged in quietly behind him, and winked at Edgar, who maintained his severe calm.

'You were late in your homecoming,' observed William sourly. 'And what is worse, Merric, you are leading this lad into your own naughty courses.'

'Give me fifty pounds and I'll set up my own workshop,' retorted Merric. 'And I promise thereafter to ask for nothing again.'

'All in good time. When I had you apprenticed to Hawes, I was his good friend and meant to adventure with him in some

clothing project. But he played me false, and now in any event
I have other interests. I am yet uncertain what it is best for
you to do.'

'I have been trained as a cloth-master,' said Merric
doggedly, 'and I am ready enough to stand by my own trade,
unlike so many persons nowadays. Which is blamed by wiser
men than myself as a prime cause of our English miseries.'

'Leave such foolishness to the wiseheads whom you name,'
snapped William. 'You are my eldest son since the death of
John.' He crossed himself. 'And I shall set your feet on the
road of a goodly fortune, whether you like it or not.'

'You need not be so angrily sure that I shall refuse your
aid,' replied Merric. 'It makes me think that you are not
yourself so satisfied with its goodliness.'

Old Fabyan, who had been following this exchange of tart
words with extreme interest, choked over a mouthful of stockfish, and Edgar at once sprang behind his chair and began
patting him on the back. William swallowed the reply which
he had been about to make to Merric; and Agnes further
distracted him by coming in, with her head bound up like
Sanchia's, though in a red cloth with gold thread. She halted
before him and crossed her hands over her stomach.

'Where is mother?' she asked.

At that moment the bells for Tierce rang out their first
peal, and there was a crash on the upper stairs. Agnes put
her hands over her covered ears and ran from the room.
Merric paled and rose from his stammel-topped stool. 'Is it
mother?'

William too had started up, but now he sat again. 'No, not
she, whoever it is. Go and see what has happened.' He cut
another slab of stockfish and chewed it with the butter-sauce
running over his chin. 'What's the flavouring?' he asked
Sanchia, who stood open-mouthed, looking up at one of the
flowers carved on the ceiling.

'Sage and chestnut,' she said in a meek voice.

'When the sky falls we shall have larks,' said Fabyan with
his mouth full.

In the passage Nest collided with Merric. 'It's Kit, your
uncle Kit,' she said. 'He's fallen down the stairs and broken
his leg.' She wrung her hands and brushed past him into

the solar. 'Kit's fallen down the stairs and broken his leg,' she wailed.

'That won't kill him,' said William, chewing.

'You've a stone for a heart,' she cried. 'Eating away here while my poor brother dies at the foot of your stairs on a Saturday morning, the first of January: which makes it worse, setting an evil pattern on the coming months, or at least on all Saturdays.'

'Merric will carry him up,' said William, unmoved. 'I'll see him as soon as I'm ready.'

Nest stood staring at him. Fabyan chuckled. 'He who goes a-borrowing goes a-sorrowing.' He looked round with watery eyes at Edgar. 'Make a good note of it, my boy. Make a good note of it.'

Jones lay abed mildly moaning in the small upper-room which overlooked the yard. William closed the door. 'No need to keep the noise up in front of me,' he said cheerfully. 'You played that very well. Everyone believed you had had a fall in truth.'

'And so I did,' protested Jones. 'I had no intention of falling till after breakfast. By no means, I tell you. I meant to partake heartily of your hospitality, and then after a decent rest I meant to fall down the stairs from the solar, in view of half the household. But instead I fell as soon as I came out of this accursed room and began descending your narrow steps. Something swung into my face, a length of rotten rope or a long cobweb, I'll swear it. I noted it yesterday as I came up with the candle, hanging from a nail, a length of old rope from the trapdoor in the roof: that's what it was. But it startled me and I grasped out at it, and so I fell.'

William was watching his face all the while. 'Can I look at your leg?' he asked. Without waiting for an answer, he threw the coverlet back. 'Where's the break?'

'I don't think it's as bad as that. The ankle is heavily sprained. I doubled it under me.'

William considered the ankle, which was obviously swelling. He gently felt the flesh, and Jones groaned.

'Yes, you've hurt it. You'll have to stay in bed awhile. I

wouldn't be surprised if it took weeks before you can move properly about. What a misfortune.'

'I regret it more than you. After all, the ankle is my own, and therefore the pain. But it won't mean so large a delay. While I lie here, perhaps you will listen discreetly and find if there is any talk about a dead abbot.'

'Tell me his name.'

Jones hesitated. 'Jerome Pym, a black-cassocked Augustinian. A fellow with great jutting brows and a wart on his flat chin.' He thrust his own chin out and frowned mightily, trying to look like the abbot. 'Hasty of temper, and much given to commerce with women, therefore miserly in all things other than those conducive to lecherous gains.'

'And he was Abbot of Langden.'

'That's what I said.' Jones went on eagerly: 'And well I recall the place. We sold all the rotten copes and bells, at a small enough price, to the king's loss and the profit of many traffickers; and the monks came out in a line with their cowls cast upon their necks for sale. We sold the tiles off the roof for ten shillings. Ah, there were bargains to be got in those good old days, and we saw that our friends got them. We dug up the leaden conduit pipes and cast them into sixty-eight sows.'

'All that is over now.' William sat on the small chest and stared out through the window where a slate filled a broken pane. 'Let us come to closer matters.'

But Jones closed his eyes and knotted his hands together over his chest. 'How clear it all seems, a yesterday seen under an arch. We brought the whole abbey down. A vaulting rose on the right side of the high altar, borne up by four great pillars, having five chapels compassed in its walls, more than two hundred feet along; and all that was put down with a dust of thunder. Then we went on to a higher vault borne up by four thick pillars, more than a dozen feet from side to side and near four times that in circumference; and we brought it all down.' William fidgeted, but Jones, with closed eyes, went on with his tale. 'We fetched from London three carpenters, two smiths, two plumbers and a man to keep the furnace, with nine others to hew the walls about. Then the carpenters made props to underset the walls while the hewers

broke up the stonework. Such a furious travail of righteous
judgment you would go far to see . . .' He sighed, shivered,
and opened his eyes at last. 'Then, brother, you'll allow me
to rest awhile in your house?'

'I have small choice, as it seems,' replied William in a bluff
voice belied by his cold eyes. 'I cannot throw you out with a
snapt ankle.' He turned away, then came sharply back. 'You
haven't forgotten the story that you told last night, I trust?
If it was all a lie, confess it now before worse harm is done.'

'Every word of it was true.' Jones slapped at his brow and
looked wild-eyed at William. 'What else cast my thoughts
back to the days of that destruction which I have recounted?'

'We'll talk more of it later.' William went to the door. 'But
you should remember that these are bad days for giving
shelter to strangers or such as may seem strangers. If I say
nothing to the servants, they will talk; and if I bid them hold
their tongues, they will talk.'

'Am I not your brother?' asked Jones. 'When you mingled
your blood with Nest's, did you not also mingle it with mine?'
William closed the door.

The clocks stood at a quarter past eight, and all the other
shop-doors had been thrown open for many minutes; but over
William Rigeley's front the green shutters still hung. No sign-
board creaked from the iron stick above the door: a year ago
the sign had been blown down and damaged and was still
waiting in a cupboard to be refurbished. William Rigeley,
Merchant Taylor, did no direct selling nowadays from his own
counter. Next door, at the mercer's, however, the apprentices
were sitting crosslegged before the window, talking in muffled
merriment; and the gingerbread wife at the corner-stall had
already gained ninepence worth of custom. A late schoolboy
came scampering with his satchel down the lane, and
all the apprentices paused to shout after him, 'You'll be
whipt!' A dog joined in the game and went after the boy,
jumping up at him and refusing to be beaten off with the
satchel. Fluff floated down from the attic window where Mrs
Wall was thumping a mattress over the sill, caught in a momentary shaft of sunlight. A rat-catcher, with a trap on the end
of a pole and two sharp-muzzled dogs, came chanting down
from Threadneedle Street. 'Rats or mice, have you any rats,

mice, polecats or weasels? Or have you any old sows sick of the measles? I can kill them and I can kill moles, and I can kill vermin that creep up and creep down and peep into holes.' One of the apprentices at a shopdoor shouted back that Mrs Wall was such a sick old sow, and laughter ran down the lane.

Ybel, who had been set to scrubbing out the dark parlour, came through the yard with a bucketful of water from the pump. His head was set on one side and his tongue was sticking out. When he saw Sanchia he tried to close his mouth and draw his tongue in at the same time, so that he bit his tongue and spilled a deal of water. She was coming out of the stillroom beside the kitchen, with a smell of mint and last year's roses.

'Give you good day,' he said, and flushed, unable to add the compliments which kept his mouth still half-open.

She looked at the clouds which had just begun piling up over the sun. 'If you call this a good day, our thoughts agree like cat and dog, and I must bid you keep yours chained in its kennel.' And then with a scornful flirt of her hips she passed him, as if she knew that he stood open-mouthed and desired nothing better than to drown himself in the bucket. She went straight into the workshop, where Merric sat moodily on a bench, sorting out teasles; but though she came in so boldly, she stood abashed before his lifting eyes.

'Who wants me?' he asked.

'No one . . . I came . . . and now my wits are so flustered that I forget why I came.'

'Then you had better stay till you remember.' The sullenness dragging at his muscles faded out, and he smiled. 'I'll latch the door.'

'O no.' She held out her arms to bar his way. 'If your mother sees the door shut, she'll beat me.' She grew yet more confused. 'I'd better go.'

'Without the thing you came to get?'

'But I don't know what it is.'

He spilled the box of teasles, and took her in his arms, with a kiss on the side of her mouth. She wrenched herself free and ran out. Merric, with a smile still flickering on his lips and eyes, tried to frown. He kicked the box against the wall.

Ybel, who had got rid of his bucket in the parlour, came in and started looking round.

'What is it?' asked Merric, frowning in earnest.

'The scrubbing-brush . . . What did Sanchia say?'

'Nothing. Don't come disturbing me with questions like that. You know what I told you about the wench.'

'I thought she might have said something about me,' Ybel humbly pleaded. He loitered. 'I heard Master Brack in the street saying something about ill news from France.'

'What does he know about France—or anything else? He doesn't even know that his wife sleeps with the prentices.' He studied Ybel's miserable face and relented. 'Besides, the news is no doubt only put out as a pretext for raising more supplies.' He smiled, pleased with himself. 'You believe everything you're told. You should learn to ask what set policy underlies the words of government. You are made to be a wench's grateful fool.'

'I don't mind what her set policy is,' said Ybel stubbornly, 'as long as it makes her kind-hearted towards me.'

'There's no curing of your folly.'

'I don't want to be cured. I only want her to love me.' He licked his lips. 'You wouldn't say a good word for me, would you? She has such a tender respect for your words.'

'Get out of here, you idiot,' shouted Merric. He gave the box another kick, and this time he cracked it. Ybel stared at him in bewilderment and went out.

II

These answers were again propounded against her four days later; and there being demanded if she would stand unto those her answers, she, Margaret Mearing, said, 'I will stand them unto the death; for the very angels of heaven do laugh you to scorn, to see your abominations that you use in the church.'

After the which words, the Bishop pronounced the sentence of condemnation against her; and then delivering her unto the sheriffs, she was, with John Rough, carried unto Newgate; from whence they were both led unto Smithfield, and there most joyfully gave their lives for the profession of Christ's gospel.

III

He was walking down Broad Street towards the Merchant Taylors' Hall. The day was in full swing, with carts and barrows rattling among the chaffering people and the yelping dogs, the squawking crows and beggars. 'Pouch-rings, boots and buskins!' A legless man in a cellar-entry plucked at the loose rail-gown of a woman-nurse, and she shook him off. A scrawny-bearded man in breeches of cowskin and red baize held up a sheaf of brooms. 'Brooms for new shoes! Will you buy any new brooms?' The various signposts of the shops swung and glittered in red and gold. At the doors the prentices were working, shouting, jostling women, annoying passers on pretence of zealously drawing them in. Mud splashed from a heavy six-horse coach, and the porters called out insulting remarks.

William was cloakt to the throat, though the sun had come out again and the sky was windily clear. He felt the touch on his elbow and looked round to see Richard Husband, a fellow Taylor, who fell into step beside him. A tall talkative man with a stoop, not so well off as he had been five years ago.

'Look there,' he said, pointing into the shops as they passed. 'Fine Venice glass, French garters, Spanish gloves. No wonder that we are a broken nation. Flanders knives, silk stocks of Italy. It is all foreign gear on sale, and sadly decreases our treasure.'

'Yet what would a country be without trade?'

'A thriving place of yeomen, making its own woollen stuffs and leathern goods. Not a den of silken apes and workless beggars.'

William shrugged his shoulders. 'No doubt what you say is true, and no doubt men will say it a myriad times. And more, they will try yet again to pass laws against these fal-delals. But your words and your laws will avail nothing.'

'Those are grievous and melancholic declarations.'

William smiled. 'What is the latest news from abroad?'

'I heard a rumour on Sunday after evensong, which I put out of my mind; and next day it was repeated as a certainty, that Calais is beset on all sides.'

'Nothing further today?'

'Not that I know.'

William hesitated, then he said, 'I heard some talk of a murdered abbot, but I scarcely listened at the time. Then, afterwards, I thought of it again and wondered.'

'I heard nothing of it,' said Husband with gossip-interest. 'What was the abbot's name?'

'I don't know,' said William hurriedly. 'Maybe I did not hear the words at all.'

Husband was going to ask more, but a neatly-dressed trades-man, with a letter folded in his hand, accosted William with a a respectful doffing of the cap.

'Pardon me, Master Rigeley, but could you tell me where the post to Bruges now lies?'

'In the Jewry,' said William with amiable dignity. 'At the sign of the White Lion.'

The man knitted his brow. 'That's the house right over against the Unicorn?'

Husband, anxious to match his knowledge with William's, broke in, 'A little further, on this side of the Goat and the Red Horse.'

'You don't know what time he's going?' said the man, turning back to William. 'If I may make so bold as to hang my questions round your neck.'

'No doubt with the first tide,' said William, now wanting to shake the man off.

But he persisted. 'Where is the wind now?'

William stayed silent and left the field to Husband, who declared, 'It is in the east, against him. Yet this morning it was north north-east.'

William strode on, and Husband hurried to catch him up. 'A civil fellow,' he said. They went to cross the street, and then paused to let a cart go by. In the cart was packed the parish hearse-cloth, on the way for loan-out to the family of some dead parishioner, and with the cloth a waxhearse or candle-frame for use in the church during the funeral service. Husband wagged his head, 'Ah, deaths increase, but at least

we have been spared the Sweat.' They crossed the road and
entered the gate of the Merchant Taylors' Hall, stepping
somewhat more proudly and easily into the garden, even
though the hedges were shabby with winter and the fountain
wasn't playing out of the conche. A dog slipped in behind
them, and the janitor went chasing it on the grassplot. The
one-eyed gardener trundled a barrow down the pebbled alley,
and a kite rose up from the bowling-green beyond the quick-
set. Several portly members of the Livery were talking on
the steps.

William and Husband went through into the Great Hall,
nodding to friends. 'There'll be another loan laid upon us,'
said Husband gloomily, 'and we're near breaking as it is. The
last corn assessment was bad enough . . .' He brightened. 'But
tell me, is it true that a man from York has been made free
of the trade per redemption per warrant of the Lord Mayor
at the suit of the Lord Chamberlain? We shall find our worths
in a sad way if this sort of meddling goes on, and all at the
cost of a mere sugarloaf.'

William saw George Heton, last year's Master, looking at
him, and bowed, taking the chance to leave Husband. He went
aside with Heton, who held him by the arm and spoke in a
voice of well-meant warning.

'Richard Husband is an honest fellow in his way, but given
to loose talk and falling away in substance. In a few years he
is likely to seem a malcontent. Don't forget that you are
marked down for the office of City Sheriff when it falls open;
and therefore avoid all company smutted with ill repute.'

William thanked him for his counsel and called Husband a
burr whom he had been attempting to shake off all the way
down Broad Street; and Heton smiled and pressed his arm.
William went across the room to talk to Luys Lloyde, asking
him if he had yet given up gambling; and Lloyde swore by
the Rood that it was so. 'Why, and what is more, Master
Rigeley, I am now a marrying man.' William laughed and
said that at least he was not marrying Mrs Lowson, that
delectable and moneyed widow. Then Lloyde laughed louder,
and said that he was fit to be called a mere mountain-goat
unless he changed Mrs Lowson into Mrs Lloyde without the
use of indictable magicks. And in less than a minute there

was a wager laid, and Lloyde had handed over two shillings and a penny to William, with the sum to be returned in double on his marriage-day.

'Where then is your oath against wagers and dicing?' said William, but Lloyde swore that they had touched hands on a Merry Bond and in no wicked gambling work, and that if such bonds were a villainy Master Rigeley was the greatest villain in all England. But in sweet truth they were no such thing, and neither was he, God forgive us in a world of whirling words.

William rejoined Heton, and they went up on to the dais and stood chatting near the buffet-recess where the plate was displayed. They looked down on the throng in the body of the hall, and William pointed to Lloyde, who was searching in his breeches for a flea. 'It is time that the rushes were changed,' said Heton. 'I myself dislodged a whole nation of fleas last week, and there are so many bones that the feet crunch as they go.' He beckoned to the Recorder and asked him when the rushes had last been changed.

'I think it is perhaps a dozen years,' said the Recorder, 'though I remember the time as though it were only a month ago. We had two women in to do the work, and they laboured for twelve days, removing sixty loads of rushes and spilt oddments. But I doubt if there is such a weight there today, since we have all become more cleanly eaters.'

A servant came in through the door opposite the recess, and asked the Recorder and the Wardens if they would go to the upper room where the Master was waiting. William followed the others and took a backward look to see whom Lloyde was talking with; and so he almost knocked into a servant who came up from the cellar with a tray of beer. In the room above, Thomas Rowe the Master was pacing to and fro, while a small group of Wardens and senior Assistants stood mutely by the window.

'My friends,' said the Master, greeting Heton and William, 'we have been asked for yet another loan. The condition of the Pale is even worse than is rumoured. The Queen's Majesty required an instant despatch of stores and reinforcements.'

'Yet it is only a few weeks since we last subscribed,' said one of the Wardens by the window, a swarthy man with a

square beard. 'It is small use to preserve a slab of land over-
seas if we ruin this larger land which is far nearer our persons
and necessities.'

His words set the others also into protests. 'Moreover, we
have received nothing back for the many loans made in the
last three years.'

'If the thing is to be done, it should have been done
months ago. Now we shall pour men and treasure in, and lose
them all by ill counsel and worse consideration of time and
place.'

William was constrained to add, 'Is the money to be paid
to the Lord Chancellor or to her Majesty's private officer,
the Chamberlain?'

'Sirs, sirs,' said the Master gravely, lifting his pale hand,
'all this is nothing to the point. If the Companies were
together in such sore straits that they must needs join in
prayer and remonstrance against the demand, it should be
done in orderly and conjoined fashion. As it is, I have already
had a word with the Lord Mayor . . .'

Then one of the Wardens, Robert Dove, known as a man
who burned many roods and images of saints in King
Edward's days, was unable to hold back a loud soaring cry,
which abruptly ended, 'I see the hand of God.'

The others sighed in the pause and drew their furred gowns
closer about them. 'I trust that we see the hand of God in all
things,' said the Master, 'sustaining or checking the un-
gracious hand of men. But that also is nothing to the point.
I regret, my good friend, that we have no choice; but so it is.
The realm lies in sudden danger, and the Queen's Majesty
calls upon us to replenish her coffers.'

'There will be corn assessments also,' said the swarthy man.

William broke in, 'Has the Lord Mayor named the sum
that the Company must pay?'

There was a deep hush, and the Master said in a low voice,
'We had better face the worst. In all it will run up to some
five thousand pounds, which our Company must bear as its
fair share.' He looked round at the stricken faces. 'The rate
of interest will be at twelve per cent.'

'But will there be any security?' asked the swarthy man.
'Will the crown lands be set against the loan?'

A hum of disputation grew up. 'The crown lands are already mortgaged against last year's loans . . .' How much would the aldermen, the wardens, and the others of the livery be called upon to pay? How much could be taken out of the common box? Then, in the midst of the wrangling, the Master made another announcement:

'There will be a further assessment for armour and the like, but that can be left for the moment.'

'And for corn, beyond a doubt,' said the swarthy man.

Robert Dove had torn a patch from his beard, and drops of blood were running down the curls on his chin. He could not resist taking William aside and whispering in his ear. 'Our Spanish King is no friend of English trade. He may well smile that the war should constrict and beggar us; and this bleeding of our money for his causes is meant to spoil our merchants from competing against his own. Nor could we expect it otherwise. But I say it is a blind goose who knows not a fox in a fernbush.'

'And I tell you, Master Dove,' said William, glancing round to make sure that no one else had overheard, 'it is a forward cock that crows in the shell.'

'There is yet more,' said the Master, and this time a deathly light glimmered in the eyes of his listeners. 'I have here a precept from the Lord Mayor, enjoining the Wardens to provide sixty good, sad and able men to be soldiers, whereof two are to be horsemen, well-horsed and armed, twenty to be arquebusiers or archers, twenty to bear pikes and eighteen to bear bills, all well harnessed and weaponed, meet and convenient, according to the appointment of our sovran lord and lady the King's and Queen's Majesty, as well for the surety and safeguard of her highness's chamber and city of London as for the resistances of such malicious attempts as may be made against them by a foreign enemy.'

A low groan came from the Wardens and Assistants, and Robert Dove stood muttering in his beard. William caught the words, 'A foreign enemy, aye, our best friends and fellows in the truth . . .' He moved quickly away in case the others might have heard.

'We must provide the men and the pressed money,' said the Master in a strained but calm voice.

The hubbub in the Great Hall fell away as the Master and Wardens filed on to the dais from the side-door. Slowly, clearing his throat and spitting into a clout, the Master came forward. His golden chain glinted and swayed forward as he bent. He held up his hand, his thin flat hand. A bone cracked under someone's shifted foot in the rushes, and made everyone start.

The Master began. 'Brethren of our Mistery, we have heavy tasks before us, which it becomes us to shoulder with a stiff stomach and a trust in God . . .'

A faint rustling, a whispering at the back of the Hall, a steady gloom of silence bearing down on them all. William frowned and and stared straight ahead, joining his hands behind his back. The Master's voice droned implacably on.

IV

Passing in through the main gate, he skirted the chapel and made for the inner gate beyond the chapter-house. The smell of the river, brown and rank and chilly, rose up in his nostrils, mixed with an acrid stink from the smouldering heap of leaves and garbage which the gardener was holding down with his rake. Half a dozen depressed monks, coming out of the abbey-church, went by without looking to right or left; but the guard at the gate gave a lavish salutation. 'Good morning, Master Rigeley.'

'Good morning, Hastings,' said Blaise, peering short-sightedly. 'Is the smoke chafing your eyes?'

'No, mostly it blows over towards the Infirmary.'

Blaise went through, a slight smile tugging at the strict corners of his mouth; and as he went, he tapped his shoe with the staff he carried between two fingers. He entered the New Palace Yard and walked through the shivering bushes towards the Exchequer House. The Deputy Usher nodded affably and continued shouting at two porters who had pulled a chest out of a cart on to the gravel path. 'Don't bump it about like that.'

Blaise went in. On the other side of the rail in the counting-house two clerks were making dotted signs on sheets of paper, while a third clerk read lists of figures out. A messenger sat sleeping on a bench with out-thrust legs, while an unoccupied clerk was tickling his nose with the end of a plume-pen. The reader signalled a welcome to Blaise by getting up on his stool and bowing, without any pause in his strings of numerals.

Blaise went on straight up the old wooden stairs, which had warped and showed many large holes where knots had fallen out. On the first floor he unlocked with his own key the small partitioned-off room where he kept his papers. A grey light drifted through the dusty mullioned windows; and when he sat down at the table he took out a pair of wood-rimmed spectacles from inside his doublet, rubbed them with a clout, and carefully set them on his long thin nose. He could hear Will Sonders next door breathing hard: which meant that he was making up his accounts, sprawled over the table and clenching his quill as though he had to dig the letters out. Blaise himself took up a quill with fastidious fingers, paused to observe an ancient fly in a cobweb, and wrote in clear but spidery characters: : *Jan. X Monday.*

A thin-headed man, with hair like moss, came shuffling in. 'What matters are afoot today, Yardly?' Blaise asked.

'Three tallies to give out,' said Yardly in a croaking voice. He felt inside his doublet and brought out a fistful of narrow shafts of hazelwood, nine inches long, shaped with four equal sides. He handled them with loving care, smelt them, and turned them over and over.

'Have you checked them?'

'Yes, Master Rigeley. Ten times at the least.'

'Let me see.' Blaise took the tallies and set them down on the table. 'Come back in half an hour,' he said, and reached for a small box on the shelf, from which he extracted the top three documents. These papers he scrutinised and set down on the table by the tallies. Yardly went out, dragging his feet. Blaise waited till he'd gone, then with a sudden smile and with quickened movements, he lifted the tallies and ran his finger-nail pleasantly along the grooves. The main sum cut in a bold notch, then on the opposite side the pounds and pence, starting from the thick end: a thumb-width, a hundred pounds; a little finger-width, twenty pounds; one pound, a barleycorn-depth. And then on the other sides, the reasons for the payment: *Writ of Allowance* . . . He checked the details with the mandate on paper. All correct. His smile deepened; and the flickering at the edges of his mouth increased.

Now the second shaft, neatly tapering, cleanly notched. The Chamberlain's Sergeant knew how to use his knife, and so he ought, after twenty years of notchings.

Blaise completed his calculations and sat with his head sunk dreamily on his hands, his eyes distant. Yet listening to every noise in the building, every creak, clank, footstep, mutter, chinkle pen-scrape sigh. Sonders had ceased his accounting. Sonders was pushing his chair back. Sonders was listening . . . He tapped on the door and came in.

'The Treasurer's gone to the upper chest-room.'

Blaise slowly closed his eyes and let his head fall back; then he roused himself and turned. 'Do you know what he's after?'

'It must be something connected with the new loans, the payments for supplies.' Sonders scratched the stubble on his cheek, and the rasping noise mixed with the creaking of the stairs as someone hurried up from the ground floor. 'Not all citizens will be groaning. Many have smiles hidden in the hollow of their hands, clothiers and ironsmiths.'

Both men pondered. Sonders sighed, and Blaise gave him a quick look. After a while Sonders said, 'How is your worshipful brother William faring, may I ask in all kindliness?'

'Prosperously as ever for all I know.' Blaise watched Sonders, who sighed again and scratched his rough cheek. 'Why do you ask?'

'In all kindliness. A friend of mine said that he had had the sight of a bill in Master William Rigeley's hand.'

'He signs many bills, I have no doubt.'

'In all kindliness,' repeated Sonders. 'No man signs bills at such a rate unless he is sadly pressed for money.'

Blaise rocked slowly on his seat. 'I have no reason to contradict your friend, and none to confirm him. He may be right and he may be wrong.'

'I thought I'd tell you. In all kindliness.'

'I'm thankful to you, very thankful.'

'Brothers don't always tell each other the truth. He might try to borrow from you.'

'I have no money to lend,' said Blaise with a short laugh,

'and so I am saved from errors. Being saved from wealth, I am saved from deceit.'

Sonders gave a dry titter. 'And how is your wife? How is that estimable woman? If I may say so in all kindliness . . .'

'As well as any woman can hope to be. She often asks after your health. But tell me, have you heard anywhere about the murdering of an abbot? I may have been mistaken, but I thought some men at Charing Cross were speaking of it.'

Sonders shook his head. But at that moment a clamour broke out on the ground floor. The two men listened intently. Sonders turned and had his hand on the doorlatch, when one of the clerks came gaping in, and knocked the door against Sonders's elbow. His breath was whistling with excitement.

'What is it?' both Blaise and Sonders asked, and Sonders, nursing his elbow, was too interested to complain.

'Calais has fallen,' cried the clerk. 'Calais has fallen to the French under the Duc de Guise.' He gulped and lowered his voice. 'Men say that there was treacherous work inside the town. Otherwise, how could the French for all their battering guns have taken the walls?' He looked from face to face, savouring the preoccupation of dismay and doubt which settled there.

'The Staple is closed for our wool,' murmured Sonders.

'So much the better for our clothiers,' replied Blaise.

The clerk was too taken up with the importance of his news to catch what they said. 'There will be more levies yet,' he cried, to reassert himself. 'England has heard no such bitter tidings since the death of King Arthur in Merlin's days.'

He hurried out, to find someone else who hadn't heard. Blaise and Sonders looked at one another for a long time; then Sonders said, 'I'll go back to my accounts.'

v

I cannot pass over a certain poor woman, and a silly creature, burnt at the stake, who, having a husband and children much addicted to the superstitious sect of Popery, was many times rebuked of them, and driven to go to church, to their idols and ceremonies, to shrift, to follow the cross in

*procession, to give thanks to God for restoring Antichrist
again into this realm, etc. Which when her spirit could not
abide to do, she made her prayer unto God, calling for help
and mercy; and so, at length, lying in her bed, about midnight
she thought there came to her a certain motion and feeling of
singular comfort.*

*Whereupon in short space she began to grow in contempt
of her husband and children; and so taking nothing from
them but even as she went, departed from them, seeking her
living by labour and spinning as well as she could, here and
there for a time. In which time notwithstanding, she never
ceased to utter her mind as well as she durst; howbeit she
at that time was brought home to her husband again, where
at last she was accused by her neighbours, and so brought
to the Bishop and his Clergy.*

VI

Rafe Heygate passed his ruffling hand over the scanty hairs
of his hand, grinned with delight, and set the book down.
Going over to the window of his attic-room, he opened and
leaned out. Yes, there was his brother-in-law Gregory going
importantly down the street with a prentice slouching in
attendance behind. Rafe took some crumbs from a small heap
on the inner sill, sprinkled them on the shingles of the roof,
and kissed his hand to the mild sun. The door burst open,
and he turned to welcome Jacint with a warning finger. 'Quiet,
my dear one, I am in an ecstasy.'

'Have you heard the news?' she asked, breathless and
dimpling. Her hazel hair slipped from its band and fell over
her face and shoulders; and she tossed it impatiently back.
'Have you heard?'

'All that concerns me,' he answered gently, closed the window, and took up his book, *Epistolae Obscurorum Virorum.*
'Listen. Someone has eaten on Friday an egg in which the
chick was already formed: tell me if his after-scruples of
conscience were right?' He turned the pages, looking for the
text. 'He writes to ask Ortwin, learned in all the Commen-
taries on the Book of the Sentences, to resolve his case. A

brother indeed told him that as what had been eaten was an egg, *essentialiter,* any other substance which happened to be present was there only as an accident and no more to be regarded than maggots in cheese, which we swallow unhesitatingly on fastdays. As against that interpretation lies the fact that a doctor of physics has said the maggots, being worms, are to be reckoned as fish, whereas the chick is the young of the fowl and therefore flesh. O, where is the page, for I spoil the tale in the telling.'

'Close the book, close the book,' she insisted, trying to pull it from his hand. 'Calais has fallen.'

'Let it fall. My jest is a better one.' He began laughing softly, half to himself, and let her take the book. 'Ah, what a labyrinthine world we inhabit. Ah, cancerous man, stinking in the fair garden. So Calais has fallen, and the pismire-heap is all a-buzz; but I snap my fingers at all your Calais. I had rather leave an avuncular kiss in the slight cleft of your chin than mangle a myriad men and raise a brazen monument to affront the sun.'

She sat down on his stool. 'Sweet uncle Rafe,' she said, 'why are you unlike all other men, and why do I love you for it?'

'Only in your brave eyes,' he said, 'am I this monstrous trumpeter of scorns. Before the rest of the world I am a silly scholar, as meek as a maiden mouse in a nunnery. But truly I am grateful for your sweet face and for city-sparrows and for witty books, so that I wear horn-spectacles to avoid the evil eyes.'

'But Calais has fallen,' she insisted, 'and father has gone to the Lord Mayor.'

'And if we have no sauce of cloves and parsley for our salt mutton, I shall be a sad man.'

She clapped her hands in anger, in a pretence of anger. 'Passion of my heart! You are a worse heretic than all those who daily burn. Are you not afraid that I shall betray your hidden mockeries?'

'No,' he said, and took her hands.

'Neither am I.' She laughed. 'But why have you chosen me for the only ear of your secrets?'

"Tell me then why you chose to make me love you, sweetheart?' His voice grew grave at last. 'For this is true above all things, that an unspoken thought can strangle a man and that when we must lie to everyone we end by lying to ourself. And so, because you wound yourself into my heart, I have found my truth and have not feared to hear my own voice in the darkness.'

'I do not understand,' she said, faltering. 'But let it be.' Then she grew animated again. 'And whatever you say, Calais has fallen, and Martin says that there were treacherous dealings in the town, and father says that there will be new levies, and Aunt Gertrude fears that the price of corn will rise.'

'And shall we have our lesson? Or has the fall of Calais scattered your wits so widely that you cannot conjugate a Latin verb, even though it be *amare,* or make an epitome of a merry song?' He sighed. 'Ah, my dear, I feel like the old man who began to learn the flute at eighty years, so that the neighbours asked if he had had news of a dance being got ready in the next world.'

'You are only five years older than father,' she said severely.

'Old enough to have my teeth set on edge. But you have not answered. Lesson or no lesson?'

'Not today.' She kissed him lightly on the brow. 'Yet it is a matter of piecrust, not of Calais, that calls me away.'

VII

William Rigeley looked up over the account-table in the small parlour. 'You have heard the great need that there is for troops?'

'I have heard it mentioned,' replied Merric carelessly. 'Also that hungry dogs eat dirty puddings, and he casts beyond the moon who has pisst on a nettle.'

'Let me hear no more of your Merlin-mumblings,' said his father angrily, rapping on the table. 'I spoke plainly, and I requ... a plain answer.'

'Sir, by ...d's truth, you did not speak so plainly as you might,' retorted Merric, flushing. 'I could not tell whether you desired me to enlist ... thought of soldiering yourself.'

'In my young days a son would have been well whipt for less than such wry and insolent words,' said William, gripping a ruler in his effort to control his temper. 'But I have long been too easy with you, and I know that sweet meat will have sour sauce and that a pretty pert child turns a pestilent man. If it is true that in this matter of the levy I have not spoken your outright name, it was because I wished to leave a space where you might thrust yourself of your own accord and with the more merit.'

'I thrust myself nowhere,' said Merric obstinately. 'My father refuses to set me up in my proper station, and I am lost in the shadow.'

'I have refused nothing. I have asked you only to bide your time.'

'The time is yours, not mine.' Merric rose and came closer to the table. 'Listen, father, since we are come to these loud words. I know you had twined all your hopes round John, and with his death you saw me step into his shoes, an unwelcome and undeserving stranger. You have grudged me my change of fortune as though I plotted his death and snared him in the sweat that slew him. But it is no fault of mine, I tell you, that I must wear the clothes fitted for another. He had a care for book-learning and I have none. He could see a silver penny where I see only a farthing token. But unless we are to hate one another, take me as I am and don't try to make a pipe out of a pig's tail. For when all is said and done, you can have no more of the cat than her skin.'

William began with irony, 'You have learned many deep sayings.' But he held himself in, and went on more mildly: 'You do me a wrong, Merric. True, John was greatly beloved by me, but it is no sin for a father to love his firstborn. That you are yourself and not John, is manifest; but I have tried to love you as Merric. Yet you keep seeing in my deeds what is not there. You suspect me of thwarting your aims when all I desire and seek is your best fortune.' Merric stirred uneasily, and William spoke more quickly. 'To overthrow you would be to overthrow my own future. Have you never thought that I may have other reasons than those you conjecture for my delays, and that those reasons may plague me more sharply than you. For you don't even know what you want, and I am

preparing in difficult darkness a better fate for all of my family
than you dream.'

Merric listened frowning. For a moment he could not speak,
then he started and exclaimed, 'Yet you counsel me to volun-
teer into the Company's levy and adventure my life to no
purpose in a war for the benefit of Spain.'

'Do not harp on that tuneless string,' said William, hardening again. 'If I suggested any such thing, it was only a stopgap
for your impatience. And now let this unprofitable conversation end. Either rest your will in mine, or look to meet my
anger.'

Without replying, Merric bowed and went out.

William turned the pages of his ledger, poring over familiar
figures and seeing nothing. An obscure curtain of rage hung
between him and the world, the records of his money-dealings.
Then, hearing a step outside, he closed the ledger and leaned
over it, brooding with out-thrust lowerlip. After a while he
rose, locked the ledger away in its chest, and left the room.
He went on upstairs, to the room on the left overlooking the
yard, where Christopher Jones lay grinning to himself in
restless discomfort.

'How does your ankle fare?'

Jones grimaced. 'I have been minded to twist it off. Ever
since I gave it yet another wrench on those stairs of hell.
Light the candle for me. The wench set it down out of my
reach.'

William struck a flint over the piece of tinder, and lighted
the candle. Jones felt about under his pillow, drew out a
sheet of paper on which he had been scribbling, and held
it over the flame. William strained to make out the words and
signs, but saw only meaningless numerals and two words:
well west . . . Then the flame caught the folded paper and
flared up. Jones held fast as the flame raced upwards, watching the black shreds whirl up and flutter in webs of smoke.
He held fast till there was only a small stub left and the fire
was stinging his fingers. Then he threw the stub on the floor,
and William stamped on it for safety, blowing the candle out.

'Why do you write things if you must burn them after?'

'Because there are many things which I cannot grasp with

my thoughts. Only when I set them forth outside my mind, in fixed words and figures, may I decide their worth and unhood their meaning. But I make a rule never to leave such papers unburnt.'

'I hear no news of a slain or straying abbot.'

Jones gave a high neighing laugh. 'Then I did my work well. I am not astonisht.'

'Yet it is strange that his absence has not been noted in any way.'

'Doubtless he is thought to have departed back to Italy in some dudgeon or misprision. He was ever a high-stomached and angry man, who had come in hope of a prosperous abbey and found that our English lords would swallow the Pope in a creed but would never disgorge their abbey-lands. Besides, if he were found bloated in the water, his acquaintances would think he had fallen into some dispute over womanflesh, suffering a likely retort—to wit, a dagger between the ribs.'

'Why then were you so aghast on the night you came hither? Also, you said that it was in the eye you had pierced him.'

'Better the eye for a water-blurring of wounds.'

'Why were you so aghast?'

'We drank together in a Southwark tavern and went up to a room jutting on the river with a small shattered balcony, and there the hare-lipt woman brought us a jug of ippocras. After which I smote him in the eye and threw him over the rotten rails.'

'At which hour?'

'How do I know? The hour before I knocked on your door.'

'And did not the woman stare at a priest hobnobbing with a rakehell such as you?'

'It is true that tippling priests are more scarce in these meagre days; but he was well-cloakt against the cold, with his shaven head out of sight.'

'And what happened after?'

'I went down and paid the scot, to prevent scandal, and told the tavern-wife that my friend had gone off in a venereal hurry to the stews round the corner.'

'You still have not told me why you were so aghast.'

'As I went out, I saw the abbot's servant prying among the drinkers in the backroom. Doubtless he sought his master. Then, though I hastily hid my face and passed into the windy street, I feared he had glimpsed me.'

William pondered, scratching his nose and hesitating. At last he said, 'Well, what courses do you propose?'

'I have been free and open with you,' said Jones evasively. 'But you cannot expect me now to name the place where the treasure lies buried. When I am well and bustling, I shall go with you to the very spot, and if you wish Blaise to come with us, let him also come. Then together we shall dig the chest and share the gold and the jewels as we have agreed.'

'As soon as you can walk?'

'Yes, after a few small matters are settled. Thus, I must first find a quiet and removed lodging of my own, to which I can go with my share of the chest.'

'But if there is nothing to do beyond the digging of a chest and the hauling of it to London, there is no need of your presence. Why cannot we set about it at once?'

'Brother Will, you know it was by a chance of the night that Blaise came into this venture—though I find no great dislike of having as companion a man so knowledgeable in the law. You it was whom I came to find with a plea for shelter, meaning to offer in return a modicum of my gains in due course. And all this I intended out of gratitude for past kindness and a regard for my beloved sister Nest, whom I have often sworn to deck with a princely sort of prosperity: if only to spite those of her marriage-kin who have looked down on me as a profitless giddy-gadder and consumer of borrowed moneys. And indeed there is surely a world of reasons in such a wish, which I leave to your unsifting. As also the manifold causes for my desiring to be present at the discovery of the treasure. Are you so little read in the dark hornbook of the sinful yet hopeful heart of man?'

William leaned wearily against the wall. 'You overbear me with your arguments rather than persuade me. I warn you that I am in no mood nowadays for any twisted stratagems. Yet if in truth you have come to my house with a baggage of gold, I pray your forgiveness for my suspicion; and surely I have a notion that I have deserved well enough of the Lord to warrant this aid in my adversity.'

'It is then true that you are pusht against the wall?' asked Jones too eagerly.

William was silent a moment. 'All that is between me and the Lord, and you had better waste no breath in rambling questions.'

'I asked you,' said Jones with an unctuous note and sharpening eyes, 'only because I thought to verify my conviction that I had been guided to you by a providence.'

'We shall judge that in good time,' said William gruffly. He turned to go.

'How is my sister?' Jones asked.

'As always, a woman torn between God and Satan, like all women, no more and no less: my faithful helpmate and a thorn in my flesh. Why do you ask?'

'I haven't seen her yet all day; and though I bade Sanchia tell her that I needed more ink in my horn, I have seen neither ink nor her person.'

'It is likely,' said William absent-mindedly.

Below in the kitchen, Agnes was cutting up sops of bread, while Sanchia scraped the trenchers. Old Gladus was muttering to herself as she sat near the hearth plucking a capon. 'You lay it out on the board,' Sanchia was saying in a sing-song voice, 'then you pin up your skirts round your waist and sit on your knees over it.' She scraped so hard that she ran out of breath, and paused, brushing her hair from her face with the back of her hand. 'And thus you wibble and wobble to and fro, afterwards kneading it with a broad rolling-pin. And the chief thing is that you sing all the while.' She chanted, 'My dame is sick and gone to bed, and so I'll mould my cockle-bread.' Then she giggled, 'Yet this is the best of all: My spell is true and cannot fail to make him follow at my tail.'

'You'll cut your hand,' said Gladus.

'No, I won't,' said Sanchia, and cut it.

'Some can sing and work the better for it,' Gladus went on, bent over her capon. 'But some can't work at all as soon as a song gets between their lips, and you're one of them, Sanchia.'

Sanchia pulled her sleeve down over the cut thumb, not

wanting old Gladus to see the blood. 'I don't care. I'd as soon sing as work.'

'You'd better not let the mistress hear you say that. She doesn't yet know you broke the little blue jug.'

'But it's true, isn't it, Gladus,' said Sanchia ingratiatingly. 'It's true that cockle-bread ties a man up in trueknots of love if a maid makes it for him and then gets him to eat as much as a crumb.'

'True as most things,' said Gladus reluctantly. 'True sometimes, at the right moment of the moon. Nowadays you wenches don't understand all that goes to a proper charm.' She gave a low throaty chuckle. 'Yet if wishes were thrushes, beggars would eat bird-pie; and if wishes were kisses, Sanchia would be no maid.'

Agnes finished her sops, pushed them into a neat pile with the knife, and went to take a bronze mirror from a shelf. 'Tell me, Gladus, was mother like me at my age?'

'In the candlelight you look her dead spit,' mumbled Gladus, 'but in the daylight you look only like yourself. For the night brings out the old cat and makes a woman hide inside herself for fear the devil may tempt her in the guise of a mouse.'

Sanchia said pertly, 'Then it's the old cat who's to blame for the night-hunting, and we need tell in the confessional only that which we did in our day-selves.'

'And how much more do you tell indeed?' asked Gladus.

Agnes went on looking into the mirror. 'Who then is the other person here?'

'Merric is the one like his father in the open face,' Gladus went on, brushing the down from her bosom.

'Who is the other one here?' cried Agnes, touching her mouth and brow. 'And whom do you see in Stephen's face?' She dropped the mirror, and bent down to pick it up, the hair falling over her face.

'Who am I to read faces like a book of words?' asked Gladus. 'No one looks on at our conceiving save the Lord, and He it is that shapes us in the darkness. If it pleased Him, He could set any face on our cooped-up soul. I heard a friar once give a sermon on such matters, saying that we wore nothing else than ill-fitting masks, which would be snatcht away on Judgement Day. Then, he declared, we should show features to the surprise of all, both for sweetness and abomination.' She fingered her own mottled face. 'Sometimes I lie awake in the dead of the dark, and touching my face I know certainly that it is no more than a painted visor, and I wonder what lies within.' She shuddered.

Agnes sat stiffly upright and spoke in a harsh voice. 'I should like to see my cousin Mary whipt bonedeep for her lack of reverence, taking a nun's veil instead of biding at home to care for her father. He is a man dismayed.'

Sanchia took up the mirror which Agnes had set down. 'I am sure that my face is my own,' she said, smiling at herself, 'and I would yield it for no one else's, much as I'd like my hair to be golden.'

Nest entered quietly and stood watching them. 'Three pairs of hands, and six of them idle. One ill weed mars a whole pot of pottage, and one chatter-wench delays a whole household.' Gladus took up the basket of feathers and went to empty it into a barrel. Sanchia ran to put the trenchers on a shelf. Agnes sat unmoving, looking at her mother, at the straight black hair combed down under a single red band, the high cheekbones and slanted eyes, the long thin sickle-mouth and the small scar on the cheek, which seemed twitching in the light reflected from the window on a polished kettle. She ran a fingernail along her own fuller lips, and suddenly shivered all over.

'It's my fault, mother,' she said, lowering her eyes. 'It was I who talked.'

The door opened, and William looked in. 'Dear wife, your brother asks for you, and in special requires some ink.'

'He asks too often and too much,' said Nest. 'I am hedged in with tasks.' She went over to the soap-barrel and dug a spoonful out. 'Better wash the skin away than add to the stains of the world.'

VIII

After their popish evensong was done, came some three score people or thereabouts and searched my house very

*strictly for me: but, as God's providence was, there was malt
a-drying upon the kiln; and they searched so narrowly for me
that I was glad to heave up a corner of the hair whereon the
malt lay, and went into the kiln-hole, and there stood till they
were gone, and so I escaped from them.*

*But within an hour after, there came a woman to my wife
to borrow a brush, and spied me through the keyhole of the
door; and there she carrying tidings abroad, immediately came
a great company of men and beset my house round about,
and I said to my wife, 'You see that the four leaders specially
seek my life; and therefore I pray you, wife, follow them and
talk loud to them that I may hear and so escape; and if they
search on the backside, I may escape on the streetside. And
be of good comfort, for our lives are in God's hand, and
though there be little help here on earth, yet there is help
enough from heaven.'*

*And when these men were searching on the backside, I
went into the street, among (as I guess) an hundred people,
and none of them laid hands on me, neither said they anything
to me; so I went out of the town, and lay there at an honest
man's house at the parish of Cobham that night.*

IX

Merric tightened the belt of his doublet under the blue
prentice-gown, and strode on down the street. Two carters,
whose carts had got their wheels interlocked, were shouting
abuse at one another. Round the corner a man in the pillory
was half asleep, with two slices of decaying bacon nailed
over his head and a placard saying that two years ago he had
been punisht for the same offence of selling bad meat. Three
small boys were collecting missiles to pelt at him. In his beard
were matted pieces of a rotten egg and mud. A stall-woman
drove away a horse that had begun crunching one of her
turnips. Merric shoved his way through the loiterers and came
within sight of the wall.

A cart went by, slowly clattering. Behind it was tied a man
who hunched up his shoulders and gave now and then a

raucous scream as the beadle lashed at him with a leather whip. Merric crossed and went under the arch of Moorgate. The broad expanse of the Fields opened before him, cut with dykes and conduits; over on the east ran the broad ditch with wooden bridges, which linked up with Tower Ditch, and in the northwest stood the stacks of the brickfield. Already the trained bands were falling in, on the archery grounds and other open spaces, mostly wearing white coats welted with green and daubed with red crosses. A few showed the city arms before and behind. Officers in royal livery of green and white stood glowering at the confused ranks from under their tall hats. On the left, where the country-levies from Kent, Essex, Surrey were grouped, there was a rowdy disorder which the loudest-voiced corporal could not affect.

Merric stood near two respectable sour-faced citizens to hear what they were saying: 'The ships that sailed out to keep the passage and the safe waftage of our army . . . so shaken and despoiled of their tackle as to be useless . . . the others dispersed or driven ashore . . . Yet they have issued orders for army to stand ready for a crossing at an hour's notice.' One of them asked if Guisnes had yet fallen. The other said that no word had come, or, if come, had not been given out.

Merric strolled over towards the country-levies. An officer was scolding Kentishmen who had come unfurnisht with white coats. One soldier wore a burgeonet with ridged crest, which was too large for his head; and whenever he made a quick movement it fell over his eyes. A drunken man from Penshurst tripped and went flat on his face. A little further on, a lieutenant was trying to get his men into files of ten. After much jostling, the files were correctly set, and he then instructed them how to double ranks. They were standing wide apart so that at the order the men in the odd ranks could move up between the men in the even ranks; and at last they seemed to grasp what was wanted. 'Double your ranks! To the left!' Then some stepped to left, some to right, others turned right round. The officer tried to correct the situation by reversing his order. 'To the right! Double your files!' The confusion grew worse.

The veterans in morions, stationed in the place of honour to the right of the line, looked on in disdain. Their square—ten

men in the front rank, with files ten deep—performed the
movements without any mistakes.

Merric moved on to a lad he knew who stood with the
trained bands' flag of argent and St. George Cross gules.
Nearby some gyved men showed that the jails had been
combed for soldiers and that no risks were taken about the
men's obedience. The pikes, ranging from twelve to fourteen
feet in length, even eighteen feet, weren't easy to handle, and
kept getting in one another's way. Men were yelling at one
another, as an officer went round examining the weapons.
'Old props with a knife hammered on,' he said in exasperation.
'We need foursquare heads of good temper.'

Merric grew tired of the noise and disorder. He moved back
towards the wall, where he knew an alehouse. But even there
he couldn't get away from the soldiers. One group had been in
the levies which sailed on the 6th and 8th of January from
Tower Wharf, and which had been driven back by the winds.
Two others were arguing about the best kind of armpiece.
Should the pieces be fixed to the gorget? or should they have
rerebraces attacht to the leather-undergarment by points passing through the two holes in the rerebrace-top? The rerebrace-
man had his points tied in a big bow-knot which a man behind
him couldn't resist plucking at. The arm-pieces fell off with a
clatter on someone's toe. Outside, a musket was discharged by
mistake, and the ale-wife complained that a hole had been
blown in her thatch.

Merric retired to the bench near the window, and looked
out at the faces of the shouters. Faces bewildered, sullen,
angry, in chilly air. A tumult of discordant purposes.

Someone threw a stone, which rattled on the buckler carried
by a captain's boy. The boy squealed and dropped the buckler;
and when he picked it up, the spike had come off. He tried to
screw it on again, but something was broken. The captain
cuffed him in the ear; and a burst of angry laughter came from
his men.

Further along, an ensign was trying to sort out the men
with muskets and calivers rusty from duck-shooting, and to
set them all round the square of pikemen. But as there were
too few, he ranged them in loose order in front and instructed
them how to fire by successive ranks. But they scarcely

listened; and when the front rank had pretended to fire, they stood there grinning or stupidly scowling, and didn't run round to the rear of the musketeer-force. And the second line showed no signs of getting ready to come up and take their places.

A horse wrenched loose and came trotting down the track, dodging a boy who tried to intercept it.

Merric turned his attention back to the talkers in the room. One was complaining that the shopkeepers were sending up the price of arms. A corselet cost thirty shillings and an arqu-bus eight: it was robbery. 'They're saying they'll send the trained bands over the seas,' a half-drunken man with a huge unwieldly sword blurted out in a momentary hush. No one answered; but when the talking began again, Merric heard the drinkers beside him on the bench:

'They can't do it, and they won't do it.'

'The Spaniards can drive up so far and no further.'

Outside, in increasing embranglement, the march to the Lord Mayor at Leadenhall was beginning.

x

Scalding Alley was made up of mean houses, and Hugh Rigeley's house was no better and no worse than the others. In the workshop the two apprentices, Stephen Rigeley and Jon Floyd, were winding up bolts of cloth. Hugh came in, watched them moodily for a while, and then asked Stephen to have a word with him. They went into the house and up to the small solar looking out of barred windows on to the street, scantily furnisht, with worn woolwork on the walls. The room was clean of dust, but otherwise neglected, with unscoured pewter on the sidetable. Hugh sat down, and motioned to Stephen to do the same. 'It's not as it used to be, the world falls away.'

Stephen thrust out his chin. 'Need it be?'

'There must be a purpose in such things.'

'And a trial for our spirits, which we are meant to meet.'

Hugh groaned, and then said, 'First, I am afraid for my brother William. He is entangled, and he strokes the deceiver. But I should not speak of this to you, who can do nothing. I am his brother and I must answer for failing to say the strengthening word at the right moment.' Neither spoke for a moment, and then Hugh went on, 'What were you saying of a trial?'

'Men are angry,' said Stephen, 'but they lack heart. They need a leader.'

'Not in tumult and violence. They had Wiat with a sword in his hand; he called and they gave back no answer. I do not blame them, I have no proof that the Lord wanted them to answer. So Wiat died on the block. They had Throgmorton, as brave a man as any Roman who never heard the name of Christ; he drew a dagger and cried out, and they did not answer. So he was racked, and died.'

'Yet we speak of these men, and are heartened.'

'I am saddened.'

'The Lord works only through the willing hands of his lovers.'

Hugh closed his eyes and groaned. 'I am thinking of Cutbert Simson, who is being racked this very day. As we talk here in peace and pleasantness he is having his body torn asunder. He testifies to the truth.' He opened his eyes and released the tears from under his lids. 'What creatures are we, grovelling to earth, while the saints speak out for righteousness. O, the pains, the travail, the zeal and fidelity of that man in caring for the congregation, and now they tear his arms out of their sockets and press hot balls upon his eyes.'

Stephen stirred uneasily. 'We shall avenge him.' His voice was hard, thin, forced from his contracted throat.

'Only the Lord may claim vengeance.' Hugh groaned again. 'I cannot get the smell of their burning flesh from my nostrils. When John Rough and Margaret Mearing were burnt a month ago, I locked the door and set the key in my Bible to prevent myself from going abroad. But a spirit came upon me, and I took the key and unlocked my fear, and I went down the road with the key held in my hand, impotent to say a word to those who saluted me.' He groaned. 'O, that good woman, I knew her well. And as I walked along Lothbury to Aldgate, I saw Sergeant, the devil who informed against her, to whose house she went asking if Judas dwelt there. No, said he. But she answered him: Does not the Judas who betrayed Christ dwell here? His name is Sergeant. And he was able to say nothing, and she went away, till next Friday as she stood talking with a friend she saw Cluney the Summoner of Bonner coming into the street and making for her house. I think surely he comes to speak with me, she said; and she came up behind him as he knocked on her door. What is it you want? she asked. And he said to her: It is you I want, you are to go with me. So he took her to the Bishop, who laid her up in jail, and the Wednesday afterwards they set her in the flame with John Rough.'

'Who told you those words of hers?'

'Henry Pond. Also he gave me a copy of the letter that Cutbert sent out of the Tower, and asked me to show it to all the faithful. That is why I brought you in. But first go and call Jon, for he is firm in the truth.'

Stephen rose and went out, while Hugh waited with his head sunk between his hands. Then the two lads came in. Hugh made two efforts to raise his head, and the third time he raised it; and then his eyes had a dimness. He drew a paper from his breast and handed it to Stephen. 'Read it, for I have no more strength.'

Stephen went nearer to the window, and read in a clear voice:

'On the Thursday after I was taken to the Tower I was called into the warehouse, before the Constable of the Tower and the Recorder of London, Master Cholmley. They commanded me to tell whom I called to the service in our English tongue. I answered that I would declare nothing. Whereupon I was set in a rack of iron, for the space of five hours as I judged. Then they asked me again if I would tell them. I answered as before. Then was I loosed and carried back to my lodgement. And on the Sunday after I was brought into the same place, before the Lieutenant and the Recorder, and they examined me. I answered as before, and the Lieutenant swore by God I should tell. Then they bound my forefingers together and put a small arrow between them and drew it through so fast that the blood followed and the arrow broke. Then they racked me twice. Then I was carried to my lodgement again, and ten days after the Lieutenant asked me if I would confess that which they had asked me before. I said that I had said as much as I would. Five days after he sent me to the high priest, Bonner the bishop of blood, where I was greatly assaulted and at whose hand I received the Pope's curse for bearing witness to the resurrection of Jesus Christ. And thus I commend you unto God, my friends . . .'

Stephen's voice broke. Hugh groaned and clawed at his face. Jon, a slight pale-haired lad of seventeen, leaned against the wall with the tears streaming from his open eyes. Stephen fought to contain himself, and read on:

'And to the word of his grace, with all who unfeignedly call upon the name of Jesus. Amen. I praise God for his great mercy shown upon us. Sing Hosanna unto the highest with me, Cutbert Simson. I ask all the world forgiveness, and I do forgive all the world . . .'

Stephen closed his eyes and threw himself weeping on the floor.

'How may we go on living?' Hugh stood up.

Stephen raised his head. 'Lord, show us the way. Tell us what to do?'

Hugh smote his breast. 'I went on to Smithfield. I saw Margaret Mearing stand in the filth of the fire which ravened at her body, O body of a saint more constant than my soul. I held the key that I had taken out of my Bible. I clenched it till it tore my flesh. I held the key, yet I did not speak. There was a seal on my lips. O God, have I denied you before all the angels? Why did I fail to speak?'

'The time is not yet come.' Stephen got on his knees. 'But it will come.' He stood up. 'It will come.'

A sense of peace descended on the room. Jon ceased sobbing. Hugh waited a moment and then said softly, 'Go back to your work, and set the world an example of sober industry.' He clasped Stephen, and kissed his brow. 'More than my son . . .' He drew away. 'My own flesh has rebelled against me, and my daughter has taken the veil of iniquity, but you have been given me instead. And I offer thanks also for you, Jon, my faithful child.' He kissed him in turn on the brow. 'Now leave me, both of you.'

XI

Blaise stood back, and stepped up onto a baulk of timber for a better view. The Messenger had already started off for Westminster Abbey, with the lesser gentry and the chancery clerks and the knights banneretts. The Trumpeters in glistening green and white swung round and sounded a fanfare. There was a passing scuffle as a Judge of the Queen's Bench was found in front of a Judge of Common Pleas, and a Viscount was taken out from the Knights of the Garter. Then the notables moved on, with heralds separating the Queen's Clerk and Hat-bearer from the Barons going two by two, and the Bishops from the Viscounts, and the Viscounts from the Earls. Then, after a press of Dukes, came the sergeants-at-arms, with their bright staves, and officials holding up on high such things as the Royal Cap, the Marshal Rod of England, and the Great Swords. And at last the Queen hurrying into her Chariot, which went with a crack of whips and a straining of harness, followed by four equerries of the stable and the Queen's footmen. The pensioners with their gilt partisans fell into confusion for a moment as the onlookers pushed in upon them; then they marched off along Whitehall with trumpetings. Behind them came a long straggle of monks.

Blaise pricked his ears. Now that the noise was thinning, he could hear what the citizens below him were saying. 'It is to be hoped that the Members of Parliament will vote money out of their own bags. London's udders are squeezed dry . . . They are scouring the wards for able-bodied men. Yesterday a thousand more were mustered, and for what? . . . Yet rogues are still thick in Blackfriars and in the stews across the river . . .' Then the crowd began breaking up, moving towards Charing Cross.

Blaise stepped down, beside an old man in a new gown of mantle-frieze—clearly one of a dozen given in charity by Master Alsop's will. Not far off stood the heavily-bearded sergeant of the royal confectionary. Blaise went over. 'My wife bade me deliver her best thanks for those candied violets.' The sergeant bowed gawkily, having a sucket in his mouth, and Blaise passed on. In the park of St. James's Manor he saw an antlered deer come out of a bush on a slight rise; and northward the scattered trees flanking St. Martin's Lane. The new gilt, which had been painted on the Cross for the Queen's wedding, still glittered in the pale light.

He turned into the Strand, with horse-hooves going clitter-clatter on the new paving-stones and beggars clustering in the shadow of the great houses. A pedlar was shouting, 'Pewter for sale,' and a ballad-singer on the shop-side of the street was monotonously declaiming: 'Pass not for ribalds which milk-maids defame.' Blaise stood for a few minutes near the Savoy, biting his nails, then he smiled and doffed his cap in salutation.

'Good day to you, Sir Francis.'

Sir Francis Ascow, a recent heir clad in mockado stained with last night's wine, made a more restrained but benevolent reply. He wore large earrings with red stones set in gold, and a flaring brooch in his hat. He flourished his hand to show off the thumb-ring, took a toothpick from the case in his pocket, and picked his teeth as he talked. A mirror hung from his girdle, and under his hat a lovelock curled over his left eye.

'Ah, Master Rigeley, the very man I most hoped to see. You are as welcome to me as a unicorn is to the lion, or a fountain of brackish water to men thirsting in a desert. I have found not far from here the most celestial pair of peach-coloured hose laced with small tawny lace, and, scarcely less desirable, a cloak lined with crimson bays, and guarded with black cloth and twisted carnation lace. I cannot endure to live without enjoying them, I promise you; and the whoreson tailor refuses me another penny of credit. Worse, he threatens to sell them to Will Privett, knowing him the last man in the world whom I could bear to possess them. For I hate him as a vulture hates an eel and as a serpent hates the smell of hartshorn.'

'Always at your service, Sir Francis,' said Blaise, bowing.

'I have proof of it, but I need yet more, unless my heart is to be broken. Speak in a word. Shall I have another fifty pounds within the hour?' He waved his hands which night-bleaching had whitened, and shifted the girdle on his pinched-in waist. 'Shall I indeed?'

Blaise looked down the road and saw Don Pedro Iniguez del Bedroso coming towards them. He answered in haste, 'It will be difficult to raise the money in so short a time; but for your sake it shall be done. Come for it to my lodgings at None.'

'I may call you my dolphin,' murmured Sir Francis, 'seeing that you preserve me in mid-shipwreck.'

'Ah, Sir Francis,' cried Don Pedro, who had come in King Philip's train and stayed at Court ever since. 'And Master Blaise, my friend from the house of treasure.' A tall long-faced fellow, with clear-cut features, he wore his clothes with so much ease and dignity that Sir Francis gave him a haughty and envious look, then began to finger his slasht sleeve with obsequious questions. But Don Pedro turned back to Blaise, bowing again, determined to complete his compliment and to air his excellent though slightly harsh English. 'With a treasure all his own, a wife more beautiful than a rose, two roses, a garden of roses, all the roses in the world, eh?' He laughed in simple admiration of his own fine phrases.

' A peerless paragon,' interrupted Sir Francis. 'I have always said so. Who, beholding her, has not been scorched with the fire of fancy, scalded with the boiling water of affection, and blistered with the beams of her beauty?' He smirked at Blaise who humbly turned up his eyes to express appreciation of Sir Francis's superior rhetoric.

'We are agreed?' said Don Pedro, and laughed so loudly that a horse shied. He took Sir Francis's arm, and they went off. Blaise stood watching them a moment, with knitted brows, then he started off back in the opposite direction, at a brisk pace. Shortly before the Cross, he turned down a lane towards the river and entered a small court. Climbing a steep outside-stairs, he reached his first-floor lodgings and let himself in with a key.

His wife, Dousabel, was waiting there. 'I saw you coming, through the window,' she said in a small piping voice, and smiled, plump and flaxen, with heavy lids coming half down over her skyblue eyes. He regarded her in a noncommittal way, then went into the room and threw off his belt. His dagger rattled against a wooden chair.

'Half a pint of wine,' he said in a vexed voice, 'I'm tired.'

She moved quickly off, light for all her plumpness, leaving a smell of ambergris. He watched her hungrily as soon as her back was turned, and sniffed, slowly smiling. Lying back on the settle, he closed his eyes, still smiling, and clasped his hands together as if he were praying. But computations about money, not prayers, were the substance of his meditative murmurs.

Dousabel returned, with a rustle of fine stuffs and amber-gris, with muscadel and biscuits on a beechwood tray. Open-ing his eyes, he dipped biscuits in the cup of wine and then dropped them into his mouth, while she stood watching him closely all the while. When he had finished the biscuits, he drank, and settled back again, with closed eyes, and dozed. Then suddenly he began talking in a drowsy pleased voice.

'Ah, Douse, I'm tired. It's a wicked world.' Smiles wreathed his face. 'But not so crafty that it cannot be beaten at its own game by one who reads in its soul. They go in their golden tumults and their lions roar out of brass, they go in their furious jewels and their summer-prides, and all the while I am watching them. They tear at each other's throats in the night, and they tread on my face, knowing nothing . . .'

Dousabel, spreading her skirts, sank warily down on a stool, holding her palms out to the brazier-glow and keeping her eyes on him all the while. When he abruptly changed the tone of his words and opened his eyes to stare at her, she showed no sign of discomfort.

'I saw Don Pedro, and he spoke of you. I saw Sir Francis also, and he spoke of you. I think it would be better if they did not speak of you. It wounds me, and I do not like to be wounded.'

She gave no answer, staring back quietly at him, and he closed his eyes again. His voice returned to its sleepy purr, its slurring of words into a rapid tumbling stream.

'Yet my time will come, and they will be forced to notice my presence. The bells are clanging, and all to no purpose. The Houses of Parliament meet, and the mice are still gnaw-ing. There is a fish which sinks to the bottom of the sea when storms are nearing, and no one knows its name but I. The world is wicked, but there are things it does not know. They cheat me to my face, they throw roses in my face, they hide in the deep waters under my bed. My own brother conspires against me with a Welsh bastard, who cheats him in turn with dangling lies; and in the end both shall be deceived. Now is the world like the scarlet apples of Arabia, which begin to rot before they are half ripe; and my rose is scattered by a lecherous wind. The gold is falling over my face, sideways. The waters are seeping through the many holes of rats, but on the last day all things shall redound to my credit, and I shall buy you a fan of great white plumes and a pomander ball of silver, and seat you on a milky cushion, naked as a peeled onion, with your feet on my face, O my Dousabel, but not a stitch of red, nothing red, nothing red do you hear?'

His voice rose in a grating sharpness, and he opened his eyes, shaking his head as if he awoke suddenly out of a deep sleep.

'Come over here, closer,' he said hoarsely, and she moved the stool beside the settle. He placed his hand on her knee. 'You are mine, mine, do you hear?' He stared hungrily first into one of her eyes, then into the other. 'Be as silent as the ravenous grave. Say nothing, nothing, do you hear?' He trembled and began caressing her knee. 'Tell me, what are you thinking? tell me . . .'

'Nothing.'

'Nothing. Are you sure? Nothing. That is right. Remember that all I do is for your sake only. Be patient . . . come closer . . . and silent as the grave. There is no other way . . .'

CHAPTER THREE

February

I

Before daybreak someone unknown hanged a cat on the gallows beside the cross in Chepe, habited in a garment like to that the priest wore that said mass; she had a shaven crown, and in her forefeet held a piece of paper made round, representing wafer.

II

The Merchant Taylors' quarterly day was a little late through the trouble over loans and assessments. In the upper room, the Master and Wardens were talking things over for the hundredth time. Robert Dove struck the table with his fist, 'Let us give what is needful for the protection of the realm, but we are lost if we pour out money for wars in Europe. Have not the Commons of Parliament set aside, and rightly, the offers of King Philip for the recovery of Calais?' He caught the gracious eye of the painted wooden statue of the Virgin behind the Master, and quailed. 'Why should we fear to say these things?' he weakly protested. 'Have not the Commons made a plain and English answer?'

'An English answer,' said the Master, 'but not so plain as some malcontents would wish.'

Robert Dove was about to speak again, but he glanced over the Master's head and closed his mouth.

Beside the window the group were talking of the coiners brought in from Cambridge. As if the coinage wasn't in bad enough state, debased and clipt, rubbed and scraped, till testons of the lion or the fleur-de-lys were not worth more than two pence and the best penny was valued at three-farthings: now forged coins were to be added to the trader's difficulties. 'The Antwerp bankerers will take advantage of it, to raise the cost of English goods.'

'They have other tricks, making the rate fall when they know a good mass of wares will be bought for England with money taken up on their Exchange. They draw in all the money on the Bourse and hold it, so that, when we want to change money for our purchases, the bankerers in conspiracy lower the price of English money, to their convenient gain and our loss.'

William Rigeley had been listening to this discussion on the coinage; but he now slipped out of the room and went down to the Hall where others of the livery were waiting. There he found the man he wanted, a ferrety-eyed trader named Olyff; and drew him into a sideroom where the clock in the wainscot case was standing. Several pieces of armour had been brought down from the gallery and stacked beside the clock, thirty muskets and a heap of mouldy arrow-sheafs.

'I shall be brief,' said William. 'I must be repaid at once.'

'I have told you that I can't do it,' complained Olyff. 'Is it my fault that the ship was taken by Algiers pirates?'

William's face darkened redly, and the jowls grew heavier. 'Then I shall sell you up and shame you before the world.'

Olyff kept looking round the room, as if he sought an escape-hole, as if he suspected eavesdroppers. 'It's not in my power to stop you, but you'll gain nothing.'

'I'll gain at least my revenge.'

Olyff took up one of the muskets and tried its trigger. 'Too loose,' he muttered. 'But you know that some of the terms are not such as the law smiles on. It would be better if you waited. My son has gone over to Antwerp to find if all is lost.'

'I am too pressed with a disaster in my own turn to spare another,' said William, standing in a swollen daze of anger. 'I have had ill fortune in more matters than one, and the burden of these new loans is too great for my galled back.'

'That is true with us all,' said Olyff. He took up some arrows. 'The feathers are decayed.'

'I put money in a clothing venture,' said William, 'in a Yorkshire sheep-run that the monks once owned, and all seemed fairly set for a fortune. But an agent has fled to Ireland with all the money, and I cannot lay the hands of the law on him. Therefore look to yourself, who are yet within the compass.'

'You will gain nothing,' Olyff repeated. 'If we are to have armour, we need an armourer, or rust will set its teeth in our metal. I beg you to wait at least till my son comes back.' He took up another musket.

'Till then, but not an hour longer. You must sell your soul if need be, for my repayment, else I shall harry you off the earth. Is that understood?'

'Yes, yes,' said Olyff, 'and I give you all the thanks of my soul for such kindly and noble words. I have always praised you as a worthy christian and now I find my words come true.' He nervously clicked the trigger. 'Tighter than is fitting. We must pay for an armourer if we would stay free from corrosions, eh? Give me your hand, William Rigeley. Till my son comes back. That is all I ask.'

William took his hand, and then drew away. 'If I am to come down, I shall bring with me as many others as I may, and you are the one whom I shall first overturn to break my own fall. Is that understood?'

'It is all understood, thoroughly understood,' said Olyff, and trod upon an arrow, snapping it.

They went back to the Hall. William joined a group who were talking about murmurs of revolt among the young men in the Yeomanry of the Company. 'Let the inner foulness break forth,' he said savagely, 'that we may lance it with assurance.' His words were so passionate that they blunted the edge of the complaints; and after a pause the others began on a different matter, the increasing insolence of the Clothworkers Company, who were once more refusing to grind shears for the Taylors and claiming the right to search in the workshops of both companies. 'Let them remain the sweaty drudges of a craft,' William interrupted again, and with such vehemence that the others looked at him and then at one another.

III

A thin dim light straggled through the window-slit in the cell. A heavy brooding hush lay over Syon House. A faint padding and scraping noise told that one of the Brigettine nuns was going past the door, and then there was nothing. Only the dim light moving in like a slow glimmering smoke. Objects in the cell were not so much picked out by the glimmer as revealed by a faint inner glow of putrescence. On the narrow bed of boards with no mattress lay a small body so rigidly arched that the chin was pressed in tightly against the breastbone.

This girl, with eyes that seemed deepsunken into blindness, spoke in a weak pleading voice, 'Are you there? are you there?' Nothing happened. A sparrow-twitter sounded for a moment outside the window-slit, and abruptly ended. 'Are you there?' the voice pleaded.

From deep down within her there came a quite different voice, a deep man's voice, which answered, 'Aye, Mary Rigeley, I am here and always here. Cannot you feel your hand upon me?'

She twisted and spoke broken words in her woman's voice, 'I won't, I won't. Go away.' Frothy spit appeared between her bitten lips. 'It's not me speaking, not me. Holy Virgin, it isn't true.'

The other voice broke in, 'You detest God and all his works, for he has deceived you with lies, and ravished you before you reached the age of understanding. Nightly he splits you like a peascod with the knife of his cruelty . . . You lie at his mercy, he comes upon you like a tempest with a myriad tongues of lightning and makes you the whore of the angels, for they see beneath all veils and thrust their wounding fingers into you . . .'

Gasping. 'Are you there still?'

'I am here, and you feel me working my way deeper within. You sow, don't you know that you have been a beast of burden all these years? I am the master, I am the head, and I shall drive you all in yoked pairs. Ah, my poor and battered Mary, you are a deceived thing. Come with me and be paid for your

shame, for your breasts are sweet apples, and there is a spring
of sweet water in your belly. Let me drink, Mary. Why should
you obey a snoring drunkard, who sets pins in your body
while you sleep? Curse God and be happy at last.'

The voice died away in low rumblings. The door opened
and a nun with a pale long face looked in. 'What is it, sister?
are you still troubled?'

Mary struggled up on to her elbows, panting. 'O, he has
made a pact with a witch to prevent me speaking to God.' She
gazed wildly round. 'Give me a piece of the holy sacrament.
I kept some and put it carefully away. O where is it? If that
has been stolen, I am lost for ever.'

'The devil has no power over the bread of life,' said the nun,
soothingly. 'Where is it?' She searched round, and found the
wafer in a wrapping of silk stuck in a crevice in the wall.
'Here.'

'Help me to hold it against my head, or I shall die,' cried
Mary. 'Against my head, using David's key to unlock my
memory.' The nun held the wafer against Mary's brow, and
slowly Mary relaxed and sank down. 'I feel better now. No
longer does he sit as heavy as a tower on my head.' She
gasped. 'Pull down the sheet over my feet, quick.'

IV

*My Lord Mayor, sitting with the Council, as most meet for
his wisdom and seeing Anne Ascough standing upon life and
death, 'I pray you,' said he, 'my lords, give me leave to talk
with this woman.' And leave was granted.*

*Lord Mayor: 'You foolish woman, say you that the priests
cannot make the body of Christ?'*

*Anne: 'I say so, my lord, for I have read that God made
man; but that man can make God I never yet read, nor I
suppose ever shall read it.'*

*Lord Mayor: 'No, you foolish woman: after the words of
consecration, is it not the Lord's Body?'*

*Anne: 'No, it is but consecrated bread, or sacramental
bread.'*

Lord Mayor: 'What, if a mouse eat it after the consecration,

*what shall become of the mouse? what say you, you foolish
woman?'*
  Anne: *'What shall become of her, say you, my lord?'*
  Lord Mayor: *'I say that the mouse is damned.'*
  Anne: *'Alack, poor mouse.'*
  *By this time the lords had enough of my lord mayor's
divinity, and perceiving that some could not keep in their
laughing, proceeded to the butchery and slaughter that they
intended before they came thither.*

v

  There was no sound in the house except a faint clacking
from the kitchen. The buzz-quiet was at its thickest in the
solar. Nest opened the door gently and peeped in; then she
entered on tiptoe and glided over to the cypress-chest. She slid
the carpet of turkey-work off, and lifted the lid. Agnes, unnoticed in the further corner, coughed, and Nest dropped the
lid with a bang. She turned with fierce eyes. 'Why are you
hiding there?'
  'I wasn't hiding. I was reading.'
  'You're always hiding. I don't like it. You're breeding lazy
bones. You steal away and sit curled up on a cushion in a
wicked dream.'
  'Wicked? What do you mean by that?'
  'You know well enough. When I see shells, I guess eggs.'
Nest stood angrily stiffened, with her mouth working convul-
sively and making little sucking noises. She came into the
middle of the room. 'I've watched you. I've seen the look in
your eyes when you think no one's looking. We weren't made
to cosset ourselves in a corner.'
  Agnes winced as though she had been struck, and put the
knuckle of her forefinger in her mouth, biting it. 'What do you
mean?'
  'Then tell me what you think about when you hide?'
  'What did you think about when you were my age?'
  'I was married, child, with a great boy in my lap and
another coming under my girdle.'
  Agnes stood up. 'And like hurdle-racers, Stephen came

head-over heels after Merric and John. You kept God busy
in those days.'

'Better keep God busy than the devil.' She turned to go.
'It's time you were married. You are not one of those who
keep well in the flower. I must see to it again.'

'No, no,' cried Agnes, 'I am afraid. Twice there has been
death in my betrothal kiss. Twice you have tried, and twice
they have died, and I will have no third time. After it everyone would point me out as accursed.'

'Nonsense,' said Nest, with a kindlier note. 'Will Machyn
was not the first lad whom a horse kicked in the belly, and
Harry Hall was only one of many thousands who died of the
pest. You were in no way blameworthy. Rather tell yourself
that third time is lucky time.'

'I have been twice widowed while yet a maid,' said Agnes,
weeping, 'and now I am lost. You have said it yourself. You
have said that you read the thoughts in my hidden mind. You
are very wise indeed. Do you know that I dreamed last night
of cutting you up with an axe?' She laughed triumphantly.
'No, you did not know that. You know nothing.'

'Dreams go by opposites,' said Nest, moving uneasily
towards the door, 'and what you dreamed of was your own
marriage.'

'I don't believe it.' She thrust her chin right out. 'And listen,
since you know so much of my dreams, I have dreamed that
I am not your child, nor Stephen. I have dreamed that the
devil meddled with the heavenly bride. As though I were an
eye in your belly I have seen a stranger get me upon your unlatched body, and I clapped my hands at the sight.'

Nest put her hands over her face. 'May the Lord forgive me
for stirring up such a beelzebub babble in your thoughts. I
meant nothing so dangerous and damnable when I rebuked
you; but you startled me into an anger that I regret with all
my heart. Let us hear no more such things, as you value my
peace and your own.'

'It was you began the questions, and now it is I must end
them.'

Nest crossed herself. 'You are becoming as swollen up with
devils as Hugh's Mary herself. Beware in time, I bid you.'

'Maybe there is a reason for it,' said Agnes, coming closer

and pressing out her chin. 'Maybe we both had the same father.'

Nest stood with her back to the door, moving her shoulders uncertainly; her eyes were fixed in a blind terror on Agnes's face. 'You never knew how he loved his Cecily, who died in bearing Mary only a few days after you were born. But all this is a madness. I should strike you in the face, but I am held back as though a great wind blew me against this door and I see you dwindling into a distance. Get you behind me, Satan . . .' Her voice weakened, died away, but her eyes were still fixed in a spell of fear on Agnes's face.

'Tell me, mother,' begged Agnes. 'Please tell me. That is all I ask.' Tears dripped down her cheeks.

Nest blinked, and the spell was broken. 'O, how wicked you are,' she screamed and hit her across the face. Then she opened the door and went out.

Agnes stood stock still, with bent head, for some minutes. Then with a long sigh she turned and went over to the settle, staring at the cypress-chest. At last she rose and went to lift the lid of the chest, but heard someone at the door. At once she rushed back to the settle. Ybel looked in.

'I'm sorry. I thought Sanchia was here.'

'No, she's gone to buy some pepper,' she said sharply, then added. 'Don't look so miserable. Come in for a moment.' He doubtfully closed the door. 'Why do you love her so much? She doesn't care for you.'

'Water wears the rock,' said Ybel, 'and I trust she will like me when it suits her.'

Agnes watched him with cruel eyes. 'Do you know that Merric could do as he wishes with her? At the crooking of his little finger she would skip to his arms.'

'I know it,' said Ybel with dogged wretchedness. 'But he is my friend, and he will not crook his finger.'

'You are so pitifully foolish,' she said with a small laugh, 'that I feel a kindness towards you.'

'Would you say a word then on my behalf?' he asked eagerly. 'She'd listen to you; for I know that there is no one more able to move her mind and her will.'

'Give me a reason for helping you, and I'll help.'

He peered at her, trying to understand. 'But you said that

you pitied me. Why should anyone want a reason for a good deed? Most of all when it costs nothing but a little breath.'

Again she laughed. 'Have you seen the world, Ybel? Have you seen the world and the things that men do? Do you still say that there needs no reason for a good deed?'

He frowned. 'I look upon you with much reverence. Is not that a reason?'

'A reason for my making use of you to suit my own purposes, not for your making use of me. Again, I say, look at the world.'

He pondered. 'I can think of no reason, except that I love her and am unhappy, and you are kind and good.'

'My poor fool, my strange and pitiful fool,' she cried, torn between tears and laughter, 'you give me reasons only for deceiving you. Go away and think of a reason, and then I am yours, do you understand?'

He nodded, but his eyes confessed that he understood nothing. He was turning to go, when Fabyan hobbled in.

'Where is my Edgar? They have sent him out on a message without my permission. This is the third time in a month, and I shall revoke the whole contract, as I am within my rights in doing; for so it runs, to prevent their taking advantage of me once the signature is dry on the parchment. I shall demand my fortune back and leave this house within the week.'

'Edgar is playing at leapfrog with some other boys in the back-lane,' said Ybel.

'Fetch him at once, at once,' insisted Fabyan. Then, as Ybel slipped out, he turned to Agnes, 'I hold nothing against you, my dear granddaughter; and if I recall the contract and disinherit my son William it will not be to the disadvantage of his children. He may have been guiltless this time, though I must sift the matter further before I acquit him wholly of ill intent, but I know he seeks to pare my rights and dignities, and if I once slacken my watch I'll be undone in a twinkling.'

'Undone in a twinkling,' she repeated.

VI

Jon knocked at the door of the dark parlour. 'A man desires to see you, master.' Hugh rose and went across, peering through the dim light at the man who stood near the street door.

'Who is there?'

The man did not answer but came closer. Then Hugh recognised him, and motioned towards the dark parlour. They went in together, and Hugh closed the door.

'Edward Benet,' he said, 'I thank God for this sight of your face. What is it you want of me?'

'I came to learn if you have left the London Congregation, or if you still cleave to the faith.'

'I am with you, now and always,' said Hugh fervently. 'The friend who told me of the meeting-places had to flee from the ungodly; and I no longer knew where the faithful met. Tell me where we meet next Sunday, and I shall come.'

'I am glad.' Benet, a small self-possessed man with large ears, wrinkled his forehead. 'As I came here, I saw the informer Banbury looking up at the windows and the signs.'

'But he lives in Stepney.'

'When he has a harm to do the faithful, he'll go anywhere, to the edge of hell, and will one day topple over. I saw him.'

Hugh listened for a moment. 'Did he see you?'

'I think not, though I sweated for a moment of unworthy fear.' He smote his chest and said in a matter-of-fact voice, 'Tremble, my body, for I shall not tremble.' Then he went on quickly with a tale. 'Three years ago I was taken up for carrying Coverdale's *Testament* into Newgate for my friend Tyngle; but I was delivered by a chance of God out of the hands of that bloody man Bonner. For we were forced to mass on a Saturday, and as we came back the porter shut the door too soon. I knocked to be let in, but he paid no heed. That day Bonner was making many priests, and there was a press of them coming out. Yet I was clearly a prisoner and a man oppressed, having one of my sleeves and the forepart of my coat burnt off in the prison-torment. Nevertheless, I went out with the new-made priests and so escaped. Then let me have no fears again, but go about the business of heaven without confusion . . .'

Some one had come into the shop, with heavy steps. Hugh grasped Benet's arm, and they stood listening. A blur of words, and then Stephen's clear voice, 'No, sir, we have no Spanish wool with a cypress band . . .' The steps withdrew, and a sigh of silence followed.

Benet said in his plain stolid way, 'You will come then?'

'Next Sunday. Where will the service be held?'

'At Thomas Carden's house, at the Blackfriars. You know it?'

Hugh nodded. 'I shall see you there. God be praised.'

VII

'Give me your shoulder, wench. It's the only part of you that I need at the moment.' Jones tottered a few steps and then leaned heavily on Sanchia, who giggled and sank at the knees, then bore him up again.

On the floor below, Nest noticed Ybel lingering on the stairs. 'Leave her to it now. We couldn't find you when you were wanted. Return to your work.' Ybel went with a backward look.

On the ground floor, William opened his ledger and closed it again. The noises annoyed him. He went to the door of his office and called, 'Must the whole house be thrown into a confusion?' But no one paid any attention. He heard Nest screeching something in alarm; and then the clumping sounds came nearer, and Sanchia's giggles. He went back to his table and forced himself to stay there till at last Jones limped into the room.

'You are up then at last?' he said with an attempt at affability.

'I am better than I seem,' said Jones. 'But Nest was so afraid I would slip again on the stairs that I have played an infirm part at her pleasure.' He sat down in the chair which William had set ready, and folded his arms.

'There are many things to be made clear.' William hesitated, then said harshly, 'There was no tide at height when you say you threw the abbot into the river. He would have fallen upon mud.'

Jones smiled. 'Well then, he fell upon mud, if you say so.'

'It is what you say that concerns us. You said that you threw him into the river.'

'I used the word river in a general way, to signify the space between bank and bank, whether or not there was deep water on every foot of it. If the tide was out, he fell into the mud; and when the tide rose, it washed him away.'

'Also, I find that this abbot of whom you speak was a dead man a week before you killed him, and died of a stroke, at the monastery of Bermondsey.'

Jones smiled and rubbed his hands. 'Ah, how shrewd they are, Will. I expected no less.'

William was taken aback. 'What do you mean?'

'Consider the wavering balances in this England and the hatred that is felt for the Spaniards and the war in which they have ensnared us. Above all, the Cardinal has no wish to bring his Romish clergy and monks into further disrepute. Therefore, having found that this abbot was a loose ungirdler of women, he has surmised that he died in a brothel-matter, and a tale that smacks of piety has been tied to his filthy carcase.'

William pondered over this argument. At last he remarked. 'You come so smartly in with your explications that my mind is in a mist. After all, you may be right. I can no longer think to the point.' He passed his hand over his brow. 'But there are so many dark and difficult twists in your story that you may not ask for my aid any longer unless you open your breast and show me all.'

'I shall do it,' said Jones, nodding, 'because I had intended all this while to do no otherwise as soon as I rose from my bed of affliction. Here then is the fact. The treasure lies in a chapel near Richmond. Of that I am sure; but there is one small point that I must yet ascertain before we dig. For we should act foolishly if we went to dig up the whole place, as though we had the leisure of a week for our search. We must go straight to the exact spot where the chest lies, and lift it out between two hoots of the owl.'

'How are you going to learn this thing? If another man knows it, why does he not dig before us?'

'He may know that one thing, and yet not know which chapel it is, or even that it is a chapel.'

'You are asking me to trust you further, and I have said that I will not do it.'

'I am asking nothing. I have told you that there'll be a brief delay, but I am asking nothing.'

'Then indeed ask nothing, and I will perhaps wait.'

'When I said that I asked nothing, I meant that I asked no money or the like. There is however another thing I ask, because of my weakness of body.'

'I have told you—'

Jones raised his hand. 'No, no, don't say words you'll repent. All I ask is the company of Merric. And this I ask all the more strongly because in his presence you cannot suspect me of playing you false or sliddering away upon any private device.'

William lowered his eyes. 'Then I agree. But at the end of a week I shall expect a report without veils and voids.'

Old Fabyan opened the door. 'Where is my Edgar? You have set him a task behind my back. Tell me at once where he is. Also, let me inform you that you owe him a new cap and a pair of hose. He goes shabby in the streets, to my disgrace and your own; but you have forgotten the agreement you signed, and its commandments. You forget the commandment of the Lord, to honour your father and mother, but you shall be reminded of the clauses to which you have set your name, because the law will support them.'

Nest appeared behind him. 'Edgar is waiting for you in your room.'

'Am I to climb all those stairs again,' complained Fabyan, 'only because you use my boy behind my back and then send him up to my room, to make my angers appear unreasonable?'

'Nest,' William called, but she had already gone away.

VIII

Blaise cocked his head on one side. Yes, more than one man was coming up the outer stairs. He looked at Dousabel. She gave him an expressionless glance in return and went out. He walked over the matting carpet, to the front-door, and opened. Sir Francis and Don Pedro stood there, arm-in-arm, in the narrow top-space with its broken rail. They grasped his arm with noisy salutations, and he led them in. Tabitha, the small dark-haired round-faced maid of thirteen, had already appeared with wine and cups which she set down on the playing-table by the small virginal.

'Why am I so honoured?' asked Blaise.

'Fie, man,' said Sir Francis with a hiccough. 'The man who is honoured never asks for reasons. He is honoured, damn him, and that's all there is to it. He can't do anything about it, can he, Pedro?'

'The honour is on our side,' said Don Pedro, with a deep bow. 'Thus the question need not be answered, I agree.'

'Where's Lady Dousabel?' asked Sir Francis, looking muzzily round. 'I smell her, but that's all.'

'My poor wife has been in sad health,' said Blaise.

'What she needs is a cup of wine in good company,' said Sir Francis. 'Call her in.'

'Tabitha,' said Blaise, 'see if your mistress feels well enough to spend a few moments here with my friends.'

Sir Francis drew him aside in the bow-window curtained with Wedmoll lace hanging from rings looped on rods. Don Pedro sank lazily into the cushions of the settle, fondling a grey cat and inspecting the painted cloths over the chimney: Mary and Gabriel at one side, and Diana surprised naked in her pool at the other.

'To be brief, I desire some more money,' said Sir Francis.

'A man of your rank and estates need never have that desire unfulfilled for long,' said Blaise, watching the cat.

'A hundred pounds,' Sir Francis hiccoughed.

'You know that I have no deep money-chests of my own,' said Blaise, 'or you should have the money at a whistle. I must borrow it for you from a usurer in Moorfields, and he declares that money is harder than ever to find in these afflicted days. Everywhere men call in their moneys to meet the loans demanded by the Queen.'

'I know, I know,' said Sir Francis carelessly. 'I shall be advised by you in any terms which he proposes.'

'This time it is twenty-five per cent,' said Blaise, intently watching the somnolent cat under the strong hands of Don Pedro. 'And he insists that you instruct your steward to act at my orders. For in this matter I am the go-between and agent of both parties, and he swears that he will deliver no more coins unless I have this warrant under your hands.'

'Draw it up as you will, but let me have the money by eleven in the morning at latest.'

'It shall be done, I promise you.'

They turned to see Dousabel come in wearing a coat of rose velvet and grey fur, with large sleeves, a waistcoat and taffeta kirtle of pale blue; on her head was a small cap strung with chrysolites. She moistened her lips with her tongue as she stood waiting to be greeted, and the poise of her head emphasised her slight double-chin.

'You are no longer sick?' asked Don Pedro rising to kiss her hand. 'But I forget that magnificent custom of you English —that you unlock your wife's lips in hospitable salute to all who come.' He kissed her on the lips.

'I also claim my mouthful,' said Sir Francis, and likewise kissed her. 'Ah, when a chance-encounter begets such bliss, what a drench of delight must he feel who owns such a sweetness by day and by night, by week and by month, by year and by year?'

Blaise handed round the cups, while Dousabel sat on the settle affording a glimpse of her cork shoes gilt with red embroidery and her open-seamed stockings.

'I am like a man,' said Sir Francis, holding up his finger and uttering the sentence with an uncertain accent, 'who, having drunk of the river Lincestic in Bohemia, is presently turned to stone; for I am enchanted beyond motion.'

'Stand there as a clothes-rack then,' said Don Pedro, 'for though I too am enchanted, I wish to learn the receit of this magic, or at least that part of which is translated into perfume. For I am not without skill in such a matter, being a lover of Ovid and desiring to know all that may be known of the metamorphoses of lovely ladies into flowers, so that some day I may find how to compose out of flowers and their scents the ladies who fled from the ancient gods.'

'Let us guess then,' said Sir Francis. He abandoned his

posture of stricken admiration, and came sniffing round Dousabel. 'Gourd water, radish and white beans,' he said with a shout of laughter.

'Fie, how clownish,' replied Dousabel with her tinkling laugh.

'Now it is my turn,' said Don Pedro. He closed his eyes. 'Flowers of glass, honey and mustard seed, with the fat of swans and the milk of goats.'

'I shall never give away my secret,' said Dousabel, tinkling again. 'Therefore I will not say which of you has touched me the closer.' She turned to Don Pedro, 'But tell me what are the latest ingredients that the learned ladies of your land are said to employ.'

He answered her lazily. 'Turpentine of Abezzo washt in nine waters and oils of lentisco I have heard praised. With cypress soap and alum scagliola. But these are doubtless long tried-out by so rich a scholar of Venus as yourself.'

She smiled, but did not answer, Sir Francis, however, drew out an ivory memorandum-book. 'An admirable varnish for the face, I am sure, well-gliddered in a gallipot. Why, the names are enough to ravish a man outright. I know a merchant who trades with Genoa and Aleppo and will gain me anything under the sun, no matter how rare or precious.'

Blaise came from the virginal where he had been leaning, and said, 'Sad as I am, gentlemen, I must now ask you to go; for I can no longer delay.' He gave a sharp look at Sir Francis who nodded, yawned, and straightened himself. The two visitors kissed Dousabel's hand, but she refused them her mouth, saying that one kiss was sufficient for so brief a visit.

'You will dine with me soon,' said Sir Francis. 'I have found an ordinary near Covent Garden, where they serve a delectable dinner in the upper rooms. You will both dine with me, or I shall be hurt beyond redemption.'

'We shall speak of that again,' said Blaise, ushering them out. He came back and sat at the table without looking at Dousabel, and began making notes in a small book. Dousabel rose and poured herself out another cupful of wine, then resumed her seat. After near half an hour, Blaise closed his notebook and lay back in the settle. He took a letter from his pocket and handed it to his wife. 'Read it out, I want to hear it spoken, for then it will feed my soul with the balm that it needs.'

She took the paper, smoothed it out on her lap, skimmed through the writing, and then read:

'Mr. Rigeley, after my hearty commendations to you, you shall understand that I have sent in the basket a couple of hens, a cheese, a dozen of puddings, forty eggs, and some apples to fill up. Also, there are four puddings for your good wife out of the bag. Goodman Birch appointed with a man to pay you certain money in London, whether you have received them or not I do not know. The small hogs have come home little or nothing better for their going; if the others prove no better we shall have no porkers, except we feed them with beans. Thorn's wife has caused the corn to be thresht out, which was distrained for the debt due to Harris (and thus to you), and Harris prays that you may see what remedy there can be had against them who did the threshing. I thank you for the oranges you sent me, but they were very much bruised. This with my hearty commendation, I leave to trouble you more at present, your affec. friend, L. Hoskins.'

She finished and set the paper aside on the arm of the settle. After a while Blaise spoke in his musing voice, 'You see that the steward and all look to me already as the master, and within six months I shall be master indeed of the manor, and more beside. But money in truth is hard to find, and I must calculate to a nicety or lose my clue in the maze. Next week I shall go down again to the manor, and speak with Hoskins to his face; for there are many matters to be dealt with, and I wish the rose-garden to be planted anew, with high hedges, for your domain . . .' He opened his eyes suddenly. 'What are you thinking?'

'I shall dye my hair again. It should be lighter for these new clothes.'

He lay back again. 'Give me the paper that I may hold it in my hand.'

IX

There were many golden images of the saints in Wykeham's College by Winton. The church door was directly over against the usher's chamber. Mr Forde tied a long cord to the images,

linking them all in one cord, and being in the chamber after
midnight he plucked the cord's end, and at one pull all the
golden gods came down with a heyho rumbelow. It wakened
all men with the rush. They were amazed at the terrible noise
and also dismayed at the grievous sight. The cord being pluckt
hard and cut with a twitch, lay at the church door.

At last they fell to searching, but Mr Forde, most suspected, was found in his bed; yet he had a dog's life among
them, Mr White the headmaster, the fellows of the house,
and the scholars crying out and railing at him by supporta-
tion of their master. Lewd men lay in wait for him many times.

X

'We need more roomspace,' said Gregory Hawes, looking
round at the broadcloths and kerseys stretcht on tenters or
hanging on poles in the open shed at the back of his yard.
'It is great shame that so many ruined churches and abbeys
stand useless in London and the Liberties, when their room
is needed for our craft.'

'Aye,' said Martin, with his eye on the solar window. Surely
Jacint had waved to him.

They went into the warehouse, where two girls with unlaced bodices were in charge of the beams and weights, weighing out wool for carders and spinners. A smell of madder and
woad came heavily from the further room. One of the girls
had her hair thick with flock, and she laughed, catching
Martin's eye and shaking wool-dust from her head. But
Gregory Hawes turned and stared at her, and she made herself busy with the sacks.

Back in the yard, Gregory Hawes gazed suspiciously round,
passed his hand over his cropt head, and snorted. 'You understand?' he asked for the third time. 'Speak cautiously and
take the lease but without a word of explanation. Give the
first payment at once, for there are many who would snatch
at the house, and you must gain it beyond argument. There
on the Surrey side the city regulations cannot reach, and the
journeyman or the small-master must dance to our tune.' He
stroked his chin, snorted, and looked with pride at the new

chimney of twisted brickwork which he had had added to his
house only a twelvemonth ago.

'I understand,' said Martin drily. 'Shall I go at once, since
the matter is so pressing?'

But his father had one more speech to make. 'I heard that
William Rigeley is in sore straits.' The snort became a laugh.
'That will teach him to know on which side his bread is
buttered. I shall discover who holds his bills, and I'll buy
them up. Then let him look me in the face. Be cautious, but
find out what you can on this matter.'

Martin went into the house, and up the stairs with the
newly carved balustrade. A servant-girl was standing on a
stool, reaching up with bare arms to dust the top of the
cupboard at the stairhead. He pinched her behind, and she
gave a discreetly inviting squeak, but he turned into the solar.
Jacint was there, dimpling as she chattered, with broad brow
and small red squarish mouth, her face narrowing under
the cheekbones. And Aunt Gertrude, sewing with quick
resolved movements, twisting her mouth to one side.

'Passion of my heart, we have strange news for your ears,'
said Jacint. 'Indeed there has been nothing stranger since the
calf with six legs was shown at the Windmill in Finsbury
field.'

'This is no matter for jesting,' said Aunt Gertrude, 'except
in so far as men jest at devils. Which I have always thought
a perilous jape, for the devil may well have the last word and
make us laugh till we weep tears of blood.'

'Then tell him,' said Jacint.

'No, you tell him,' said Gertrude. 'There are certain things
which my tongue cannot bear to utter, and ingratitude I have
always rated the blackest of sins.'

'In a nutshell, our father is to marry again.'

'I cannot credit it,' said Martin, with a deep frown. 'I have
heard no whisper of it. He said not a word in my hearing to
hint at such a rashness.'

'He has fallen topsyturvy into a passion,' said Jacint.

'That is beyond all bounds of reason.'

'With a widow's jointure.'

'Ah, that is possible.'

'It is proved and abominable,' said Gertrude, spitting out a thread. 'Did he need the money to save his fortunes, I should forgive him; but never has he prospered more widely.'

'That is why he lusts after the widow's coffer,' observed Jacint. 'For gold is a catching disease.'

'But which of the gilded widows is it?'

'Mistress Pernel Wicke, the richest and the most resigned of them all.'

'I won't have it,' cried Martin, unable to hold his rage in any longer. 'I'll tell him so.'

'Neither will Tace have it,' said Jacint, with her gurgling laugh. 'She rebels at having kept a bed warm all these years for a crackt and patched-up widow, who is held together only by a glue of gold.' She saw her aunt signing to her to stop, but she went on, 'Surely we may now acknowledge Tace as his well-flesht bedmate; for though we have misliked her empire while it lasted, we must all combine now in lamenting its undeserved fall.'

'Why must he disgrace us before the world?'

'No, Martin, the world will think it no disgrace. The world will hear only the chinkling of her inherited treasure. The world will gratulate our father on his decrepit bride as on a reinvigorating goddess. The world will laugh, but the world will admire.'

'I shall never permit it.'

'Then go and tell him.'

'You know I cannot do it. But I shall find some other way to break the match. I'd rather marry the dribbling widow myself than let him do it. She has a sickly son, who lives at her country-place, and I hate him even more than Merric Rigeley. She would never cease till she'd filched our heritage for his scrabbling enjoyment.'

'Yes, steal her from him,' Jacint pleaded with a gurgling laugh. 'After all, you have excellent warrant. Did not Launcelot carry off his master's wife on his saddlebow? Did not Sir Tristram lie with the wife of his Uncle Mark? And did not Sir Lamerock with a rash courage invade the bed of his own aunt, the wife of King Lote?'

'Fie,' said Aunt Gertrude, 'you will put him in danger of his soul, dear lad.'

'We shall take counsel together,' Jacint went on, 'and we

shall even if need be, admit Tace to our righteous plans. But
by hook or crook we must defeat this marriage.'

He nodded and was going out, when she added, 'Why did
you speak of Merric?'

'I saw him again at the review in Moorfield, and he sticks
in my thoughts.'

'You knocked him again to the earth?'

'No, he looked the other way, and I let him pass.' He
studied her face for a moment, and went out.

'Merric, who is that?' asked Aunt Gertrude. 'Ah, yes,
Merric Rigeley, who was prentice here. Have he and Martin
been fighting again?'

'Now and again.'

'What fighting-cocks these men are.' She shook her head.
'They cannot let things be. If God hadn't told us otherwise,
I'd have sworn that Adam meddled first with the apple and
beguiled his wife into the fret of sin. But it cannot be that
this Merric still dares to desire you. Your father would never
agree to a union of Rigeley and Hawes bloods.'

'Neither do we agree to a mixture of Hawes and Wicke in
bed or bond; yet maybe for all our striving it will come
to pass.'

'Sometimes I think you talk only to cause misunderstand-
ings, Jacint, and today I am too weary and disturbed for
your play.'

She grew serious, 'I am sorry, aunt. You have lovingly
laboured in this house for years, and truly it is on your
behalf, at least in good part, that I resent this marriage-
project and hate Mrs. Wickes as heartily as you yourself.'

'I hate no one, Jacint, but the enemies of the Lord,' said
Gertude hastily, 'and as to whom those are I say nothing
and will not be trapt. I leave it to the Lord Himself to
determine, and if that is heresy, who is safe from the fire?
But I am within my godly rights in despising a flighty and
abject woman who should have turned her thoughts to ghost-
lier things than a double-bed, God forgive us all, sinners as
we are.' She sighed and agitated the hairy mole on her chin,
sniffed and wiped her reddish nose.

'Never doubt my affection, aunt,' said Jacint humbly.

'I pray then that I have misjudged you. After all, there's a look of your dead mother in your face when you lower your head like that; and it's clear to me that if she hadn't died, there'd have been no second marriages to divide the household. For she always urged me to come here, even when she was still alive; and thus when I did come after her death I felt that I had her ghost on my side. For many months I had a constant sense of her presence at my left shoulder, telling me what to do, so that I often spoke out aloud my answers and was adjudged a madwoman.'

'Tell me more about her,' cajoled Jacint, clasping her hands.

'I've told you all that I remember.' She pondered. 'She had a birthmark on her left knee in the speaking likeness of a dove. But I told you that before. Also, she loved applepie with custard more than anything else in the world, even more than a carol with claspt hands. But you knew all that before. I have told you everything.'

'Everything,' repeated Jacint. 'Then tell me again about the day she was startled with a leaf blown in her face and dropped me out of the solar window, and I fell by providence into a basket of newly-washt clothes on the ground.'

'What a day was that!' Aunt Gertrude raised her hands and stared up at the plaster ceiling with its recent ribbing and patterning in heavy relief. She lost the trail of her thoughts. 'I liked the painted flowers better.'

Jacint sprang up. 'I haven't told Uncle Rafe yet.'

'He'll only make a mock of it,' said Gertrude sadly. 'Though he's my brother, I know him for a convinced mocker and gleeker, who bites his thumb at the blessed angels. I only hope and pray that the angels are better-mannered and never bite their thumbs back at him.'

Hawes in his counting-room was talking to an agent from Norwich about the efforts being made to compel country-clothiers into bringing their wares to Blakewell Hall in London for first offer. 'The towns may rage and pass as many regulations as they will,' he said, 'and their drapers may set themselves up as kings of the Bridewell, but for long-seeing men the countryside is the loadstone of money.'

'We are of one mind,' said the agent, laying his finger on his bulbous nose. 'You will understand that in Norwich I

must go with the tide on the Council and vote for setting the
workless men and women to tasks within the city. They talk
of giving each spinster six pounds of wool on a Saturday
and sending the constable after her if she bring it not back
spun by nightfall next Saturday; and such enforcements are
indeed required to spare the Council's money from maintain-
ing idle rogues.'

He leaned forward and lowered his voice, pointing over
some horizon of profit. 'But it is further afield, among the
villagers, that cloth can be most cheaply made, and with
least outlay.'

Hawes poured out some claret. 'Taste of this, I have no
finer wine, and I chose it to match your foresight. Men make
so many lamentations over the decay of towns and the spreading of sheepwalks that they spend their wits in unprofitable
schemes.' He set a book up on end and knocked it over.

'The cottager, with his patch of arable, will work for returns
in money that would fail to keep a journeyman alive in one
of our cities. Only with his cloth can we gain our markets
abroad.'

The Norwich dealer drank the wine and smacked his lips.
'There is just the right tang of borage.' He raised one eyebrow and went on, 'The town lives by regulations, and though
we set the assize of wages as low as may be, we must set it
higher than the rates for the cottager. Therefore look to the
countryside, in Norfolk and in Wiltshire, in Yorkshire and
its valleys.' Again he pointed at the wall and traced map-
configurations in the musty air, winking. 'But with a decent
discretion, for there are many enemies of this policy, as you
know better even than myself.'

Hawes clapped the man on the back. 'We are opportunely
met, my friend.'

Jacint burst into the attic without knocking. 'Uncle Rafe,
father is marrying again, a painted and mouldering widow.
What shall we do about it?'

'Drink the best wines at his wedding,' said Rafe without
looking up. 'And let Martin throw her down in the race for
her garter.' He looked up at last. 'Will she want my attic, do

you think? No? Then I give her my blessing thrice over
and return to more serious things.'

'There is nothing more serious. We are all of us enraged.'

'Marriage is the venture of taking an eel from a bag in
which there are twenty snakes for one eel. Having said that,
there is nothing else to say. As for your father, he'd have a
good wit if someone else had the keeping of it.'

She took hold of his ears. 'Look me in the face.'

'When the Grecian girls took hold of a man by the ears,
it was to hold him securely for a kiss.'

She kissed him. 'There then. Now you must talk with me
of serious things.'

'Serious things? Listen then. There are today in England
three religions. That which the Bishops hold, and that which
their opponents hold, and that which the generality hold,
which is to say one thing and believe another. And if I were
to declare this in the street, all three religions would combine
to burn me. Which proves that I am right and all the others
are wrong.'

She put her hands to her ears. 'That is the worst thing
you have ever said.'

'But not as bad as the things I shall yet say.' He tossed his
books about till he had found the *Colloquia* of Erasmus.
'Listen to this, my angry girl. A man tells of a shipwreck,
and you must know that the shipwreck is our world in its
blinded fear.' He read out, 'I heard one with a clear voice
promise Christopher, who is at Paris on the top of a church,
a mountain more truly than a statue, a wax candle as big as
himself. When bawling this vow at the loudest of his voice
again and again, he was nudged by the man who stood next
to him, and was warned that he should have a care what he
vowed; for though he made an auction of all his goods, he
could never pay for such a candle. Then he lowered his voice
lest the saint should hear, and said: Hold your tongue, you
fool, do you think I speak from the heart? If once I touch
land, I'll not give him a tallow-candle.'

'He was a coward and a liar,' said Jacint, 'and I hope to
be neither.'

'Ah, we lie because we fear, and we fear because we lie,
and then we are lost. For we set our courage upon a lie and

our truth upon a fear, and are bold in the wrong cause and
shrink from the truth as that which rends us.'

'I say only what you have taught me.'

'I have taught you nothing.' He smiled sadly. 'Forgive me,
my beloved, the good I have done you; for you will find it
a grievous burden outside this small room.'

'I shall still seek to break my father's marriage.'

'Then do it, not from malice, but from merriment, and all
shall be forgiven. I mean, you will be able to forgive yourself when you have failed or succeeded.'

After a while she said, 'I am afraid.'

XI

The wind had come up again, blowing from the south-
west with an unending cloud-host. Well-muffled, Merric and
Jones went down New Fish Street, and then turned along a
lane towards the docks. A constable was measuring the height
of a low pentice-roof, saying that it was at least a foot less
than the prescribed ten; and the housewife, wrapped in a
fustian blanket, was howling and wringing her hands. 'It is
as great a pity to see a woman weep as to see a goose go
barefoot,' observed Jones. Further along, some lads were
shooting with a crossbow at a cat in a leather bottle. A girl,
looking from a window, threw a piece of candied peel at
Merric and hit him on the cheek; and he almost fell over a
hairy man with a barrow of charcoal. 'This way,' said Jones,
and they turned into a wider street.

The black waggon of a hearse was trundling by, going to
the house of the recently-dead Lord Mayor. No coffin bumped
about in it, but a heap of dark cassocks for distribution to
women mourners, and an empty barrel. Over a near door a
scutcheon declared that a nobleman was lodging there: Jones
examined it, but could not make out whose the arms were.
'You never know what knowledge may save your life.' Then
he nudged Merric, 'Do you see that gallant with a swelling
on his cheek? He is older than he seems, blacking his hair
with a leaden comb; a gambler who has lost more money
than you will ever save. It was to him that our good King
Harry lost a throw for a hundred pounds against the Jesus

bells hanging in a steeple not far from Paul's, as great and
tuneable bells as any in the city.'

They turned into a lane again, nearer the river. A man
sitting in the door of his shop was reading aloud from a book
held close against his eyes. Jones quickened pace and drew
Merric on. 'He was reading a forbidden book,' he muttered.
'The fool will be under arrest by the chimes of noon.'

Merric looked back. 'Why must men rush on death for the
sake of a word? Is he mad that he reads in the street, and
aloud, if read he must?'

'We all have our own way of wooing death,' said Jones. He
pointed to the painted lattice of an inn, and they entered.
'Yes, we all hug our mistress,' he went on, 'though there is
death in the marrow of her bones.'

Inside, they settled at a table in a curtained recess, but
did not draw the curtain. As the tapster brought them their
wine, they looked out unspeaking on the other drinkers. A
tall girl attracted Merric's eyes because of the pretty crudity
with which she was painted: her eyebrows broad lines of
black, her mouth a bright red, and on her cheeks the same
red in simple patches. More, her lowcut dress showed most
of her breasts, their nipples boldly painted with the same
red. And yet she was proudly young, with no slackness or
wrinkles. A small morose tradesman held her hand.

After the wine was set on the table, Jones said, 'You don't
know why you have been delivered up to me as my companion.'

'To watch over you, that you do not break your ankle again.
Also, that you do not flee.'

'Ybel or Edgar would have served for that. No, it is a more
violent matter, Merric; and I have taken a fancy to you as my
dear sister's favourite child.'

'That I am her favourite child is news to me indeed. Now
I think of it, I should have said that she owns no favourites,
but that she dislikes Agnes most.'

'You are mistaken, nephew, and I have a mind to make
your fortune. Another fancy of mine is that your father does
not treat you justly, and I find no reason why you rather
than he should not benefit from my discoveries.'

Merric grasped his cup tightly. 'It is true that I have not

been justly treated, but I have never complained, nor shall I.'

The notably painted girl saw Merric, and gave a broad smile. He smiled back, but turned away to Jones, who said, 'I have much gold at my fingertips, but not yet in the palm. I propose that you help me and set aside all other claims upon your honesty. I shall then give you a third of what we gain, and keep the rest for myself. Unless of course you wish to hand your third over to your father and take nothing.'

Merric pondered hard. 'Is this a true offer?'

'As true as this wine. The matter is simple. Who is to get that part of my treasure which I do not get myself? You or your father?'

'But is not Blaise a partner as well?'

'Your father has excluded him, and now I propose that we exclude your father. It is justice.'

Merric laughed bitterly. 'And with whom will you propose that I in turn am excluded?'

'With no one. I have given you my reasons; but if you set them aside, you yet have a good reason for trusting me, since we are the ones who will find the treasure with our own hands and heads. Therefore you will be on the spot at all times, and I could not cheat you if I wished it. Which I do not wish.'

Merric pondered again. 'Well then, here is my hand upon the contract. And if you cheat me, I shall cut your throat.'

Jones gave his hinnying laugh. 'Those are words that I respect, and we shall prosper together.' They pressed hands over the table. A lurching drunkard who had been watching them came up and leaned on the table. 'Give every man his due and give him no more,' he said, 'by failure of which aphorism the world falls away into maggots.' He slapped himself on the chest and almost slid under the table. 'I am Roaring Rickword of Colchester. Now answer me or be damned for dastards.'

'We are deep in business, Master Rickword,' said Jones.

'Do you refuse to drink with me?' bellowed the man. 'That is the greatest indignation which can be offered to a man, and were he yet godlier given you would make him swear out his heart's blood. No, I'll not hear another word till you have drunk with me.'

'Then you shall drink with us, and honour will be satisfied,' said Jones, pouring wine from the jug into the man's jack.

'You know, I hope, that I have drunk all the alehouses in Colchester dry, and therefore have come on to London. I have drunk them dry and laid the taps on the table when I've done. Blood, I'll challenge all the true rob-pots in Europe to leap up to the chin in a barrel of beer, and if I cannot drink it down to my foot before I leave, and then set the tap in the midst of the house, and then turn a good turn of the toe on it, let me be counted a nobody, a mere carthorse, a squeamish titterer. Aye, let me be bound to drink nothing but small beer for seven years after, and then I had as lief be hanged.' Looking round in squint-eyed defiance, he noticed a friend signalling to him from the other side of the room. 'Forgive me, companions, but I must go. Remember well what I have said. A pound of care won't pay an ounce of debt, and that's the end of it.' He staggered off.

'Our bargain is then fixed,' said Jones. Merric nodded, and Jones went on, 'I need not tell you for the moment more than this: that I have knowledge of a chest of gold hidden in the earth. How and why, I shall leave to a later telling. What matters is that I have quarreled with a certain man who shares the knowledge with me; and in the haste of our parting we have each gained a half of the paper that sets the story out.'

'You don't know where the treasure lies?'

'It lies in a chapel, which I know. But to dig at hazard would bring unwelcome eyes upon us. This other man of whom I speak knows the place in the chapel where the chest is buried, but he does not know the chapel's name.'

'Then you must find the man, I see.'

'That we may find the paper on him, and know all.'

Merric drank. He looked over again at the big-breasted girl, and drank to her. 'I heard the rumours in our house, as you have guessed. Who then was the abbot you struck down?'

'Another matter,' said Jones, grimacing. 'Let us leave him out. Our concern is with a sailor, who captains a ship now tied up to a post near Botolph Wharf. That it still floats there, I have the word of Ybel, whom I sent to bring me word of it yesterday.'

The girl threw off the hand of the morose man, and came

with unsteady steps over to the table. 'If you are a man, prove it,' she said in a northern voice, thrusting out her breasts.

'He must prove it another way,' said Jones, standing up.

Merric sat sprawling, with his eyes lockt in the girl's; then he too stood up. 'Sadly I must go,' he said in a weak voice, and pushed a shilling in her hand.

At first she seemed to take it; but with her slow wits she understood at last, and screamed, throwing the coin after him and striking him in the back of the neck. 'Go then, you gagtooth jack,' she called, 'you codless cheat.' Merric slipped quickly out.

'What then are we to do?' he asked uncertainly.

'Not to Botolph Wharf,' replied Jones, walking close against him and pressing him into the wall. 'We can't climb into his ship and ask him questions. Rather, we must find him in a less periculous situation. To wit, alone in a backlane, and preferably too drunk for fast running.'

'But how? Shall we invite him thither?'

'We must trust to our fortune and to the fact that sooner or later all men go walking in the dusk, especially sailors who have no home but a tavern-hearth and a harlot's bosom. Let us then frequent the streets by the Wharf and leave the rest to the devil's contrivance; for he has had a longer experience in such matters than either of us.'

Merric laughed out aloud. 'I am glad that we have met in this venture.'

'We shall do many things together, lad, and yet be buried within the church's ground. Now tell me something of yourself.'

Merric paused, and then the words tumbled out of him. 'You know I was apprenticed to Gregory Hawes in the old days when he worked hand-in-glove with my father, and John was yet alive to step into my father's shoes. Now I am fallen between their angers, and my father refuses to set me up or confide his purposes. Sometimes I think he has a sore lack of money, and then that he hates me. Whatever the reason, I am lost.'

'All the more cause then for your taking a third of the treasure.'

'As I truly think. For my troubles are more entangled than I have yet said. Jacint Hawes and myself plighted our troth in the old days, and I cannot get her out of my thoughts. Sometimes I hate her, and then I die with tenderness for her face. I feel that if I lose her I have been wholly defeated by her father and mine.'

'Take another wench, and sluice this Jacint from your flesh. Then she will fade from your thoughts.'

'But I don't want her to fade. It would break something in my life to lose her now. You have seen the wench at home, Sanchia, who sighs in my face on the stairs. I know that if I snapped my fingers all her laces would break in a breath, and yet I cannot do it. True, Ybel lies under her feet, and he is my friend. But at moments when the devil pricks me on, his melancholy makes me want all the more to throw her petticoat over her face. And one day I will do it, to end the torment in which I live. For my father would take it to heart and say things of such a fury that we would quarrel past redemption. Her father, you see, was a journeyman who died in his service and left the maid to his care.'

'Then look for a Sanchia outside his walls.'

'No, I must win my Jacint, else I'll shrink from looking myself in the mirror-face.'

'Right then. Forget all your Jacints and Sanchias for a week or two, till we dig our treasure up from the dead bones in the chapel. After that you will be rich enough to start on your own. But not a word to your father, or he will spoil everything. Was I not a true friend in offering you his share? For you are Nest's dear son, and he is only her pestilent husband.' He held out his hand. 'Let us shake our hands once more on this excellent accord.'

They shook hands. A monk came yawning out of the house ahead, and stared at them suspiciously. 'Any wood to cleave?' a ragged man was shouting through cupped hands.

XII

As Hugh was coming into Blackfriars, a man stepped out of a doorway and halted him. Thomas Samson, the deacon.

'Not this way, brother,' he said in a low voice. 'Carden's house is being watched. Bearde the informer is lurking at hand. Go instead to Seamler's house at Aldgate.' Hugh nodded and turned back. At the corner he met Stephen and Jon, who had been coming behind him at a distance. 'It is not here after all,' he said, 'but rather at Aldgate, a house I know. Follow not far in my rear, so that you may escape if you see me arrested.' Then he walked off, with a thoughtful frown hooded over his eyes, going faster and again faster.

They came to Aldgate, to the priory of Holy Trinity, which had been thrown down near twenty years before and sold for building materials; and now there were bushes sprouting from the cracks in the levelled walls. Hugh paused, losing his direction for a moment, then made for the glass-house and went down a narrow lane. He stopped uncertainly at a side-gate, and entered; but came back and waited for the lads. 'It is here,' he said, and they went into a large shed where already a couple of score men and women were waiting in quiet, many of them old women and three being young wives with child. A few whispered together, but mostly they bowed their heads and seemed to read signs in the straws upon the ground.

'Greetings in the Lord, brothers,' said a stalwart woman.

Hugh went aside, to meditate against the wall. Stephen looked round and saw Tom Hinshaw, a blithe roundfaced lad of nineteen, apprentice to a bookseller in Paul's churchyard; and drew Jon over to the bench where he sat. Tom made room.

'We used to come here last year, but I think you went to John Rough's house at that time. Then at last we were suspected, but had warning in time. When the constable came with his men, the housewife said that a dozen of good fellows had visited her for breakfast and then had gone a-maying. But now we are returned.'

Stephen looked round with anxious eyes, and at last settled his gaze with an eagerness of repose on the bench opposite where a frail milkfaced girl sat with her mother, bending a little forward with her hands claspt on her knees. Her hair was coloured with the palest gold, like dried-out hay in the sun or certain wines, and mixed its glistening with the milky light of her small face.

Tom laid his hand on Stephen's knee, and drew his attention back. Stephen trembled and then murmured, 'Before I came I opened the holy book for a word of guidance, and I read at once these sentences out of Jeremiah. Make bright the arrows, gather the shields . . . set up the standard on the walls of Babylon, make the watch strong, set up the watchman, prepare the ambushes . . .' He trembled again. 'Could a command sound more clearly, as though it spoke with trumpets?'

'Make bright the arrows,' repeated Tom with kindling eyes. 'You were indeed led by the spirit. Aye, prepare the ambushes.'

'We must read the prophets with new eyes,' said Jon, stammering and flushing. 'Where they wrote in the flesh, we must read in the spirit. Where they wrote in the law, we must read in charity.'

'The words are plain,' said Stephen. 'Besides, as we came along, I cried out in the spirit for guidance, and when we reached the lane to this place, I besought as follows: Lord, if I am to take your command in the manifest sense, make the number of my steps even, and if in the allegoric sense, make them odd. And lo, I took forty steps between that cry and the threshold of this meeting.'

'If we tempt God, we waken the devil,' said Jon. Tom was so stirred by the dispute that he tore at his hands, cracking the fingerjoints; and many of the people nearby looked round at him. But at that moment the minister Bentham came in, and there was a rustle of gladness and expectation all over the shed.

'Brothers,' he said, setting the tips of his fingers together, 'we shall meet here on Sundays until the spies drive us on. There will be two services, the first between nine and eleven, and the second between one and four in the afternoon. And before we begin our worship, let me make some needed warnings. No more services will be held at the Swan in Limehouse or at the Kings Head in Radcliff, as we know that the informer Roger Sergeant has notified these places to the Bishop of London. But there are still weekly meetings at Horsleydown beyond Battle Bridge, and at Master Church's house in Wapping by the waterside.'

The service began. Bentham, a stocky man with a heavy chin and slow voice, made a short prayer, and then addressed the congregation. 'My dearly beloved, may the angel of the Lord pitch his tent about us and defend us in all ways. Amen.'

The congregation answered, 'Amen.'

'O my dear ones, we are met here in sad tribulation, which is our glory and election, like a dark and ragged cloak that shows for lining the red of a satin bright as blood, gorgeously signifying a reversal and a jubilation. O consider, if we are the true servants of Christ, then we may not in any wise make agreement with his enemy Antichrist. For there is no concord between them, say the Scriptures, and a man cannot serve two masters, says Christ. Further, it is prefigured for us in the old law where God's people are most strictly commanded that they shall not mingle themselves with the heathen, and are forbidden to eat, drink, or marry with them.'

Stephen tore his eyes from the minister and looked over at the pale girl, Mabel. Her hands were still claspt over her knees, only her face was turned towards the minister, so that he saw her faint profile, her small snubnose and slightly retreating chin, the long silken lashes laid glistening on her lily-cheek. Her heavy-bodied mother at her side was listening with mouth wide open, panting regularly; with one broad hand resting on her huge bosom as it rose and fell.

'. . . . and so often as they either married with their un-circumcised sons or took their unsanctified daughters in marriage, so often there came a great and ponderous wrath of God on his own people, to overthrow them and their cities, with the holy sanctuary itself. And he brought in strange princes of a false religion to govern them, so that they were sure of hunger, sword, pestilence, and wild beasts to devour them; and such punishments never ceased till the good people of God were separated out from the idolaters.'

'O Lord, separate us out,' cried a woman, Mrs. Baker, a fishmonger's wife of Fish Street.

'Dearly beloved, this was written for our learning, that through patience and comfort of the truth we might have hope. Look around on this realm of England. We behold the faithful held in derision and trampled underfoot, and the cities, towns and houses where they dwelt are inhabited by those who have no right thereunto, and the true owners are spoiled of their labours. The sanctuary of the blessed word is laid desolate, till the very foxes run over it and the owls hoot in the pulpit. Yet is the truth the very food of our souls; and where it is not preached, there the people perish.'

Hugh groaned deeply. Jon was swaying forward, as if he were about to fall. Stephen put an arm round him, and Jon sank back against his shoulder.

'But the prophet has told us, the man who refrains from evil will be spoiled. Why then should we stand abashed at our fate, seeing that it was foretold?'

Mat Osborne, a weaver of Lambeth came forward. 'We are spoiled, and who can expect otherwise? But I remember, he who chastised the money-lenders from the temple has told us that he came to bring a sword among men, and that they who take to the sword shall perish by the sword.'

Bentham raised his hand. 'Wait till I have done, brother.' He brought out a paper from his breast. 'Here I have the very letter that was written by Ralph Allerton to Richard Wroth with his own blood, a few days before they both testified in the flame.'

The congregation hushed and leaned forward, while Bentham held the paper at arms length level with his eyes and read:

'O dear brother, I pray for you. For I hear that you have been divers times before the bishop in examination. Wherefore take heed for Christ's sake what the wise man teaches, and shrink not away when you are enticed to confess an untruth for hope of life; but be ready always to give an answer of the hope which is in you. For whosoever confesses Christ before men, him will Christ also confess before the father; but he that is ashamed to confess him before men shall have his reward with the deniers. And therefore, brother, go forward.'

Bentham pressed the paper against his heart, and said in a choking voice, 'Praise God, he went forward into the fire with unfaltering faith.' He burst into tears and sat down on the stool near the table. A man took the paper from him and passed it round. Most of the congregation were weeping and sobbing; and when Jon was handed the letter written in blood, he fainted. Stephen and Tom laid him on the bench and chafed his hands. Mearing, grey-haired and grey-eyed, was going round with a cap, collecting for the poor prisoners in Marshalsea and the Lollard's Tower; while others were preparing the communion table. Bentham, wiping his eyes, was taking a loaf and a bottle of red wine out of a bag.

A rap on the door struck everyone motionless. But Samson came in, saying that he had seen the informer go away from the Blackfriars house with his hat pulled over his face. Stephen, leaving Jon to Tom's care, moved across the shed towards Mabel; but she kept her eyes fixed on her unshifting hands, and he passed her by, making for the weaver who had spoken of the moneylenders.

Two shopkeepers were arguing with him. 'You are no better than an Anabaptist who endangers the souls of the godly with snares no less deadly than the Pope's. We must submit to the laws of the world and the princes, except insofar as matters of conscience are touched. And even then our resistance must be that of the turned cheek and the mild answer.'

'No, no,' protested Mat the weaver, 'what you say is what the Popes and their popelings have taught as Christian practice, to ensure their own power. How much do you think the Pope cares for turned cheeks? No, he cares for acts which lessen his power. Otherwise we are no better than faggots which warm his feet against the cold.'

'Then you justify the papists when they say that a heresy, by which they mean a testimony of the truth, is a treason?'

'A treason against all laws but those of the liberty of love. A treason against both the Bishop of Rome and the lords of our land who are ready to whip us to the stake of fire, but who jealously guard in a vizored obedience the lands which they have stolen. Men who will have the Pope but abhor Peter's Pence: men who go with the wind and are to be scattered.'

Stephen lunged forward, opening his mouth to speak and clenching his hands; but the minister had finished cutting up the loaf, and the communion table was set ready.

'Brothers and sisters,' he said, folding his hands, 'here is the table which we appoint as a memorial of our Lord's death, and in no superstitious fear. For we are not of those who think that God can be made of dough and that he sits huddled in a pyx instead of heaven.'

'No Round Robin or Jack-in-a-Box for us,' called one of the men.

'We must speak further,' said Stephen aside to Mat Osborne, and then went over to help Jon. The Congregation was moving in single file towards the table.

XIII

Blaise strolled up and down the gallery, with hands behind his back, pausing every few paces to stare with blank eyes at the painted cloths of tortured saints and amorous nymphs. Then, at the patter of many feet and the hectoring call of the usher, he stood humbly aside and bowed his head. But the slight glance he threw down the gallery told him who was coming, and the lines tightened round his mouth. A gentleman with a rod went stiffly in front, and a troop of maids came after, and between them walked the Lady Elizabeth in a tight bodice, with her bosom uncovered, as was right for a maid, and a necklace glinting round her straight neck; her fardingale outspreading red brocade. Blaise backed against the cloth that showed Daphne bursting with a rash of leaves; but with one quick glance up through his lashes he took in her high poised head of reddish hair, her calm face with aquiline nose and light blue eyes, her lips closed tight against unwary words, her slight imperious body gliding under the pomp of clothes. Then she was past, and the last waiting-maid had waggled her rump by in the hurrying train. Blaise looked steadily after them, till all were through the further door; then he rubbed his chin.

Then he was humbly bowed again. A bare-footed friar approached him. 'Who was that?' the friar asked in quavering tones.

'The Lady Elizabeth, I think.'

'You are not of her train?'

'No, I am a clerk of the Exchequer, who have come with a message for the Lord Treasurer.'

'You are a good son of the Church?'

'Yes, father. I made my confession last week.'

'The peace of God be with you.'

Blaise looked up and saw two piercing dark eyes fixed upon him. He lowered his head, and the friar went silently on.

No sooner was he out of sight than George Stoddard came in. 'I am sorry to have kept you,' he said, bustling importantly. 'I had found a shortage of charcoal. Someone has pilfered. Well, what may I do for you, my friend?'

'I have a message for the Lord Treasurer, but I wished to see you first.'

'I think he has gone by barge over to Lambeth.'

'Then I have lost my trouble. But I wished also to speak privately of other matters. You have a Chancery case against the copy-holders at Hadlow manor, and I can help you to witnesses.'

'My claim is sure,' said Stoddard. 'The two sons of the main lease-holder sold their rights to a man, who sold it to me, and I have his hand for it. That they owned the right to sell is proved by the steward approving their inheritance of the land.'

'Yes,' said Blaise, 'but the elder son contests your tenant's occupancy, alleging glass windows in your bond through lack of dates and places. You see, I know your position well, and think I can remedy its weaknesses; for in the Receipt we meet many men and learn many things.'

'We shall talk of it later with my lawyer' said Stoddard gratefully. He came closer. 'The Queen has declared again that she is with child.' He paused, and they looked at one another, faintly grinning. 'She is angered at the Kentish recruits,' Stoddard went on, 'for lacking white coats.'

'Her confessor spoke to me. He came along the gallery after the princess had passed.'

'Ah, many tongues are clacking.' He beckoned to Blaise and they went out of the gallery, to a small room near the stair-head. Stoddard sent a servant for wine, and they sat sipping and chatting.

'I need some more money from the same place,' said Blaise at last.

'It will cost you fifteen per cent,' said Stoddard. 'I have never known money so hard to coax out of the dark.'

'Then let it be fifteen,' said Blaise, fingering his lower lip.

'How does Mistress Rigeley fare?' said Stoddard, drawing

crosses on the table with some spilt wine. 'My wife complains that these winds have planted daggers in her reins . . .' He put his head close to Blaise's. 'There will be a crop of libels as soon as the Queen's reputed pregnancy is whispered around, and that will make her more angry than ever. It has been reported that men in a Suffolk town declared she bore a monster, which she keeps in a box and feeds with bloody hearts. More books are being smuggled in from Amsterdam, and the authorities will shortly be instructed to search them out and burn them before all men's eyes. I heard the Lord Chancellor saying last week that if the principles set forth in such books were spread into men's heads, there would be an end of all order; for they debate on such forbidden matters as the nature of tyranny, and if subjects are permitted to argue whether a prince, a landlord or a master is a tyrant, then each by his own fancy and supposition will decide the question. After that, what Lord of the Council may ride quietly-minded in the streets among such desperate beasts? what minister shall be sure in his bedchamber?'

'I am glad that the Council has such deep matters of our safety under their hands,' said Blaise.

'Wickedness gains apace,' said Stoddard, drinking a full cup in a breath. 'Ah, I knew there was a thing on the tip of my thoughts. Do you remember Tom Handicot, once a servant of Rossey who kept the Star Chamber? He was never caught when the others were arrested for their attempts to steal treasure from the Receipt. Well, he was murdered early last month, and his body was found villainously hackt in the Great Ditch. A farmer's dog sniffed it out, and the carcass was thought at first to be that of a Dutchman, because of a book in the pocket and the cut of the beard; but later it was proved to be Rossey's man, who had long been sought.'

'This is news to me,' said Blaise, flickering at his nose.

Stoddard leant back and looked round the room. 'Yet I cannot forbear to smile when I think that a month ago, by candle-light, I saw a certain lady of the court in this room, whose face was red with wine and the scratches of a tinsel-cushion, lying breast down across the table . . .' He gave a belly-laugh. 'But no names and no mischief.' His voice sank. 'And our good Queen dreams nothing of such things. About Christmastime the Lord Chancellor was talking to the maids-of-honour and came to Mrs. Francis Neville. My pretty whore, he says, how do you? For that, you know, is his noisy manner of talk. Then, after he had gone, the Queen came from behind the traverse, and her fardingale was loose at her feet. So she signed to Mrs. Neville to pin it up, and then, taking her by the chin, she said: How do you, my pretty whore? But Mrs. Neville blushed, and asked her: Mistress, what have you said? I have said only what I heard Lord Howard say, the Queen answered. May I not be as bold with you as he? Then Mrs. Neville told her that the Lord Chamberlain was an idle gentleman. We respect not what he says or does, she declared, but your Majesty has never used such a word before. Tell me what it means, said the Queen, for I thought it was only a word of endearment. O, a whore is a wicked thing, said Mrs. Neville. Then you must pardon me, said the Queen, for I meant no harm.'

Blaise finished his wine. 'You have given me much to think about, Master Stoddard. I thank you.' He rose. 'Never was it more requisite for all men of good will to stand together.'

'I am in a perfect accord,' said Stoddard, also rising, with a belch.

XIV

In the inner room of the apartment, Dousabel sat naked in the shallow bath while her maid Tabitha sponged her with warm water from a ewer, in which a few drops of scent had been measured. She tucked some straying wisps of hair back under the canvas cap, and then bent forward, to the fire. Tabitha dipped the sponge and squeezed it with the utmost care, then rubbed it up and down her mistress's spine as though she feared she would break the bones at the least roughness. 'Is that right?' she asked earnestly.

'Rub, rub,' said Dousabel, and closed her eyes, drowsing into the warmth. 'Don't be afraid . . . what do you think I'm made of?'

Then at last she woke with a sigh and stood up. 'How fat I'm getting.'

'O no,' said Tabitha angrily, and towelled as vigorously as she had sponged with cautious admiration.

'That's better,' said Dousabel, standing with legs wide apart to keep her balance. She read out the posy over the chimney-piece. 'Have you a friend as heart may wish at will? Then use him so to have his friendship still.' She sighed again. 'How often I read those words out. I am near hating them.' She raised her arms. 'Ah, now is the moment. Rub the snake-fat in, Tab . . . Then wipe it off. Dab a finger of wool in rosewater and wipe it off. O, what a thing it is to be a woman, cursed as a slut or a wanton. Twenty-four hours are too short in a day for the nurture of these failing things, our bodies.'

'You glisten all over like an angel of red and white,' said Tabitha, clenching her hands and giving a little jump of joy.

'Then close the curtains,' said Dousabel with a small tinkling laugh, 'or I may float over this astonisht city of London, the fattest of all the angels that ever descended a shaft of light into a picture on the wall.' She yawned. 'O that I had married at least a beadle who would whip me now and then. Anything rather than this man of mine with his ravenous tongue. Man do I call him? Fie.'

'He frightens me, mistress,' said Tabitha in a whisper, 'when I hear him talking away to you as though he were asleep on the other side of a screen or had a spirit wagging at the root of his tongue; and all the while he lies as helpless as a wicked baby in a cradle.'

'How true that is. You have hit the mark, my child. I am sorry to teach you wisdom before your time.' She kissed Tabitha, and then returned to the steel mirror in which she was examining her face. 'He is what you say, and yet a man in his capable malice.'

'O mistress,' cried Tabitha, 'never send me away, and I will do anything you ask. I will do anything, I say.'

'While you are faithful,' said Dousabel coolly, 'I shall keep you. And now hand me the other towel.'

'I'll poison him or push him down the stairs.'

'Hush your mouth,' said Dousabel sharply. 'If I have need of such services, I'll ask for them; but take nothing on yourself, and above all keep your mouth tightly closed. These are not pretty things you see and hear in this household, and I do not wish you to injure your soul unless I find it necessary.'

'I'll be as mum as the grave,' said Tabitha, pinching her lips together.

'Take the bag of chalk and dust me with it.'

Dousabel stepped out of the bath on to the towel. 'I haven't made the least splash,' said Tabitha with pride, looking round at the linen-panels decorated in green and vermilion designs.

Dousabel sat on a small stool of needlework chequered with white, blue, and tawny crewel. 'Now put on my stockings.' She thrust out her short heavy leg with the toes pressed close together. Tabitha, holding her breath and showing the tip of her tongue, drew the cloth-stocking on and buckled it under the knee. Then Dousabel lifted the other leg, till it too was stockinged and buckled. 'Now fetch the blue paint, and pick out the veins on my breasts,' she said lazily, yawning with her head thrown back.

'O yes, please,' cried Tabitha.

XV

Bishop Bonner: 'Why, will you take on yourself to read the Scripture and yet can understand never a word? For you have brought a text of Scripture, the which makes clean against you? For Esdras speaks of the multitude of you heretics, declaring your hate against the catholic church, making the simple or idle people believe that all is idolatry which we do; and so entice them away.'

Ralph Allerton: 'No, not so, my lord; for he makes it more plain and says on this wise: They shall take away their goods and put them out of their houses, and then shall it be known who are my chosen, for they shall be tried as the gold and silver is in the fire. And we see it come to pass, even as he has said. For who now is driven from house and home, yes and his goods taken up for other men who never sweated for them, if he does not observe your commands? Or else, if he is taken, then must he either deny the truth or else he shall surely be tried, even as the gold is tried in the fire. Wherefore all the world may know that you are the bloody church, figured in Cain the tyrant, neither are you able to avoid it.'

Dr. Morton: '*I promise you my lord, now he speaks plainly.*'

Bishop Bonner: '*Marry, sir, as you say indeed, he is plain; for he is a plain heretic, and shall be burned. Have the knave away! Let him be carried to Little-ease, at London, until I come.*'

CHAPTER FOUR

March

I

OLD FABYAN, with Edgar pushing behind, came breathless on
to the five foot way along the top of the Wall, grass-grown
between the stones and fleckt with the first small white
blossoms of the spring. 'Here stood the archers,' he said as
soon as he gained his breath, and Edgar looked gravely round.
The bright sky was streaked with fine hurrying clouds that
sent a skein of delicate shadows over the fields beyond. Below,
the ditch showed full of rubbish, broken with small pools of
greenish water in which ducks dabbled. 'Tell me what you
see, Edgar?'

Edgar looked for a long time, while his master regarded
him with a kindly smile. 'I see a boy riding a goat,' said Edgar
at last, and laughed a clear merry laugh.

'Godsbones, it's true,' said Old Fabyan. 'Though a man
lived ten thousand years, he would still find something new to
delight his eyes. Yet those ditches stink. Ah, Edgar, when I
was a young lad of your shape, they were deep with shining
water, and we used to swim therein. Also, many people came
fishing, though they caught little. But I recall one summer's
day when my father by some mishap hooked a great green
frog, which he brought home in a jug to my mother, to her
indignation.'

'He caught a frog,' cried Edgar, and laughed again, until
old Fabyan joined in.

'Give me a clout, for my eyes water,' he said, and wiped
his face. 'We used to run along this wall where we now stood,
from gate to gate; and often I came first.' He stared along

the wall. 'Once we stole the offertory box from a shop; for in those days there used to be boxes in all the shops, to take offerings for the religious. But there was nothing inside except some pebbles, so we broke the law to no purpose, and it would be well for men if all wrong-doing were so harmless to the innocent and profitless to the guilty.'

'Why were there pebbles in it?'

But Fabyan now heard only his own voice. 'All day long the churchbells were ringing. The monks have tried again to make as loud a noise, but their chimes are a poor jangling to that tumult of sweetness. Well, frost and fraud have foul ends. But I am sorry for those who never heard the bells. They rang for a thousand things and were friends of men from the childbed to the grave. Bells, it was bells all the while, bells and bells, ringing from church to church, from college to chapel from spital to nunnery, in festival and fast. Why, never a good girl lost her maidenhead but to the clapping of the bells, and every christian man breathed out his soul into the bell-mouth. You could tell London from miles away by the ringing of the belfries.'

'How could you tell the time if the bells rang all the while?'

'Ah, it's a sad world you've been born into, Edgar, and I grieve for you. What kind of a world your children will find, I cannot think, but I grieve for them even more. And as for the children of your children, I dare not think of the world they'll inherit. I am almost of a mind to beg you forswear the getting of children; but I know how vain are such requests. For no matter how the devils swarm, a lad and a lass in the dark will fall to the fashioning of men, without further consideration. And doubtless there was a good reason for implanting a defiance of all prudence in the loins of men; for who would beget a child if he could foresee all the troubles that it would cause him.'

Edgar ignored this disquisition; and they walked on westward. Old Fabyan meandered through his maze of memories, and Edgar held the dinnerknife slung round his shoulder like a dagger. The bright sky went rushing on over them, and no one else was to be seen on the wall.

At last Old Fabyan tired. 'Now let's go down. If I stay any longer on this high place I shall talk like a bird of the air and fall into prophesying. Aye, let us go down and see how my poor old friend Hugh Wokins is faring. Five years younger than I am, and bed-ridden since last Easter, poor old fellow. It's sad the way that some cannot bear their years. Let me lean on your shoulder, Edgar, and don't forget that I am leaving you all the contents of my chest with the Flanders lock, which is opened by order of certain letters known only to myself. I mingle other letters with the needful ones, and nobody can read the enigma . . . And learn from my example, Edgar, give nothing away to your children unless you have a covenant duly signed and witnessed by the Master of your Mistery.'

'Can't we go and see the muster in Hyde Park?'

'No, it is too far, it is not worth seeing,' said Old Fabyan.

II

Then they got a candlelight at one of the neighbours' houses and came in, and in the entry met the woman who had answered them at the window, and said she was afraid of spirits. Argentine, the informer, looked upon her, clapped her on the back and said, 'You are not the woman whom we seek for.'

So entered they the house and searched the parlour next the street, where the woman lay who was his mother's tenant, and a young child that sucked on her breast, and not only in the bed, turning it down past all honest humanity, but also under the bed, behind the painted cloths, and in the chimney, and up into the chimney; and finding the bed hot, asked who lay in the bed. The woman said, 'I and the child.'

'And none else? said they.

'No,' said the woman.

When they could find nothing there for their purpose, they went in an inner parlour, in which stood the cupboard wherein Agnes Wardall, whom they sought, was hidden. And they searched the parlour, which was a small one. And one of the company, laying his hand on the cupboard, said, 'This is a fair cupboard, she may be here, for anything that is done.'

'That is true,' said another of them.

*Notwithstanding, they looked no further, but went from that
into the chamber aloft wherein the said Agnes had lain, and
then into all the other rooms and chambers.*

III

They stood round in the cold of early morning, clapping
their hands and gloves, with curdling breath under the bell-
clangour that brought the heavy sky closer over their heads. A
woman in a black velvet hood set a five-pound taper before
the cross at the north door of Paul's Church. Three women in
threadbare gowns were kneeling on the chilly pavement with
knotted hands. Drawing back with small jerky bows, the
velvet-woman took the linen cloth which her maid held out,
and wiped her almond-smelling hands. The music swarmed
like unquiet bees in the vaulting; and buzzed round the head
of the bishop seated inside the pulpit on the top of the stairs.

Constables and beadles, with bills and poles, stood round
the open space under the torch-stanchions. Porters in leathern
shirts or ragged doublets were piling up faggots and kindling-
wood before the Rood of the Northern, and monks came up
with armsful of books. 'Cast them on,' said the subprior in
charge. 'And light the fire.'

An old monk struck steel and flint, and coaxed the sickly
flame into a blaze. The monks came running up with books,
spilling them on the way. One of the onlookers kicked a couple
of the fallen books behind a pillar; but a beadle saw him
and ran over with a shout. The man dodged away. The
beadle picked the books up and added them to the bonfire.
The subprior took a pole from one of the constables and poked
at the books, seeking to open them so that the flames would
burn more easily.

'Here is that devil Calvin!' shouted one of the monks. 'And
Melancthon, with Zwinglerius. Shall not the books burn when
the writers of them are already stewed in the cauldrons of
hell?'

A half-burned copy of an English Bible toppled out near
a man in a flat cap, who took it up. A monk snatched it from
his hands, but he caught at one of the covers and tugged the

book back. Then the cover ripped, and the book went into the flames.

'If my Lord of London had been his judge, Saint Paul must have borne a faggot,' the man cried. 'Ah, it had been a good sight to see Saint Paul with a faggot on his back, at Paul's Cross, and my Lord of London sitting under the Cross as his persecutor.'

Monks came rushing up to seize him. The first slipped on a book and fell forward on his face, so that the others closed round and beat the man down on the stones. The onlookers drew away and huddled on the further side of the fire.

Then the man was seen again, crawling from under the feet of the monks. He twisted free and ran towards one of the buttresses, shouting, 'Have you then come up out of Sodom to silence me? Ah, you kites of Rome that live on the world's offal!'

'Peace, you varlet heretic!' yelled a burly monk, and felled him. Two constables came over and caught the man by his ankles, dragging him away.

Hugh had shrunk back with the others of the crowd. Now he opened his mouth and seemed to shout. The close pressure saved him from falling to the ground. He shouted. The flames burst up with a great crackling, and on the other side the faces of the monks were red with a flickering smutted haze.

IV

The two men were talking about the Lady Elizabeth. She had driven through the city that morning in a closed carriage, making for Hatfield again. Merric was straining to listen, and failed to see Jacint and her maid until they were almost across Chepe. Then, as he went to follow, there was a scuffle in the road, and for a moment everything was confusion. A woman on a horse led by Bridewell beadles had come up, surrounded by jeering youngsters. From a garland on her head there hung small fishes on strings, and clusters of fishes were tied to the horse's mane and rump. The beadle was calling that she had been found guilty of bringing into London the young fry of divers sorts of illegal fish. A brewer's cart ran athwart this procession, and the horse reared. The woman almost fell, but managed to grasp the mane. One of the nimble boys smacked the horse, and it reared again, knocking a man down. Everyone was shouting advice, and a beadle tripped over his own staff, so that another of the boys made off with his hat.

Merric skirted the brawling crowd and reached the other side of the road. Jacint was nowhere to be seen. The uproar grew worse; for the beadles were restoring order with their staves. Merric turned to look and almost missed Jacint again; for she came to the door of a near draper's shop, wanting to learn the occasion of the noise. Seeing Merric turn towards her, she smiled her dimpling smile.

'Good day, Master Rigeley, I am surprised to find you here. I heard that you had married an heiress and become a portly merchant.'

She was wearing a chamlet doublet trimmed with silk, and over it a sleeveless jacket. Looking in her tasseled purse, she moved back into the shop. Recovering himself, he came after. 'You go too fast for me, mistress. I am left behind.'

'Then it is clear we were never meant for fellow yoke-beasts. Goodbye, Merric.'

She went, and he followed. Her tall, bony maid Lettice gave him a timid smile and looked away. An apprentice came hurrying up. 'What may I show you? We have some first-rate London green, lady.'

'Then bring a fair French tawny.'

'We have no more of that, I fear. But surely we can please you with another cloth.'

'Show me a large crimson, a fine one.'

'Ah, that I can do.'

He dashed off, and Merric came close to her shoulder. 'Fast as you go, I am still unlost.'

'I must be a very calf,' she said without looking round, 'since I trail such a tail. At least frisk me all the flies away.'

'It is early in the year for flies.'

'Then you are no use at all, sir. Goodbye again.'

The apprentice came running up with a bolt of cloth. 'See, this is the best in all London, a make of excellent breadth. Hold it up to the light and you'll see I speak the truth.'

'Fie, there is something that blocks my light,' said Jacint, turning. 'Ah, it is Master Rigeley.'

'Let me hold the cloth for you.'

'Yes, hold it up, Master Rigeley. You are good enough as a tree for hanging the clothes-line. If you come next washing-day, we shall use you well and spill no more water down your neck than ensures a good day's work.' She took the cloth from him again and gave it back to the apprentice. 'It seems so-so.'

'Handle it, mistress,' said the apprentice. 'The colour is in grain. The stuff will never lose colour, I warrant you.'

'Then it is scarcely fit for this world, is it, Master Rigeley? For such constancy is out of fashion here. Let us have stuffs that fade with our oaths, and let every new love have a new dye.'

The apprentice scowled at Merric, not sure how to treat the intruder. 'I have never yet heard complaints at a cloth for wearing too well.'

'Then you live out of the world,' said Jacint. 'But tell me, how do you sell the stuff? by the ell or the whole piece?' The apprentice, still keeping a wary eye on Merric, hesitated; and she went on impatiently, 'by the half yard or the full gown-length? Tell me.'

'As you wish, as you wish,' he stammered. 'Ten shillings and sixpence the yard, fifteen shillings the ell, sixteen and eightpence the ell and the halfquarter.'

'How well he reckons,' cried Jacint, addressing Lettice, who had shrunk between two chests, a long thin-shouldered girl with curly hair and frightened eyes. 'What a pity that we cannot take men by the piece, when so often the full length of them is too much for our stomaching.'

'You are over-modest,' replied Merric. 'For I am sure that you never choose a gill of wine when you hold a pintpot in your hand. And as for myself, I am always at your service, the whole of me or as many inches as you fastidiously require.'

'A hit, a hit,' she cried, with her gurgle-laugh. 'Did you hear him, Lettice? His wit is growing fast, and in a few years it may outweigh a mustard-seed. It is true that I purposely stretched the mark until none but a blind and palsied man could have missed, yet he shows a coming disposition and nicked me beyond cavil in the white of my point.'

The apprentice had given up trying to follow the conversation. 'How much, mistress?' he begged. 'How much?'

'Measure out five ells and a half, and make it a good measure, I bid you, since I am a woman who likes always to get even more than she bargains for. Did you hear that, Master Merric?'

The apprentice retired to the counter-table, where he measured the cloth with a rod. 'One, two, three, four, five and a half. That is good measure I trust. Two inches more than you'd get anywhere else in London. I trust you will give our shop a good name among your acquaintance, mistress.'

'Two inches, a thumb-length of charity. By so much I shall praise you.' She handed him the money.

'Thank you, mistress. Can I show you a pretty stammel for petticoats, which has come in only this morning?'

'No, I am burdened enough. Make the crimson up in a parcel and present it to my maid here.'

She went towards the door, and Merric followed.

'Jacint, I have long been praying to meet you.'

'Then you are one of the rare petitioners who find their prayer granted. We are now parting; and I do not see how we could part unless we had first met.' She half-turned over her shoulder, and he saw the smile dimpling in her cheek. 'Next time pray more adventurously, and who knows what may happen?'

'Jacint, I must see you—'

'You are still looking at me, and yet you ask to look again. This is a pleonasm, or I have learned my grammar upside down. Passion of my heart! If you must beseech a favour, speak it in good English; for I have grown a scholar since you left the house.'

'Meet me somewhere. I must talk at length with you. I have so much to say.'

'Why?'

'I am unhappy.'

'Why?'

Angrily he retorted, 'I love you.'

'A reason at last; and I am glad to hear you so sharp about it. Why didn't you speak up at first, and prevent all this waste of breath? Though, now I think of it, the reason is not so

striking or singular, neither.' She called to Lettice, who came
shrinkingly out of the shop, stooping a little, with the parcel
hugged in her arms. 'Do you love me, Lettice?'

'Aye, indeed, mistress. I should be ungrateful if I did not.'

'Shall I ask the apprentice? I do not doubt but that he
loves me too; for he gave me more longing looks than Merric
did. When so many love me, why should I choose one more
than another?'

'Please let us meet again . . .'

'Then make an appointment through my brother Martin,
and I promise I'll keep it. He also loves me, as I well know.
But I hear that you have taken to knocking him down whenever you meet; and that is unkind of you.'

She signed to Lettice, and went off. Lettice gave a smile at
Merric and followed. Merric made a few indecisive steps in
the same direction, but Jacint said in a cold voice over her
shoulder, 'If you dog us after the next corner, I shall be angry.'

He stopped at once and turned back, colliding with a priest
who held a pyx and cup on his way with the sacrament to
some sick man. The boy with cross, bell, and light stumbled:
the light went out, the cross fell to the earth, and the bell
rang. 'Hey, you ruffian!' the priest called and Merric took to
his heels.

v

Nest set the nosegay on the chest. 'It will do no harm,' she
said and went out. William gave a scowl at the pink flowers
and returned to his ledger, checking entries with various bills
and memoranda. He ran his fingers along one of the neatly-
recorded transactions, speaking the money-sums aloud:

For the loss of £60 taken up in London of Wm. Sherry-
man at 22s. 2½d. remitted from Antwerp, and bought again
at 21s. 1½d., wherein much is lost, making in all £62 1s.
more by account which I owe him for that he had paid since
last clearing £3 7s.

His brow wrinkled and he read the entry through again,
then made some computations on a scrap of paper, sighed,
and underlined the entry. Then, taking up another scrap of
paper, he made a new entry on a fresh page.

J. Clint to W.R.: 4s. 5d. being for my nightgown furred, sold to him, to pay at his day of marriage, and if it please God I die before him or his marriage, then he is to pay nothing for it.

Under that he entered from a third slip of paper:

F. Harrison, Merchant Taylor, to W.R.: 3 sables of the very best which shall come from Russia, where now he is going, and is for a gown otherwise called a Doudge, with all things thereto belonging, or to pay me at his return as aforesaid £20.

That stirred his interest; for he looked at it a long time and then began turning over the sheets of the ledger. His nose twitched as he read by chance:

£15 in the way of money lent for Corn for the City, through the Company, to be recovered when I can get it.

He wrote under it these words, 'Never,' and then turned on to the entry he had sought.

Arthur Edwards to W.R.: £24 10s. He owes me at his return from Russia for a sword-girdle, 2 marten skins; for a long gun called a fowling-piece, 3 sable skins of the best, or else a good fell to make a cloak of; for a spaniel called Trivey, 4 sable skins; for 2 lbs. white sugarcandy which he promised would be sold there for 30 Roubles or more a lb., so that he has promised 8 French Crowns for it at the least, or the value thereof. More, for a pair of sails which he left to pay for on his coming back from Russia, where the ship is now gone by no bill of his hand for lack of time £15 13s. 4d.

He ran a line through this entry, and added: 'Through no fault of his own he died of cold and vomiting. God save his soul.'

On the same page he crossed out another entry:

Nurse Sturmsand to W.R.: a red Spanish blanket, which cost 19s. for which she has paid me 9s.

He added: 'No further hope.'

He turned back to the page of new entries, and wrote:

N. Small, clothworker, to W.R.: £5 for a grey gelding, to be paid at his next child born, £7, or at his day of death, £5. Then, after a pause, he appended a note:

This is the last Merry Bond that I shall undertake, so help me God, since my heavy losses in the ship *Cockrobin* have shown me that my works are no longer blessed by providence. Also S. Farles not dying when I had £400 from him on bond eight years ago to take that sum from him at 20 per cent yearly as long as he lived. Now I have paid him back in 5 years the whole sum and £240 in three more years, with another £80 falling due in a month's time.

He ruled a line under this note, as if to emphasise its finality. 'Come in,' he called, in reply to a low but clear rap on the door. Blaise came in, throwing his hat on the chest beside the nosegay.

'Well, brother, how goes our Welsh goat? I thought that such had a surer footing. Has he stirred to any purpose?'

'He has stirred, but I cannot say to what purpose. He goes with Merric every afternoon on a round of taverns, at which they drink many pints and return reasonably merry in the evening. They are satisfied, but no one else.'

'He is a convicted and bottomless liar,' said Blaise, plucking at his loose lower lip. 'Yet the night when he came running to your door, he had certainly frightened himself with more than bugbears and malmsey-ghosts.'

'That it was which made me trust his story. I felt that he came in truth from a murder, however he glossed it. But now I am sure of nothing except his lies. He plays with us for his own purpose, which he has not yet disclosed.'

Blaise pulled at his lip, and then let it smack back. 'We must find the means of tripping him up, so that he lets the hidden thing out of his hand. I have good use to make of this gold that he promises; and if he truly can find it, we must bring him to the point.'

William sucked his breath in. 'I too have good use to make of ready money.' He turned the pages of the ledger over. 'I have been making up my accounts, and I find that fortune has never shown herself a worse whore in her ticklish dealings with me.' He struck the table. 'Yet if I only laid my hand on new money within the next few weeks, I could go far to changing her tune. But these loans and subsidies close up all credit except to the great men. Otherwise I had felt no need to look for help in so risky a quarter as this brother-in-law of mine.' He ended with less emphasis and looked sharply at Blaise, to see how he took the words.

'We must press him hard, brother, press him hard. Maybe the tale is altogether a lie, and then we lose only what we put into it, our breath and our patience. But if there is the least glint of a golden truth in its darkness, then we gain much. And at a moment when one pound is worth two.'

William frowned. 'I don't see what more I can do. I have spoken hard words to him. He knows that he cannot for long now make promises without performance.'

'Have you asked your good wife to sidle into his confidences?' asked Blaise with a wriggle. 'I have always thought that he loved her with an inordinate fondness.'

'Not so fondly as all that,' said William grimly. 'Not so fondly that he would tell her the truth when a lie served his occasion better. I think I know his soul by now.'

'Are you sure, brother? He makes a show of fondness; and then we scratch him and find a ribald rogue and liar under the fond brother. But I have a fancy that under the rogue and liar there is yet another man, who is the fool of his own ribaldry and no wittier than a child.'

William pondered. 'That is keenly urged, brother, but still wide of the cast. For your words are true of us all, seeing that we play a certain game before the world and ourselves, yet are undeceived after all. Under the bond from which we think we can withdraw, there lies a bond from which we cannot withdraw despite all our reservations. Therefore are we most entangled when we think ourselves most free, and so on. I remember when our father died . . .' He paused abruptly, and put his hand to his throat.

'What then?'

William went on, in a hasty withdrawn voice, as though he feared to lose the thread of his thought and at the same time was listening to himself, afraid of what he might say.

'I mean only that a man may be too shrewd. For if we think long enough, the walls of our thinking fall down, and we cannot tell in what place our minds remain. Thus a thing appears as its opposite, and all syllogisms are confounded. No man knows how the world stands, and thus we come upon heresies and rebellions, figuring a man who stands on his head or turns his clothes inside out. This way all things fall apart, and death comes among us with a deafening rattle of bones.' He breathed deeply, and ended in a quiet voice, 'No, there is no way to the truth by such devious subtleties.'

Blaise sat twisted sideways on his seat, intently listening. 'Yet I hold that we may dive into this rogue's intentions if we set his sister to ensnare him with a Delilah's devices.'

'I shall consider the matter,' said William stiffly.

After a while Blaise sat upright. 'Have you found out anything about the abbot whom he cited?'

'I believe that he died at Christmastime, of an apoplexy, in Bermondsey. I meant to tell you before, but I have had so many matters to consider.'

'Have you also heard of another death, closer to the night of our rogue's coming?'

'No,' replied William, with interested brows.

'A servant of Rossey was murdered and thrown in the Ditch.'

'Rossey that was keeper of the Star Chamber?'

'Aye, Rossey that let the conspirators into the Receipt for the theft of moneys. He took Dethick and Bedell into the Treasury, and they weighed the chests there, to decide which they should carry off to the riverside. Do you remember? They meant to hide the chests underwater beside the Bridge or among the rushes on the southern bank.'

'But how can we link Rossey's plot against the Queen with the ravelled lies of our Welshman?'

Blaise shrugged. 'I made a throw in the dark.'

'It is possible,' said William slowly. 'Yes, I see that it is possible. Yet even if it were true, we should be no nearer to our gold.'

'We should have better reason for believing that he knows something and follows a true trail.'

'I thought that Rossey and Dethick were caught and executed as traitors before they stole the treasure for their rising.'

'There was more in the matter than was spoken abroad. Though I was in the Receipt, I learned very little more than others knew; but I know there was much secret talk between the Treasurer and the Council.' He closed one eye and swayed in his chair. 'Think now. Dethick went to William Hinnes and besought him to use his skill in alchemy to turn foreign coins into gold: to which Hinnes objected that though it was not treason yet the noise of the hammers would be heard and would bring shame and rebuke on their heads. Then Dethick offered to transport him to Captain Tybald's castle adjoining the sea . . . Can they have made gold after all? . . . No, it is more likely that there was truth in the rumour I heard of a chest being spirited off.' He grimaced in the effort to check his feelings. 'A chest holding spoils from one of the abbeys, which a great nobleman paid in as his subsidy-money under certain seals of secrecy . . . But if that were so, Rossey or one of his creatures removed accounts and papers, and the matter was husht up.'

'It is possible,' said William, 'but we can only break our head against conjecture in such matters. Rather let us lay our hands on the thing itself; and whether it comes from an abbey or a great man's coffers, from the Receipt or an alchemist's still, its market-value is the same, eh?'

Blaise was still thinking about Rossey. 'The chest would have been taken into Rossey's garden by the riverside and buried there, or carried away on a boat.'

'Let us hope so. Yes, I will press my wife to find out what she can from her loving brother.'

There was a knock on the door, and they both started and drew themselves up. Hugh came in. He looked round at his two brothers, and as neither of them spoke, he came to the point at once.

'Brother Will, I came to ask if you would lend me ten pounds till next quarterday.'

'I am sorry, but I can't.'

'You are peremptory, brother. Is it because you fear that you might weaken and do a kindly act?'

'I haven't got the money. I am more hard-driven than you think.'

'It is the same with me,' said Blaise. 'I myself came to borrow from William, and he has been explaining his difficulties. That is why he spoke a trifle bitterly when you touched a rawness in his thoughts.'

Hugh considered their faces. 'Then there is no more to be said. If you cannot lend the money, you cannot. But I am sad to be treated like a dog. I do not say beggar, for we are all beggars in Christ.'

'You think the world has nothing better to do than to hearken to your sickly complaints,' said William, reddening. 'You are not ready to wrestle with the enemy except in prayers. It is not right to fall forever on the charity of those who have more foresight and endeavour.'

Hugh answered calmly, 'When I came in, I smelt the devil; and the sweat of money. I was sorry that I came. Now I am more sorry, for I have no wish to quarrel with my own kin. I leave it to the Lord to decide whether I labour enough in the vineyard. Also whether I choose to eat bread salted with my own tears or with the tears of the widow and orphan.'

'You infer,' said William, 'that my bread is of the latter sort, yet you would borrow it if you could, and no doubt would find it more nourishing than the loaf of your own thin leavening.'

Hugh went to the door. 'I see that usury is turned evening wolf and swallows the bones down to the very marrow, and, having consumed the poor man, turns upon the master.'

He left the room. 'He will come to a bad end,' said William, 'and it is no use trying to help him.'

'This dispute had to come sooner or later,' said Blaise soothingly. 'Now it has come. Let him go his own way, and we shall go ours.' He rose. 'You will send to me if you learn anything?'

William nodded and pursed his lips. 'That fool Hugh has vexed me. Good day, Blaise. I shall do as we said.'

Blaise lifted his hand. 'I can let myself out.' He went.

William returned to his ledger, and glanced through the slips of paper. He began to write, but dropped the pen. A sweat broke out on his upperlip and he groaned, taking his head between his hands. Nest slipped in, and he at once blinked and reached for the pen. 'What is it?' he asked. 'I hate people who always wait to be asked.'

'There is a poor maid come to the backside,' she said hastily, looking only at the nosegay. 'I knew her once to be a good and industrious girl; and she is to be married as soon as she can win the cost of it. So I have promised her a few shillings.'

'Then my wife must redeem her word.' He opened a drawer and took a purse out, then he opened the purse and slowly took out some coins. 'Here.' She came swiftly over, with her head inclined forwards, and he closed his hand. 'Wait a moment. I should be pleased if someone could find out what Christopher means to do; for he has told me many things that fail to tally one with another. I wish to do the best I can for him; but it is hard while he confuses me with cloudy tales. Further, he is my wife's brother; and if he cheats me again, I shall feel as though she had done it herself, and be accordingly sad.'

'He means no harm,' she said, with quivering mouth. 'But he goes such a long way round to come into the next street that he often forgets what he set out to do. Otherwise, he means no harm, and he does none.'

'Find out what you can, for his own sake.'

She nodded, puckering her mouth, and he opened his hand. Without looking into his face, she took the coins and ran out. He sighed and returned to his ledger, this time writing with a firm hand:

To a young maid poor to be married: 3s. 4d. Praised be God for his manifold mercies and forebearances, Amen.

Nest counted out the coins carefully into the girl's hand. 'Spend it in as godly a way as it was got; and turn yourself to a good and prudent wife. For a man must make his own fortune, but his wife can mar it.'

'Yes, mistress,' said the girl in mournful gratitude out of her large straw-hat. 'I'll pray for you daily.'

'Once a week will suffice,' said Nest, and dismissed her. She turned back into the kitchen, where both Agnes and Sanchia were watching her. 'Let it be a lesson to you both, that marriage is a sorrowful matter.' She went out.

Sanchia tossed her head. 'If I had to beg the charges of my wedding, I'd stay a maid.' She raised her brows and stood listening to the echoes of her own words.

Agnes said thoughtfully, 'No, if I had to beg, I might humble myself to the other thing as well. For a woman lies as low as she may, on the lap of the earth, and would lie lower still, but she cannot.'

'You are bitter, mistress. I would lie on the earth in summer, it is true; but a married woman is more likely to lie on a mattress, and it is certainly more proper and virtuous that she should.'

Agnes smiled. 'May you never know better. But tell me, child, do you know that Ybel loves you?'

Sanchia tossed her head again. 'He gives me little of chance of knowing anything else. He lives in my shadow and puts posies of love in my combs. When I hear the wind sighing in the chimney, I am sure that he has climbed there to pester me. He spoils his beer by weeping into it. He has cut my name on a beam in the loft and on the timber behind his bed. He drew a picture of me on a piece of slate with a rusty nail and mended its unlikeness by adding my name in inch-high letters.'

'I think you should be kinder to him.'

'I have done nothing. I am neither kind nor cruel; but I cannot bear a whining voice and a face in the dumps.'

'It is better to have your griefs early and pass on to sweeter times, than to fall on the pricks after wilful years.'

'Some grieve early and still grieve late. If I laugh now, I know at least that I am not one of those who never laugh at all.'

'Laugh then your loudest,' Agnes stood up. 'Go on, laugh while you have the time. Laugh.'

Sanchia shrank before her cold voice. Then Gladus came in from the still room, with her hands tucked under her apron. 'Lazing again! Find me the toasting fork, Sanchia.'

VI

Dr. Martin: 'You rebel whore and traitor heretic! you shall be racked inchmeal, you traitorly whore and heretic, but you shall confess before a judge before you go: yes, and you shall be made to confess how many books you have sold, and to whom.'

Elizabeth Young: 'Sir, I understand not what an oath is, and therefore I will take no such thing upon me. And no man has bought any books of me as yet, for those books that I had your commissioners have them all.'

Dr. Martin: 'You traitorly whore, we know you have sold a number of books, yes, and to whom; and how many times

*you have been here, and where you lie, and every place that
you have been in. Do you think that you have fools here?'*

Eliazbeth: 'No sir, you are too wise for me; for I cannot tell
how many places I have been in myself. But if it were in
Turkey, I should have meat and drink and lodging for my
money.'

Dr. Martin: 'You rebel whore, you have spoken evil by the
queen, and you dwell amongst a sort of traitors and rebels,
that cannot give the queen a good word.'

Elizabeth: 'I am assured that no man living upon the earth
can prove any such thing by me.'

Dr. Martin: 'You rebel and traitorly whore, you shall be so
racked and handled that you shall be an example to all such
traitorly whores and heretics, and you shall be made to swear
by the holy evangelists and confess to whom you have sold all
and everyone of these heretical books that you have sold: for
we know what number you have sold and to whom; but you
shall be made to confess it in spite of your blood.'

Elizabeth: 'Here is my carcass: do with it what you will.
And more than that you cannot have, master Martin; you can
have no more but my blood.'

VII

Many Members of Parliament were riding up from Westminster, past Whitehall. A few went strolling on foot. One,
a tall gaunt man with sunken eyes and long hatchet-face, was
walking beside a fat ginger-whiskered man, listening and looking round with quick jolted gestures which every now and
then he tried to turn into a flourish. Seeing Blaise near the
palace-gate, he made his farewells to the fat man, who was
holding forth in a shrill seesaw voice; and came over.

'Master Popham,' said Blaise, 'I could not see anyone who
fits more aptly with my mood.'

Popham squeezed his arm, made a shambling movement to
the right which he sought to correct, and half-fell against the
post for tethering horses. 'Yes, we are breaking up, and I for
one feel that we have not wasted our time. We have most
loyally supported the Queen's Majesty in everything; and she

in her benignity has recompensed us by refraining from all requests that might have discomposed our spirits. She has graciously given up asking us for an army to sail abroad in support of her husband's wars, and she has made clear again that we need not fear for our land-titles . . .' He flipped his hand in the air and all but struck Blaise on the ear. 'Ah, noble and regal lady.'

'I should like a few words alone with you,' said Blaise, walking beside him towards Charing Cross. 'You know that I hope shortly to have a small estate close to your own more notable residence.'

'I have heard of your good work in that place, Master Rigeley. Our friend, George Stoddard, has engaged my love for you. If I can be of any aid, ask me, sir, ask me.' He swerved round suddenly upon Blaise, regained his balance in time, and shot ahead. Blaise hurried after.

'Your words chime in exactly with my hopes. The manor has been left to rack and ruin, and the copyholders have greedily fastened upon their holdings, asserting rights against me which would sorely hamper my use of the property.'

'Then you have been hardly treated, Master Rigeley, and nothing would please me better than to teach the upstarts a lesson. I cannot bear deceit or restrictions upon property. Our realm has sad need of men like you; and the best way to set you in a position to serve it is to make you a J.P. in a county. For which you need first a pleasant estate. And how can you find such an estate if lousy leaseholders are permitted to plague you with their stale claims and outdated formulas. This is a matter well understood in Parliament, let me tell you, Master Rigeley; but I need say no more than a word to a man of your intelligence.' He shook hands, bobbing and nodding. 'I shall return to London in a fortnight's time. Come and talk with me.' He floundered away, straightened himself up, trembled in the knees, and then sped off at a good pace.

VIII

Nest came running down the stairs, 'Lord save us, Fabyan your father has been sick upon two or three sage leaves eaten in the morning, which he has now cast up in his chamber; and Lent is upon us.'

London in Lent. The fishmonger three doors off rubbed his scaly hands on the forty days to come, with fish-eating a duty both civil and religious. Eat fish, stop the slaughter of beef and mutton, preserve the herds and flocks, keep money in the country, give employment to sailors, raise a goodly fleet, revive the ports, strengthen the realm, and obey the church. All in one breath.

'Here is my licence to eat meat,' said Gregory Hawes to Gertrude, 'which cost me six shillings and eightpence for the year, and which permits me to choose whatever diet best suits my bodily infirmity—namely, boiled chicken. But because men are envious and censorious, I shall eat my Lenten dinners in my private room; but see there is enough hake, haddock, herring and bloatfish for yourself and the others.'

The Lenten hangings were brought out in the churches. The white and the blue cloths covered up the images and pictures, marked with crosses and the emblems of the Passion. The Lenten veil was hung between choir and high altar.

In Coleman Street a mob dragged out a plasterer and his wife, who were seen defiantly eating bacon, and trampled them in the mud. After which they set them upside down in a pillory; and a friar preached on the Second Coming.

The procession came from Aldgate, the Mayor and aldermen in violet gowns, and the ladies in black. The sheriffs came with banners and drums, and a score of giants large and small, and a host of hobbyhorses. The horsemen came in velvet coats with gold chains round their necks, and men in plump suits of armour. The morris-dancers came in a hurlyburly of little bells, in a whirl of windy ribbons, in a medley of cross-garterings; and then the whifflers with busy cheeks. The sergeants in velvet and the yeomen on horses came, with green and white ribbons; and the Lord of Misrule in a splendour of gold chains and with rings on his fingers.

The devil came with a handful of squibs and a barbed tail, with ears painted red and a pigs-snout. The sultan came behind him, swaggering in yellow silks, with a stuffed peacock on his head and a black face. And last came Jack of Lent himself, with a herring in his cap, riding on a great horse, and a priest running beside to shrieve him. And running behind, his blubbered wife cocking up her hairy leg and drinking from a green flagon; and with her, Jack's doctor in zodiac-gown and huge spectacles. And every time that Jack died, his bearded wife set up a lamentation and besought the doctor to save him for a thousand pounds. Which was done with a magnificent pill, after they had debated the matter with brag and bargaining to the laughter of the crowd; and so Jack was thumped back to life, saying that he had been in a country where the fish jumped into the fryingpan and the pigs ran in the streets with knives stuck in their backs, crying *whee-whee, come eat me*. Then he fell sick again, was shriven, and died; was lamented and brought back to crowing life for a thousand pound. And all men lustily cheered.

Then said Mr Winchcombe, 'Take pity on your golden years and pleasant flowers of lusty youth, before it be too late.'

Julius Palmer: 'Sir, I long for those springing flowers that shall never fade away.'

Mr Winchcomb: 'If you keep at that point, I have done with you.'

Then was Palmer commanded again to the blindhouse, from which he was soon after led to be burned.

Next day the Lord Mayor and aldermen were bidden to the Guildhall, to make another loan to the Queen's Majesty; and there sat the Lord Treasurer and the Lord Privy Seal and the Lord Bishop of Ely, as Commissioners, with the Lord Chancellor and others of the Council. But the Queen's Majesty had gone down the river to Greenwich for Lent.

In the churchyard, a girl in a red skirt was riding a bear. A monk tore a bill from the churchdoor and cried that some heretic had nailed it there. All the people ran away.

In the solar at Frickes Lane, Nest sat painting an egg with stripes of green and red. 'I shall set a hen upon it,' she explained, 'and she will hatch me a chicken of these colours.'

Agnes bit her lip and went out. O where?

Now the arum thrust its folded green from brown earth, and the ground-ivy stretched out its long red stems feeling for the light. On upland fields, where the plough lay idle in the last stubborn furrow, the coltsfoot scattered its leafless flowers. In sheltered hollows, primroses were mustering. Cones of the great alder by the weir, hanging all year soberly from every spray, were lighted up with the fresh tints of opening catkins. Waterwash had unbared the roots and made a thick refuge for water-rail when the reeds were thinned and beaten down. Titmice with ringing notes scrambled in the hazel and loosened small fleecy showers of gold.

'You must eat some early lettuce if you cannot sleep,' said Gertrude to Gregory Hawes, but he made no answer.

IX

'What more could I have done?' muttered Merric. He scowled across the tables at Jones, who drank his beer unconcerned. 'Tell me,' Merric repeated, 'what more could I have done?' He coughed. The weather had become cold again.

'We could always have done more,' said Jones, 'or to put it another way, we could always have done less; but it would have come to the same thing. Therefore, that which matters is merely what we did. We must begin from that, and having carefully considered all possibilities we may proceed to make the same mistakes again.'

'No, no, that I'll never do. Next time I'll bring her pride down.' He stared at a stain on the wall: a tree, no, a cat.

'Good, then you need fret no longer; for your mind is resolved, and you can turn to other matters.'

'Have you ever been scorned by a woman?'

'More times than I can well remember. But I can laugh louder and scorn more scornfully than any woman born; and thus I laughed her into silence and scorned her into anger, and then we agreed or did not agree. But either way I have forgotten her and the colour of the kiss. If you cannot forget your viperous Venus, I shall lead you willnilly to the treadmills of Turnbull Street—'

'I've told you it wouldn't help.'

'Since when did the physician heed the sick man's prescriptions? If you keep mewling and appeal to me for a cure, you must abide by my medicines.'

'Then tell me one of your villainous stories.'

Jones thought for a moment, then gave his hinnying laugh. 'Here is one which comes to my mind because it deals with medicinal matters.' He settled forwards. 'I was going from Metz to Chalons, which you are to understand is a low base city of timber and clay with many pleasant islands outside the walls on the west; and I was robbed by two soldiers. They took my inner doublet, cloak and shirt, and exchanged my good hat for a deep French one, all greasy. But they never guessed that I had sixteen crowns in the bottom of a wooden box, covered up with a stinking ointment for scabs. Another six crowns I had lapped in cloth, wound round with divers coloured threads, in which I stuck needles, as though I were a husband to my own needs and thriftily mended my own clothes. And these too they missed. I had thrust both box and thread-ball into my hose as things of little worth—' He stopped and peered again through the window. 'Come on.'

Merric tossed a coin to the tapster, and in a moment they were out in the street. A man was hurrying with bandy gait towards the river, wrapt in a dirty yellow cloak, with a striped seaman's cap sideway on his head. Jones began quietly running, and Merric followed. Before the man had reached the corner, they had caught him up. Merric sprinted and ran full-tilt into the man as he turned. They fell over against some stone steps.

Shaken by the fall, Merric got up on his knees in time to see that Jones had grabbed the man by his ankles. Jones tugged and the man's head thudded on the stone. Merric lurched over and took one of the ankles. Together they dragged the man down into a small blind-alley.

Merric leaned over and sat him up. The man made clucking noises and clutched weakly at the cloak round his throat, which was half-strangling him. Merric loosened the cord, while Jones stood close with his drawn dagger.

'So we meet again, Ben.'

Ben gasped. 'What d'ye want, Kit? . . . Been looking for you . . . True as hell . . .' His face was so slasht with scars that it looked as if it had been sewn together, but his eyes were virulently alive, small, shifty. He gasped again. 'Never

meant to do you out of your share, Kit. Swear it, Godscods
. . . Shouldn't have quarreled. Your fault. Suspicious all of a
sudden . . . Damn you, Kit. All in self-defence, eh?'

'Stab him in the eye if he calls out or tries to get away,'
said Jones. Holding his knife between his teeth, he began
roughly searching Ben's clothes. Some copper coins in a wad
of dirty cloth he threw down in the mud; a dagger he put
in his own belt; some hemp-string and a latten spoon he threw
down. Looking up, Merric saw a woman with unbound hair
leant on a windowsill straight above, quietly watching them
at work with a mild interest. 'What's this?' said Jones. He
wrenched at something in an inner pocket and brought out a
leather-wallet. Fumblingly he found a shred of paper inside,
and a gold ring. 'Now we have it, you foul liar, Ben.' He
raised his dagger, but Merric caught his wrist. Ben lay unmoving. He stared up without a blink at the dagger-point.
'We can throw the body in the river.'

'No, we're being watched,' said Merric. He glanced up at
the woman, who was yawning.

Jones drew back. 'All right. You can go, Ben. But remember. We've done nothing wrong. I've only taken what belongs
to me.'

Ben said nothing. He lay there unmoving with wide-open
eyes. Jones and Merric turned back up the alley. At once Ben
leaped to his feet and ran after them. Drawing a second dagger
from a loop of rope round his calf, he flung himself on the
nearest one, Merric, and stabbed him in the back, then dodging on, he ran round Jones and off down the street.

x

'Take your time,' said Cluney the keeper, and wiped his
nose with the back of his hand. 'We have all the day before
us.' He sniggered, and then wiped his mouth with the back
of his hand. 'And all night too, if he still longs for Meg's
embraces.'

One attendant was tying Cutbert Simson's wrist to the
ropes of the upper beam of the Rack; another was tying his
ankles to the ropes of the lower beam. Cluney, with his large

bushy beard and pale sharp eyes, stood back and blew through
his keys. A young monk and one of the bishop's officers were
talking beside a pillar, giving side-glances now and then at
the man being set in the Rack.

'Are you ready, sirs?' said Cluney at length in a brisk voice.
The officer looked at the monk and then nodded.

'Give him a few turns, lads,' said Cluney cheerily.

The men took crowbars and inserted them in the slits on
the outer ends of the beams. Setting their right feet on the
crowbars, they pressed down. The ropes tautened and made
a slight humming noise. Then, holding the crowbars underfoot to prevent any slacking, the men inserted, on the left,
other crowbars, which they pressed down in turn to tighten
the ropes yet further. Something in Simson's clothes tore.
Blood dripped from his ankles. The upperlip was drawn back
from his clencht teeth.

The officer spat, took a roll from under his arm, and began
to read in a droning voice. 'You, Cutbert Simson, have
uttered and spoken deliberately these words and sentences
following, videlicet that though parents, ancestors, kinsfolk
and friends, yes and also yourself, before the time of the late
schism here in this realm of England, have thought and still
think that the faith observed in times past here in this realm
of England was a true faith, though in the church it was set
forth in the Latin tongue, and not in English, yet you believe
and say that the faith and religion now used commonly in
this realm, not in English, but in the Latin tongue, is not the
true faith and religion of Christ, but contrary and expressly
against it . . .'

He paused and picked his teeth. The monk had gone over
and stooped close to Simson's face, watching his eyes. He
now stood up and folded his hands. 'Do you confess to these
treacherous words and thoughts, you abominable rogue?' he
asked in cold even tones.

Sweat was beading thickly on Simson's brow. His face had
turned a greenish pallor, and his eyes were turning up into
his skull. He said nothing.

'Give him another turn, lads,' said Cluney. 'There's some
good strong beer coming down for you in a moment.'

The small bones of Simson's body cracked. Blood dripped

anew from his ankles. His eyes were almost lost to sight in his skull. His mouth was wide open. The ropes creaked.

'He is about to speak,' said the monk in a husht voice.

'I have said it . . . I have thought it . . .' The voice came very small, very clear. 'God, forgive the world . . .'

'Write down that he confesses it,' said the monk.

'Give him another turn, lads,' said Cluney. 'He's an obstinate fellow, and deserves worse treatment, the whoreson pricklouse.'

The ropes creaked and strained. Simson's body was flat as though all the joints were pulled out. The monk was narrowly watching, to catch the least motion or word. A young apple-faced girl came down the stone steps with a tray of drinks, which she set on the table against the wall. She smoothed out her apron, took a long bleak look at Simson, smiled with big mouth at Cluney, and curtseyed. There was an over-emphatic swaying of her hips as she went up the steps, as though she knew all the men had turned to watch her go.

'One more turn, lads,' said Cluney, 'and then you can deal with the beer.'

'Item,' the officer read out, picking his nose with his little finger, 'that within the said city and diocese of London you have wittingly and contemptuously done and spoken deliberately against the rites and ceremonies used here . . .'

'O my people . . . O my people . . .' moaned Simson in so low a voice that the monk had to bring his ear within a few inches to hear the words.

XI

Rafe sighed, set his book down, and pushed the spectacles up on to his brow. Jacint came in without knocking. 'The sun is out,' she said. 'It's time you also showed your face abroad. Walk to the Bridge with me.'

'I grow daily to love my attic more desperately,' he replied, with a slow smile, wrinkling the corners of his eyes. 'Tempt me not out of Eden.' He laughed gently. 'Though I am both Snake and Adam within a single skin, tempt me not.'

'But you scarcely ever go out now,' she said with a pout. 'Not even when I ask you. One day you will forget to depart from within the covers of a book, and then you'll be shut up there for ever, in a world of gibbering shadows.'

'Ever since I was sick last year, I have lost my taste for gossip and the stir of things. I am afraid of my tears.'

'But you are the happiest person I know,' she said wonderingly. 'That is why I cannot leave you alone. I want to learn your secret.'

'It is a sad secret,' he said. '*Lachrymae rerum.* What you consider my happiness is my lack of hope.'

She went down kneeling before him and leaned on his knees. 'No, no, Uncle Rafe, that would break my heart.'

'It may be that your heart will be broken,' he said gently, 'for you are a loving girl underneath your show of scorn; but I shall not be the one. It will be a younger man.'

They were silent for a while. 'Tell me about yourself,' she said at last, stroking the slight cleft in her chin. 'Why did you never marry?'

'Do I ever tell you anything except matters of myself?' he stroked her hair. 'And I never married because you are the first woman ready to listen to me.' He sighed. 'As for my life, you know it. Many years of teaching logic to headstrong children at a meagre salary. For it is commonly seen nowadays that most gentlemen will give better wages and deal more bountifully with a fellow who can train a dog or reclaim a hawk than with a well-qualified and honest man to bring up their sons. Thus it is that dogs are able to make syllogisms in the fields when their young masters can conclude nothing at home, if occasion of argument or discourse is offered at the table.'

'It is true and sad,' she replied, 'but you are not one who looks to money and its pleasures.'

'Maybe I had my worldly hopes once, but certainly such hopes soon fade away from the master of a freeschool with a stipend paid halfyearly by the auditor. One who, going in the street, is pointed out as a schoolmaster or maybe one of the blackguard scullions of the palace. But my complaint does not truly lie that way. If I regret the lowliness of my vocation in men's eyes, it is because I regard highly the work of

reducing the spirits of men and erecting their minds to a lofty
view of the world.' He sighed again. 'All that, however, is
over now; and I am glad that my failing health led me to a
pensioned cranny here, where I might call myself your tutor
and Martin's, and forget the world. Ask me nothing more.
I have a satchel of oblivion at my back for all such matters.
Yes, I thank heaven for giving a coney's memory in all that
concerns myself, so that I may remember better the great
things of the world—a dozen lines of Lucretius or the dimpling of your smile.'

'No, but tell me why you are so grieved today? More than
these old matters are hurting you. When you can help others
so well, why cannot you help yourself?'

He smiled. 'My name Rafe is from Randulf, which as
Rodulf signifies Help-counsel, not differing much from the
Greek Eubulus; but it is true that my counsels are a chair
with a rickety leg when I seek to sit in them myself.' He
mused. 'Indeed our names are fanciful tags, and perhaps a
pole on which the wandering vine of our lives is trained,
Jacint my Jewel . . . Cutbert signifies not Cutbeard, as some
take it, but Famous and Bright, as the line declares: *Quique
regit certum Cutbert de luce vocamen . . .*'

'Who is this Cutbert?'

'A disreputive tailor I knew a little, a man forward for
the English Bible and such reformations. I have argued with
him, for logic's sake, now and then, in the old days; and I
liked him for all his young angers. Now he is in the Tower,
I have heard, and they rend him as a pastime.' His voice rose
in an unintended indignation of pity. 'What are we to do with
such a world? You see why I have no taste for its streets.
Yesterday when I went out, I heard two men in the barber's
shop who spoke of this Cutbert and his mangling . . .' Tears
came into his eyes. 'They spoke as though he were being
birched for a truancy. A jesting matter, with games to follow
in the twilight. I cannot think that men were made for such
jests.'

'You may say to me what you will,' said Jacint, rising. 'But
promise me that you will keep such dangerous words for my
ears alone.' She put her hands over her ears. 'What have
you done to me, Rafe?' She went hastily out.

XII

'I'm so glad that I haven't a whole house to look after,' said Dousabel, snuggling into the settle-cushions and taking care not to disturb her headgear of netwire, cloth-of-gold and tinsel. 'Go down to the girls in the kitchen, Tab.'

Nest, stiffly composed on a panelback oakchair, looked round the solar as if seeing it for the first time. 'It's not the things I do that tire me out; it's those I don't do. All the while I feel I've forgotten something, and I can't sit down.' Below in the yard sounded the pounding of clothes with wooden beetles, and a low murmur of women's laughter.

'But what does it matter if you do forget something?'

Nest considered the question with a dumbfounded face; but was saved from having to answer by Agnes entering with honeycakes and marchpane. She pointed to the painted fruit-bench, and Agnes set the tray down there.

'How prettily you grow,' cried Dousabel. 'Come here and give me a kiss, Agnes. I always feel it's lucky to be kissed by a comely maid.' Agnes inclined her head, but said nothing. 'How pale you are. If you were a vain creature like myself, I'd swear you'd been eating gravel for your complexion. Look up, girl.' Agnes raised her head high and looked away. 'Time you were married, sweetheart. Then you wouldn't need these melancholic airs and angers.'

'Yes, she's nearly eighteen years and a half,' said Nest. 'It's shameful to stay unwed at such an age. But she won't listen to a word I say, only because there were some natural misfortunes over her betrothals.'

Agnes went out. Nest and Dousabel looked at one another. 'She's brooding,' said Dousabel with a light laugh, languidly caressing her slight double-chin.

'What a family of brooders I've brought into the world,' said Nest, with a note of friendliness at last in her voice. 'John was an easy-going son, who would sooner laugh than cry; but as for the others—you see for yourself. Agnes broods in a corner, Merric broods in a tavern, Stephen broods on a book.'

'Blaise said that your Merric had been hurt. One of the reasons for my coming was to ask about him.'

'Hurt? Aye, hurt enough to make a deal of work for us

all, but that's all. He goes out without as much as good-day and then come back with a sleeve full of blood. First there was Kit with his broken ankle, and now there's Merric with his cut shoulder. What comes next I fear to think; but I know it will cause more labour for my hands and not a word more thanks.'

The door had opened, and Jones stood there, bowing to Dousabel. 'You were talking of Merric? I have just come from his bed.'

'Is he resting?' asked Nest.

'No, he is raging. He will soon be well enough to rise, but it will be many weeks before he can knock a man down with his right fist.'

Dousabel patted her mouth. 'Fie, an aging man like yourself to draw a youth into such bloody courses.'

'Not so aging, mistress, as all that,' he said with a sneer. 'Neither so bloody. Tell your husband that all will yet be revealed, to the comfort of the virtuous and the distraction of the wicked. And you, being so beautiful, shall be enabled to buy crimson shoes, so that if you walk in blood nobody will know.'

'You always liked to wrap up a simple tale,' said Nest with satisfaction, 'till you forgot what lay inside the covers. Once, when another lad blacked your eye, you told us all that you had been carried under a hill by the Mothers and set fighting with a great red bull. After which you grew so persuaded of your own story that you have been seeking the hill ever since.'

'Sister, you are all astray. I found the hill again with ease; and who was there, dancing with the very bull, save you yourself? However, that I might not shame you in so reverend a company, I stole out before you saw me; but not before I watched you draw tears from the bull with your proud words.'

Nest gave a little scream and put her hands over her eyes. 'I think indeed that you must have visited my sleep; for now I believe that I have dreamed of that red bull and his weeping eyes.'

'Leave my dreams alone,' said Dousabel, yawning, as Jones turned to her. 'They are thick enough with monsters without your fiery face.'

'A sister and brother may share a dream unrebuked,' said Jones, 'but if I intruded on your darkness, I might be taken without the breeches of custom and forced to pay too large a sum of manhood.'

'You know too much or too little.'

'I have forgotten,' said Nest, and went out in agitation. Jones approached the settle, where Dousabel sat smoothing her lap and looking him boldly in the face.

'You are a jewel worth a golden setting,' he said.

'So many think. But I am one that holds a plain framework best shows off a flaring diamond.' He took up her plump hand, but she drew it away. 'You know too little.'

Nest came back, flapping her face with a handkerchief. 'What did you forget?' Jones asked.

'What did I forget? O, nothing . . .'

Dousabel rose. 'It is time I went home.' She yawned. 'But not to dream.'

Jones was still in the solar when Nest came back from seeing Dousabel out. 'Why did you take my clothes away?' he demanded angrily. 'Why did you leave me these things that don't fit me?' He plucked at his doublet and breeches. 'You saw how strangely she looked at me. Where are my clothes?'

'Gladus took them down while you slept. She wanted to clean them, and I thought you'd be pleased . . .'

'But Ybel told me that he saw you with them on the stairs.'

'How dare he tell lies about me! I'll box his ears.'

He caught her arm, but she shook him off. 'Why did you take them?' he asked.

'I told you. Gladus wanted to clean them.'

He strode to the door. 'You will learn nothing that way!' Then, as soon as he had closed the door behind him, he grinned and ran up the stairs to his room. Inside, he bolted the door, went to the bed and moved it about a foot, lifted up a board and took out Ben's wallet. He extracted two slips of paper and set them down carefully on the bed. Then he read the writing out in a low whisper:

> therefore bring up the c . . . art by the old
> rutted roadway at the b . . . ack of the
> chapel near yngford th . . . en from the door

walk straight along tow . . .ards the altar xi
steps and then to the l . . . eft ii steps
after which you will li . . . ft the slab

He smiled and moved the two pieces of paper together and apart and together again, clapping his hands to see how exactly they fitted their torn edges. Excitedly he prowled round the room, touching things, muttering to himself; put the tips of his fingers together and raised his hands over his head on to the nape of his neck. Without breaking the contact of fingertips he brought his hands over again in front of his face, so that he stared between the fingers as through the slits in a vizor. Chuckling he went to the window and looked down at the yard, where Sanchia was bending to pick up a clothes-peg. Returning to the bed, he fitted the ragged paper-edges together once more, then put the two bits back in the wallet, hid it under the board, and restored the bed to its normal place. Then with resolved stride he went out of the room, down half a flight of stairs, along a short passage, up half a dozen steps, and into Merric's room.

'Don't let Sanchia come up with my meals, or my mother,' said Merric irritably. 'Send Agnes.' He was sitting up in bed with his right arm and shoulder in plaster and splints. 'And let her bring a book and read to me.'

'Heal yourself, heal yourself fast,' said Jones, bright-eyed. 'The gold tingles against my fingers. I cannot sleep for its chinking in my ears. I taste its sweat in my wine. Heal yourself fast.'

'What have you told my father? He comes and looks at me without a word.'

'I have told him only that we now know what we needed to know; and that as soon as you are whole, we shall go for the treasure.'

'And he wants you to go without me?'

'Yes, but I have refused.'

Merric reached forward and grasped his uncle's arm. 'Swear that you're not playing me false. As I lie here, I can't help thinking. Why should you stay true to me when you're lying to all the others?'

'I've told you, lad. Also, I need you. Also, I love you. I love only you and Nest in all the world.'

'Then tell me the truth.'

'It's true I made up the story about the abbot. Rather, I set the facts in a different order. But we'll leave him out for the moment, and turn to another man, who was his servant. And to the treasure itself. I saw a list of the things in the chest, lad, and the words themselves were enough to set your heart on fire. A cross of silver gilt garnisht with great coarse emeralds and a chalice of gold, a collar of gold with sixteen fair diamonds and fourteen knots of pearls, four pearls in every knot. Think of it, think of your hands getting among such wealth. And what could be more rightful than that I should gain it, seeing I gained so little in the days of the destruction of the abbeys? For I was green in the world's ways then, and let many chances slip through my fingers.'

'What of the abbot's servant?'

'I'm coming to that. I knew him as John Faxy, but I have reason to think he had answered to other names in his time. A gross man who sweated at the least breath of heat or exertion, with furry hair above his ears. Somehow or other he had filched this chest, I think from the Receipt of the Queen or from some great man's strongroom. That he took it with his own hands is unlikely. He half said that others had taken it and then had fallen under the law, leaving him cockawhoop with a disproportionate treasure. Also, I suspect that he had been a spy of the Council and had somehow cheated his masters. However that was, he had the gold, and he desired to sail with it to Flanders. That was in large part why he met with Ben and myself.'

'And why was that?'

'I cannot set forth every detail, lad, for some of the secrets are not mine, and it would endanger your head to hear and mine to tell. But the main point is clear. He came to us because we had a boat that slipped across to Flanders more often than the Queen's officers knew. Not, indeed, that he came to us with a plain question. Rather, we came to him about another matter.' He scratched his head. 'I cannot make out where to begin in this crisscrossing story. In part I met him because I was watching the abbot his master; for it is true that I had been at the spoiling of Langdon in the old days and believed that the abbot had hidden the best of his ornaments, as so many of them did. But I never came to the question; for when John Faxy let me into his master's chambers, I found nothing.'

'Why did he let you in?'

'How many questions you ask, and none of them to the point.' He scratched his head again. 'By this time, you must understand, Faxy was afraid of denying me, and I had a notion that I might find something to set me on the trail. Also, there was a cupboard that Faxy was too great a coward to force open. Then, as I was forcing it with a bar, the abbot came in and I struck him down.'

'It is true then that you killed him.'

'No, he fell in a swoon and did not die till three weeks after, when an apoplectic visitation came upon him, the Lord's work and not mine. Yet his untimely coming meant that I gained nothing, for he cried out as he fell and I was compelled to flee.'

'Are you sure that the treasure which Faxy had was not the abbot's after all?'

'All things are possible.' Jones laughed. 'You are a shrewd lad. I have thought since that Faxy may have drawn me into the attempt on the cupboard and then sent the abbot to the room, so that I might be nabbed or the abbot killed. For he knew that the abbot was an old choleric man, liable to fall dead at a mauling. But let that pass.'

'Why should Faxy wish you out of the way?'

'He wanted to cross into Flanders, and he said too much to us; for he was a man unable to bear his drink. He told us things that he had better have kept to himself. I think he had been set as a spy on the abbot by the Council.'

'But why?'

'You know that Cardinal Pole is at odds with the Pope who hates the Spaniards so hotly that he is ready to lose England again rather than see Philip swallow it. The abbot had certainly come with letters from the Curia, connected with the Pope's desire to depose the Cardinal. You know that the deposition was prevented before, only because the Queen stayed the Pope's envoy in France and refused to let him take boat for England.'

'I know a little of such rumours; but how should they mix

with this Faxy's fears and your own resolves?'

'Faxy was playing both sides false. He was the sort of man who cannot resist a price. That may have been another reason for his wanting to see the abbot dead. Now he wanted to flee to Flanders, and he had news of Ben from another source, which I may not mention. Therefore, finding his weakness, we filled him with wine till his belly gurgled and gaggled. Thus we learned certainly about the treasure, and decided that our most politic course would be to throw him overboard in midsea.'

'What honesty was there in that?'

'Had he not told us twenty lies for one true word? If he had come to us with an open offer, he would have tied our hands. But what we learned, we learned in his own despite, so that we owed him no oath or truth. He blabbed when he was drunk as an ape, and we swore to nothing.'

'You have sworn nothing to me, neither.'

'Then that's something we must remedy, lad. I'll come up later with a pint of charnico and nick our wrists to mix the blood in the jug. Then we'll drink the wine, and that's an oath no good man would break. For if such solemn bond were mocked, all fellowship would fail on earth and we might as well go hang ourselves.'

'Will you do it?' asked Merric eagerly.

'Here's my hand on it. But I have sworn no such oath to your father or to Blaise. Neither had I sworn it to this Faxy.'

'But what of Ben?'

'Ah, there you touch me on the raw and show the excellent reason why this Faxy had to die. For in his morning glooms, though he cannot have remembered all he said, he knew well enough that he had said too much. Therefore he tried to buy each of us to his side and to set us one against the other.'

'How did he do it?'

'I'll tell you. He took us each aside at different times and swore that the other had begged him to join in a cheat. I think he thought to set us so busily watching one another that we should find no time for him. Also, he tried to deceive us into taking a false chest, promising himself to come along on another boat.'

'How did you discover his stratagems?'

'At first I did not discover them. I believed what he said, or much of it. Therefore I went aside to Ben and declared that I detested this Faxy beyond all words. Let us find out all he knows, I said, and let us push him into a quag or set him drunken in a stye of hungry pigs. Ben answered me that he saw no good reason against my plan. Only, he said, let us make sure that we know where he has hidden his treasure.'

Jones paused, exhausted; and Merric, who had been watching closely all this while, said, 'Thus, both of you wished to see how far the other would go?'

'You understand it all,' said Jones, reviving. 'I knew that this Faxy had a paper in the pocket inside his doublet, for I had watched the way his hand went straying, and once, when he fell over, I felt the paper through the cloth. And later, when we went out to make water against a wall, I saw him take it out to make sure it was not lost.'

'Then what happened?'

'We killed him.'

'But you must tell me how.'

Jones gave a sigh of reluctance. 'I hate this turning of dead matters over and over, and find it hard to set the acts in their right line, one behind another; and that makes you mistrust me.'

'You have told me so much,' cried Merric, 'I beg you to finish it.'

'Thus it was,' said Jones resignedly. 'Ben agreed with what I said, but his face still showed a distraction. So I thought to push him yet further, and I said: Let us kill the rogue tonight, for I cannot bear the rattling of his breath any longer, nor his fumbling hands. Then I saw Ben look darkly, but he agreed. Therefore the three of us went to an alehouse beyond Bishopsgate in the fields, and we drank all day till we were near mad with hatred and wariness. But Faxy couldn't take his drink, and twice he vomited out of the window and grew maudlin, saying he had been circumcised by the devil in his youth, so that all women scorned him. And I hated him, but I hated Ben yet more, for many things seemed to confirm my suspicion of him, until towards seven of the evening the reckoning was brought in, and the hostess said that if we wanted further drink we must command a bedroom for the night. Then may you wallow, she said, when you can stand no more. So the chalked-up sum was brought in, and we spent much time counting the cost, till Ben and I disagreed and come to blows.' He paused again and cried, 'Why cannot I shorten this endless tale?'

'Go on,' said Merric, watching him closely.

'Then the tapster pulled us apart, and no sooner had he gone than we turned on Faxy. First I pushed him down on the floor and set his own cap in his mouth, and then I drew the paper out from his pocket. To make sure what it was, I moved towards the door, where the light was better, and Ben thought I was turning to make off. He grasped at me, and I thought that he now proved all my suspicions true. He caught my hand with the paper in it. I drew my knife and slashed at his fingers. He let go, but took away a half of the paper. Now he too had his knife out, and we staggered round the room. I felt the burden of the drink on my brow, and my eyes burned with hollowness, but I was sober enough with fear to keep myself from falling facedown. Then the fool Faxy, dragging the cap out of his mouth, looked up and saw the knives. He climbed on to his feet and came floundering between us. Ben fell over a stool, and Faxy waved at me with his pudgy hand. So I struck out and pierced him in the throat, and that was the end of him.'

'And what of Ben?'

But this time Jones needed no urging. 'I leaned back against the wall and watched him fall with a spout of blood. Ben was lying on his back under the table, trying to catch hold of the table-legs. Then for the first time I thought that I had made a mistake, but as yet I had no way of telling what or why. So I turned and ran out, and came in through the Gate back to the city, and in due time I reached this house.' Breathing with difficulty, he added, 'It's the truth, lad. It's the truth, as near as I see it. And after I had come in through the Gate, I found I still held my half of the paper.'

'What happened to Faxy's body?'

'That I can only guess, and your guess is as good as mine. Ben and the hostess must have thrown it out somewhere or dug a hole in the fields.' He made a weary gesture, then after a while added, 'I knew that Ben wouldn't go till he found me, because I knew that I wouldn't go until I found Ben.'

'I see . . .' Merric put his hand over his eyes. 'I feel there's more I want to ask, but my mind is broken.'

'I'll go and get the charnico at once,' said Jones, rising with a quick smile. 'And we'll swear our blood-brotherhood. I can't bear to have you mistrusting me a moment longer.' His voice grew soft. 'I know you'll look after your mother in her old age, and so, what I give to you I give to her.' He went lightly out.

<h1 style="text-align:center">XIII</h1>

'Why have you come so far round, to walk through this street?' asked Jon.

'I have a purpose,' said Stephen, refusing to look Jon in the face.

'It is another of your wagers. You have broken your promise,' said Jon sadly.

'I did not promise,' replied Stephen obstinately. 'I said only that I would tempt God no longer.'

'Why have you come this way?' Jon looked round. 'This is the street in which the Hudleys live.'

'It is nothing to do with them,' protested Stephen. Then he halted and leaned against a post supporting a three-storey house. 'You have been right to rebuke me, for my shame has made me lie to you.'

'How then do the Hudleys concern you,' asked Jon in a weak voice, 'except in so far as they are godly folk?'

'I wished to see if one of them showed at a window.'

'And what would that signify?'

Stephen did not answer for a moment, then he asked very softly, 'Yes, what would it signify?'

'Have I also lied to my brother?' said Jon. 'Stephen, do not make me say that to you which I refuse to say to myself. I cannot tell what my thoughts would be if we lived in quiet times, in a christian world. I often think that then there would be no taking or giving in marriage; and at that, instead of comfort, my soul finds gall. For one voice says that we should be as innocent as babes; and another voice says that we should lie in another's arms without jealousy, or particular claims, or separation. One temptation is sweet and icy, and the other is sweet and burning . . . But I stray from my meaning. I set out to say that in times like ours there can be no love of husband for wife, no love of father for child, which is not a betrayal of Christ. We must set all thoughts of our comfort and solace aside, and prepare only for death.'

'I too have had these thoughts,' said Stephen, 'but I am often far from your conclusions.' He stood with sunken head.

After a while, Jon spoke in a cheerful and kindly voice, 'Then let us go on.'

They walked slowly down the street. As they passed the house of Mrs. Hudley, Stephen looked up and he saw through an open window on the first storey the face of Mabel Hudley for a moment. She passed the window whitely and was gone without noticing him, but he smiled and walked more blithely. At the end of the street the two lads stopped.

'I saw her passing,' said Stephen.

'I did not look up,' said Jon.

They went on in silence.

XIV

A low indrawn sigh came from the crowd as the tumbril hove in sight. Three Londoners stood in the tumbril: Cutbert Simson with his ragged beard all tangled and turned up at the edges, Hugh Foxe, a small man with a blackened cut across his brow, and John Cavendish, sick with fever and upheld by the other two. Cavendish's head lolled on his shoulders, and he stared up as though he marked a presence in the sky; but Hugh Foxe stared rovingly out at the people, as though he sought for someone familiar. Cutbert had a stern face of repose, Foxe had a wild and anxious face, and Cavendish had a face which already looked beyond it all. One stood enclosed in his own deep meditation, one looked out on the world, and one looked through the world, and all were blessed. Dressed bleakly in old shrouds, they came along the track in a tumbril dragged by a grey horse and a roan; and there was a smell of dung from the tumbril.

The tumbril lurched on the stones and ruts and tussocks of grass; and the three men swayed, but did not fall, these three Londoners, grasping the wattled barrier at the side of the tumbril. Two men held the barrier, and between them they held the third man, who looked only upward. And as they swayed and swung at the tumbril's lurching they were like three figures in a painted cloth on the wall, which may waver in a wind but cannot fall. Always they came back to their upright position, enclosed in meditation and looking straight at the world and looking right through the world; and the people watched them, with intaken breath, as the tumbril came rattling into Smithfield.

A little dog with his hair combed on either side of his back sprang up yapping, till someone kicked him; then he yelped and was mute again, and a large cloud like a man's hand was standing over the steeple of Paul's. Porters were coming up still with bundles of faggots and dropping them on the mound, around the stake with its three rings of iron. Nearby stood the three-posted gallows, with ropes dangling in the wind, next to the battered oaktree. Boys had climbed it, clinging with their legs and riding in the sky. Also, not far from the stake was a cauldron already simmering, with an old woman at watch over it; and round the stake on its mound stood the soldiers with pikes, burly in jacks and morions. And the tumbril came on, led by a clown with a whip, and guarded by soldiers, sergeants and monks.

'Let the earwigs burn,' said a Catholic. A monk turned smiling; but no one else of those at hand made a response.

The crowd opened to let the tumbril through, and then formed its circle again. The tumbril jerked to a stop. The wattled fence at its back was taken down, and the clayfaced man with the whip flicked at the prisoners. First Cutbert came down, and stood for a moment with closed eyes. Then Foxe, looking keenly around; and Cavendish, falling into the arms of his companions with tottering knees and head still thrown back.

A porter came with a tar-barrel and set it in the midst of the faggots and rushes; and then two others came with tar-

barrels, and set them carefully down. After which they stood
aside, like men who have faithfully discharged a task.

A monk with a tall crucifix called loudly on the prisoners.
He represented their sins to them and asked whether they
wished in contrition to make their peace with the Church,
their loving mother, that offered them every mercy. But they
stared at him and said nothing.

Then Cutbert Simson, seeing his wife in the crowd of faces,
cried, 'O, my beloved,' and turning to the monk, he said
with an aloof courtesy, 'Do not trouble those who have made
their peace.' And to his companions, 'I beseech you now be
of good cheer and count the cross of Christ greater riches
than all the vain pleasures of England.'

'Amen,' said Hugh Foxe. 'The cup is blood; and if we
believe, we must drink.'

John Cavendish looked quietly round at the people with
a smile, and those who met his eyes, burst into tears. 'There
is no other wine of life,' he said.

The monk who had spoken saw that the porters had now
completed their work, and he muttered to a sergeant. An
officer threaded chains through the rings on the stake; and
others brought the three condemned men to the faggot-mound
and set them against the stake, lifting the barrels over their
heads. So the three stood there, covered by the barrels to
the waist, in grey shrouds, chained under the arms and round
the throats. The monk began speaking again, but his voice
was drowned by the rising hum of the people. For a tall
fellow came up with a pinetorch kindled from the cauldron-
fire, and plunged it among the rushes under the feet of Cutbert, and then among those under the feet of Foxe, and then
among those under the feet of Cavendish; and the flames
curled and writhed upward, and smoke-plumes whirred from
the seams of the barrels.

And the drums beat, and the voices of the people rose.
Each man and woman cried out, and did not know it. The
flames crackled and leaped in a twining mess, and the plumes
of smoke beat the three men in their calm faces, and pieces
of rush went threshing in the fiery wind. The three men
lifted their heads and the flames beat up towards their chins.
Then a line of burning tar ran over Foxe's feet, and he

screamed through his blackened mouth, and it seemed that a flock of white birds went startling up the sky. A handful of flame lighted on the thick beard of Cutbert, and the hairs caught fire, licking up over his face, and then went out. Now the flames got up inside the barrels and roared with the tar, biting deep into the flesh of the three men, who screamed and screamed. But the cry of the people rose higher, though no man knew that he cried. The faces, transfigured into masks of mad anguish, showed momentarily through the smoke-flurry, hung on loops of iron chain.

Hugh Rigeley raised his eyes at last from the blackening foot of his friend Cutbert, which showed under the charring edge of the barrel in a red heart of fire. He looked on the streaked face, in which the eyes seemed white hells of burning, and he cried out, 'Take me, I too wish to drink the cup of blood, I too believe.' But no one heard him, or heard any of the others who cried the same words.

XV

Agnes stood at the side of the window, peering between the window-frame and the curtain at the room across the street where a man was looking for something in a cupboard. He stared out, and, though he could not possibly have seen her, she stepped back, knocking against a small table, which rattled. She caught the bronze basin as it was sliding off, and set it back with the earthern ewer and the ball of sweet-soap. Returning to the bed which showed the dint of her body, she sat down, reached to a shelf for an ivory case with boxwood combs, but did nothing with it. Then, dropping the combcase on the pillow, she stood on the edge of the bed and felt about in a cavity at the back of the shelf. From it she took a paper written *I love you, love you, M,* an ivory figurine of Virgin with Child, a long red candle, an oval pebble, a key, a stained ribbon, a soft-leather glove, and a rough woodcut of Adam and Eve naked in the Garden before the Fall. The cutter had meant to hide the loins of Adam and Eve with flowers, but had given the effect of a rose actually growing from their bodies.

Hearing a slight noise, she replaced the things in the hole, slipped down from the bed, and sat down with a book in her leather-seated chair. Her mother looked in. 'I thought you were downstairs, helping Sanchia with the conserves.' Then, as Agnes gave no reply, she came in softly. 'What are you reading?' She took the book and read the title out slowly, holding it at arms length. '*The Birth of Mankind* newly translated out of Latin into English.' She blew through her nostrils. 'Why can't you be content with reading the Herbal after dinner? I've never read anything else, and I don't see why you should go setting yourself above your mother. But whatsoever you read, why must you pick such a book as this? I told you before to put it aside. It has things in it that I never knew, though I'm a married woman who has borne four children and five abortions. It isn't decent that you a virgin should read things that make you more learned about childbed than your mother.'

'Even a virgin comes from a woman that was no virgin,' said Agnes.

'That's as true indeed as the skin between your brows; but what it signifies I leave to the wise hare to instruct me, and then I'll be no clearer. Your father tells me that Master Olyff's son has been proposed as a husband for you. If you will show yourself obedient in this, I shall forgive you many things, and you may read all the lewd books you desire.'

'No, by Saint Ann.'

'Yet you have never seen him.'

'Reason enough.'

'There, you admit that you have nothing against him, and you make it an excuse for hating him. Won't you at least look him in the face?'

'I don't want to marry anyone.'

Nest raised her hands in dismay. 'No, you want to become a burden on your parents, who have spent their goods in raising you to become a mock and a bitterness for their old age.'

'I must go against the stream with the crab,' said Agnes, 'and feed with the deer against the wind.'

Nest raised her hands again, and went out. On the way down she met old Fabyan, who stood outside the solar, clicking his tongue and groaning. 'What ails you now?' she asked.

'I've the ache of the teeth again,' he complained.

'You have the least teeth of anyone in the house,' she said, 'and you get the most pains in them. But as a man grows old, he reverses the course of nature. Come down to the kitchen, and I'll roast you a clove to lay on the guilty tooth.'

He followed her meekly down, and then began complaining once more. 'I had a clove last time. Cannot you give me a new and mightier cure? For this tooth is larger and the pain is more sharp. My mother used to boil henbane roots in vinegar and rosewater.'

'No,' said Nest severely, 'there is no better cure than a clove roasted in the embers and then brayed.'

'A clove will give ease,' said Gladus, who was setting tarts out on a pewter plate. 'But there is only one lasting medicine. A bean with a louse in it, tied in a piece of taffeta and hung round the neck.'

'O, that the season of beans were here,' groaned Fabyan. Nest set some cloves on a stone near the fire, and then began mashing up some burnt mice-heads as toothpaste. 'O, what a castle-come-down is the whole world nowadays,' Fabyan went on. 'I feel so amazed that I keep looking seven ways for Sunday.'

XVI

Jacint leaned from the window and called to her father, 'Don't forget to bring me some Spanish oranges.' Then, making sure that he had gone up the street, she closed the window and hurried downstairs. In a shed near the warehouse at the back she found Martin sharpening his knife on a grindstone. 'He's gone. Stop that noise and listen. What are we going to do?'

'Bear it as best we can.'

'I won't. Listen. What do you say to buying a bottleful of fleas and tying them under her chair?'

'Fleas are no respecters of persons. They may decide that your lap is a sweeter harbour than the widow's.'

'Still, it would be clear that the fleas migrated from under her rump, and that could hardly make her seem delightful in our father's besotted eyes.'

'It would also be clear that she had enemies in the house.'

'At least let me drop a spider down her neck.'

'If you and the spider agree, who am I to object? But I think that more will be needed to discourage her.'

'It's your turn to say something.'

'Only two things would break the marriage. Dissolve her money-stores or marry her off to another.'

'Then marry her yourself.'

'I desire indeed a golden double-bed, but my bride I'd like with nimbler legs for the marriage-dance.'

'Lettice has learned from her Prue that she is afraid of frogs. Let me put a frog in her wine. Lettice says that once a frog jumped in her face as she was riding and the horse threw her. Also, once she found a frog in her shoe as she drew it on, so that she fainted.'

'Stick her with a bodkin and have done with it,' he said, offering her the knife he had ground. Then he laughed and kissed her; but she drew away.

'Speaking of fleas, I promised Aunt to strew the parlour with wormwood. But I warn you, Martin, unless you help me against this widow, I shall look elsewhere for my succours and comforts.'

XVII

Tabitha, with wetly gleaming face, peered into the pot of boiling honey, kneeling before the brazier with dress pulled up over her knees. 'Shall I take it out now, mistress?'

'No, leave it awhile,' said Dousabel in a muffled voice. She was seated on a quilted stool with pins in her mouth.

'There are marvellous lights of gold,' said Tabitha in an awed voice, trying to get closer.

'That is a reflection of the honey,' said Dousabel, 'it proves nothing about the jewel.' She thrust the pins into a little yellow cushion, and stood up, yawning. 'I shall wear only my coat of new scarlet.'

'Yes . . .' Tabitha couldn't take her eyes from the slow heavy bubbling of the honey.

'He will come at three o'clock, by the backway. See that the front door is bolted. And look out of the little window up the lane before you open . . .' She yawned. 'Not that I fear any interruptions. I take precautions for no reason other than custom. I am secret, so that I may feel secret; and the whole while I truly feel that I am in the open street, under all men's eyes.'

At last Tabitha looked up, wide-eyed. 'Mistress, I find it hard to credit. How could a man do such things?'

'Must I tell you again that he is no man? He mates with a succuba of gold, not with me. I am his miraculous virgin, who changes the world into alchemic gold for his purse; and yet at times I feel that he hates me for it.'

'I hate him in turn so much that it hurts me,' said Tabitha, clenching her small chubby fist.

'Then hear the strangest thing of all,' said Dousabel. 'None of these matters have been put in words between us, and I know that he would kill me if I said them outright. Yet as clearly as though he wrote it down in plain commands, I know what he desires me to do and he knows that I know. He knows that I entangle this Francis in his net, he knows that I receive him here and take his gifts, and yet if I accused him of it, he would wish to strike me dead.'

'How can such things be?' whispered Tabitha.

'You know little of the dark hearts, child. Maybe, among the poor, with nothing to do but work and starve, things are different, and love or hate is a simple and manifest matter. Then fear may show an ugly face yet it is known for what it is, and men are so much the safer and happier, no matter what hardships they feel. But when men become the masters of money, then are they truly mastered. Then are they inveigled into schemes which they devise with much craft and which serve only to cheat them in the end themselves.'

'I cannot understand . . .'

'I am glad. See that you never understand.'

'But why does he do it? why cannot he enjoy the delights that heaven and earth have given him? Why must he strive to put butter on bacon, only to spoil his stomach?'

Dousabel yawned. 'It is dull and wearying. Help me out of my clothes. I am in a mood to surprise this Francis.' Tabitha came close, unbuckling her belt. 'I am in a mood to surprise myself.' She yawned, lifting her arms. 'I think sometimes I know that man of mine through and through, and then he says or does a thing which shows I know nothing . . .'

'Mistress, cannot there be a kindness between man and woman?'

Dousabel dropped her skirt round her ankles and then kicked it away. 'Not where money has come between, even though the man thinks he wants it only to gild his woman's flesh. There is only a snare, and they are enemies who share a darkness.'

Tabitha shivered. 'He makes me afraid. I have never said it before, but my flesh feels a chill when he touches me. I thought you'd be angry if I told you.'

'It shows only that you are a good girl.'

Tabitha pulled the shift over Dousabel's head. 'Mistress, you will never leave me; never turn me away?'

'I shall take you wherever I go.' She laughed. 'Strange, I was thinking only a few moments ago that I am tired of this England with its broken men and its market of flesh and blood. I should like to cross the seas and set a length of water between myself and a thing I fear.'

Tabitha ran to the pot of honey. 'O, it's boiling over.' She took a spoon and felt about in the pot, then drew out a large red stone which she dropped on to a towel.

'Rub it well,' said Dousabel, 'and then we'll see if it shines more preciously or if it is a glass-cheat.'

XVIII

'When they bury them, the monks pour soap-ashes on the ground; and after they say that God will not suffer grass to grow on a heretic's grave. Then many of the Balaamites come to see and testify to the same.'

'I plucked the fellow from the altar as he was about to make his god.'

Stephen was trying to listen to both conversations at once. This Sunday the Congregation met in a clothworker's loft at the end of a narrow lane near the Great Conduit; for the house at Aldgate had been noted by the spies.

'. . . suffering the images in the church, the idol hanging in a string over the altar, candlesticks and tapers, and the people honouring the idol.'

'Do as I did, brother. I took up a cowturd with the spade and clapped it on the monk's new-shaven crown. Before long, I said, all of you will be glad to hide your tonsured pates.'

'That was scarcely mannerly,' said a woman. 'We must behave decorously, or give our enemies a weapon of scorn against us.'

'Satan is no prince of mine,' retorted the man, 'that I should think any ceremony his due save a buffet and a sharpened word.'

Master Bentham came slowly up the ladder and through the trapdoor. 'This is the first time we have met,' he said, dusting his shoulders, 'since our dear friends died in the fire; and they are deep in our thoughts. We are no papists to say masses for the souls of the dead or set up our faithful as images of prayer, but let us thank the Lord for granting us such signs of his grace and such lanterns of strength to guide our steps at this dark turn.'

A man called, 'They have gone up in a fiery chariot, Elijah-rapt to heaven!'

A woman began chanting, 'In the way wherein I walked have they privily laid a snare for me. I looked on my right hand, and beheld, but there was no man that would know me. Refuge failed me, no man cared for my soul. I cried unto you. I said: You are my refuge and my portion in the land of the living.'

Another took up the cry. 'Attend to my voice, for I am very low. Deliver me from my persecutors, for they are stronger than I. Bring my soul out of prison that I may praise your name.'

'Lord, we thank you,' said Bentham, 'we thank you for the lives and deaths of these three brothers . . .'

They took up the thanksgiving, the prayer, the lesson. One and then another spoke, man and woman, old and young. They sang. They sang as they spoke.

Mrs. Hudley came late, Mabel with her. They sat on a box some paces ahead of Stephen and Jon. Stephen glanced at Jon and found that he'd averted his eyes. Feeling about in his

pocket, he took out a coin and glanced at it. Head or tail?
Head it was. Jon, he saw, had an unwilling eye on him.

Stephen put the coin back in his pocket. When the last
prayer was said by Bentham, he walked past Mabel to the
other side of the room, where Tom Hinshaw stood. Jon came
after. Then Mat Osborne joined them.

'Is your mind yet clear?' Mat asked.

He spoke to Stephen, but Jon answered. 'Others have fought
with carnal weapons. But what have they won?'

'They struck for a Lady Jane or a Lady Elizabeth,' said
Tom, 'not for righteousness. I am against lurking in rat-holes
till we are driven out with iron rods. I am for an open battle.'

'But how?' asked Stephen. 'They have the weapons.'

'There are a hundred ways. And yet if there were only one
way, and that hopeless, I should choose it rather than a weak
waiting on their cruelty. I should march on the devil's fortress,
the palace of the bishop, and knock on the door with a shout
for vengeance. Aye, they'd sieze and burn us. But if we came
day after day, they'd grow afraid, and the stink of burning
flesh would drive the people into arms against them, against
the Dagon in their churches that eats men alive. And with
their fall all the Dagons of the world would come down in a
crash.'

'We might be called on to testify in some such way,' said
Jon, musingly. 'I speak of the knocking on the door.'

'I speak of the throwing-down of Dagon,' said Mat.

'But are there enough of us?' asked Stephen.

'Which of us has counted the faithful, save him whom they
serve?' answered Mat. 'I warrant you that our master can
raise up all the defenders he requires.'

'We must beware of a wrathful spirit,' said Jon.

Stephen looked round and saw that Mrs. Hudley and Mabel
had gone. He turned towards the ladder-hole, but came back
to the disputers. 'Therefore let us agree,' he said angrily, 'for
then there is less danger of error and waywardness.'

'The people are discontented,' said Mat. 'But they lack
hearts. I think they were near an uprising after the news came
of Calais; but now the war has fallen into such a contempt
that the Queen dares not send an army abroad, and the people
are damped down again. They hate the Spanish alliance which

has brought them only misfortune, risen prices, and decay of trade. Five years ago there were many who welcomed the return of the old religion, thinking that it signified the putting-down of the bitter lords who have taken the land, and the merchants who have trampled on the fellowships of craft. But now they know otherwise.'

Hugh joined the group, 'Ah, but I fear the unruliness of the people, who are driven by fear and anger, by pain and hunger, but not by a desire to behold the sun of righteousness.'

'He who speaks ill of the sheep speaks ill of the shepherd,' said Mat. Hugh paled and stood with trembling hands.

Suddenly someone shouted from below. Those of the Congregation who still lingered in the loft fell silent. Mat tiptoed over to the ladder-hole. He peered down, then made a friendly sign. The others began talking again, in husht voices.

XIX

Cicely Ormes in Norwich came to the stake and laid her head on it and said, 'Welcome the Cross of Christ.' Which being done, she looking on her hand and seeing it blackt with the stake, wiped it upon her smock; for she was burnt at the same stake that Simon Miller and Elizabeth Cooper were burnt at. Then, after she had touched it with her hand, she came and kissed it and said, 'Welcome, the sweet Cross of Christ,' and so gave herself to be bound thereto.

CHAPTER FIVE

April

I

WILLIAM WAS looking at an almanac; Jones sat on a stool, hugging his knee; Merric leaned back staring at the ceiling. A knock, and in came Blaise with a sly solemn smile. 'I trust I find you all in good health and godly inclinations. Let us put aside all compliments and gossip, and turn at once to our solemn purpose.' He nodded to William, and took the empty chair.

'I trust your wife's stomach is easy,' remarked Jones.

'No compliments, I said,' Blaise protested.

'But I meant it in no complimentary sense,' replied Jones, with an air of pert innocence. 'Yet let it pass.' He blew his nose.

'Well, then?' Blaise looked at William for a lead.

'You sound dry and grating,' said Jones. 'Let us at least drink to our fortune.'

Without a word William took up a flagon from the floor and filled four mugs that stood at the end of his table. Merric handed them round.

'To our fortunes,' said Jones, 'and since a man's best or worst fortune is his wife, that means Nest and Dousabel for you two, and the gold for Merric and myself.'

William drank, ignoring Jones's words, and turned to Blaise. 'Kit declares that he has now completed all his enquiries.'

'With Merric's aid,' interposed Jones.

'And now he wants to make the final arrangements before he goes for the gold.'

'Since Merric is now well enough healed—or will be in a week,' Jones interposed again.

'Well, then?' asked Blaise, licking his lips.

'We shall need a river boat, large enough for three men and a chest. Because of Merric's half-healed wound, we desire Stephen to come with us.'

William frowned. 'That means asking a favour of Hugh.'

'He has refused to share in the treasure.'

'The less he knows the better.'

'We must have at least one more man. Merric must not strain his wound open, slight as it is. Who could be better than Stephen? or would you take the matter outside the family?'

William nodded reluctantly. 'No. Let it be Stephen then.'

Jones ticked the articles off on his fingers. 'We shall need further two crowbars, a strong sack, and five pounds in money.'

'Why the money?'

'For various small matters, such as a pistol.'

'No killing,' said William sharply. 'I want no hue-and-cry ending on my doorstep. What an honest man dare do, I dare do; but no more.'

'We have no thought of killing, but we must be able to defend ourselves if need be. We must trudge near half a mile to the chapel, and that is a fair distance, even in the dead of night.'

'How will you carry the chest through London,' asked Blaise.

'We shall not carry it. As we row down the river, we shall break it open and hide the things in special pockets in our doublets and cloaks. Then we shall sink the chest. I have considered every point most carefully.'

A pause: then Blaise, after consulting William with a glance, said to Jones, 'I agree. I shall pay you tomorrow half the sum you ask. That is, two pounds ten shillings.' William nodded, and Blaise went on, 'There is only small matter of information left out. You have not told us where lies the place you seek.' He looked again at William for support.

'If you do not tell us,' said William heavily, 'it seems as though you do not trust us, or mean to overreach us in some way.'

'To that I have two answers,' replied Jones, leaning eagerly forward. He touched his forefinger. 'One, it is my certain experience that the less people who share a secret the greater the security. Now this is not a matter of deceit and villainy, but of the chances of things—above all, the chances of the tongues of men. Two honest men can keep a secret safe. Four honest men are likely to make some slip among them. If there were any need to tell you, then I should be forced to take the risk and hope for the best; but since there is no need, I wish to hold my own counsel.'

'What is the other answer?'

Jones touched his second-finger. 'This other answer most pleasantly supplements the first and prevents any suspicions on your part. For I am not prosing to go alone on this treasure-quest. No, I shall have Merric with me, who knows as much as I do of the whole matter. Further, I shall have Merric and Stephen to carry the chest from the moment it is found till it is broken open and shared among us. And lastly (which note well) I shall be one among three, so that if Will superintends the sewing of the special pockets with a masterful eye, I shall have only a meagre share on my person of the things we uncover. If you can devise means to hold me more strictly in your service, I ask you to set them forth; for it seems to me I have outdone myself in the invention of knots and curbs to ensure your gains.'

Blaise and William looked at one another. At last William said, 'You seem indeed to have dealt honourably in these proposals; and therefore I agree.' Blaise nodded. 'Let us once more make clear what the shares are to be.'

'Half to me, and a quarter each to you,' said Jones, with a glinting smile towards Merric.

'Out of your portion you will pay us back the expenses we have incurred on your behalf,' said William.

'Two-thirds of them,' replied Jones with another glint at Merric. 'For it is not just that I should be held responsible for all the expenses. Two-thirds is enough.' He raised his cup and drank.

'Two-thirds then,' said Blaise, plucking at his lower lip.

II

When Joyce Lewes had thus prayed, she took the cup into her hands, saying, 'I drink to all them that unfeignedly love the gospel of Jesus Christ, and wish for the abolishment of papistry.' When she had drunk, they that were her friends drank also. After that a great number, specially the women of Lichfield, did drink with her; who afterwards were put to open penance in the church for drinking with her thus.

When she was tied to the stake with the chain, she showed such a cheerfulness that it passed man's reason, being so well coloured in her face, and being so patient, that the most part of them that had honest hearts did lament, and even with tears bewail the tyranny of the papists. When the fire was set upon her, she neither struggled nor stirred, but only lifted up her hands towards heaven, being dead very speedily.

III

He walked for the third time past the Cross in Chepe, watching its glistening gold, and went to the draper's shop where he had met Jacint. A fattish gawdily-painted city-mistress was the only customer, and her snarling spaniel, with uncut claws that clattered on the floor, bared its teeth and flopped out of the maid's hands that sought to catch it up. Merric withdrew and made again for the Cross. Lutesong from a barber's shop in a side street almost drew him down, but he moved on and encountered Dousabel, his Aunt, who stood with a young round-faced maid before a goldsmith's. Doffing his cap, he went to pass by; but she beckoned him to come nearer. 'There is no one I could be happier to see,' she said; and he stood looking a little defiantly into her sleek face, waiting for her to go on. 'You might be mannerly enough to offer your services. I should like you to accompany me into Master Herrick's shop, where I have a purchase to make.' He smiled and nodded. 'My husband is wound up in his unending business at the Receipt.'

'It is a new sort of labour for me,' he said, inclining his head.

'You use a weighty word for a light matter.'

'Because I wish to show my zeal and to ask for yet more exacting tasks.'

'Fie, where have you learned such courtliness?'

They went in. The hawk-nosed Master came forward, raising his tufted eyebrows, and Dousabel told him her name and said that she thought him acquainted with her husband. He expressed his pleasure at having Mr. Blaise Rigeley's wife in his shop, and asked what she wished to see. A ring, she said, or an earring of passable value. He clapped his hands, and an apprentice brought a tray of trinkets and rings, from which he selected a pearl pendant wrought in a vine-pattern. She turned the others over with slow and dainty hand. Yes, the pendant was pleasant. Its price? The Master smiled at his ridiculously low charges before he said, 'At a word, two crowns.'

'You ask too much,' she said casually, 'let me see other things. Show me a black pendant of jet after the manner of France. No, show me a fair topaz set in gold.'

'I have no topazes today worthy of your choice, but here is an excellent turquoise.'

'Is it oriental?' she asked, and turned to Merric with a smile.

'It came in a cargo from the East beyond India,' said the Master importantly and vaguely. 'Not far from the region is the imperial state of Cathay. Ah, here is one of the rings from Venice with a crystal in the collet, and under the crystal a little scorpion of iron wagging his tail very artificially. A pretty toy for a gentlewoman on a summer's afternoon.'

'I weary soon with toys,' said Dousabel.

'Then here is a ring of gold weighing a crown and a half, with a diamond cut in Cairo.'

She weighed it in her palm, put it on her finger, and asked the price. The Master, who prided himself on bluntness, told her, 'At a word, eight crowns.'

'I'll take it for five,' said Dousabel negligently.

In the end she bought it for seven and had it made up in a small parcel, which she handed to Merric, telling him that not the weight but the virtue of the contents was what she handed to his discretion and protection. Holding the parcel high, Merric winked at the maid, Tabitha, and followed his Aunt out into the street.

When they arrived at her apartment off the Strand, she asked him in. After some words of hesitation and surprise, he bowed and went in with her. She took the parcel from him, opened it, and asked him to put the ring on her finger. 'Now you have consummated your duty,' she said with her small tinkling laugh. 'Tab, bring my good nephew a sip of wine. And you, my good nephew, sit in one corner of the settle, and I shall sit in the other; and let us have an edifying conversation. For though I am your Aunt in law, I am closer to being a Sister in age and fancy, I think; and therefore I am somewhat undecided, now that we are alone together for the first time, whether I should romp with you or bid you join me in a prayer. Or shall I merely whisper a secret in your ear. On Saturday, I shall be twenty-five years old; and I have bought this ring so that my husband may give it to me as a surprise.' She rose. 'Make yourself at home. Blaise will be detained for at least three hours more in the Exchequer. I shall be back soon in a day-gown, to continue with the prayer we decided on. Meanwhile Tab will feed you with wine and sops.'

She went out, and the next moment Tabitha came in with the wine, looking down at her shoes; and when he took her hand, she pulled it free and hastened out. Merric drank, and then wandered round the room, looking under cushions and covers, and finding in a cypress-box an Italian book with wood-cuts illustrating Ovid, of ringleted ladies running fat-legged and dimpling-bottomed from brawny gods with riveted muscles or sprawling broadly-creased under goatish satyrs. Hearing a rustle, he slammed the book back and skipped to the settle.

She entered in a watchet gown buckled with a broad silver belt, and sat beside him, asking for wine. They drank; and when she caught his unwilling eye, she laughed and asked him what he thought of her. He faltered and could think of nothing to say.

'You are afraid of me,' she said in a challenging tone. 'I am your Aunt, and that is a dreadful thing. I am your naughty

Aunt, and you are afraid of what I may do to you.'

'I'm afraid of no woman.'

'Then look me in the face.'

He raised his eyes and then dropped them again. She laughed and he made a movement of angry discomfort. 'Well?'

'You were not afraid of my Tab. In the shop you eyed her all the while; and when she brought you the wine, you tried to kiss her.'

'Did she tell you?'

'No, neither did I spy on you. But I know your ways.' She smiled, and this time he looked at her without being bidden. 'No, I am not a jealous woman. If Tab wanted it, I should bring her now into your arms. Strangely I am a woman without jealousy. Yet you think me wicked beyond conception.'

'No, no,' he said. 'It is only that I do not understand you. In part perhaps I am confused because you are my aunt; but not only that.'

'I'll tell you more, since you know so little of yourself. You think there are two sorts of women, one who is chastely virtuous, and one who is wanton. You have never respected me much, but you have scarcely set me among the wantons. Now I behave with you as only a wanton could, and yet you are not sure, because you feel that I laugh at you. There is something which prevents you from feeling yourself in all simplicity my better. You would feel at ease with a girl in a bawdyhouse because you despised her and felt above her in the very act that made you one with her.'

'I don't know,' he muttered. 'These are not matters to think about, let alone to debate . . .'

'Why not?'

He turned his head angrily aside. She poured him out more wine, which he took unwillingly, and then drank at a gulp. Then he looked her full in the face at last. 'I am not so callow and bewildered as you think; but I like to look over a wall before I leap.'

'Look as long as you like.' She kicked her slippers off. 'Take down my stockings, Merric. I love the fire on my skin.' He knelt before her, unbuckled one of her stockings, and drew it slowly off; then the other. 'Now I feel a free woman,' she said, smiling down at him. 'I love all warmths. Someday I shall go to a land where the sun thrives. I die in the cold and the shadow.'

He stared up at her still, and she poured him out another cup of wine, which he tossed off. 'I'll buy you jet earrings in a fortnight,' he said thickly. 'I'll buy you one of those Venice rings.'

'I care rather for a bird in the hand.' She held out her open palm. 'Give me a penny for alms of love, and you have bought me. No, I mean it in truth. A penny, a penny.'

He felt in a pocket and found a penny, which he put in her palm. 'But I'm not boasting. Within a fortnight I shall be a rich man.'

'And I shall be a virtuous lady.'

'No, it is true. You see me as a youth hanging on my father's frown, with no more than a penny in my purse. But I tell you I am made for better things, and I have another man within.'

'No doubt. You shall show him to me at leisure.'

She set her finger on his lips. He shook it away. 'You do not believe me.'

'I believe everything I hear; but I hear very little. What were you saying?'

'I shall make you listen.'

'Why not? You have only to say something which commands my attention.'

'Listen then.' He caught hold of her chin. 'You're mine.'

'I think I heard that,' she said with a small laughter, fixing her eyes fully upon his and pressing against his palm. 'But if seeing is believing, it is only when the claim is sealed and pressed to its conclusive point that I credit my ears.' She yawned and lay back.

'Listen.' His voice roughened. 'I am not to be treated so contemptuously. At this moment I am indeed a nothing, but I know where a treasure lies.'

'Being so near the prize of my womanhood, you are likely to speak the truth when you boast of a treasure within your grasp.'

'No, this is a treasure of ordinary gold, and lies not far from London, where I shall gain it, within a week or two.'

She laughed. 'If you must tell me of it, tell me and have
done with the foolish matter. But I warn you, I shall still
think you closer at this moment to a mine of delights than you
are likely to be within any weeks of distance from my person.'

He hesitated, and she yawned again, showing the red of her
wet mouth and the top of her curled tongue. 'You shall not
misjudge me,' he muttered. 'I am a nothing now, but I know
how to astonish you . . .'

She put her hand over his mouth. 'Be silent or say all.
Which is it?' She looked from one of his eyes to the other.
'I see the hidden thing still angry to come out, like a snake
in your eyes that would strike me down in the dust of Eve.'
She laughed again. 'Know then that whereas the serpent
tempted Eve, I tempt the serpent and thus requite the ancient
ill of women. Come, dear fool, tell me what is to make you
a mighty man with a sword of gold for the wounding of ladies
on a Saturday afternoon. Speak or be shamed.'

'You think that I boast like a green prentice with the next-
door serving-maid,' he said, frowning. 'But I tell you I speak
soberly of money that lies in a known place. Listen, I say. In
a chapel not twenty miles from your venus-hill, to wit Richmond.' He faltered again. 'Can you keep a secret?'

'No,' she said. 'What is there secret about me?' She threw
her gown quite open. 'Yet I can be secret as to what I share
with another, though I blab it otherwise. Here is my secret,
and now it is yours, and no one else may share it because no
one else may occupy the same place as you at the same time,
except for angels, who crowd a cranny beyond all our estima-
tions.' She took his hand. 'Are you afraid now? Tell me the
secret you desire to tell, and thus we may meet in a simple
circle of charms, shutting away the world which is in no senses
angelic . . .' Her voice softly sank. 'Tell me, since you wish it,
so that we may share our hidden gold.'

'I know exactly where it lies,' he said with closed eyes and
head thrown-back. 'On the left side under the altar. I see it as
a smouldering fire. In that chapel of covetousness.' He opened
his eyes, and gripped her arms hard. 'There lies my liberty, in
the cold earth. But I shall dig it up and come again to you. I
shall pour it into your lap.' He trembled with the strength of his
angry desire. 'Now do you believe I am other than I seem?' His

voice rose. 'You said I feared you. No, it's not true, but I wanted you to respect me. Could I stretch out my hands to your sweetness, only to earn a knuckle-rap?' He let her arms go and touched her on the face, the shoulders, the breasts. 'No, I wanted to come with that in my hands which would make you cry out and kneel to me.' He trembled again, but held himself back. 'I have desired you ever since one day I saw you kiss Agnes, and I thought I had never seen a kiss before, so sweetly you lengthened it in a soft and innocent way. I used to think of meeting you in a lonely place of trees and tearing your clothes or climbing into your bed-chamber on a stormy night when you lay alone. But I never thought of this. Within a fortnight I shall pour gold within your lap.'

She reached sideways and took up the jug and poured the remnants of the wine over herself. The red wine ran, over her breasts and then down her plump tight stomach and downwards. 'No, today.'

IV

The Wardmote was being held in the yard of the parish church of St. Peter the Poor; for the day was fair, with small white clouds sown in a clear blue sky. Old Fabyan came bustling in, on Edgar's arm. 'You should not have come,' said William. 'I thought you had ear-ache.'

'I'll not have the clerk fine me a fourpenny absence unless I have worse troubles than worms in my ear,' said Fabyan. He coughed and sat on the gravestone which Edgar found him. Hugh came up and stood behind him without a word.

The alderman took his seat on the trestle-table fixed against the church wall, and the rich men of the ward gathered round, William among them. Several standers-by called for quiet. The Clerk, getting up on the table, read the warrant of the meeting; and then the beadle, from below, read out the name-roll of ward-residents. The crowd listened attentively, and a couple of names were questioned; then at the end a man complained that he had been left out. But the beadle showed that he had been given among his street-mates. The names of those absent were ticked off for fining.

Next the ward-constables came forward with the jury-panel
of the respectable men of the ward. The names were called,
and the jurymen gathered on one side of the trestle-table,
where they were presented by the Clerk with articles of
enquiry.

'I need not detail them,' the thin-legged Clerk said, scratching his nose with a quill-pen, 'for they are of immemorial
custom out of mind but I will briefly remind you that you
must see to the keeping of the peace of God and Holy Church
and the King by clerk and layman, rich and poor. That no
strangers be received in inns or lodging-houses for more than
one day and one night. That lewd and loose-living women
be driven out of the bounds of the Ward or else locked in the
Compter. That all furnaces and chimneys, all lepers and
usurers, and all night-walkers male or female, be kept under
control. And that no wakes be paid at a higher rate than the
assize. You will give your full verdict by the last day of this
month, so that the Alderman may bring before the Court of
Common Council all matters needing correction.'

The Alderman cleared his throat with majesty, and con-
gratulated the jury on their appearance. 'In these worsening
days a jury too often turns a deaf ear even to a threatened
fine, so that the coroner is forced to bring in a writ *decem
tales de circumstantibus*. But the men of Broad Street have
ever set an example to all England.'

Householders in the crowd began shouting out their complaints:

'There is a broken pavement before St. Anthony's whereby
lives are endangered in the dark, and a man ripped his nose
open.'

'A noisome drain in Howell's house.'

'The cage is noisome too.'

'Badcock's wife is a scold.'

'Mistress Spence is a common whore.'

'The haylofts in Scalding Alley are a menace in event of
fire.'

The Clerk was busily noting the grievances. 'All these
matters will be lookt into with a straight eye,' he called. 'And
now to further business. We have many officers to elect. The
scavengers and the officers for sealing weights and measures

and for bringing all freemen on the roll. Also for putting the oath of frankpledge.' He looked round with red-rimmed eyes.

A man in a poor blue cloak raised his hand. 'How are we to maintain good custom nowadays when the whole realm is perverted, and superstition reigns hand in hand with greed?'

The Clerk peered in his direction and the beadle shouted. A tumult began, the constables ran to the spot where the man in a blue cloak had spoken, and the dogs barked. But the man was gone, no one knew where. 'Which of you knew his face?' the Clerk cried.

Someone answered, 'He was not a man of this Ward.'

Merric sat on the wall with a couple of young men whom he knew slightly, members of the Yeomanry of his Guild. They were only a few years older than he was, but they were already masters in a small way. One of them, Peter Larch, eyed him unfriendlily. 'I had angry words with your father the day before yesterday,' he said.

'I know nothing of it,' said Merric uneasily. 'And I am unwilling to enter into a second-hand quarrel, even my father's.'

'He offered me starveling terms for a job of work, and I told him what he and his like are bringing England into.'

'I cannot stay to hear my father abused,' said Merric, getting down, 'even though I know nothing of the matter.'

'You shall hear more from us later, whether you like it or not,' said the other man, 'and whether you know anything or not.'

'England is become a commonwealth of caterpillars and cormorants,' said Peter.

'I wish you no harm,' said Merric, turning away, 'or I could bring those words in against you.' He went over to his grandfather Fabyan, who was cleaning his ear by twisting a piece of wool into it.

William walked faster and caught Hugh up. 'Will you come aside into a tavern and speak with me?' Hugh shook his head and said that he did not enter taverns. William went on, 'I am sorry that we had hard words the other day. I have brought five pounds to lend you, and I beg you in charity not to throw them back into my face.'

Hugh bowed his head. 'I thank you, brother. They are more than five hundred to me.'

They went on towards his house. 'Have you any complaints against Stephen?' asked William. 'Do not spare him because he is my son and your nephew.'

'He is closer to me than that,' said Hugh.

'What do you mean?' asked William fiercely.

'In Christ.'

William scowled and was silent for a moment, then he spoke again in a flat voice, 'Will you lend him to me for a day or two? I have need of his hands in some work.'

'So be it that the work is honest and godly.'

'How should it not be? What an honest man dare do, I dare; and not an inch beyond. You know that well. Has there ever been a whisper against my name?'

Hugh groaned. 'How easy is it to accuse.'

'I accuse nobody. I stand in my own good name.'

'The world entangles the best of us. Forgive me. I see the way in which you deceive yourself, but my own lies I cannot decipher.' They turned into Scalding Alley. 'And yet there is so much good in the world. On Monday I heard a poor man of my acquaintance say to his wife: Woman, if you were sparing, you might have saved me a hundred marks more than you have. And she answered him lovingly: O, man, be content and thankful, for we have enough if we can see it. Alas, good husband, she said, I tell you truth, I cannot firkin up the butter and keep my cheese in the chamber, to wait for a great price, while the poor want.'

'She acted according to her lights.'

Hugh answered angrily, 'You merchants trade always with the devil, whatever the proxy-names on your ledgers.'

William spoke slowly and decidedly, 'I tell you that hope of gain makes men industrious; and where no gain is to be had, men will not take pains. As good it is to sit idle as to take pains and have nothing. Merchant's doings must not be overthwarted by preachers and others who cannot understand them; and this overgreat curiosity of some, to meddle in other men's matters, I must tell you plain, is even the right way to undo all in the end. Therefore, say what you will, I shall amend, so I may live every day better and better, by any means, I care not how. Yes, I will make hard shift with the world and strain my conscience narrowly before I shall starve or beg, both I and my children after me. Provided always that I do not come within the compass of positive laws: and this I know well, that by all laws a man may take as much for his own wares as he can get, and it is no sin for one man to deceive another in bargaining, if he carries things decently and proportionately. For a bargain is a bargain, let men say what they will.'

They had halted before Hugh's house. Hugh stood with bowed head, listening. Then when William had finished, he said, 'I do not require that money of yours, nor ever shall. But if you wish to speak with Stephen, come in.'

William checked his tongue, and they went in. Rosbel, the slatternly housekeeper, called out in a rough voice, 'You are back then, and in good time, or the meat would be as dry as rope.' She shuffled about within, and then called again. 'Have you company with you? Have you brought more beggars to eat you out of house and home?' She appeared tangle-headed in the doorway, saw William, and stood open-mouthed, disconsolately waving a ladle. Muttering something, she turned away, showing a rent down one side of her red petticoat and a burst armpit-seam.

'I shall bring you Stephen,' said Hugh, and followed Rosbel out. Her voice could be heard remonstrating, then sinking into a sullen soliloquy over the joint on the jack. William looked round the room with contemptuous curiosity. A few lengths of undyed cloth on the shelves, a large ewer of water, a measuring rod, a dank earthy smell. Rosbel came and peeped in again, but finding herself observed, shrank back. Then Hugh returned, with Stephen slowly wiping his hands on an old clout.

'Your father wants your services for a few days.'

There was a pause for near a minute. 'Will you come then?' said William at last, in a voice that sounded hollow.

'How should I refuse?' said Stephen and looked at Hugh.

'It is to help your brother bring some goods down the river,' said William impatiently.

'Shall I take my cloak and come now?'

'No, come tomorrow afternoon. That will be soon enough.'

He stared at his brother and his son with a defiant glitter in his eyes, a sagging anger in his jaws and mouth. No one spoke. 'That is settled then,' he said savagely and turned to the outer door. But before he went out, he looked round, 'Judge not that you be not judged, my righteous brother.'

'Amen,' said Hugh.

William wrenched himself away. 'You think that he wants my hand for some bad matter?' asked Stephen.

'If it is bad, you will refuse to do it, without my bidding,' said Hugh. 'Doubtless it is no worse than other works of the world, which are counted honest.' He sighed. 'Ah, Stephen, we are indeed in a snare.'

He put his arm round Stephen's shoulders, and they went into the kitchen. 'So you've come at last,' said Rosbel, sniffing. 'You didn't ask your brother to stay, eh? You think he'd soil himself at our poor table. You let him trample upon you and you beg his pardon, I have no doubt. Tell me, if you're a man, why shouldn't you talk as loud as he does? I'll take an oath that he's cheated you out of a hundred pounds . . .' She pottered about, knocking a gridiron over. 'What's the use of talking to a pair of dumb dogs?'

'Call Jon in,' said Hugh quietly.

v

An honest good simple poor man, one William Nichol, was apprehended by the champions of the Pope, for speaking certain words against the cruel kingdom of Antichrist, and on the 9th day of April, anno 1558, was butcherly burnt and tormented at Haverford-west in Wales.

This William Nichol was so simple a good soul, that many esteemed him half foolish. But what he was, we know not; but this we are sure, he died a good man. And the more simplicity and feebleness of wit appeared in him, the more beastly and wretched does it declare their cruel and tyrannical act therein.

VI

'Come in, come right in,' said Blaise patiently, as the clerk Yardly halted in the doorway of his office-room. 'I see you

have something of importance to tell me,' he added, as Yardly
shut the door with sudden agility and came over to the table,
bending and muttering to himself.

'No, Master, nothing at all, nothing much,' said Yardly,
rubbing his moss-like hair. 'But I happened to hear something.
Nothing much, but a shrewder man than myself might make
something out of it.' He looked Blaise in the face with a
quick jerky smile. 'One such as yourself, with greater gifts
than myself.'

'Out with it, Yardly,' said Blaise patiently, sitting back and
picking his teeth with pen-point. 'You're not so weak-witted
yourself, you know. No, don't say you are, for I won't be contradicted in such a matter. I know you better than you know
yourself. Yes, I do.'

'That only proves how much shrewder you are than I,'
said Yardly with a dry chuckle. He rubbed his thick crisping
hair. 'What was it now? Don't say I've forgotten it after all.'
He felt in his pockets and at last found a scrap of paper.
'Ah, yes, Faxy it was. Handicot it was. Dead man, a great-
haunched liar, a man who dribbled in his wine and wept
penny-tears at will. I remember him as well as my own little
finger. You wished to hear any news of him.'

'What then of Faxy alias Handicot, or Handicot alias Faxy?'

'Besides waiting on the abbot, he made many journeys up
the river. I found a wherryman who once took him to Richmond and beyond.'

'And how did you find him?' asked Blaise, picking his nose
with leisurely enjoyment.

'A known rogue. One who rows between Southwark stews
and Savoy backstairs. A confederate of traders who seek to
evade the tax on cloths. A notorious finder of drowned men.'
Yardly shook his head. 'I claim no merit for finding him. As
simple as finding the navel in a bared belly. But having found
him, I had harder work to draw out his memories of the aforesaid dead man.' He chuckled. 'But I knew certain things to his
discredit. Not things, master, that would harm him in the
eyes of the law; for such things would be over-easy to find.
But things which would harm him in the eyes of malefactors,
murderers, shark-thieves and others whose good esteem he
craves.'

'Where did this dead man go?'

'To a certain pier beyond Richmond, used by poor fisher-men.' Yardly turned the paper over. 'I have it here drawn out in terms capable of confusing an architect of labyrinths.' He handed the paper over to Blaise, who scrutinised it with much interest.

'To find this landing-stage should be possible.'

'Having landed, he went to a Chapel inland, with a crowbar under his cloak. My wherryman followed him, but is too cowardly a fellow to creep up at close quarters.'

'You have done well, Yardly,' said Blaise. 'You have done very well, and I'll see you don't lose by it.'

'No, no,' protested Yardly, rubbing his hair. 'What I have done is nothing. I can't make sense out of it. Not at all, master. It takes a man shrewder than myself to fit things together and see what picture they make in their dangerous conjunction. I'm content to stand aside and say nothing. Thank you, thank you, Master. Now I'll go back to my work and leave you to your thoughts. Good-day, good-day.'

VII

'She's coming,' said Tace Kemp agitatedly, entering with her hands folded over her breasts. Her coarse black hair was standing out all round her head in elfknots. 'I won't stay to be despised.' She dashed out again, with flapping slippers.

Aunt Gertrude felt carefully at her cap and gave a quiet cough. 'It's a judgment on me for some of the harsh things I've said about poor Tace. Now I couldn't feel angrier if I was marrying him myself.'

'Shall you, myself, Rafe and Martin be defeated by a witless widow?' said Jacint, who was dressed in her richest gown of damask. 'Shall a single pismire outfront an anger of eagles?' She was looking round for further similes when a sound of voices came from the stairs, and she bit her lip. Aunt Gertrude stood up and sat down again.

'I have a lace coming loose somewhere. O what an unfortun-ate woman am I.'

The door opened and Mrs. Pernel Wicke came in, ushered by Gregory Hawes and followed by a whey-faced maid. She looked round, giggled, and put her hand over her mouth to hide the gaps in her teeth. 'Come and kiss your mother,' said Hawes to Jacint.

Jacint rose. 'Are you married already, madam? or does he mean that you have anticipated the ceremony?'

'We are contracted, we are contracted,' said Hawes, glowering.

'As one woman to another,' said Jacint, taking Mrs. Wicke's hand, 'you know what I mean, and take no offence, I am sure.'

'No offence indeed,' giggled Mrs. Wicke. 'Rather I take it as a compliment, Gregory.' She simpered at him. 'There are worse faults in a lover than a rash and passionate urgency.'

'Take her to bed at once,' said Jacint. 'How can you be so cold-blooded, father, when your mistress is as complaisant as she is beautiful, and as amorous as she is wealthy-pursed?'

'No, we are to be married in September,' said Mrs. Wicke hastily, seeing Hawes's growing annoyance. 'There is some lawyer's reason for the date, and so it is fixed.' She giggled and put her hand over her mouth. 'Love must wait upon law.'

Aunt Gertrude, who had begun by trying to efface herself in a corner, now fidgeted and coughed into her hand. Hawes turned sharply. 'You too are here.' He spoke in his hand to Mrs. Wicke, 'Here sits Mrs. Heygate, my dead wife's sister.'

'There is no need to notice me,' said Gertrude. 'I am nobody in this matter, less even than your poor daughter. I am a shadow, which gives way to the sun; for the shadow is cold, but the sun is gold.'

'I am pleased to know you,' said Mrs. Wicke, 'and wish only to know you better. For I desire all to learn that I intend no harm of any sort, but to make happier what is already happy.'

'Ah, indeed,' said Gertrude darkly, 'intentions may be of the best, yet the effects may seem otherwise. By these means we are reminded that on earth we are generally the devil's playthings. Not that my opinion could concern anyone, and least of all, you.'

'You are wrong in that,' said Mrs. Wicke, seating herself on a stool of tufted taffeta. The paint had cracked under her eyes and round her mouth; and out of the gawdy mask her eyes looked in pallid glassy fear.

'No doubt I am wrong,' cried Gertrude with increasing confidence. 'We all know that. What would be more usual than to find myself wrong, as you say? If only I could be right for once, I should die happy. But no, Gregory says I'm always wrong, and there's no going against his word, for it's law in this house and no other writ will run. Therefore I was glad to hear you say that you set law above love; for when you're Mrs. Hawes, you will get a bellyful of law and no love worth mentioning.' She shook her head at Hawes, who was trying to get a word in. 'It's no use denying the truth. I've always laid down under you, but now I think I must quaver a sentence in my own behalf and let Mrs. Wicke know the truth of this matter. Look at him, Mrs. Wicke, and judge for yourself.'

'Hold your tongue, Gertrude,' said Hawes. 'You speak like a fool.'

'You see, Mrs. Wicke,' said Gertrude with equanimity. 'He can't bear being contradicted.' She turned back to Hawes, 'but that is no reason why you should try to shout me down when I desire to tell Mrs. Wicke how lucky she is at being a quiet and longsuffering woman like myself. I had meant to advise her against the marriage, but now I see that she is the best-suited woman in the world for your bed and board, one who will never want her own way in anything, one who will be happy to bend under your least vagary.' She smiled sadly, and looked again at Mrs. Wicke. 'You won't ever find any trouble with Gregory, as long as you always give in to his demands, however outrageous they may be; and I can assure you that until you have lived with him, you have no notion of the unreason of a man, morning, noon and night. But I see plainly that you are a woman with a proper sense of her own sinfulness and therefore ready to be martyred, asking nothing of the new-fangled things that wilful wives rate as pleasureable.'

'Why have you made all this up to shame me?' Hawes spluttered.

'Perhaps you will tell me to my face that I am lying?' cried Gertrude, standing up from her chair of blue velvet. 'Yet I won't complain, Jacint, for I prefer that Mrs. Wicke, poor soul, should see the way he behaves in his own home, roaring and rioting like a whole harlotry of Herods. If she has learned the worst before she comes she cannot cry out afterward. Take some sugared fruit, Mrs. Wicke, or let me help you to some wine. You see how Gregory neglects you. I should have thought he'd attempt a better pretence of courtesies until he has you in his clutches; but at least he shows you his true face of rage and tyranny.'

Hawes stood facing her with clencht fists, red and staring-eyed with his need to shout her down and his fear to seem the person she described. 'It's no matter,' said Mrs. Wicke, in kindly tones. 'She means it in good sort, I am sure.'

'She means it in malevolence,' said Hawes hoarsely. 'She has planned it all to disgrace me. Jacint, your mother-to-be has brought you a ring. Go and receive it.'

'It's a token of my own betrothal ring,' said Mrs. Wicke placatingly. 'One for me, and another for you.'

'I don't know why our men haven't thought of ringing us like sows with a ring in our nostrils,' said Jacint, and took the ring so carelessly that it fell on the floor and rolled under the cupboard. The whey-faced maid, who had kept in the background, tried to intercept it and slid on a carpet, falling on her back. Jacint laughed, and her father, in a burst of fury, went to slap her face, but thought better of it. 'Go down to the kitchen!' he shouted, 'and take care that I do not banish you there for longer than an hour.' Jacint laughed and turned away.

'You will see such sights hourly,' observed Gertrude, 'and hear such names twice as often. But sticks and stones will break no bones, and names will never lame you. Therefore, it would be foolish to mourn unduly at a harsh word; and indeed you will find that you grow used to them, till the names you wept at will seem little worse than endearments. But he is to be pitied rather than blamed, for I have always said that a hasty temper is as much an affliction as a racking cough, and very like in its manifestations, being an excess of the choleric blood in the spleen.'

'You pair of cross-grained bitches!' he shouted, 'have I reared and fed you all these years for such ingratitude? You will torment me out of my senses.'

'You see,' said Gertrude solemnly to Mrs. Wicke, 'he thinks that he is still in his senses. From that you may judge the degree of his judgment. Above all, never believe that anything you say will please him; for the harder the try, the more you will bring out his devils of contradiction.'

Jacint had gone to help the maid up, and they were poking about with the tongs under the cupboard. Hawes made a final effort to show his reasonableness; and Mrs. Wicke, glancing fearfully from him to Gertrude and back again, tried to grimace in general agreement, dissociating herself from all unkind remarks and thanking everyone for not being worse than they were.

'If I were this tyrant of your fancy,' said Hawes, 'would I have brought Mrs. Wicke to hear your slanders? and further, would you dare to say such things to my face?'

'To such deceitful pleas,' said Gertrude crushingly, 'the answer is simple. First, you did not think we would dare to utter the truth; second, you forgot that even a female worm will turn. Still, though I know you well in all your naked rudeness, I am astonished that you make so slight an attempt to hide your tyrannical disposition from this poor lady whom you have bewitched into accepting your adulterous hand. Do you not fear that when she has seen you as the Great Turk among all your ravisht damosels, she will refuse to marry you after all?'

A tremendous crash from the kitchen below anticipated Hawes's fury. Mrs. Wicke squeaked and put her hand over her mouth.

'It's poor Tace Kemp breaking a pot in her terror,' said Gertrude, 'but who can blame her in such a house, badgered from top to bottom as she is, by day, by night, and even on Sundays? Once when he found that she took a hot stone to bed in the cold nights he hung it round her neck for a whole week, and when she ran you could hear it thumping on her breastbone.'

'That was to prevent the danger of fire, you fool!'

'Don't shout, Gregory. I can hear every word you say. You don't know the strength of your voice. O, Mrs. Wicke, you can't think how wearying it is to have a bull roaring up and down the stairs and telling you to brush the crumbs from the table.'

Hawes rushed to the door, rushed to the window, tore at his hair, and then said in a cold controlled voice, 'Leave the room.'

Gertrude folded her hands over her belt and went to the door. 'You'll remember those words, Mrs. Wicke. You'll remember them at midnight—' Then, seeing Hawes's face, she went out. Jacint gave up trying to find the ring with the tongs. She brushed her hair off her face and said in loving tones:

'I'll send up Tace with the currant-cakes and wine.'

'No, they'd choke me.'

'O Gregory dear, I'd like some,' said Mrs. Wicke with a flutter of her eyelashes.

He gestured to the whey-faced maid, 'You go down and bring the things up. I've had enough troubles for one afternoon.'

'O father,' said Jacint, 'why should you think that Tace would add to your troubles? She's only a kitchen-maid.' She went out and the maid followed her.

Mrs. Wicke giggled. 'You do get worked-up,' she said to Hawes, 'but I like a masterful man.'

VIII

About this time was one Joan Seaman, being of the age of three-score and six years, persecuted by Sir John Tyrrel out of the town of Mendlesham, because she would not go to mass against her conscience; which good old woman being from her house, was glad sometimes to lie in fields, bushes, groves, and sometimes in her neighbour's house, when she could. And her husband being at home, about the age of eighty years, fell sick; and she, hearing thereof, with speed returned home to her house again, not regarding her life, but considering her duty; and showed her diligence to her husband most faithfully, until God took him away by death. Then by God's providence she fell sick also, and departed this life within her own house shortly after.

And when Master Symonds the Commissary heard of it, dwelling thereby in a town called Thorndon, he commanded straitly that she should be buried in no christian burial (as they

*call it), where-through her friends were compelled to lay her
in a pit, under a moat's side.*

IX

Skirting the draught-nets held by poising stones, the boat
came swishing quietly through the reeds to the small half-
rotted pier. A faintly oily glimmer of starlight rocked on the
waters. The men in the boat whispered as they roped the
boat fast, then they stepped out, one, two, three: Jones,
Merric, Stephen. On the pier they counted over the things
they held and Jones went back into the boat for a missing
crowbar. Then they moved carefully ashore.

'This is not the kind of work that you told me,' said
Stephen.

'It's too late to withdraw,' said Jones in an urgent whisper.
'But there is no crime intended, I swear to you by the Virgin
—or by Saint Paul, if you prefer it. What do your professors
swear by?'

'We do not swear at all,' said Stephen quietly.

'It is true, I remember,' said Jones in surprised dismay.
'Then, with or without an oath, I promise you that we intend
doing no man any evil and that you endanger neither body
nor soul by accompanying us.'

'Come along, Stephen,' said Merric in impatience.

Without another word, Stephen took up his spades and
sacks, and followed Merric down the track. Jones came in
the rear. The night opened and took them in. Under a darkness of trees they trudged along a narrow way, brushing
bushes and overhanging boughs. Their feet squelched in a
small pool. On the right there was a scuttling of thicket-
creatures; and an owl hooted.

They halted. 'Soon we turn to the left,' said Jones from the
darkness at the rear. 'I've been counting my steps.'

Then after a while he said, 'If the map is true, it must be
here.' They turned to the left and walked into a bank. Feeling
their way with their hands, they went slowly on.

'Here it is,' said Merric.

They went down a lane, which descended more sharply

than they had expected. Leaning back, they chose their steps with care. The bars and spades on their shoulders gave a slight clank now and then, and their breathing was heavier. More small creatures of the undergrowth slithered away. A trickle of wind came down through the treetops but scarcely seemed to shake the lightest bough. All the forms were graven with black acid on a dim sky of iron. 'One more turn,' murmured Jones. Then the ground began shelving up again, and Merric stumbled. The owl hooted a second time. Stephen kicked a stone and grunted.

Something fell through the branches. A bird of stone. 'Now.' They turned to the right. Merric walked into a bush and Stephen bumped against him. Then they found the ruts of the track again. The stars lay along the thin boughs like a faint tinselling.

'Stop. We're there.'

Only a distant sigh, a crackt twig. They moved on slowly and saw the chapel looming up and came suddenly under its wall. Merric felt the stone and moved round till he came to a small door. Groping for a latch, he pushed harder than he had meant, and the door fell in with a clatter. They all halted, listening.

Merric stooped and went in, and the others followed. 'Strike a light now,' said Jones. Merric struck steel and flint, and in a moment had his small lantern lighted. They all held breath as the flame sank down, flickered, rose up again. Then they looked round and found that they stood in a narrow back-chamber. The door leading into the chapel proper was half-open. Merric went cautiously through. 'Go up to the further door and measure from there,' said Jones, following close.

They went across the floor littered with leaves, broken benches and fragments of masonry. Lifting the lantern high, Merric began to pace out the distance from the door towards the altar. The hoops of light wavered. Then they had found the place, and knew it at once by the sick apprehension that gripped their hearts. There lay the stone slab tilting upward . . . Merric thrust his crowbar beneath and turned the slab over. An empty hole.

Jones made an inarticulate animal-noise and kneeled beside

the hole. He thrust his arms down and felt about on every side, though the lantern had shown that nothing was there. 'Lower the light,' he muttered.

Nothing. Only the dank earth and some coiling flat root-ends. 'See,' said Merric, 'they have grown like that against the side of the chest. Who has taken it?' He stared closer. 'You can see where the chest rested on the clay. It looks to me as though it had been taken recently away . . .'

'It's gone,' said Jones, still on his knees, looking wildly round. 'It's gone.'

'Did you slip ahead of us and take it?' demanded Merric, holding the light near to Jones's face.

Jones drew his knife. 'Say that again, and I'll dig your life out, no matter who you are.' Again he looked wildly round. 'Are you listening?' he said to the unknown enemy. 'I'll cut your heart out if it takes me ten years.' Tears rolled down his cheeks. He leaped up. 'I've got to kill someone for this.' Merric laid his hand on his own knife. Stephen stood quietly by all the while, studying the rage and despair on the faces of the other two.

'You have deserved nothing better.'

Jones turned and would have thrown himself on Stephen if Merric hadn't caught his wrist. 'What do you think you're doing?'

'Let me go,' said Jones. 'I won't hurt him, but don't let him say things like that. I've got to find the man who did this to me, do you hear?'

'We'll both find him,' said Merric. 'It's as hard a blow to me as you.'

'No, no, no,' said Jones furiously. 'How could it be? I've been seeking that gold for more than twenty years, and you've only begun. You don't know know what you're saying.'

They paused. Jones put the knife back in his belt. Merric lowered the lantern again into the hole, and then examined the space around. Signs of trampling feet could be made out, but that was all. 'If it is gone, whatever it is,' said Stephen, 'let us return to the boat. I am tired of this place.'

Jones snarled a curse, then weakened. 'Let's go then.' They went back into the rear-room, and out into the night. Stephen took a deep breath. After getting his bearings, Merric put the lantern out. They went about twenty paces when Jones's spade caught in a nuttree-bough. 'Damn the thing,' he said. 'Why am I carrying it?' And threw it away into the night.

'They're good tools,' said Merric.

'No, he is right,' said Stephen. 'We came with them for a foul purpose. Throw them away and let a cottager find them, who will put them to better uses and purify them.'

'Throw them away because they're a nuisance,' said Jones, 'and someone else paid for them.'

They threw the bars and spades away among the bushes, then set off walking, now without caution, towards the river. Jones walked into a sapling and screeched. 'O, you devil, you she-devil,' he cried, and drawing his knife he gashed the tree several times.

x

A masterless boy was being whipt along the street by a beadle. His cheeks were dirtily streaked with his tears, and there was blood on his brow. A group of six Augustinian monks went by, dressed in black copes with fur-lined hoods hanging over their shoulders, and with foursided caps on their heads. 'I heard them saying the Queen is ill again,' whispered Sanchia to Agnes as they stood for a moment by the kennel. 'No one believes that she's with child.' Agnes nodded but did not reply, and Sanchia went on, 'What is worse, Master Jones and Merric didn't come home all last night. But they took Stephen with them, and I cannot believe that he would join in any naughtiness.' Again Agnes nodded without replying, and they crossed the street. An apprentice shouted at them, 'Very fine hose, fit for an angel, costing an angel.' Two gallants were discussing a horse that had just gone by. 'A horse of Naples or Ferrara, I cannot be mistaken . . .' The other wagered a quart of wine that it was a Spanish gennet. 'You saw its mincing pace, going a while overthwart, left side, right sift, touching the ground only with the top of his hoof: a fine frisker . . .' They left off their argument to stare at Agnes, but she walked past. And at that moment Jacint and her Uncle Rafe came round the corner: she and Agnes looked at one another, halted, and then quietly moved on.

Sanchia was about to ask a question; but Agnes silenced her with a gesture of displeasure.

At Syon House the porter recognised her; and then, though she knew the way, she was led in by a little friendly nun with great dark eyes and dusty feet, who ran ahead like a playful dog, looking back to make sure that she wasn't going too fast. Sanchia trailed behind, wrinkling up her nose; but Agnes looked round with sharp interest, trying to catch glimpses of the nuns in their cells or the garden. Glancing up, she saw two nuns watching her through a grill, and hurried on.

Old ivy grew gnarled round the door. She bent her head and went in leaving Sanchia to sit on a bench in the sun. For a moment she saw nothing and felt dazed. Then she made out Mary on the plank-bed, Mary with her long thin flat face, crying, 'Are you there? Are you there?' The little nun leaned over, and shook her head, then stood back.

From the belly, the deep male voice answered, 'Never fear, I am here,' And as it spoke, Mary's face subtly altered. Agnes leaned forward, intent.

Mary's voice answered, 'Is it you or I? which is it?'

'It all began through her hiccoughs,' said the little nun. 'She began and couldn't stop. She hiccoughed all night, and in the morning the devil was inside her. That's how it began.' She nodded knowingly. 'And then she screamed and bellowed, she neighed and bleated, she hissed and squawked. It was like all the beasts in Noah's Ark come coupling into her body and trying to get out. Father Paul the exorcist thinks that it must be at least a thousand devils, but the cook says one devil would do it all.' She shivered. 'It was worst when she crowed like a cock. You'd think she was going to burst open. It came out of her throat like a sword.' She crossed herself. 'Holy Virgin, don't let it start again, please.'

Mary shuddered all over and opened her eyes. She stared at Agnes for a moment, while the little nun prayed to herself.

'Agnes,' said Mary in his own voice, very tired, 'I knew you were coming. I told Sister Orabilis.' She looked at the little nun, who nodded earnestly, still praying. 'He comes at me from over there,' she went on in an aggrieved way, 'just where the Sister's standing.' The nun hastily moved away from the spot. 'A man, coming out of a dark cloud. He speaks to me: Will you at last give me an answer? Will you? Take care, he says, I shall torment you. It's no use, he says, I'll enter you now in your own despite. Then he comes over at me and makes for my left side. I feel a cold hand on the back of my neck, and he's inside me . . . through the wound . . . the wound . . .'

'Please don't,' sobbed the little nun. 'You'll entice him again.'

'He stops me doing anything,' said Mary in her weak voice. Then she screamed, 'Go away!' The nun kneeled down, praying. Agnes stood calmly and intently watching. Mary whispered, 'Listen. I'll tell you what I'm afraid of. He'll make me fat. I know he will.'

'No, you'll fast and drive him out,' said the nun.

'Poor little Mary,' Mary went on gently, 'O poor little Mary, kiss her for me. Kiss poor little Mary, she never harmed anyone, and she's so sad, so sad. There's no one to comfort her . . .'

'I can't bear it when she talks like that,' said the nun, whimpering. 'I'll be back soon.' She went out.

Mary opened her eyes and looked round. 'Come closer, Agnes. I don't trust her. She keeps something under her clothes. I can hear it . . .' She spoke querulously. 'Why didn't you come yesterday? I had a thing of the greatest import to tell you, and now I've forgotten it.' Tears ran down her wasted cheeks. 'It's terrible, Agnes, I feel as if another person was being drawn out of me. As if my lips were being stretcht out to make new ones.' Agnes came a little closer. Mary spoke in a sinking voice, 'O, I am in the same case as father Adam when his wife was taken out his side.' A slow sly smile came over her face, then died away, and she whined. 'He's just like me. You couldn't tell us apart. He speaks as I do, but always of a contrary opinion. He turns my head to a block of wood.' She moved her head weakly from side to side. 'Cut it off. Please cut it off for me. I'd be so happier if it was gone. Cut it off, please cut it off . . .'

Agnes came yet closer, with wide unblinking eyes.

Mary looked at her again. 'Give me a penny,' she said. 'I must set money aside against a certain danger . . .' She half sat up.

Agnes felt inside her glove and took some money out. 'Here is a penny.'

Mary took it greedily and sank back, once more turning her head from side to side. 'I press my lips so that the words won't come through, but it's no use. He twists my tongue and mocks me.' She looked at Agnes again, 'Tell me, what am I to do?' Her voice roughened with suspicion. 'Did he send you? Why doesn't he come to see me any more? I'll kill him some day . . .' Her face suddenly grew contorted and Agnes watched in passionate absorption. Mary's face was strangely like her father's. 'It was I who came with the voice of Gabriel . . .' Her voice changed to the deep male bass, and she laughed hootingly. 'I deceived you. I lay with her . . . I lay with her all the while . . .' The sheet slipped yet further and showed her leg with a blood-encrusted garter of iron, set with nails, that had scarred her flesh under the knee.

XII

William was pacing up and down the counting-room. Nest looked in and closed the door again without a word. William shouted after her, but she did not answer or come back. Then someone rapped on the door, and Blaise entered. 'You sent for me, brother? I have been so busy at the Receipt this last week. What is it?'

'They went last night to get the treasure, and still they are not back. Now it is near Vespers.'

'But you didn't tell me they were going.'

'Wherein lay the need? I thought to send for you this morning and show the gold and the jewels. You knew that they would be going one night this week.'

'I still think you should have warned me,' said Blaise. 'But you say that nothing has been heard of them. What can have happened? Where did they go? Was there a chance of ambushes?'

'I cannot answer any of your questions. You know that he told neither of us anything.'

Blaise gave him a keen glance and looked away. 'Did they take Stephen with them?' He added sarcastically, 'Or was this matter also revised behind my back?'

'Of course they took Stephen,' said William irritably. 'It was agreed among us. Nothing was done behind your back. I have sent Ybel to Hugh's house, to see if he too is missing.'

Blaise settled down in his chair. 'Then we can do nothing now but wait.'

'You take it very easily,' said William. 'It will go harder with me if they have miscarried. My brother-in-law and my two sons together on a thievish venture . . .'

'You should have thought of that before. An enemy of yours might say that you had tried to keep the matter under your sole thumb. I still find it strange that I was not told of their going . . .'

'I have explained all that!' shouted William.

Blaise watched him for a while, and then said, 'Let it pass then. You have heard of the ambassador from the King of Sweden?'

'I know the common rumour: that he comes to ask the Princess Elizabeth for the Swedish Prince.' He frowned with the effort to turn his mind from the thought of Jones and the treasure. 'But no one believes that he will gain her, since it is known that King Philip desires another Spanish marriage for her.'

'And the Queen is known in all things as a dutiful and loving wife,' said Blaise.

'Why do you speak of this matter?' William stared hard at Blaise.

'You said there was nothing more to say of Jones, and I wished to ease your mind. I can see that you had no sleep last night.'

'How could I sleep?'

'Yet you kindly saved me from a pestered night by telling me nothing. Thus I slept as on all other nights, with a clear conscience.'

'Why do you harp on that matter? What kept me waking was no darkened conscience, but a fear of unforeseen mishaps.'

'Since my advice was not asked, I refuse any share of the blame and can deny without falsity that I knew nothing— if the Council or the Star Chamber make investigation.'

'What reason have you for thinking that?'

'Only your speech of mishaps.'

William glared at Blaise. 'You are trying to make me angry.'

'I have said little of what I might. I think most men would have shown greater offence at finding they were called into a matter only when it became endangered and dark. Is it my fault that you are afraid of meeting trouble from the Council?'

'I am not afraid.' William struck his table. 'Further, I think that my reputation in the world's eye will stand brightly against yours.'

'I trust before the end of the year to become possessed of a small but pleasant estate in the country,' said Blaise mildly, 'and to attain with the name of Justice of the Peace my loftiest ambition. But you, brother, are known as a usurer.'

'I am no usurer,' shouted William, 'which is a morally infamous term, and one that brings a man within the compass of the law! True, I have helped a few friends with loans at permissible interest, taking only *poenam conventialem,* which is a legal fine, and something for *damnum,* an indemnification against the better uses I could have made of the money, with a *titulus morae* against delays in repayment and a modicum for *periculum sortis,* the risk of throwing the money away. All of which is allowed by civil and canon law.'

'You have the words all pat,' said Blaise with a grin, 'yet in an unjust world men call you usurer.'

'Do you then never lend money?'

'In a small way, but I labour to keep money within the realm and so am a good citizen, unlike the merchants who squander the wealth of Queen and Commonwealth, growing rich on the importing of toys and vanities.' He sneered. 'Not indeed that all grow rich, seeing that some overreach themselves and fall on their faces.'

After a heavy pause, William said in a strangled voice, 'I will not be mockt.'

Blaise rose. 'Then I had better go.'

But Stephen knocked at the door and came in. 'You sent for me, father.'

'You went with the others last night?' Stephen nodded. 'Then what happened?'

'We found the place they sought, but the thing in the place was gone, and they came away with empty hands. Others had been there before.'

William sat in stunned silence. 'It was gone, the chest?' Stephen nodded. 'But where then are Kit and Merric?'

'We rowed back to a landing near the Bridge and there I left them.'

'Did they say where they meant to go?'

'I am not sure. I scarcely listened, but I know they talked against a ship's captain named Ben, and grew angrier all the while, and I think they went in search of him. Also, they spoke of knocking up a familiar tavern for wine.'

Blaise asked, 'Did this Jones seem truly surprised by the loss of the gold or did he perhaps act a counterfeit part?'

'God alone sees the heart,' said Stephen. 'I see the face and hear the voice. The face was angry, and the voice was angry. The motions of the man were angry, to the edge of madness. But that is all I know.' He looked at his father. 'Do you still want me?'

William shook his head, and Stephen went.

Nest was waiting for him. 'I had no chance to talk with you yesterday, my son. Tell me, are you in good health and ease of soul with your Uncle Hugh?' She laid her hand on his arm and looked fearfully and curiously into his face.

'He is a good man, and I dearly love him.'

'I am glad, though I should rather like to hear my son speak as warmly of his parents as of a stranger.'

'Hugh is not a stranger.'

'No, it is your parents who are the strangers.' He lowered his head, and she added, 'I am not rebuking you, my son.'

'Then let us break the wall of estrangement, mother,' he said eagerly. 'I have long prayed for you.'

'What would you have me do?' She drew back against the wall.

'That which cuts us apart from one another is the fear and the worldliness that cut us also from Christ. When we turn to Him we find in Him the love of all the others, and are united.'

Her face set into hard lines and she spoke in a withdrawn

voice, 'That is true, my son. Now go back to your Uncle Hugh. Your place is at his side.'

'Have you any word for him?'

'O no!' she cried with her hand against the high cheek-bones of her face. 'No, no!'

A knock on the outer door. William left the room in haste, and Blaise quickly stepped over to the table. Peering short-sightedly, he tried to look through the papers, listening all the while. Hearing voices and steps, he scuttled back to his seat. William entered with Jones and Merric. Jones was wild of eye, with dishevelled beard and torn coat-sleeve. Merric had a mud-smear over his cheek and smiled sleepily, brushing from his nose flies that weren't there. 'We come with a sad and dementing story,' Jones began, staggering and recovering himself with a blink of dignity.

'We know of your defeat.'

'Who told you? Who told you?'

'Stephen was here a moment ago.'

'Ah, Stephen.' Jones relaxed his grin of fury. He struck himself on the chest. 'We were forestalled. Some villain had been there before us. We found a gaping hole under the altar and nothing more.'

'Who is the ship's captain named Ben whom you sought?'

'Who told you? Who told you?'

'Stephen, who was here,' said Merric, yawning.

'Ben is an old friend of mine,' said Jones evasively. 'I met him in Amsterdam ten years ago.'

'What made you think he had taken the gold?'

'Ben is a shrewd man, and has supped with the devil. If anyone took the treasure, he is more likely than another.' He plucked at his beard. 'Moreover, he knew a little about the matter.'

'Did you find him?' asked Blaise.

'No, his ship had gone.'

'A week ago,' added Merric, yawning.

'But maybe it went no further than Gravesend,' said Jones. 'That is yet to be discovered. And now you have heard all that we can tell you. The gold is gone, through no fault of mine. If you desire to throw me out, now is the time. But I warn you, if the man who took that gold is within earshot, soon or late I shall tear his heart out.'

'How do we know,' said Blaise, 'that you didn't go up the river weeks ago, with this Ben of yours or another man, to rifle the gold?'

'You do not know it,' said Jones, moving towards Blaise and speaking close into his face. 'But you accuse other men of villainy with too easy a tongue, you weevil. I have never wanted you in this matter, and I have said so.'

'You have talked against me behind my back?' said Blaise, rising with loose underlip. He pulled at his long nose and stared round.

'He spoke in a general way against the multiplication of hands in the venture,' said William. 'No particular person was named.'

'Yet I have been named now; and since I am no longer wanted, I'll go. But before I go, let me say, Master Jones, that I never believed much in your Merlin tales of dragon-gold and abbots; and now I believe even less. What you intended by your many tales I cannot tell, but I am sure that they brought gain to yourself and none else. So farewell, and if my brother Will is wise, he'll echo my words.'

He went out. William looked doubtfully at Jones. Merric yawned, 'Let the fool go. I spit on him for a pithless husband, who cannot content the body of an amiable wife, thereby driving her to set up a bawdy sign at her backdoor.'

'You speak too disrespectfully,' said William.

'For the moment we must drink,' said Jones decisively. 'Otherwise the misery will madden us. Tomorrow I shall start with Merric on the trail of the thieves. But tonight we must save our souls with wine.'

'Aye, wine and again wine,' said Merric, trying to smile through a yawn. William regarded the pair for a moment with a frowning helplessness.

XII

Perotine, who was then great with child, did fall on her side, where happened a rueful sight. For as the belly of the

*woman burst asunder by the vehemency of the flame, the
infant, being a fair man-child, fell into the fire, and eftsoons
being taken out by one W. House, was laid upon the grass.
Then was the child had to the provost, and from him to the
bailiff, who gave censure that it should be carried back again,
and cast into the fire, where it was burnt with the silly mother,
grandmother, and aunt, very pitifully to behold.*

XIII

In the darkness of the shed the three lads were seated on
the straw of the ground, talking in low and pondered tones:

Said Stephen, 'I believe that it is laid on us to cast out evil.
That is certain. But how to do it is a cloudy thing.'

John, 'We must be long suffering. The burden on our
shoulders is always the burden of the cross.'

Tom, 'Yet not all our burdens are of Christ. The money-
lenders were not driven out forever, but are still to be driven
out. The poor were not bidden to starve, but were given the
miraculous feast of plenty and the water was turned to wine
at the marriage, signifying that man inherits the earth and
its fullness. Yet they are not fed, and they thirst for the
sweetness. The mighty were told that they shall be pulled
down, and the poor shall be set in their place. Yet the mighty
grow mightier, and the poor grow poorer. Therefore the
mighty are now to be pulled down.'

Jon, 'But these are tokens of the end of the world which
comes daily nearer.'

Stephen, 'What confuses my mind is this. There have been
many risings of the poor people for Christ's fellowship; but
they have always failed, and the rulers of the world, the lords
and the bishops, have darkened the earth with blood. What
is the reason?'

Tom, 'The reason is plain. The hearts of men have never
wholly sought for brotherhood. They have sought to displace
one lordship with another. When men claim the entire birthright, the hedges of division will fall down, like the walls of
Jericho at Joshua's godly trumpet. But not till then.'

Stephen, 'If only I could be assured that we are the men.

Are not our hearts also darkened?'

Jon murmured assent. After a while Tom Hinshaw began to talk about the renewed efforts being made for the lowering of wages. Outside, Rosbel's heavy steps and then her grumbling voice were heard. 'Where has the devil hidden you all? Why didn't you come when I rang the bell?'

XIV

St. George's Day was kept in holy fashion at the Queen's Court, with monks chanting and all the outer court strewed with rushes as far as the gate and processions led by Master Garter and Master Norris, Heralds, and the Dean of the Chapel in a cope of crimson satin with a red cross of St. George. Also there walked eleven Knights of the Garter in their robes, and the Queen's Grace in a magnificence of furred velvets, and all the guards in their best clothes. And so back to the Chapel; and after the service, through the Hall to her Grace's chamber.

Stoddard, Popham and Blaise stood talking in the court-yard. 'The Queen's Grace is in good colour,' said Stoddard piously. He lowered his voice. 'Today she has spread her belly in all men's sight, and we may well pray to the Holy Virgin that this time her hopes may not be deceived.' He screwed his eyes up and peered round.

'Aye,' said Popham, standing first with one knee bent and then with the other, 'as a general thing I should advise that you present a case against a tenant in Trinity term when the corn is upon the ground, since then you have the best means of gaining satisfaction for your rent. If the injunction goes in too soon, it may hinder him from sowing.'

Blaise stood listening, with a polite smile.

After the Queen had rested a while she went to dinner with her lords, and was served in gold and silver. And after she had eaten, there came to her Lord Grey de Wilton, the new Knight of the Garter, and then all the heralds in their coats of armour, Masters Clarencieux, Lancaster, Richmond, Windsor, York, Chester, Bluemantle, Rougedragon. And Jane Dormer, her Grace's darling, found a piece of hay on her

collar, which a sparrow had dropped as they came from the
Chapel; and she plucked it off with a word about the nests
of the year, which made her Grace smile through her sadness.

'What would you say to a price of fifteen pounds for
twelve three-year-old bullocks?' asked Blaise, going through
the palace-gates.

'A fair price, a fair price,' said Popham. 'If I were buying, I
might say rather fourteen pounds, and perhaps get it; and if
I were selling, I might say sixteen pounds, and perhaps get
it.' He laughed, and Blaise laughed, and Stoddard, coming
up from behind, also laughed.

And in St. James Manorpark was a muster. Also on Moorfield. But no one cheered. A sharp wind blew up with small
torn cloud about three o'clock in the afternoon. Merric,
coming out of a tavern in Billingsgate, joined a small crowd
in an alley and found that an exorcising monk was at work
on a possessed woman, who clucked like a hen and shook her
skirts to get rid of the eggs. 'Lay us a golden egg, you goose!'
called a butcher. Merric went away; for he was late in meeting Jones.

Near the pump by St. Benet's Church, Ybel met Sanchia,
and asked her to come·for a moment into the church so that
he might speak with her; and she said that she would go if
he carried home her basket afterwards. But in the yard he
pulled her behind a bush and begged for her love, till she
put her hands to her ears. And then, turning, they saw under
a hollybush against a wall a lad and his girl making the
double-backed beast, so that Sanchia cried out in surprise and
fell against Ybel, who sought to kiss her on the cheek. But
though he kissed the lobe of her ear, she broke away from
him and went off with her basket, and all he gained was a
tear in the breeches, as he found later from some thorns in
the bush.

Then in the evening apprentices pulled down a bawdy-
house in Southwark, and set the whores naked in a tree, to
be pelted with horsedung. Also, a Flemish weaver was murdered outside the Red Lion in the Strand by two roarers,
who struck him twice between the ribs and once under the
ear. Also, a sadler's wife, seeking to dislodge a starling's nest,

fell from an attic window in her shift and broke her head on
the cobbles. Also, before daybreak many were born in London,
and many died, and a lawyer hanged himself. So, said someone, the day was not unprofitable.

Merric, having missed Jones, was to spend an hour in a
bowling alley. A cross-gartered man on stilts was blowing a
flute with a devil's head at the end. Under a covered trellis
Merric played with a noisy prentice at shovelboard. Taking
his four flat metal-weights, he flicked them one by one down
the board, trying to send them past the line but not over the
edge. The first fell short, the second well over the edge with
a slither, the third halted half on and half over the line, the
fourth stayed between line and edge. 'You need practice for
this,' Merric said, and took a draught of beer. 'I haven't
played it for months.'

'Then what have you been doing with yourself?' asked the
prentice in astonishment.

Merric winked. 'I know a place where sits a woman warming herself at the fire for my comfort.'

The other spat. 'Womanflesh is cheap. Also, dear.'

'No, this is a proper loving wife, who costs me nothing,
however much her husband has to pay for it.'

The other spat again. 'If she doesn't cost money, she'll cost
something worse. Across the road from our house lies a wife
of the sort you paint. She unbuttoned her placket to the
journeyman, and he thought he owned the luck of the world;
but secret lovers ever turn reckless lovers, and one day they
were caught in the stable on a creaking sack of hay.'

'I'll take my chances.'

He watched while the other made his casts, and then said
moodily, 'Find another. I'm in no mood for games.'

'You hear your mistress calling you over the housetops?'

Merric nodded and went off, walking quickly for the
Templegate and the Strand. Reaching the street off which
Blaise's house lay, he halted to fix his belt and compose himself; and then sauntered down, into the courtyard, where he
climbed the outer stairs and knocked at the door. After a
while Tabitha came and asked through the still-bolted door:

'Who is there?'

'You know who I am.'

'My mistress is not at home. She has not bidden you at this hour.'

He beat on the door. 'I heard voices within.'

'Go away. You do yourself no good.'

He beat louder, and shouted, 'Dousabel! Dousabel! Where are you?'

The door opened, and Tabitha said, 'Go away, go away.'

He pressed the door fully open and went in. Tabitha hit him with her fists, and he laughed. Dousabel came in her loose watchet-gown from the further room, buckling the belt. 'Stand back, Tab.' She faced Merric with her face heavy in scorn. 'Why do you come with this riot against my door? For shame, nephew. I thought you had a better sense of yourself and me. But since I see that I was mistaken, I want nothing further with you. Now leave me at once.'

'Let me come in and talk with you more closely.'

'Leave me at once. My husband will return at any moment. But even if that were not so, I should refuse to admit you after this tumult.'

'I'm not frightened of Blaise.'

'Then be frightened of me.'

'Three words at least.'

'No, nephew, you have shown me your true face, and I see you have no respect for any slight kindness. Therefore, go and stay elsewhere. Your welcome here is ended.'

She pushed him out, resisting his fumbled effort to catch her hand. She shut the door on him, and bolted it. He knocked once, and stood irresolute. Then he went down into the yard and looked up at the window. Hearing steps and the tapping of a stick in the lane, he stood aside; but the sounds went past. However, after one more look up at the window, he passed under the built-over arch into the lane. There, he hesitated between left and right, and, going down with a knot of people, he found a bear-pit near the river, for which the others were paying to enter. He too paid and went in.

A Merryandrew was talking down at the blinded bear in the pit, warning him that his Wood-Majesty was about to feel the might of Englishmen; and the man next to Merric nudged his friend, reading a political allegory into the words.

'. . . Pope or Philip . . .' Then the Merryandrew changed his tune and spoke in commiseration, 'Alack, poor Robin, how you are betrayed to a beastly blindness and beggary. How you are lured from your lairs and wandered from your woods? What a great fool were you to flee from the undergrowth of leaves to the usurers of London. Tell me, my poor Robin, were you chased by your cruel children? Were you drawn to barter a birthright of green for a brittle bait of gold? How are you fallen, uncle, into a pit of profligacy, and now you are burnt and blinded . . .'

The bear growled weakly and rattled the many chains which held it to the central stake in the pit. Five men, stript to the waist, went one by one down a wooden ladder lasht to the side; and then, after they had muttered together, a boy threw their whips down after them, and, at a word from the Merryandrew, began tapping on a tabour.

The men with the whips circled the stake. Then, at a louder beat, they halted, stretched out the arms with the whips, and slashed together at the blinded bear, who yelped and wrenched at the chains, contorting himself with attempts to get at the whippers. The men whipped on regularly; and as the baffled bear winced back to the stake, one of them skipped up close and slashed him across the face. The bear flung himself in the man's direction, snapped out of the smaller chains, and managed to scratch the man's calf. The spectators howled with delight. The bear found the whip which the man had dropped, caught it up, tore it to small pieces. The boy threw another whip down to the cursing man, who joined the other four in their regular slashing at the bear.

Merric rose and went out. Reaching the open space by the riverbank he sat down on a stone and stared at the waters flowing past. Tears came into his eyes. 'What have I lost?' he murmured; and then, blinking, began to doze. A wherryman's shout roused him. He sat up and hailed the man, and getting into the wherry, took the oars and set off vigorously rowing. 'Good weather for drowning cats!' he said with a laugh.

XI

This time the Congregation was meeting in a cooper's house in Pudding Lane. The numbers were smaller, mainly because a hasty change of meeting-place had once more meant for the moment a breakdown of organisation. Stephen looked round, but Mrs. Hudley and Mabel weren't there. Tom Hinshaw came in and sat beside him. Then, Hugh Rigeley, after a short prayer, asked a brother from Ipswich to tell them of the persecutions and sufferings there. A stumpy weaver came from his seat and stood by the table. He clapped his hands, stared at the ceiling a moment, and then began in a rusty voice.

'I'll tell you the tale as it happened, friends. For that's the only way I can tell it. They brought in Will Seaman, a farmer of Mendlesham, after a neighbour informed against him. His wife, with three small children on her hands, had all her goods seized and her corn sold by the manorlord's orders. Also, Thomas Carman was taken by the Bishop, and Thomas Hudson of Aylsham, a glover, who learned to read that he might read the Gospel, and now is to be blinded; for he cried out against the draff and darnel put into the service instead of wheat. He went travelling around, to escape their hands; but when he came home to comfort his wife and children, he was informed against and the constables sought to seize him. His wife hid him a long time under the faggots, but the vicar came and threatened to burn her unless she told him where her man was hidden. Which effected nothing, and Hudson sang psalms and many folk of Aylsham flocked openly to hear his vehement prayers. Then at last he walked abroad in the town crying out against the mass and such trumpery, till in the end he came home and sat down upon his knees, reading his book and singing psalms continually for three days and nights together, refusing meat all that while. So John Crouch his neighbour went to the constables in the night, and at daybreak they came to take him.'

'Let us praise God for Thomas Hudson,' said Hugh.

'When he saw the constables, he said: Now my hour is come, welcome, friends, you shall lead me to a new life. So they took him before Berry, the town's vicar and commissary;

and Berry asked him where he kept his church for the last
four years, and Hudson said: Where I am, there is the
church. Then Berry examined him about the transmutation
of the sacrament, and Hudson said: It is worm's meat, my
belief is in Christ crucified. Then Berry examined him about
the mass and its taking away of sin, and Hudson said: It is
a patcht monster and a disguised puppet, more longer a
piecing than ever was Solomon's Temple. So Berry smote
the earth with his staff and sent Hudson to the Bishop. At
which one Richard Cliffar, standing by, prayed him to be good
to the poor man. But Berry raged and cried that he must have
this Cliffar bound in a recognisance of forty pounds for good
bearing in word and deed; and as for Hudson, he lies in
Norwich jail this moment, awaiting his death.'
'How long, O Lord, how long?' a plasterer cried.

XVI

In a sidestreet some boys were blowing up a bull's bladder
for a game of football. On a doorstep sat a beggar leisurely
looking for fleas in his shirt. An apprentice in watchet-hose
and an old cloak went by, lugging a woolpack. An oysterwife
was shrilly laughing. A serving-maid slipped into the thatched
house where lived the wisewoman known for restoring lost
goods and maidenheads with palm-reading and alum. A gaunt
man was coming slowly along the street, holding on to the
house-walls. As William approached, he fell to the ground,
moaning, 'Master, for Christ's sake, alms . . . I have been
thrown out by my master because I am sick, and I have
nowhere to go . . . Have pity . . .' William threw down a
silver groat and strode on.
In Cornhill a whore was being drawn on a hurdle behind
a flea-bitten horse, while a portly beadle was lashing lazily
at her bloody back. Two gallants went briskly by, one saying,
'I feel sick of purse, lusty of body, and ready to go to breakfast . . .' William moved his bloodshot eyes from side to side,
and was about to cross the road when he heard his name
called. Looking back, he saw Blaise hastening his way. He
scowled and would have gone across the road, but a horse-

man came by; and the next moment Blaise had him by the
arm, panting. He looked at Blaise and said nothing.

'Brother,' said Blaise, 'I have thought over the other night.
I hold no malice save against Master Jones. He wickedly and
intendedly embroiled us.'

'It is no matter of great moment,' said William, shaking
Blaise's hand off.

'What could be of more moment than the falling out of
brothers? Did not Cain and Abel begin the strife that echoes
on in our sinful hearts this moment?'

'You spoke bitterly.'

'And so did you, brother.'

'Then let us keep apart if we both speak bitterly. What is
there to be gained by such abuse? It makes me suffer. I have
been sick of a fever.'

'Why are you not open with me about your debts and
troubles?' asked Blaise reproachfully.

'I am as open with you as you with me. Yet I make no
complaint.'

'Nor I, but I wish to help you.'

William spoke dully. 'Only one help can touch me now.
Money, which can be seen, felt, weighed, and assayed. I need
money, not airy and unmarketable words.'

'What then if I offer you what you want?'

William ceased his restless glances and looked at Blaise at
last. 'Do you mean only to torment me?' He gave a hoarse
laugh. 'Show me this money that you offer. Let me see, feel,
and weigh it.'

'Who carries gold in his pocket? Yet I have ways of finding it in other men's pockets. My office gives me many chances
of encountering money that lies idle and needs a strong man
to make it engender. I can promise nothing, but I think I
will not fail you.'

William spoke suspiciously, 'Why didn't you offer before?'

'I thought that perhaps your Master Jones might indeed
bring you a sack of gold. Your mind was turned towards his
dreaming cheats. And even now you have rebuffed me when
I come to aid you.'

William's face quivered all over. 'I will trust you, brother,
and turn to you in this moment of my great need. I can keep

my creditors at bay no longer. My promises have lost all currency.'

'I feel sure I can save your credit, brother, but you will have to uncover your whole position.'

William again gave a dull rough laugh. 'I can lose nothing by it now. But tell me, on what security am I to gain a loan?'

Blaise took his arm and they crossed the street. 'Let us go to your counting-room, and consider more exactly what you need.'

'On what security?'

'I shall stand for a part, but you will have to throw in all your remaining substance and credit, I have no doubt.'

'The substance is dwindled, and the credit is lost. Otherwise I should not need your help.'

'No, you are wrong. I hope to find ways of new credit and thereby of new substance. If you pass this danger, you will be able to put forth trails in many directions. Most of all, if you have me and a friend or two beside to work with you. You will be a Sheriff next year if you hold your good name, and many new trading ventures will be open to you. I am interested in your next year, brother.'

'You are shrewder than I thought,' said William grudgingly, 'though I knew that of late you have come out your lurkhole in the Exchequer with golddust glittering on your person, like a badger who has dug unawares into a wealthy mine.'

'Not altogether unawares, Will.' They laughed in friendly tones; and Blaise went on, 'Let us go quickly now to your place, for I cannot think clearly about money-matters unless I have a pen in my hand.'

XVII

'O what a trouble I find to drive my brood to bed,' said Nest. 'Now, maidens, is all my nightgear ready? Take out of the way the pewter candlestick that is so foul. Make ready the silver candlestick with wax candles, and we'll play at being rich for once. Where's the snuffers and the warming-pan? Where is the white lace to bind my hair? And you, Ybel, go light the bedroom-fire. Edgar, take the plaster of red colewort and camomile up to your master, and tell him that I will look in shortly to see that he has laid it on the right place. Agnes, hand me my new-washt shift that hangs before the fire. No, I'll get it; but first give me my pantoufles, for fear I catch cold. O, what a world it is to get to bed, and what a world to wake in the morning: and all of it left to a woman in the end.'

CHAPTER SIX

May

I

SWALLOWS RETURNING, CHIFFCHAFF chattering in the wood-land. Small beetle of the sun going madcap over a patch of sandy soil, green nipper-beetle wheeling past and lost in the green. Shrew faintly crying, grass-snake rustling by. Linnets alighting and bending the swayed topmost bough of the beech in time with their singing, blackbirds restless and rapturous in bushes below. Robin flitting from dead leaves into the dwarf oak with single plaintive note, and going into his rounded nest in rock-hollow, hidden by three fronds of harts-tongue; mouse nibbling where wood-sage unfurls its wrinkled leaves. Now was the May of the Year.

II

All over London straw-mattresses were creaking. From some of them rose Catholics devoutly dressing for the Matins at Midnight. The monks of the few restored houses slipped from their narrow couches and moved trancedly down the passages of stone darkness. But mostly the risers were young girls, rustling naked with slow yawns under tousled hair or leaping with resolved mouths from the blanket-warmth, snatching up smocks and shifts and putting them on back-to-front in haste, tearing them, bumping heads and feeling round for truant shoes. Candles were lighted, and eyes blinked under the shocks of hair. Heads flung back, ribbons ringed the rebel ringlets and the streaming lengths of various gold.

213

Candle-flickers urged them on, with a throb and a bob. No stockings on May morning, but a gown over the smock buckled with a plaited belt and a snood to catch the uncombed locks. Find the lost shoe and wriggle toes into its clammy cold. Then tiptoe downstairs.

But parents still snored in rooms curtain-muffled against draughts, deep-sunk naked in mattresses with caps pulled over their heads. The watchlight guttered on a ledge made by the bed's head-carvings. And if the house was wealthy, there were curtains round the bed, tester, valances and fringes; feather-mattresses and coverlets of patterned yellow and green. The parents snored and turned over and turned back again, making animal dream-noises in their throats. Or, if they rose, rose only to the chamberpot, and then clambered heavily back to flop with a groan into bed.

Sanchia, with hair braided all ready over her brow, tugged at Agnes from her truckle-bed, then rolled over and slipped under the sheet. 'Time to rise . . .' 'I'm not going.' 'Please, please.' Thin arms closing round, small hard chin pressed against nape of neck, slender body closely pleading. 'Please, please . . .' Weakening, a yawn. 'You promised.'

Jacint lifted arms over head and deliberately yawned. 'Lettice, are you there?' A muffled yes from Lettice with belt in mouth, tucking something in. She swung lightly out with feet close together. O, feet on splintery boards, missing the small piece of carpet. She swayed, fell back with a laugh. Bed creaked.

Tab tied a blue ribbon round her right thigh, a little above the knee. Blew on her copper mirror and rubbed it, but still could not see at all clearly. Combed her hair with a wooden comb.

Nest sat up suddenly in bed, sniffed, and then lay down again. She felt about under the bolster, drew out a piece of biscuit and began slowly chewing it. William snored softly at her side.

Rustling of girls all over London. Tiptoe.

'Don't drop anything,' said Jacint, 'and don't fall down the stairs as you usually do.'

'Only twice,' said Lettice, and caught her by the shoulder, 'O.'

'Be careful. If aunt awakes, we'll never get away. Did you tap at Martin's door?'

Tab slid some bread and cheese in her wide sleeve.

Agnes said, 'I'm a fool,' sitting on the edge of the bed with her hands dangled between her legs. Sanchia pulled the smock over her head. 'Wait till I put my arms up,' murmured Agnes. Sanchia left her to deal with the smock and went to the shelf, looking for something behind the jug.

'The bottle for the dew is gone. Did your mother find it?'

'It's in the cupboard.'

One by one, from various bedrooms they crept downstairs and out into the dark streets. Jacint and Lettice along Fenchurch Street, Tab up St. Martin's Lane between the hedges, Agnes and Sanchia with Merric towards Moorgate. Thousands of girls. Out through the gates of the City and along the alleys of the Liberties, for the nearest piece of woodland, the fields and slopes north of Holborn, the muddy lanes and closes. Sensible girls in wooden shoes, others slithering and losing their shoes of leather in the pot-holes, laughing, clutching one another round the neck, climbing on the banks, falling back, standing on one leg on a tree-stump, getting caught in discourteous bushes, climbing trees to kiss on a forked bough, sharing a cloak till sunrise, scanning the thinning heavens of night in the howl of distant dogs.

Suddenly light. A wash of faint light stealing in from nowhere, everywhere. A dimming of darkness rather than an advent of day. Then a greening of the dimness, and a deepening of the green and the grey. A warming tint, and then at last the turn to day, a cloudy light, and then light dissolving the clouds. A faint breeze of day. The couples huddled closer.

Then they moved into the shadows, under the greenery full of tingling glints, a rosy sky and birds singing, with the steeple of Paul's in the distance. Merric went moody with Agnes quiet at his side and Sanchia running on ahead and running back to Agnes with some small hedgeflower. Daisies scattered in meadows and bluebells drifted in the copses, daffodils lost in the hedges or skirting the woods, bobbing over a stream or climbing the hills. Wood-violets pale in the shadows and feathery larchtufts, ladies-tresses with sweet spikes of green

amid grass, and a spread of celandine leaves with bits of dis-
carded gold strewn around. Come.

'What is on your mind?' Agnes asked at last. 'I gather that
something has gone wrong, and Uncle Christopher is at the
root of it.'

'Yes, everything has gone wrong.' He looked back to where
Edgar was strolling in self-possession, peering now and then
into the crannies of the bank. Ahead, Ybel was trying to keep
up with Sanchia without repeating her zigzag course. 'Kit
isn't to blame. Somebody deceived him. But he's not a man
to take a cheat without replying . . . Still, I don't suppose
it'll help me.' He lowered his voice. 'If the gold had been
there, all my difficulties would have been ended. But don't
say a word of that to anyone.'

'No, no.' She pressed his hand gratefully. 'But why don't
you ask father?'

'Never.' He stiffened. 'I'll be hanged before I ask him for
my rights again.'

'Let your anger go. I wish I were you with only a matter
of money to keep me awake at night.' Before he could ask
her what she meant, she went on, 'And father isn't sleeping
well. Mother has been putting henbane leaves under his
pillow and rubbing of the soles of his feet with dormouse-
grease at night.'

Sanchia came running back. 'What's the name of this
blue flower?'

'Eyes of Agnes,' he said with a laugh.

'It isn't?' cried Sanchia, half-believingly. She compared
the blue flowertint and Agnes's eyes. 'But it ought to be.'

Agnes gave a shy cry and put her hands over her eyes.
'You make me afraid of blindness when the flowers die.'

Merric drew her hands away. 'No, look upon this day of
all days.' His voice grew tenderly blithe. 'Surely we are
already old, my dear sister, when we have to look back over
the years for our happiness. And yet now I am suddenly
happy because I have remembered how happy we have been
together and what Mays we have seen.'

She looked wonderingly round. 'The earth is as lovely
still. Put your hand on my mouth and wipe the bitter words
away.'

He laughed. 'Come, crawl under this maybush, right through, into the young years.' He drew her under the bush and they crawled through into a patch of daisied grass beyond. 'Now we are free, having little white flowers of sweetness in our hair.'

She spread her skirts on the grass. 'Now I am eleven again, and you save me with a wooden sword from the forest-monster, to wit, a straying heifer with a garland of red blossoms.'

Sanchia came crawling halfway through the maybush. 'Am I to come too?'

'All may come,' said Merric. Reaching out, he caught her hands and pulled her through. Sanchia slid across the grass, laughing and crying out that he would stain her petticoat with green, and one of her shoes came off, and her hair was un-done. 'Take down your hair also,' said Merric to Agnes, 'so that she may have no grievance. And unlatch one of your shoes.'

'If justice is to be done in all things,' said Sanchia, sitting up, 'let her snap one of her boddice-strings in addition: for I am certainly unstrung.'

The lads and girls were breaking boughs off the trees and making small bowers or binding tall plumes of greenery. The girls were brushing the dew off the grass and rubbing it on their faces; some thrifty ones were collecting it in phials and little bottles. Tab was in a field gathering dew for her mistress and every short while putting a dab on her own cheeks. Then, seeing the bottle half-full, she drew up her skirts and sat down on the cool wetness of the grass, saying, 'Under and over, by full moon send me a lover, late and early, with hair straight or hair curly.' Couples were creeping under the bushes and into the built-bowers singing, singing. A horn blew and boys came running with sticks, knocking a round stone.

Twelve girls danced with bare knees round a garlanded bull tied to a post. The drums beat under all the hills and out of the risen sun. The tall girl was wreathed and wreathed again. Morris-dancers jingled in the daisy-ring, and boys ran cross-gartered in the turf-maze for the young bride with open

arms astride at the stone-heart of it. The fife shrilled above
the birdsong. The basket-women were standing at the cross-
roads with pie and pease and tarts.

Jacint tucked up her dress and sprinted long-legged down
the hill.

III

A few of the revellers had dutifully returned to deck the
fronts of their houses with green boughs and wreaths of
flowers hung from windows. Hugh was walking with bent
head down the street to Cripplegate. A few paces behind came
Jon and Stephen still arguing whether the sword of righteousness was purely spiritual or could become a sword with biting
edge against the evil of the world, a sword wielded in the
hand. The revellers scampered by, and the foreman of a
morris, with gold-laced cloak, leaped in front of them; and
yet they scarcely noticed him. A girl threw a flower bud at
Stephen, and he put his hand to his cheek, but did not look
round.

They came out through the wall-gate, and Hugh spoke to
them for a moment, asking if they knew Islington. 'It is years
since I went to that township, and I am told that we must
seek the fields on the left side of the lane beyond the church.
Our people have met there before and suffered no hindrance,
but this is a strange Sunday.' They looked round at the
hobbyhorse chasing the girls along the street before them,
the boys with drums, the lad loosing an arrow at the sun.
'The informers have found all our trysting places along the
sad river, but perhaps they will lose our tracks in this day
of many noises.'

They walked on towards Islington, with troubled faces.
And came to the town, a handful of houses and closes, and
found the lane they sought. Past a line of elms they found
the entrance to the field of meeting, a gate with an archway of
vines and an aged holly tree, and went down a narrow path
between hedges which turned into a large closed field. Already
about thirty persons were there, sitting quietly on grass or on
their spread cloaks, reading the English Testament or meditat-
ing. On the further side was a tall fence and more elms; and

somewhere beyond it was a dancing place, for the bells and the singing reached the close in a gentle tinkling burden.

Mrs. Hudley and her Mabel were seated on the slight rise in the further corner. Stephen turned to see if Jon had noticed them, but Jon's eyes were downcast. 'Mrs. Hudley is here with Mabel,' he said in a strained voice, 'and Mr. Polard her brother is with them.'

'There are also others here,' said Jon, closing his eyes.

'Tell me if you love her, and I will give her up,' said Stephen in an anguished whisper.

'She is not yours to give up,' retorted Jon in the same tones. 'If I have looked on her with desiring eyes, I beg the pardon of heaven.' He dug his nails into his palms. 'And in truth my eyes have desired her. Why should I strive to tell God a lie when my friend has read the truth in my mind, however much I have striven to hide it? But she is not mine and never will be. I have scarcely spoken a word to her.'

'Neither have I.'

'Then what right have we to talk of taking her or giving her up, as if the possession of another's soul and body lay in our choice? But even if I knew that she would marry me I'd say the same as now I say. The end of the world is near, and I have only my own death to cherish.'

Stephen drew slightly away, and a smile flickered at the ends of his mouth, which he checked. 'I spoke in friendship, because I cannot bear that anything should come between us. But now my conscience is cleansed.'

'I fear that you are laying a snare for yourself again,' said Jon, raising his eyes at last.

'No, no,' said Stephen hastily. 'The choice is not mine.'

'The choice is ours, and is not ours. But we deny it when we should accept, and accept it when we should deny. Ask your own heart which you have now done.'

'I have done neither,' said Stephen stubbornly. He moved round so that they came closer to the Hudleys. Mabel, with her frail long face, was staring as always at something unseen by others, straight ahead, with nothing moving except her slow hands plucking at the grass or a thread of her dress. Mrs. Hudley was talking behind her palm to her brother, a stolid man with a mottled face. Stephen went on speaking, as if he

continued the same debate, 'Therefore we are told that it is
better to marry than to burn. An unmistakeable counsel. If a
man encloses his desires entirely in a single bed of marriage,
he has cut off all bond between his body and the world's
uncleanness. Otherwise we should be told to pour a bitter
water on the fires. And by the same truth a man must find his
fellowship, not by quenching all his wraths, but by wedding
them with an entire justice. Thereby he gains a banner under
which to fight against the world's evil without himself entering into evil. To counsel a false peace is to pour a bitter water
on the innermost fires of man . . .'

Jon lay down, shuddering, on the grass. 'No . . . For me a
woman is a sister or a devil's poppet.' The ringling of the
morris sounded louder on the breeze, and a blackbird
screamed in alarm-cry.

Stephen looked round. A man had come down the hedgeway
and stood looking interestedly at the company in the close.
Bentham was not yet arrived, so Hugh went across to the
man and asked him who he was. 'We are Londoners,' he said,
'who have come to rest here for a short while before we return
home. If you know any reason against our quiet continuance
here, tell it, and we shall go.'

'Sit here as long as you like,' said the man, 'for all I know
or care. You seem to me such people as intend no harm.' And
with that he went.

Now the sun came over the elms and warmed the green of
the grass. Stephen left Jon and strolled nearer to Mabel, who
was dressed in a close-fitting boddice and a skirt of rusty-
tawny. Her hands plucked at the long grasses. He looked over
and saw that Tom had joined Jon, and strolled back to them.
The morris-noises swelled, and the happy fear-scream of a girl
rose above them, and then the thudding of the drum was
strongest. 'I have been talking to a man in Queenhythe . . .'
Tom began.

Everyone was looking at the hedge-entry. The man who
had interrupted them before was there again, and now beside
him stood a constable. The constable came forward. 'My name
is Robert King, Constable of Islington Town, and I desire to
know what you are doing here, and what these books are
which I see in your hands.' He went over to the nearest reader

and took the book from his hand. After reading a few lines
with some difficulty, he beckoned his companion, and read
stumblingly aloud: 'No man can serve two masters. For so he
shall hate the one and love the other: or else he shall lean to
the one and despise the other. You cannot serve God and
Mammon.' He shook his head. 'I am sorry, but this is treason-
able and blasphemous stuff, and you must answer the Queen's
Majesty for it.'

'It is the word of truth,' said a man mildly.

'Say you so?' said King. 'Then you shall cast the lie in the
teeth of the Queen and the Lord Cardinal; but I am a simple
man and cannot tell how such fustian folk as you have learned
more than the ones whom God has set over you.' He nodded to
the other. 'Fetch me all these forbidden books. Bring them in!'
he called to the people around.

'Shall we let them take us without a blow?' cried Tom
Hinshaw; but no one answered him.

King whistled, and several men with bills and bows came
running down the hedgeway. 'You shall all come to the Justice
of the Peace,' he shouted to the people, and signed to his
men to move round and drive the congregation down the
hedgeway.

'There are no more than eight of them,' said Stephen, 'and
near forty of us.'

'Would you spoil it all with an unseemly riot?' asked an
old man, Dick Bailey, a woolpacker. 'We are Christ's chosen
and must abide in his longsuffering love.'

Jon, who had got up on to his knees, said softly, 'Amen.'
A baby, held by one of the women, began screaming. King
raised his voice and shouted. The three men with bows fixed
arrows in the strings, and about a dozen of the congregation
obediently moved over to the hedgeway. Stephen pulled Jon
to his feet. 'Come along,' he said, and moved across to where
the Hudleys stood. 'Mrs. Hudley, there is no time to be lost.'
He took her and Mabel by the arm and drew them aside to a
place where the fence was broken. Their movement was
hidden from King and most of his men by the group who had
obeyed the command to come before the J.P.

He wrenched at the paling and tore two of them out. Then
he pushed Mabel through, and followed her. Turning back,

he took Mrs. Hudley's hands and pulled her through. 'Come along,' Stephen cried, and took Mabel's hand again. An arrow flew over his head and snapped on a bough. Looking round, he saw that two of the billmen were trying to prevent others of the congregation from escaping through the hole. Hugh was one of those who had come out. He was helping Mrs. Hudley.

Several of the congregation, who were making no effort to escape, had gathered round the hole, to prevent the billmen from following the fugitives.

They ran over the open close and came to a stile. Stephen jumped it and helped Mabel to cross. Then they found themselves among fruit-trees. A dog, chained to an apple-tree, leaped and barked. Two lovers, kissing in a tree, stared down at the running pair. 'What has happened?' the lad called, but Stephen answered only with a vague gesture. Mabel was panting, holding her side. 'A little further,' he said. They came out of the orchard on to a small grass-grown lane, and climbed into a meadow, where three cows were grazing. Beyond, a clump of woodland stood in all its green promise of refuge.

'My feet are hurt,' she complained. 'I've lost both my shoes. I untied them in the close. They were made for me by my uncle, with laces and ribbons, and I'd never worn them but once before.'

'Only a little further.'

They halted a moment, and he took her up in his arms. She said something he didn't hear. Then he hastened on. When he told her to put her arms round his neck, she obeyed. At last they reached the first shadows of the trees, and he walked in with straightened back. Over on the left stood a cottage with a blue twist of smoke rising from its hearth-hole; and in the woods invisible revellers were singing of Robin Hood, the babe found yearly in the green cradle.

'It is a sin,' said Mabel, mildly, without resistance or rebuke. 'The songs are a sin.'

He took no notice and still carried her. They passed a group of girls weaving a flower-chain, who laughed and pelted them. He went on, saying only, 'I hear water . . .' And soon he found the stream wandering among brown rocks and ferns delicately beaded with wet. He set Mabel down on a tree

that had fallen across the water. 'Put your feet in the water,'
he said, and she obeyed.

Only, she said, 'Where's my mother?'

For answer he plucked at her torn stocking till they came
off, and her legs were bare. She stared down at her legs with
her mouth falling open. He washed the torn and dirtied stockings and set them out to dry on the bank. 'We are safe,' he
said. She was still looking down at her feet in the water, the
cool frills of the running water, her narrow white feet. 'We
are safe,' he repeated.

'We should have stayed,' she said in a small sinking voice.
'I dreamed last night that I stood in a fiery hole of the earth,
till it swallowed me to the waist. And then I floated in a cloud
of wings. We should have stayed and testified . . .'

'We shall yet testify,' he said. 'Set your heart at peace.'

'What are we doing here,' she asked quietly, 'while the world
is burning?'

'We are testifying in another way.' He tore up some grasses.
'Today we are reprieved, and I have had a sign which foretold
this moment and a covenant which justifies it. And on it many
things depend.' He lifted her up off the log and set her on the
ground. Then, taking her feet in his hands, he dried them with
the grass and warmed them between his palms. She watched
him without resistance.

'Are you sure of your sign?' she asked in a low voice. 'Is
the covenant clear?'

'I am sure,' he answered. 'You are given me as my wife, and
this moment is a seal both of lost Eden and regained Paradise,
whereby I may enter back into the world for all men and
rejoice in the war against the world's evil.'

'I had rather be burnt,' she said with her hands over her
breast. 'For I have given my thoughts to that, but not to this.
Yet I believe in your sign and covenant, though I do not
understand.'

He took a handful of grass-blades and twined them into a
ring. 'Give me your hand.' He set the ring on her marriage-
finger. 'I take you as my wife in the eye of the Lord and the
Angels.'

She stared at the grass-ring and repeated, 'I take you as my
husband in the eye of the Lord and the Angels.'

'Now are we man and wife, in a special place and in a special way. For I wrestled with the Lord in the close, and was told that if he gave you to me, it would be a sign that we may fight with a manifest sword against evil and that the meekness of the sacrifice lies in the wholeness of the will to fight and endure for the truth's sake. Now I know what is permitted, and I rejoice; for my long and weary wrestling is done, and I am accepted, and I know what work is set to my hands. I am thereby securely told that we were led to this green place as a token of both Eden and Paradise, into a new innocence, from which our strengths must grow.'

She watched his eyes and mouth with an entranced look. 'It is true, because you say it and the words are true.'

'I shall beget a child of promise on your body,' he said, taking her hands from over her breasts. 'I know it all. You are mine and I am yours, whatever may come. For this is our Eden, but in the world we must take blow for blow with Satan; and this moment may never return. But that is not a matter for our thoughts. We are here, and return into the first innocence, yet take with us the knowledge of the defeated Fall.'

'Now if we burn, we burn together.' She lifted her face to his kiss.

They stayed long in a calm kiss and then he helped her to unlace her boddice and drew her shift over her head. 'We must come together in the nakedness of the spirit.' The rippling whisper of the water mixed with a distinct warm cooing of doves and a faint May-song from the edges of the wood.

IV

Jacint waved her bough entwined with flowers. 'There's Uncle Rafe,' she said to Martin, who looked, said 'Yes,' and looked away at the girls dancing in the field round a hobbyhorse. Jacint ran on ahead and kissed her uncle.

'I thought I'd catch you at the Gate,' he said, 'if I waited long enough. I wanted to see you against the green, with the dew on your mouth.'

'You should have come with us. We climbed a fairy-hill and ate sillabubs and honey-bread.'

He took her hand. 'It is enough that you have been there. Enough that I have stood here and watched the youngsters at their tumbling laughter.' He raised her hand and kissed it. 'I kiss here the spirit in man that makes a Saturnian Garden in the world despite the angry darkness. When I see such a holiday, I feel that it needs only a single word, only a single thought, to strike all the fetters away and restore the Hesperidean sweetness, when man lies down with the lion of his own heart and is happy. What is there in man that sows such flowers of delight and then cankers them with greed and cruelty? Tell me, you who are washt in the dew of this day and have its dances yet merry in your legs. Do you cast your voice for a Golden Age of innocence renewed, or do you desire a return into the Iron City?'

'Ask Martin,' she said, with dimples of complicity. 'You know I am on the side of the poets.'

Martin came up and saluted Rafe. Then Lettice, stooping with her light curly head, a pale blue distance in her eyes. She stood behind Jacint, took a leaf from her hair, and meditatively gave it a little bite. 'What is it?' asked Martin curtly.

'Shall the world be always as happy, or must we strive one against the other on a bed of thorns?'

'It's not you or I who have the last word.' He shrugged rather wearily. 'Wintry winds come at last on the earth of May; and even on a festival we cannot fill our bellies with the scent of flowers.'

'Therefore,' said Rafe, 'we must watch the poor weeping in the streets, and worse still . . .' He cut himself short. 'Nevertheless, I am for *Saturnia Regna,* and pay my homage to a lost liberty and laughter. *Terra prevalebit, magnus ab integro saeclorum nascitur ordo . . . redeunt saturnia regna . . . aspice.'*

'Say it in English,' said Martin, with his eye on Lettice.

'It must be translated by many voices,' said Rafe, smiling at Jacint. 'Or no translation will be true.'

v

Stephen knocked at the door. Mabel stood straight and quiet behind him. 'If your mother is not here, you must come

H

back with me,' he said, and she nodded. But as they were turning away, the door opened a few inches, then opened further, and Mrs. Hudley called. 'I have brought your daughter back,' said Stephen. 'I am glad that you are happily preserved.'

'Come in at once,' said Mrs. Hudley to Mabel.

'I shall come in a few days to see you,' said Stephen. Mabel made a slight inclination to show that she had heard, and went inside, lifting high her swaddled feet. Mrs. Hudley closed the door at once.

Stephen went slowly back through the dusk to the house in Scalding Alley. Rosbel let him in. 'Has Jon returned?' he asked. 'Or my Uncle?' She shook her head, and her sombre eyes looked with enquiring fear into his face. He closed the door. 'They came to arrest us at Islington.' He leaned back against the wood.

'The Virgin save us all from the Pope,' she muttered, crossing herself.

VI

'I shall not go to Hull until I have tried every tavern in Wapping and St. Katharines; and perhaps after that we shall go on to Deptford.'

'Have it your own way,' said Merric. 'There are worse journeys than this, which passes through all the sailors' boosing-kens between Blackfriars and Hell.' He stretched out his legs under the table.

'I have such a memory for faces,' protested Jones, scraping on the table-top with his knife-point, 'that if I see any one of his men I shall know him at once.'

'And will he know you?'

'It is possible, though I have changed the cut of my beard. Also, at that time I wore a green flap over my eye and a wide-brimmed hat of beaver.'

Merric yawned and looked at the tarnisht bravos and buxom sluts around them in the tavern. 'Why should he linger, if he has the gold?'

'The ship is not his own, and the man from whom he must take his sailing orders is not yet returned to England. A month ago he crossed the Irish Seas from Chester.'

'And is your Ben so obedient a servant? I should not have thought so.'

'He serves only one man, and to that man he is indeed obedient, in so far as he loves his life.' Jones sunk his head and looked round. 'For the master of whom I speak is known throughout the narrow seas as a man dangerous in anger.'

'A pirate?'

Jones frowned. 'Not so loud. Some call him by that name, but he is indeed an honest trader and a valiant soldier.'

'Then will you make me known to him on his return, for I begin to have some inclination to a sea-life?'

'We'll talk of it later.' He drove the knife into the table. 'Wounds, I may be driven to it myself yet. Keep these words as close as your life, lad. The man of whom I speak is as generous as he is sharp of temper; and is a notable benefiter of our trade by opportune removal of its rivals. I have a notion that Ben was told to await his coming hither. If so, then Ben is near, gold or no gold.'

'I am near a hatred of this city and its women,' said Merric thoughtfully, and drank. 'On one side a wench with a giddy brain slights me, and on the other—' He drank again, hesitated, and then burst out. 'I have a mind to take a revenge on someone and then laugh it over on shipboard.' Jones was now regarding him with keen eyes. 'That damnable Dousabel—'

'Have you burned your fingertips in her prickling fires?' Jones asked eagerly.

Merric drank again and called to the tapster for more wine. 'I don't know if I want to speak to her, except to say that I hate her for her loose betrayals of my uncle.'

'Ah, but did she betray him with you yourself?'

'That would surely make it worse, since I am his nephew.'

'Did you tell her so to her face, after you had done your best to get a cousin for yourself under her girdle?'

Merric stood up. 'Let's get out.' The tapster came up with the wine, so Merric drank a cupful off without sitting again. A dark-faced girl came sidling to him, and said something. For reply he poured the remnants of his cup redly down her corsage, and she squealed. 'Now I shall know you again,' he said, 'you are marked mine.'

They went out and turned down towards the river. A beggar held a box in their faces, saying that he had been maimed in the wars. A noseless woman lay sprawled on a heap of wood, with a kite circling overhead. Through a window without curtains or shutters in a tenement they saw a woman in child-labour with her shift pulled over her face and a blousy midwife drunkenly wringing out a cloth beside her; a young girl in a torn blue petticoat stood watching at the foot of the bed, leant against the wall with a finger in her mouth. Coming out of the lane, they saw a crane at work on a wharf. A bull with his head in a hempen net was being led down the road by two men, each of them holding a rope tied to a horn.

Kit grabbed Merric's arm. 'There's one of the rogues.'

A sailor in a tasseled cap of wool and great boots was walking half drunkenly ahead. 'I'd know him anywhere. He's Pierce Codring, a silly murderous fellow, whose brains have long run out of his ears. Now we shall find where the ship lies.'

VII

Woodman: '*While I was in prison, I had leave of the Council to go home to pay my debts; and then I went to a fair to sell cattle, and there met me divers poor men that I had set awork, and of love asked me how I did, and how I could away with imprisonment. And I showed how God had dealt with all them that put their trust in him; and this they called preaching.*'

Bishop of Winchester: '*Judas and the devil are your masters. For the devil is master where hell is, and you said you had a burning hell in you. I pray you tell me, how you can avoid it but that the devil was in you, by your own saying.*'

Woodman: '*The hell that I had was the loving correction of God toward me, to call me to repentance.*'

Bishop: '*What a naughty fellow is this.*'

So he was judged by sentence of condemnation and deprived of his life; and with him were burnt nine others.

VIII

Near a dozen men were gathered round the barber's shop, watching a man have a tooth pulled out with a pincer. A carter shouted as a barrel came rolling off his dray, and a tumbril full of cabbages got its wheel caught in the dray's wheel. William Rigeley edged his horse into the only passage-space left, and found himself facing Gregory Hawes, also mounted. 'Sir,' he said with dignity but without offence, 'I am more than halfway through this narrow lane and you are just entering. I beg you to withdraw.'

'I'll withdraw for no man,' said Hawes, 'and least of all for you.' The men left the barber's shop and crowded round, urging both riders to stand firm. A tailor's apprentice, recognising Hawes, cried, 'Down the Clothworkers!' At once both William and Hawes stiffened.

'As a warden of the Merchant Taylors Company,' said William, 'I must insist on my rights.'

Hawes shouted back, 'Though you belong to the Firking Botchers and are King of all Dunghill Roosters, you shall not pass here.'

'The Taylors,' said William, still trying to keep his dignity, 'were long an honoured mistery of St. John when the Clothworkers were a mere pack of straveling journeymen.'

The crowd cheered, and Hawes replied, 'If you are indeed warden of your Company, I bid you keep better watch and ward against covert bankrupts and usurers who assume a merchant's face to gloss over their filthy frauds.'

William drove his horse forward, till it reared, neighing with fear. Hawes in a cursing fury tried to draw his dagger, but found that he must drop either dagger or reins. He fell forward over the neck of his bay-horse. William drove the spurs into his own horse's flanks; but at that moment the carter rolled his barrel away from under the feet of the crowd and a space opened, into which William moved. Hawes hadn't given way, but he had been pressed to one side, and William was the one who first got through. So William seemed the winner, and the crowd cheered him.

Then at the further end of the street appeared a Maypole slowly moving on a wain drawn by bullocks. A long yoke of bullocks, twenty of them, with a posy of flowers tied to each horn. The pole stood upright, held by many ropes and hung with greenery, dabbed with paint and streaming with ribbons. Girls were singing and dancing in the wain and all round it.

One man, standing at the corner, cried out, 'Let it bring luck to the earth. For we need it.'

'Fie on the stinking idol,' said another.

Hawes rode on to his house, approaching by the backlane. He handed the horse over to the stable-boy and strode angrily towards the house. As he passed the drying shed, one of the cords broke and several broadcloths fell on the ground. 'Who is in charge of this line?' he shouted. At first there was no reply. He shouted again, and a sick-looking man came from behind a stack of poles. 'Out at once,' cried Hawes, 'and don't let me see your face again.' Then, ignoring the man's pleas, he went on into the house.

Jacint, peeping from the solar, saw him coming, and ran out, up to Rafe's room. 'Father has come home in a raging fit,' she said to explain her hurried entrance, 'and I shall leave him to Aunt Gertrude who will madden him till his nose bleeds.'

'England is the paradise of women, the purgatory of servants, and the hell of horses,' he observed. 'Or so the Frenchman tells us. Do you then feel yourself a woman, a servant, or a horse?'

'Something of them all.'

'Tell me the meaning of the latin adjective *fastosus*?'

'No, no lessons!'

'A rare word, but I feel better used of your father than *superbus*. Spell me the word *Complexion*.'

'C. o. m. p. l. e. k. s. i. o. n. e.'

'Near enough. It is sad that we can agree how to spell latin but not our own tongue, where a variety of pronunciations has brought in such diversity of orthography. A Welsh friend of mine at Cambridge reported to the derogation of our tongue and the glory of the Welsh that a sentence of English, penned out of his mouth by four good secretaries, was so set down by them that all differed one from the other in many letters; whereas so many Welsh, writing the same likewise in their tongue, varied not in any one letter at all. Well, I will not abuse the good fellow's credit, yet I could never happen on two Welshmen together who acknowledged they could write their own language.'

'Call me Welsh,' she said, 'and test me with no more words.'

'Yet spell me love in Jacinthian terms.'

'I think it begins with M,' she said. 'And it certainly includes a I and a R.'

IX

The kitchen had grown dark, but neither of them rose for a light. The fire had gone out. Rosbel spoke first, in a low rumbling voice, yawning and scratching herself. 'You're so silent there in the dark that I begin to think you must have gone away, though I know you haven't. If Mrs. Tanner next door was to look in and find us in the dark, she'd think the worst . . . But I'd have done the same once. I'd have thought a man and woman couldn't sit alone in the dark, in a deserted house, without the devil getting between their legs, as the saying is . . . What do you think has happened to him?' She gasped, with voice dying away, but her stool went on creaking as she moved about on it.

'Jon is arrested, but I can't find out anything else.'

They were silent again. 'The Virgin save us—shall I light a candle?' she asked after a final gasp and creaking.

'It's all one to me.'

She rose from her stool and felt about in the darkness. Her hand touched his face and she gave a cry. Then she put her hand back and touched him again. 'Not for carnality's sake,' she said, 'but for the comfort of a companion. For a moment you felt like someone else.' She took her hand away and struck a light. 'But who that someone was, I have no more notion than a babe in the cradle.'

As the candle-flame grew, a knock sounded on the outer door. Stephen went and unbolted. For a moment he failed to make out who stood there. Then he stood back to let Hugh come in. 'Where have you been?'

'I stayed with a friend who lives in an alley near White-chapel Church.'

'We thought you were taken as well as Jon.'

Hugh groaned. 'My heart failed me.' He went on into the kitchen. Rosbel gave him one look and then went into the larder. 'My heart failed me.' He sat with his head sunken.

'The constables and the soldiers took the others off to the Justice, who lived nearby, beside Islington Church; but he was away, and so they went further on to Sir Roger Cholmly, putting their prisoners in a brewhouse. But in the going and coming many slipped away, till only twenty-seven were left for Sir Roger and the Recorder. And those two, calling them one by one, sent them off to Newgate. But five more got away from the brewhouse, so that there are twenty-two in the jail. This much is certain. Among them are Bailey the woolpacker, Roger Sandby, and John Mills. Also our Jon.'

Rosbel came in and slapped a slice of pie on a platter before Hugh, but still said nothing. He tried to eat, but gave up after a while. Stephen continued in swift confessional tones:

'Also Mrs Hudley's brother was taken, and lies in Newgate.'

Hugh sobbed. 'My heart failed me.'

'As for Mabel Hudley,' said Stephen, in the same swift flat tones, 'she is safe, and we are married.' Hugh cried out in a spasm of pain so that Rosbel came and stared in his face.

'Go straightway to bed,' she said harshly. 'Do you hear me? To bed.' And he rose, lurching.

x

Blaise stood in the garden outside the Receipt, talking with Popham, who kept trying to reach for an elm bough. 'Ah, Master Rigeley, a wise man wants to hold the leases of his own land under his own hand, and while the copyholders abide by such fancies and ghostly defences as immemorial usage out of mind, a landlord never knows where he stands. Thus he cannot improve his land to his own profit. A strange and prodigious inequity, which the law should exist to rectify.' He gave up trying to reach the elm-bough, and instead reached down to pluck one of the daffodils that lingered along the grassy edge.

'I shall act as you bid me,' said Blaise meekly.

'As follows.' He twirled the daffodil. 'You already hold a lease to half the manor, the part which is cut off on the north side of the church, eh? Yes. You have told me that there is a man owed by the estate the sum of thirty-three pounds, since promised yearly payments of fifty-three shillings and four pence have not been paid, and other matters have fallen in to his advantage.'

They went strolling on the path towards the river, passing the small ivied tower. At the side of the Queen's House stood a small ring of soldiers and court-officials. Popham raised his brows and swung in that direction, taking one of the daffodil-petals and crushing it between his fingers. 'But I have bought the bill from the man,' said Blaise.

'No matter, we shall use him or another as a stalking-horse. Is he a trustable man?'

'I think so. I hold him under obligations and debts.'

'Then we shall get him to invade your part of the manor and seize various goods from it, to your harm.'

Someone was howling inside the ring of guards. Popham walked faster, tripping over a half-buried brick. 'But why?'

'Then you shall take action against him and gain damages, also claiming forfeit of the land because of molestation in your holding. The cause of such molestation being the lord's neglect. The lord will certainly lack the money to meet such a charge, and will thus be forced to sell outright at a loss. For I suppose you have not made such an error as signing a lease without preferment of purchase.' He tore the rest of the flower and threw it away.

Blaise grinned. 'I have the preferment.'

They came up to the group, and some of the under-officials made way for them. Inside, by a block of wood and a brazier of coals, stood a weeping tavern-gallant, who had his right sleeve torn off. 'He was drunk, drew his sword, and wounded another in the precincts of the Court,' said the court-surgeon to Blaise. The man screamed, but the Sergeant of the Wood-yard caught his right hand and bound it with cords to the block. The Master-Cock delivered to the Sergeant Larder a dressing-knife. At a nod from the Marshal the Sergeant Woodyard hacked the offender's hand off at the wrist. At once the Sergeant Larder slashed the head off a cock; the surgeon seared the stump with irons heated by the Sergeant Farrier; and the ripped body of the cock was bound round the stump. Two other sergeants stood round with bread and red wine, to refresh the maimed man; but he swooned away, and the Marshal himself drank the wine.

Blaise nodded to him with a smile, and resumed his stroll with Popham. 'Justice must be done,' said Popham and veered back towards the river. 'Have you any news of the Queen's Majesty?'

'She steadily expects her child,' said Blaise, and lowered his voice. 'She also daily expects King Philip.'

'What is a woman without a man?' asked Popham of the sky, then he corrected himself. 'Yet a Queen is a Queen, vested where necessary by God with a masculine will and a single efficacy of potence.' His cold withdrawn gaze moved over Blaise's face, as if disowning the earnest voice.

XI

Thus (said Edward Underhill) became I so despised and odious unto the lawyers, lords and ladies, gentlemen, merchants knaves, whores, bawds, and thieves, that I walked as dangerously as Daniel among the Lions, yet from them all the Lord delivered me, notwithstanding their often devices and conspiracies by violence to have shed my blood, or with sorcery destroyed me.

Methink I see the ruin of London and this whole realm to be even at hand, for God will not suffer any longer. Love is clean banished; no man is sorry for Joseph's hurt.

XII

'There she lies,' said Jones, pointing through the misty dusk at a boat hawsered to a small wharf. 'I'd know that masthead anywhere.' He studied the situation. 'We'll hide in that shed over there, and wait till Ben comes out.'

'And if he doesn't come out?' asked Merric.

'We'll come back tomorrow. When he comes out, we'll knock him down or track him to some place where we can ask him questions.'

They went round the back of the wall and came out at the broken gate by the shed. Drawing his knife, Jones slipped in, and Merric followed. The shed was dimly lit by holes in its sides. Jones stumbled on a block of wood, and then sat on it. Merric went and peered through the holes on the river-side.

'Keep your eye on me,' pleaded Jones in a rasping whisper. 'I'm afraid the sight of him may send me mad; and if I kill him now, I'll cheat myself out of all that gold. Also, I'd like to put a proper fear into his stinking soul before the devil swallows it. So, keep your eye on me, lad, and don't let me do anything rash.'

They stayed there, with no more words. A man came up on the boat's deck and threw some rubbish overboard, and then lighted a lantern hung from the mast. Shortly after someone came ashore down the plank. Jones crouched down to see him against the evening sky. 'No.' The man went whistling across the wharf.

Then nothing happened for a while. Suddenly two men were coming down the plank. 'Now,' Jones hissed. Still crouching, he moved out of the shed; and Merric followed him. They kept close to the wall. Something slid away under Jones's foot, a piece of tackle, which rattled. Jones fell over sideways against the wall. One of the men ran straight across, was on top of Jones in a moment. Jones struck up at him, still half off his balance and miscalculating in the uncertain light. Shouts, and the second man running over, a skurry on the deck. Merric lashed out and hit the second man on the face, then bent and tried to pull Jones away.

The second man recovered and swung over him, striking askew, but falling and bearing him to the ground, where they lay struggling beside the other pair. Men were running down the plank. In a moment Jones and Merric were kicked, punched dragged aside, and then, at a word from Ben, who had been half strangled by Jones they were hauled up the plank, on to the deck.

Ben lifted the lantern over their faces. 'I thought so. Bring them down.' The sailors pulled them up and dragged them into a rear-cabin with a large port. Ben sat in a small recess, looking with malicious satisfaction at the huddled prisoners. He made a sign, and the others went, except for a broad-chested fellow with a snippet out of his nose, who closed the door and leaned against it, knife in hand.

'Search them, Tobias,' said Ben.

Tobias searched them, turning them over and ripping their clothes with his knife when he wanted to make sure nothing was hidden in a pocket or a seam. But he found nothing.

'That'll do,' said Ben. 'What were you doing out there, Kit?'

'Looking for you, Ben. No call to be so bitter. We came along in a friendly sort of a way, to talk with you. Isn't that so, Merric? We wanted a quiet word with Ben, that's all.'

'Well, now you've got it.'

'We only wanted to ask you for a fair share of the gold—'

'Gold!' shouted Ben. 'What's this about the gold? Give him a clout across the jaw, Tobias, and teach him to clean his mouth out.' And then, after Tobias had struck Jones, he went on, 'It's you Kit who's going to talk about the gold, and soon.'

'Would we come hanging round your ship if we had it?'

That surprised Ben. He scratched his nose and snorted. 'Why do you think he's come, Tobias?'

'What's it matter?' Tobias spat. 'Some dirty trick. If not one, then the other. What's it matter?'

'I came in good faith, Ben,' said Jones in his most wheedling voice. 'Did I try to run away? No, I came to talk, and you've no right to threaten me. Would I come if I had a blot on my conscience?'

'He didn't come,' said Tobias. 'He was brought.'

'Yes, Tobias, but he came to the wharf. Why did he do that?'

'What's it matter? But whatever you do, don't ask him. You'll only get lies.'

Merric fell over on his face. Tobias kicked him, but he didn't move. 'Leave him alone,' said Jones. 'He's sick.' Then he went on coaxing. 'Ben, I sailed with you a dozen times over to Ostend with the cloths. You'd have been cheated if I hadn't shown you what to do. You know you can trust me.'

'You're a nine-men's-morris,' said Ben. 'Nobody can follow all the motions and the ins-and-outs.'

'What's it matter?' repeated Tobias.

'I came to ask you to set our disputes aside,' said Jones. 'I came to join with you, so we might share and share alike.'

'There's one way of proving your words,' said Ben. 'Start sharing out what you stole.'

'But all we have to share is our goodwill.'

Tobias guffawed. 'You see how he lies.'

'Let's forgive and forget,' said Jones. 'You know we always prospered when we worked together.'

'True enough: till you began your double-dealings.'

'Slit their throats while the tide's going out,' said Tobias.

'But I came of my own free will, Ben,' protested Jones. 'Why did I do that if I wasn't your friend? Maybe I've got something to tell you that nobody else ought to hear.' He jerked his head at Tobias. 'Maybe I want to warn you against something you don't know. You were always too trusting, Ben. Would we ever have quarreled if you hadn't trusted those who lied about me?'

'They didn't lie.'

'I had to come and tell you, Ben.'

'What? Speak out in front of Tobias or I won't hear you.'

'I've got a message from someone you know in Ireland.'

Ben stared sharply. 'What's that? Orders for a voyage? Why did he send to you and not to me?'

'I don't like being treated so suspiciously, Ben.'

'The last time we met,' said Ben surlily, 'you knocked me down and tried to put a dagger into me. The time before that you did the same. And now you complain I'm suspicious. Why, to sit here and talk in a civil fashion to you is a christian act you don't deserve.'

Tobias broke in, 'What's it matter? why waste time when the tide'll turn in half an hour?'

'It'll ebb and flow after that again,' said Jones. 'No need to fall out with old friends. I admit I've been hasty; but I wasn't the only one. I admit I struck back; but I wasn't the first to strike. Ben, I've got a message for your sole ears.'

Ben scowled. 'You searched them proper, Tobias? They haven't any hidden knives? . . . Then go up on deck for a quarter of an hour. I'll give him every chance. Then, if he hasn't told me the truth, I'll let you flog him before you cut his throat.'

'Let me light fires under his feet. That's the best way to make a liar talk the truth.'

'I'll leave it to you. Whatever you like.' Ben pointed to a bell on the table. 'I'll ring that if I want you.' Tobias glared at Jones and went out. Ben drew his dagger and placed it across his knees. 'Now talk, Kit, and don't cause everyone a deal of trouble.'

'I came to tell you that there's a traitor aboard.'

'I carried you eight voyages, Kit, and still stayed alive. I'll not be so easy killed. Don't try to make up a lying story against Tobias because he wanted to cut your throat. It won't do, Kit. Only one thing'll save your life, and that's the truth about the gold.'

Merric moaned and turned over onto his face.

'I don't know, Ben. Honestly I don't know. Would I have come to your ship if I had it? We went down to the Chapel marked on the paper, and the chest was gone.'

'Then he was lying to us all the while?'

'No, I don't think so, Ben. Someone had been there a few days before, and the hole under the altar was empty. The gold had risen from its sepulchre.'

Ben scratched his chin. 'Then I'll let Tobias have his will with you.' He reached out his hand for the bell.

'No, no,' said Jones, appealing. 'Let's join together and find who it was that overreached us both alike.'

'I can't make you out,' said Ben in confusion. 'I can't make you out at all, Kit.' Merric groaned again, and Ben pushed him with his foot. 'Get up, damn you.' He reached down to prick him with the dagger, and Merric reached suddenly out, gripping him round the throat. Jones at once caught hold of Ben's wrist and twisted the dagger away.

'Knock his head on the wood,' said Jones. 'No, that might make too much noise.' He took up a jug from the floor and smashed it on Ben's head. Ben collapsed and Merric let him fall to the floor. Jones and Merric listened to hear if Tobias was coming. They heard a noise like a step, and Jones set himself at one side of the door with dagger ready. But no one entered. 'Get the port open.'

Merric went to the back of the cabin and unlatched the stern-window. Lifting the carved frame, he hooked it open. Jones leaned out at his side, over the dark water lapping and clucking in the piles.

'Don't jump in,' said Jones. He climbed out and lowered himself as far as his arms would allow. Then he slid down into the water. Merric followed him. They swam cautiously up the river, to the next wharf, and climbed the rotting stairs. Jones let out a curse as they stood a moment, squeezing the water from their clothes; and Merric asked him if he was hurt. 'We should have finished Ben off with his own dagger while we had the chance,' muttered Jones. 'It'll take more than an earthen pot to knock the life out of that skull of his.'

XIII

'Can you tell me the marks of good honey, Edgar?' said Old Fabyan. Edgar stood listening dutifully, but made no attempt to answer. 'Let the honey be of a yellow colour, pleasant smell, pure, neat and shining in every part, sweet and very delightable to the taste.' Fabyan wrinkled up his face and nodded. 'Mark it well, Edgar, let there yet be a certain acrimony or sharpness, of an indifferent consistence between thick and thin, hanging together in itself, in such sort that being lifted up with the fingertip it keeps together in the manner of a direct line, without any breaking asunder. And that which is gathered in the spring or summer is much better than that which is gathered in winter. Also, the newer it is, the better: clean contrary to wine, which is more commended when it is old than when it is new.'

He looked hard at Edgar, who answered in noncommital tones, 'So indeed it is said.'

'But this is not so well known,' Fabyan went on, 'that, as wine is best at the mid-cast, and oil at the top, so honey is best towards the bottom. And now bring me some in a cup;

for it prolongs life in those of greying years as also in those
of a cold complexion such as yourself. Therefore despite our
ages we may equally profit from its virtues and may draw
many moral lessons from their workings. Now go and wash
your face.'

Edgar nodded and went out. Nest, who had entered the
solar near the end of her father-in-law's eulogy on honey,
came forward. 'Did I leave my needle-case here?'

'I sat on something,' said Fabyan, 'which Edgar set on the
mantel; and if it was your needle-case, I must complain
against your carelessness. For I have still enough flesh on my
bones to know whether I sit on a needle-point or an honest
cushion.'

Nest went to the mantel. 'Someone stole it.' She looked
inside the case, and her voice lost its sharpness. 'The Holy
Virgin be praised for small mercies, all is well.' She turned
round to find that Agnes had slipped into the room. 'Don't
stand there behind me without a word. If you do it once
again, you'll find me angrier than you think.' Holding the
needle-case tightly, she pushed past Agnes and glided out.

'Hang the bell about the cat's neck,' said Agnes.

'I am waiting for my honey,' said her grandfather. 'Tell
Edgar that I am waiting for my honey. Go and make sure that
Nest does not send him out on some kitchen-errand, I beg
you.'

Agnes went slowly downstairs, with one hand behind her
head, and caught Ybel peering through the latch-hole of the
door leading to the kitchen. 'Is the sight so worthy?' she
asked close behind him. He straightened with flusht face, and
put his finger to his mouth. Agnes withdrew into the front shop-
room, and he followed her. 'Well?' she asked, with head on
one side, and loosely-hanging arms, softly closing and un-
closing her hands.

'You know I was looking at Sanchia,' he said, looking up
with bent head. 'She mocks me for looking at her when we
are together; and this time she was standing where the light
fell prettily across her face . . . Why do you scorn me for it?'

'To peep at a girl through a hole in the door,' she said
coldly. 'That is scarcely a sign of courage. You will never
gain her.'

He crossed himself. 'Mary Mother may take pity on me and incline her to kindness.'

'Poor fool,' said Agnes in a half whisper, almost tenderly, watching his eyes. 'Tell me how such love is born. Tell me that, and I'll do all I can to help you.' She pressed her hands over her heart. 'I cannot understand it. I look on people as they pass, men and women, and I ask myself: Is it possible that such a one should love and be loved? I see only a hidden animal, which fear has tamed. But the dangerous smell is not so easily wiped away. I would sell my soul to learn how to love, even though I were as wretched and shameful a lover as you, unloved and weakly.'

'How can I tell you,' said Ybel shiftily. 'Love is no knife, to leave a bloody hole where it entered. Yet it strikes hard, and it draws blood.'

'A flea or a louse can do as much,' she said, and left him.

XIV

'What would you say if I told you that I had married Mabel Hudley?' asked Stephen.

'I should call you a sad jester,' said Tom Hinshaw.

'Yet it is true.'

Tom stared into his eyes. 'How could it happen?'

'The spirit descended on us . . . But now I don't know what to do. I can get no further guidance.'

'In these dark times we have no right to the least of comforts, if it distract us from our great task.'

'That is what Jon said, though he spoke more bitterly.'

'You have wounded yourself, when we need all our strength to resist the wounds that the enemy give us.'

Stephen covered his face with his hands. 'I don't know any longer; but I am sure I did right. If I was mistaken then, I am mistaken in all things, and I am delivered up to the devil. No, it cannot be.'

'What torments you then? Do you still yearn for the fleshpots?'

'I yearn to know what we must do to be saved.'

'That we know. Otherwise, what have we been doing? You have said it yourself.'

'Then why have I become so shaken with fear?'

Before Tom could answer, Hugh came into the workshop. 'You too are here, Thomas? That is good. I have had news of our three brothers in Norwich jail. They have passed through the fire in the place called Lollards Pit. Thomas Hudson felt dolorous at first, not through fear, but because he lost a quickening sense of salvation. So he kneeled on the ground, and after a while rose up with a cheerful face, as a man changed from death into life, and cried: Now I am strong again. And so with joy and constancy went into the flame.'

They were silent. Then Hugh added, 'I cannot understand why the sergeants have not come to search us.'

'Jon has said nothing.'

After Tom went, Stephen took his cap and walked through many streets sometimes speaking to himself. At last he came to the house of the Hudleys, and looked at the windows, and went close to the door. But he did not knock, and soon departed, walking uncertainly because of the blurring of his eyes.

xv

In the trellised bowling-alley in Blackfriars men were trundling bowls at the two small cones against the wall. The red-boddiced girl with plaited hair brought two jacks of bordeaux-wine, and Merric took his turn with the bowls. His cast was ill-judged, and someone who had come up behind him made a jeering noise.

'So the Rigeleys stoop before all men's eyes for a bad throw.'

'Yet the Hawes fall flat in disgrace.'

Merric, still half-kneeling, dived for Martin's legs and brought him down falling on him. Then he stood up, drained his wine, and walked off without looking back or waiting for Ybel. Martin must have been half-stunned or winded; for he didn't rise and come after.

As soon as he was out of the alley and round the corner, Merric quickened his pace. Turning into a lane, he ran till he

came out into Fleet Street. Then, at an easier pace, he went on
westward. Half way down the Strand he paused by some
burnt-out houses on the northern side, and saw a dead cat
mouldering among a heap of nettles. Going to a near haber-
dasher's shop, he bought a small box, returned to the nettles,
and put the cat in the box. Then he walked on till he saw a
scrivener's office. Here he paid a penny for a sheet of paper
and the use of a pen. 'To Mistress D. Rigeley: I smell a Rat
. . .' He meditated and then added some rhymes. 'So said the
Cat. Now tit for tat, here smells the Cat.'

When he neared Charing Cross, he called to one of the
ragged boys playing in the fields and gave him a penny with
instructions to deliver the box at Blaise's apartment. 'The
mistress there will be much pleased and will reward you
further,' he said. Then he walked briskly off, back towards
the City.

In Broad Street he met Ybel, who said that shortly after
the brawl in the bowling-alley the sheriff had come with his
officers and searched the premises. Two workless men were
found there and arrested; and so the Sheriff condemned the
place. Declaring that the law against harbouring vagabonds
had been broken, he set his men to break up the alley with
mattocks. 'I got away through a hole in the trellis, into a
backside,' said Ybel with pride.

'What about Martin Hawes?' Merric asked with an effort.

'When I came out of the privy, I found him leant in a
window, cursing. Then he went.'

'I knocked him down.'

'O, did you?' asked Ybel with awe. 'I wondered why you'd
gone.'

XVI

The Corpus Christi processions in the parishes were thinner
than last year; but in the dusk many streets were bright with
the staff-torches borne by children, and the canopies. Near
Smithfield a man attacked a priest with a dagger and was
carted to Newgate; but all Westminster was loud with singing,
and the bell-ringers of St. Margaret's earned sixteen pence.

The thin bald wrinkled clerk, making up accounts in the vestry next day, noted that one staff-torch, left by a boy, had burnt up with a loss of 4s. 2d. and tenpence had been paid to the man who bore the great streamer; 4d. for flowers and 19d. for bread and beer.

Rafe and Jacint, strolling in the afternoon with Lettice a few paces behind, came upon a knot of talkers and stood on a crackt doorstep to listen. A soldier whose right arm was missing and who wore a green sarcenet flap over one eye was holding forth in a loud drunken voice. 'How then did the commonweal profit by such things?' he demanded, flourishing a paper. 'Now I have a licence to beg, and no constable in all the realm may touch me for whining; yet my mother had other thoughts for me when she lay on the groaning-bed.'

'What shall we do?' asked a journeyman with an ulcer on his cheek.

'Many things can be done,' said the wounded soldier. 'We might tear the bodies of such Spaniards as remain in London, flaunting in our faces the gold they have filched from our pockets.'

'You are a traitor to say such things,' said a pug-faced shop-keeper who had paused to listen.

'The traitors are the men who sell our realm to those wishing to use us only till we sink in poverty and perdition.'

Rafe took Jacint's arm. She resisted for a moment, then let him draw her away. 'The people are no fools,' he murmured, 'but how shall their voice be heard above the clashing of swords and the chinkling of coins? *Res publica res populi.* I am converted to this doctrine as a last resort of hope.'

'For what do you hope, uncle?'

'For my quiet room with books, for your too-young face, for a death in my sleep.'

XVII

Betwixt six and seven of the clock in the morning, were brought from Mote-hall unto a plat of ground hard by the town hall of Colchester, on the outward side, William Bongeor, William Purcas, Thomas Benold, Agnes Silverside alias

Smith, Helen Ewring and Elizabeth Folkes; which being there and all things prepared for their martyrdom they kneeled down and made their humble prayers; but not in such sort as they would, for the cruel tyrants would not suffer them; especially one master Clere among the rest (who had sometime been a gospeller).

When they had made their prayers, they rose and made them ready for the fire. And Elizabeth, when she had plucked off her petticoat, would have given it to her mother (who came and kissed her at the stake, and exhorted her); but the wicked there attending would not suffer her to give it. Then taking the said petticoat in her hand, she threw it away from her, saying, 'Farewell all the world! farewell Faith! farewell Hope!' and so taking the stake in her arms, said, 'Welcome love!'

Now she being at the stake and one of the officers nailing the chain about her in the striking-in of the staple he missed the place and struck her with a great stroke of the hammer on the shoulder-bone; whereat she smilingly turned her head.

When all the six were likewise nailed at their stakes, and the fire about them, they clapped their hands for joy in the fire, that the standers-by, which were by estimation thousands, cried generally almost, 'The Lord strengthen them.'

CHAPTER SEVEN

June

I

WILLIAM CAME down the lane counting the doors. Mud-smeared children were playing and shouting about, with a small black pig excitedly getting mixed up with their legs. Women sat at the doors on stools or benches, in torn shifts, some with babies in their broad laps. One was suckling her baby while drinking from a beer-mug, and the beer, spilling on her bared breasts, ran with her milk into the baby's mouth. A short dark girl, yawning heavily, naked in a window and rubbing herself on the ribs, beckoned to William. He strode faster on, then stopped and hastily counted the doors again. A fat woman with a warted nose chuckled through her toothless mouth. 'You want Humfrey Lock, eh? I thought so. Come in. This is where he lives.'

She led him through the house and out to the back, then pointed to some outside-steps going up to a built-on room. 'Up and knock for yourself. I'm not made for climbing ladders nowadays.' She chuckled and slobbered a little. 'If you want to see me on the way out, just give a call. Susan's my name. There's many fellows who prefer a woman to have same padding on her bones. Hang dogs! though I'm a poor woman, yet I'm a true one.' William went up the steps and knocked at the door. 'The man you were expecting, Master Lock!' the woman called from below.

'But he wasn't expecting me,' said William, looking down.

'Yes he was. He told me that a large fair handsome man would be coming.'

The door opened, and a small man with quick fragile hands and white fluffy hair said, 'Come in, come in.'

'I am told that you are a scrier.'

'That is so, Master Rigeley.' He waved William in. 'I can invocate the spirit into the crystal glass. Also I can deal with the ring that has the Great Name thrice written on it, to wit, Tetragrammaton.'

'How do you know my name?'

Lock bowed and smiled. 'Also, I can find where stolen goods are hidden. Not a day passes but citizens frequent me for that purpose.'

'You have touched my intention. Certain goods have been stolen from me, though I never had them in my hands.'

'If you never held them, the work is more difficult; for what a man takes in his hands, he makes in some sort a portion of his life. Yet I do not despair of success, if the right time and way are chosen. Tell me what these goods were.'

'I prefer not to say.'

'That again increases the difficulties, though the matter is still possible.'

He turned towards the window where stood a square tall table, with its legs set on wax seals and a red silk cover tasseled at the corners. In the centre, on a large red seal, rested a crystal ball. A green chair stood by the table. Lock touched the table-top, standing on tiptoe with the light straw-golden on his hair. He lowered his voice.

'Here are written the seven names of God, which are unknown to the angels, neither can they be spoken. They bring forth seven angels, the governors of the heavens nearest to us. Every letter of the angelic names brings forth seven daughters, and every daughter brings forth her own daughter, and every daughter her child brings forth a son, and every son begets a son.'

He sat in the chair and signed to William to stare into the crystal. After a while William said, 'I see nothing.'

'Yet stare. You will help me to see.' He touched his brow. 'Unless the matter is too difficult for simple scrying. Then we shall need sword, ring, and holywater.'

William swayed giddily, and moved away, to sit down heavily on a bench. Lock leaned forward and stared in turn

into the crystal. 'Ah, you have a strong spirit. I see an impress
at once, a milky cloud of presences . . .' He murmured, 'He
takes the darkness and wraps it up and casts it into the middle
of the earthen globe. The black cloth of silence is drawn . . .'
A hush fell on the room in which the shaft of light seemed
to utter a seething sound, and the buzzing of a fly grew
louder and louder. William loosened the collar of his coat.
Though the day was warm, a brazier was burning in the
room. 'I see someone close to you.'

'Has he a pointed beard?' William asked hoarsely.

'A burning babe, which moans and looks steadily at you.'
He gripped the table. 'He holds a key in his hand and desires
to turn it in your heart. He says that the thing you seek is
closer than you think. He sets three knives point-to-point and
they turn as a flashing wheel. There is only one heart of fire,
and the knives are the key. Now I see a lamb in a befouled
nest.' He shivered and drew away. 'Now he is gone.'

'This is a matter of men, not a babe's bauble,' said William
sourly. 'Ask him where it lies in precise terms.'

'He is gone. I told you that it would be a difficult project
to command. As for the babe, he is emblematical and to be
understood through a glass darkly. Yet I tell you, Master
Rigeley, this babe in his rose of fire is known to you, and has
evil eyes like a man looking through a visor-slit, which looks
furiously upon you. There were spots upon his body like ink.
He is also to be understood as the Lamb and its Slayer.'

'You shall find no gain from me, until you see more than
emblems in your glass.'

'I have bargained for nothing, Master Rigeley, and I trust
that a man of your virtue will not hold a single failure against
me in such a dark search. If you come again, I may get closer
to the significations of the vision; but I can promise nothing
unless we have recourse to sword, ring and holywater.'

'And what then would you promise?'

'Only, that such a powerful spell has never been known
to fail, so far as I have heard, except when it acts too mightily
and summons up a great gusty wind of spirits that blow out
the light and break the circle. For such a mishap happened
recently at a conjuration in Templesham in Sussex, where an

oriental spirit named Baro was drawn up in a black storm to the perplexity of the scrier.'

'I shall consider the thing further,' said William, going to the door. 'For I think that this sword, ring and water of yours would need a large outlay of money, eh?'

'The holywater must be bought from a priest,' said Lock, 'and priests know the value of such a commodity which they hold in monopoly.'

'I shall consider the thing further,' said William, going.

As he came down the stairs, the fat woman appeared at the backdoor. 'Would you like a cup of wine? No. Or your future read from the book of your palm? No. Then let me tell you there is a quieter way of going and coming than the gossip-street.' She pointed to the gate in the backwall. 'Now, when you come again, you know how to cheat the eyes.'

William went to the gate; and as he lifted his hand to the latch, the gate opened. He stood aside to let through a citizen's wife cloakt to the faintly-rosy nose.

II

A PROCLAMATION BY THE KING AND QUEEN. Whereas divers books, filled both with heresy, sedition, and treason, have of late and be daily brought into this realm out of foreign countries, and some also covertly printed within this realm and cast abroad in sundry parts thereof, whereby not only is God dishonoured, but also an encouragement given to disobey lawful princes and governors: the King and Queen's Majesties, for redress hereof, do by this their present proclamation declare and publish to all their subjects that whosoever shall, after the proclaiming hereof, be found to have any of the said wicked and seditious books, or finding them, do not forthwith burn the same without showing or reading the same to any other person, shall in that case be reputed and taken for a rebel, and shall without delay be executed for that offence, according to the order of martial law.

Given at our Manor of St. James's, the 6th day of June, 1558.

III

Hugh went to answer the knocking at his backdoor, and found Harry Daunce the Whitechapel bricklayer there. 'Here come I, old Harry Daunce. What can I do for you, friend? Did you send for me that I might set brick on brick together or that we might join in a joyous song?'

'I sent for you, Harry,' said Hugh, leading him into the house, 'as a man I may trust.'

'In brickwork and in godliness you may trust me.' Harry nodded his head of glistening silver. 'Only this morning Will Grey the baker, a good man though a Catholic, spoke up to me as I passed, and cried out: Does it not make you think of the Lord when you see the Blessed Rood? Why, I answered him, it is an idol of man's contrivance. How much rather ought the creatures and living handiwork of the Lord call you to remembrance? Or the grass and the trees that bring forth fruit?' He laughed. 'Ah, friend, when I walk along the street, I am so filled with a spirit of love for all living that I fear I may break open like an overfilled jar.' He clapped his hands and made ungainly dance-steps. 'How then shall I be ravisht to behold the angels at their carols.'

'It is strange that you are left when so many are taken, and no man so loudly glorifies the fount of all life as you do.'

'There is no need for sadness,' said Harry, still hopping about. 'It will come, it will come.' He paused and spoke in an astonisht voice. 'Yet once I was the worst man in England. I swore with such oaths that my companions declared they must come from hell, since they smelt of sulphur.' He clapped his hands. 'And now I am justified. When last the devil came to me, I asked him if he thought he had a little place for me in hell where I could sing a song. For you can't burn me, devil, there's no grease in me. So I told him.' He looked round. 'Now what can I do for you, Hugh Rigeley?'

'I have seen the informer John Avales in the street five times in three days; and I have a mind to hide away the good books till a better turn of things.'

'How could there be a better turn?' asked Harry in surprise. 'What is there to prevent our testifying? May we ask more than such a privilege?' He shook his head when Hugh didn't reply. 'Still, have it your own way. What am I to do?'

Hugh led him to the chimneypiece. 'You see there is a space here, easy to be brickt in.'

Harry examined the recess with a shrewd eye. 'It can be done.'

'There are bricks in the shed at the back, and some mortar. You can set to work at once.'

Harry took the trowel from the rope round his waist. 'I'll finish it before nightfall.' Hugh gathered the books from a shelf and stacked them in the recess. 'I don't speak against books,' said Harry as he went out. 'But for myself I have it all here,' he tapped his silver head, 'lockt up like singing birds that sing for the day when the Lord will open the cage, O glory!' He hobbled out.

IV

Jacint looked up from her samplar as Martin entered the Solar. 'Did Merric ask you for permission to see me?'

'What do you mean?'

'I have only just learned through Lettice that you met with Merric in a bowling-alley—'

'He set upon me from behind.'

'Of course. How otherwise could he have brought you down? But what I wanted to know was another thing. Did he speak of me?'

'He knows better. Why are you trying to make me angry?'

'I want to know why you hate him so much. When I last met him, months ago, I told him to gain your permission if he wanted to see me again. I said it to torment him and to prove that I loved you. Now I am not so sure that my love isn't for him and that you aren't the one I wish to torment. The world and my heart grow more topsyturvy every day.'

He took her wrist. 'You are a wilful girl. I'll make you beg me for a kiss like a spaniel for a piece of sugar.'

She wrenched her wrist away. 'You have released me from my vow.'

'What vow?'

She laughed. 'Now I am no longer afraid of you, so I shall beg for the kiss.' She threw down the samplar, stood up, and kissed him. 'Go your way for a sturdy fool.'

'I cannot follow out your meaning.'

'If you could, it would no longer be mine but yours. Farewell, my sullen brother.' She turned round on her heel a full circle. 'Now I am gone away, now I am returned, and kindlier. Listen.' She laughed to herself. 'Yesterday I leaned from the window as our mother-to-be knocked on the street-door, and I dropped on her headgear a dusty spiderweb. Which she failed to notice till our father sat beside her and cried out on the filthy streets.'

'And therefore he has decided not to wed her,' said Martin with heavy irony.

'It is her moneybags on which he hopes to breed.'

Aunt Gertrude came in with folded hands and a grim look on her face. 'I have composed my mind at last. As soon as I have conscientiously seen the new Mrs. Hawes set in her bridal bed, I shall go to my sister in Dunmow. This morning I had a letter from her, brought by a carter from Blossoms Inn, an excellent man who agreed with me about the hardship I suffer in being driven from a house built up on my very breastbone.'

'No, aunt,' said Jacint. 'Stay and sow prickles in her bed.'

'She'll find them there without my sprinkling.'

Hawes came in, and a gloomy silence settled down on the room. Martin went over to the window, Jacint picked up her samplar and began work again, Aunt Gertrude turned up her eyes to the ceiling. 'So you are here?' said Hawes, unnerved.

'And where else should I be? You needn't make it so manifest before the others that you pant for the day and hour of my departure. I am not so despised that I must sleep in the street if you turn me out of your favour. My widowed sister writes daily to me, begging that I should leave such a house of iniquity; but I have answered that I cannot leave till I am thrust out. Otherwise my conscience would fret me for abandoning a man who was once my brother, while there is still a meagre hope of bridling the lusts that drive him headlong.'

'I said nothing.' Hawes tried to find a jesting tone. 'I said you were here, and you are indeed here, unless all my senses deceive me, and glad I am that this is so, because, being here,' he stared round for a suitable phrase, 'in a manner of speaking, you are not elsewhere, but are here, all of you.'

'There is no need to multiply your insults,' she said, 'making a hundred skulking words abet the villainly of three. For yourself I say nothing, since I know that ingratitude brings its own punishment; but for these poor children I cannot forbear a grieving exclamation. True, I am here, as you have so basely remarked. I am not ashamed of it, but I knew your baseness too well to think I should escape having my situation flung in my face. I am indeed here, and while I am here, I must speak the truth, however little you like it. In body I am here, and in law I am here. For though I disregard the claims of kinship and the many years of toil spent under your roof, yet I cannot forget the words you said to me in the presence of witnesses, who have set their names to a paper drawn up by the scrivener in Threadneedle Street. For in those words you bade me stay here as long as I desired, and never thought of defaming me with sidelong sneers—'

'Enough of this!' he shouted. 'The sooner you go, the better.' And left the room with a slamming of the door.

'Then I shall not go till he puts me out,' said Aunt Gertrude. 'You see how I am treated,' she turned to Jacint, 'and if there is one thing I partly regret it is that in the past I smote down Tace's pride. Perhaps the Lord has brought this strange woman into the house because I did not cherish Tace; for her moderate fornications prevented such an outbreak and invasion before, and tamed Gregory to a proper acceptance of his widowed state. Perhaps by complaints and hard looks I made him uneasy in her bed, so that he reached out for this painted Babylonian.' She sobbed. 'But if I had my time again, I would light him to his fornicating peccadilloes and leave Tace to her small triumphs of lasciviency.' She shook her head and added, 'Amen.' Then, as the door opened and Tace looked sulkily in, she uttered a little gasp of surprise.

'The pie has been burnt again,' said Tace with satisfaction. 'There must be a devil in the oven who turns every crust to a black coal.'

Aunt Gertrude gave a cry of anger, and Jacint slipped out,

up to Rafe's room. He was reading Suetonius, and tried to make her translate a sentence or two. *Mox Romae circa Sigillaria* . . . She closed the book, and sat on his lap. 'Do you think I am very cruel, fickle, and wanton?' she asked, putting his spectacles on her own nose. 'Now I squint and see the world as it is. Heaven preserve us all. Do you think I am kindly, constant and chaste? I warn you that whether you lie or tell me the truth I shall still love you.' She laughed and swung her legs. 'Let him marry the widow. What do I care?'

v

The storm came suddenly up out of a brazen hush. Five repentant heretics were doing penance by bearing faggot, candle and beads in processional round St. Paul's; and the wind came on them with a buffet that blew out their candles, tore the beads from their hands, and dashed the faggots in their faces. A noblewoman, crossing the road in the Strand, had her skirts blown up over her head, and the servants had to run to her help, pull the skirts down, and hold them round her ankles. A few minutes after eleven the thunder broke. In Chick Lane two tenements fell down and killed sixteen persons. A bolt smote down many large stones from the battlements of a church near Ludgate upon the leads, and burst the leads and boards as well as a great chest under them. Then a fire rose and burned the beam of the steeple-bell, so that the bell fell on the tomb of an old bishop. And a mouldered traitor's head was blown from Ludgate.

Sanchia ran into Merric's room to close the window; and not till she had made everything secure did she turn and notice that he lay on his bed, raised on his elbows, looking at her with drunken eyelids. 'Come here,' he said. She went over and watched him shyly.

'I thought you were still out,' she murmured.

'Who cares any longer whether I'm in or out? I don't care myself. I've no longer got a place in the world, and I don't want any. I'm going to live by trick and knife-edge. Come closer.' He reached out and caught her round the waist, then lost his own balance and pulled her over, laughing. 'Why haven't I done this before? I'll tell you, Sanchia. It's because I've been afraid. I've let a niggardly scruple tie my hands. But that's all ended now.'

'Let me go,' she cried, growing afraid. 'There's nothing loving in what you say.'

'No, my sweet fool, you can't deny me. I know you can't.'

'You're drunken. You don't know what you say.'

'Look me in the eyes.' He put his hand under her chin and raised her face. 'Kiss me.'

He kissed her and she shivered under his hands, weakening. Then the door opened and Agnes came in. She grasped Sanchia by the shoulder and half-pulled her from the bed. Sanchia sobbed, escaped from Merric's arms, and ran from the room with her hands over her face.

'Why did you do that?' asked Merric savagely, trying to rise. Agnes hit him across the face, first on one cheek and then on the other, and he fell back in astonisht pain.

'Do you still ask me why I did it?' she said between her teeth, standing over him. He cowered. She bent and kissed him on the brow, then left the room.

'Why did you do that?' he muttered. 'O Agnes, have pity on me.' He lay on his back, weeping silently and the tears tickled as they ran down his cheekbones, over and behind his ears.

VI

The others turned to see Mat Osborne climbing the ladder into the loft. Mat threw down the coat he was carrying over his arm and stretched himself. 'Three of us plucked down a couple of gallows during the storm.' The others stirred and asked questions that they didn't finish, looked at one another, and then waited for Mat to go on. But he merely sat down on an upended earthen-pot. 'Who was speaking?'

'Edward Torkey,' said Stephen. 'He's telling us that we're bound by no law to serve this tyrannical queen.'

Torkey, a printer with deepset eyes, gave Mat a searching look, then resumed. 'God has blinded their eyes and suffered them to build on false ground, which can no longer stand

than they are propt up with rope, sword and faggot. For the
Queen's first Parliament, by which they sought to overthrow
King Edward's work and establish their own tyranny, was a
thing of no force or authority. For perceiving that her enemy's
stomach could not be emptied nor her malice spewed on the
people by any good order, she committed a great disorder.'

'Her vile and damnable work we know,' said Tom, 'but
surely it is legal. Is not legality the very sign of evil?'

'Her work is not legal,' retorted Torkey, in his flat argu-
mentative voice. 'By violent snares she has taken away from
the commons their liberty. For, according to our ancient laws
and customs, we should have free election of knight and
burgess for the parliament. But she well knew that if any
Christian men or true Englishmen should be elected, it was
not possible for her to succeed as she intended.'

Tom was going to speak again, but Stephen touched his
hand. Torkey went on, frowning as he marshalled his
arguments.

'In divers places many were chosen by force of her threats,
men ready to serve her malicious affections. Thus her parliament was no parliament but may justly be called a conspiracy
of tyrants and traitors. For most of those by whose voice and
authority things proceeded in that court, by their acts manifestly declared themselves such. The others, being good
Christians and true Englishmen, were unable to resist or
prevail against the many voices and suffrages of men false to
God and traitors to their country.'

'We are then absolved from all allegiances,' said Stephen.

'Aye, many burgesses, orderly chosen and lawfully returned,
were disorderly and unlawfully cast out; and others, without
any order of law, were placed in their places. Dr. Taylor of
Lincoln, a true Englishman, was lawfully called to Parliament, yet was violently thrust out. Alexander Nowell and two
others, burgesses of shires, true Englishmen and lawfully
chosen, were returned and admitted, then by force put out
of the Commons. Therefore this Parliament is void, as by the
precedent of the Parliament held at Coventry in the thirty-
eighth year of King Henry Sixth, as I read in Chronicles.'

Hugh came up the ladder, and Torkey waited till he had
taken a seat before going on:

'Further, the third Parliament called by our Queen and her infected husband omitted the style and title of Supreme Head of the Church of England, which by statute was necessary. So, as a woman can bring forth no child without a man, these writs can bring forth no good and sure fruit, because an ordained part of the King's title was left out.' He blinked and stopped suddenly. 'You see.'

'All legalities are of the devil,' said Tom; and Jack Bennett, a plasterer, seated aside in a corner, growled agreement.

'Some legalities are of love,' replied Torkey, 'and of liberty. They are needed in a world of sinful greed and force, testifying only to the love beyond law. Such are those which speak against usury and all the devious defilements of money, and those which assert the immemorial rights of the people to the earth of their labour.'

'Once you talk in such a way,' ejaculated Bennett, 'you come to terms with the enemy and speak his language. Let us away with law, and love will know its own children. Let us away with force, and men will know their own hearts and the hearts of their fellows.' He seized a piece of rotted sailcloth on the wall and tore it down, then stamped on the spider that fell with it.

'That is true,' said Stephen. 'But meanwhile must we not fight to maintain such rights as look towards the perfect liberty of love?'

The voices were about to rise in argument, when Hugh broke in: 'Two of our friends in Newgate have died under the tortures.'

VII

Mabel answered the knocking on the door. When she saw Stephen on the doorstep, she smiled gently at him, but said nothing. 'May I enter?' She nodded, and he followed her into the parlour. They stood looking at one another with slow smiles, swaying, but still not coming close.

'I knew you would come today.'

'I have wanted to come every day. Every moment of the day. I have passed by the house twice daily and looked for a sign of you in the windows.'

I

'Yes, I knew.'

'You are my wife,' he said wonderingly. 'You are my wife.'

'You are my husband.'

He hesitated. 'Does your mother know?'

'No, she scolded me, and then turned to other matters. She is afraid and has gone to confession once more.'

'Have you gone?'

'No, but she seeks to make me go, and now she has asked the priest to call and talk with me. She is afraid. The searchers came and frightened her, and she swore that she was the enemy of her brother.'

'He still lies in Newgate.'

'Yes. I knew you would come today, for I need your counsel. Tell me what I am to do. Am I to run away or am I to stay and defy the priest to his face?'

'You have no thought of obeying your mother?'

She smiled and shook her head. He came a little closer and reached out his hands. She too reached out her hands, and the fingertips touched. He came closer again, and held her hands. 'Where is your mother now?'

'She is visiting a friend in the Vintry.'

He leaned towards her and she lifted her mouth to his. They kissed quietly, without embracing. 'Take me up to your room,' he said in a hoarse whisper. She led the way up to an attic room with a narrow bed, sarcanet curtains, and a pewter bowl on a stand. 'So this is where you sleep?'

She smiled and sat on the bed. 'At first I thought you would never come and we had been granted only that one day in the wood. Then I knew that we should meet again, but in what sort I couldn't tell, and even now I am confused. Tell me.'

'We are one flesh.'

The smile irradiated her pale face with a faint golden warmth. He sat beside her and took her in his arms. She at once loosened her slight body, though her eyes remained open. He kissed her, but could not let go. Rather, he tightened all over. For a while he held her loose body in his taut embrace; then he said in a stifled voice:

'This place is not for us. It murders our marriage. Let us go out into the fields.'

She rose and took a cloak from a small chest beside the window, and they went downstairs. Silently they walked along the streets to Moorgate, and then, with quickened pace, they went north into the open country. Now they went hand in hand, except when they paused to buy draughts of milk from a farmwife going towards the city. After a while they came to rising slopes, and a pocket of woodland in a hollow. They followed a bridle-track and came to the green shadows.

From a rock overhung with holly a blackbird swung out from her nest cradled in a coil of knotted ivy-stems. A wren, a small ball of brown, seemed to fall out of a treestump and went singing with ringing song ahead. Footsteps grew noiseless under the little hasty gushes of the woodwarbler's call. The ringdove, brooding on white eggs aloft, did not hear the intruders till they were close under her tree and then crashed out with a loud chatter of startled wings. The trunk of a grey old ashtree, hewn down years ago, lay half-buried in the soft earth. Shell-like fungi, marked with faint waving lines of green and yellow, clung thickly to the crumbling bark, and bramble-sprays arched over. Behind it meadowsweet was springing.

They turned aside into a little nook, where woodruff was already scenting the air, and sorrel hung its hundreds of pretty bells. She spread her cloak on the ground, and they lay there. 'Now we are home,' he said. 'Now we are one, my bride.' He brushed the whitegold hair back from her face, and she smiled up at him, already unbuckling her green belt.

VIII

The guard was coughing. Jon began coughing too. The other two prisoners stirred uneasily. 'The coaldust sticks in my throat,' muttered Mills, and he also was racked with coughs. The door opened, letting-in a dim shaft of light.

'Stop that noise,' said the one-eyed guard. 'You're to go before the Lord Bishop.'

The three prisoners came out, bowing their heads in the low doorway. Two attendants were waiting. One of them had

a lathe, with which he tapped and beat the prisoners' clothes
to get the worst of the coaldust out. Then he pointed down
the passage. Climbing some back-stairs they came into a
gallery, and on into Bishop Bonner's study. A page, who kept
trying to pull his short sleeves down over his wrists, told
them that the Bishop had changed his mind and gone out into
the orchard. So they went down the main stairs and came out
through the front-entry into the orchard-garden on the side
near the river.

Bonner sat in a loose red gown, with a close-fitting cap, in
a small summer-arbour, heavyfaced with a liquid glitter in his
half-closed eyes. 'Are you there?' he said without turning.
'Are you there?' Then he turned slowly and stared at the
three prisoners. 'One at a time. That fellow first.' He pointed
with a stick at Jon. 'Leave him here and take the others under
the appletree till I am ready for them.' Then, as the others
withdrew, he called to Jon. 'Come here, young man, and have
no fear of me. You seem a comely and simple creature. Why
cannot you enjoy your life under the safeguard of the
Church's sacraments and give over addling your brains with
matters you cannot understand? I am always sorry to see a
comely young man who neglects to enjoy the sweetness of his
years; for grief and impotence come fast enough.' Jon did not
answer, and he asked, a trifle sharply, 'Tell me, do you believe
in the Scripture?'

'Yes.'

'Why then, St. Paul says that if a man sleeps the woman
is at liberty to go to another man. If you were asleep, having
a wife, would you be content for your wife to lie under
another man? And yet this is to be read in the Scripture. I
tell you, if you will believe Luther, Zwingli, and such, then
you cannot go right; but if you trust to my words, you cannot
err. I am in myself nothing, but in my voice is the voice of
the Catholic Church; and if you refuse this, you shall go your
way to destruction. As truly as you see the bodies of them in
Smithfield burnt, so truly do their souls burn in hell.' All the
while he spoke, he was flicking at the feathery grass and the
flowers with his stick. 'Look up, boy. Are you afraid of me?
They call me bloody Bonner, I know, but they lie.' His voice
grew thick and bitter. 'A vengeance on you all. Speak, boy.'

He slashed more angrily, and with a sudden twist struck out at Jon instead of the grasses.

Jon gave a startled cry of pain.

'Cry out then, if you will not speak.' His voice grew weary. 'I'd be glad to have all this ended, but you have a delight in burning. You will not be saved despite the love we bear you, and all our forbearances.' He spoke shrilly. 'Rather, if I had my way, I'd sew your mouths and put you in sacks to be drowned.' He beat out at Jon, who was ready this time and did not cry. 'You are obstinate, eh?' He beat at Jon again and again, over the legs, the loins, the belly. Then he sank exhausted back and called to the officers, who came running to the arbour. 'Take all three and set them in the stocks,' he said in a blurred dull voice.

About two hours later he came to visit them in the stocks at the entrance to his Fulham Palace. They were shackled and could not stand squarely on the ground; and Mills, a small blunt-nosed man, was hanging with full weight on his arms. 'How do you fare now?' the Bishop asked. 'Do you like your lodgings and your fare?'

'If I might have a chair to stand on,' said Mills, 'I could praise God with more comfort.'

'Ah, but you will show no token of a Christian man,' said the Bishop, 'and so you prevent all my love for you. Nevertheless I have come with your wife to see you, and a kinsman of yours who is yet a good Catholic. Come hither, Mistress Mills, and show your belly to your heartless husband.'

Mrs. Mills, large with child, came weeping up, and Mills's kinsman Rouse hovering behind her with cap in hand. 'Let him go my Lord,' she begged. 'For I cannot bear his child without him.'

'Let him repent, and he may go with you.'

'My Lord, I am stricken with dread; and if you hold him still, I must lie on your doorstep and bring forth my child there. For I cannot return.'

'Do you hear, you heretic?' said Bonner jocularly. 'If your wife miscarry, or the child with which you have filled her, the blood of them will be required at your hands.'

'If the choice were mine, it would be so,' said Mills. 'But the choice is beyond my will, therefore look to yourself.'

Bonner turned and lumbered away a few paces, then he came back in response to Mrs. Mills's cries. 'Can you teach him better than I?'

'At least let me hire a bed in this town of Fulham,' she begged with clasped hands, 'where he may come to me on the morrow. Master Rouse will stand pledge for him, and will take him afterwards to your house in Paul's or here.' Rouse came sidling up, gazing into his cap and gulping.

The Bishop gave him a long look, smiled, and turned to Mills. 'You may go for three days under your kinsman's charge if you will cross yourself and say *In nomine Patris*.'

'How can I cross myself with my locked hands?' asked Mills.

The Bishop signed to an officer, who unlocked Mills's stocks. Mills at once fell to the ground and lay there groaning. The officer dragged him up, and Mills managed to keep on his legs, leaning against the stocks; but his arms were stiff and he could not move them. 'Move his hands for him,' said the Bishop, and the officer took Mills's right hand and moved it roughly crosswise. Mills groaned again, and would have fainted if the man had not held him up. 'Say then *In Nomine*,' repeated the Bishop.

'In the name . . .' began Mills in a mumbling voice, with sweat thick on his brow.

'Say it in Latin!' shouted the Bishop in a fury.

'Is the Latin good and true?' asked Mills with lolling head. 'Tell me cousin Rouse, though you are Catholic . . . There is no deceit mixed in the words to catch my soul?'

'No, no, the words are good words,' protested Rouse; and so Mills repeated the Latin phrases after the Bishop. His arms were beginning to tingle and hurt him, and he had to bite his lips to keep himself from crying out.

'Bring him to me at my house in Paul's after three days, Master Rouse,' said the Bishop, glancing at Mrs. Mills's blotched face and swollen body. 'And teach him more Latin and more obedience while you have him in your charge. If he flees, you shall answer.' He strode off, laughing.

IX

Tabitha handed Sir Francis his belt, and then stood with the comb ready. He buckled the belt on, took the comb, and began combing his hair before a small mirror hanging from a nail. 'Yes, your mistress is a marvellously gifted woman.' He tittered. 'I am not without knowledge of the varieties of Venus, but she surprises me more every time that we meet.' He took Tabitha's hand and kissed it. 'Otherwise I should not have been so unstirred by the charms of her maid.' Tabitha took her hand away and stood back.

Dousabel came in, wearing a loose red gown, with her hair tied back in a single red ribbon. 'Haven't you gone yet? Hurry, I tell you. He'll be back any moment now.'

'How grateful am I to that good man of yours for supplying me with money so that I may fitly enjoy his wife.'

'Then remain grateful and go.'

'If you are the wind, then I am as constant as a weathercock, for I turn with all your vagaries. Say that I may come at the same time tomorrow, and I'll go at once.'

'Tomorrow then.' She patted him on the cheek. 'Off, sweet monster.' A slight noise came from the front of the house. 'See him down the backstairs, Tab.' He tried to catch her hand, but she evaded him and pointed to the door. 'Away you go.'

'Help me with these points,' he said to Tab, who led him out.

Dousabel went through into the front-room. Blaise stood there, taking off his belt. He bared his teeth in a quick grin. 'And how has my dear wife been laying out her time? Profitably, I hope.' He gave her a sidelong glance and sank down on the settle. She brought him a cup of wine, without a word. He drank in rapid sips, holding her close with his free hand. 'Don't go . . .' Closing his eyes, he caressed her without looking up, and her face tautened with a look of distaste.

'We have not yet begun . . . I have always told you that we should begin only when I had defeated my enemies and gained a footing on the earth. Next year all will be in my hands. Then you shall go to the manor-house and live there

in ease and greatness, watching that no one cheats me. I shall
have a new-cut garden and a terrace. I shall built a turret,
and set pilasters with cornices over the old doors. Also a new
long window interspersed with pilasters, and a new chimney-
piece in the hall instead of the fire against the reredos. You
shall stand in a garden of coloured earths set round with
tall hedges . . .'

She stiffened again and tried to move away, but his hand
held her. He sniffed rapturously, and his voice ran on in a
low rambling meditation:

'Wages, Richards, fifty shillings a year, Bordman, forty
shillings. Others, twenty-six and eightpence twenty shillings,
thirteen and fourpence twice twenty-six and eightpence again,
five shillings . . . For money is a maze deadly beyond the
magic of a Daedalus, and you the white kernel of its rough
shell. Seven score twelve pounds of beef, fifteen shillings and
tenpence; two cheeses, two and eightpence; well-bucket,
twelve pence; pitch for marking the sheep, three and six . . .
Turn twelve more acres of arable into sheep-runs. Chilton
Rents nineteen pounds five and threepence. Into your hidden
mouths I pour the wine of my money, the seed of my credits.
Two pheasant-nets fifteen shillings, a wet way in a wilder-
ness warily and wearily wandering. You shall rise at cock-
crow and set the tasks, watch the cat doesn't get into the dairy,
make candles on all possible occasions, raise walls and hedges
all around. Only a bad housewife has clean fingers. Diana
of the Ephesians. A calf is fortunate with so many paps to
suck. Fine the cook sixpence if the dinner is late. A tunnel
of lard in a nest of bones, and we shall begin at last, I have
waited all these years, trading further afield to Russia and
India, there's the answer, and William tied in a neat knot of
bonds and bills for my discretion. For he that kisses his wife
in the marketplace shall have many teachers. In the end the
door opens, the hole in the river-mud and the beard of ooze,
but a man may always wear gloves and slip onwards, as long
as the walls and the hedges rise higher still and you my wife
are enclosed at last behind the stones of my power, with a
coppice of forty acres at four pounds per acre besides a
hundred and twenty trees at four shillings . . .' He ground
his teeth. 'I'll not be thwarted, I tell you. For they live who

say that not in fire or water is a bed of dark repose. I am safe while you are safe, and thus at last I shall set you in the marriage-maze forever lost and found as I come home . . .

XI

Agnes, in her bedroom, set down on the bed the little box with a cover embroidered NEST and turned out the contents. A ringlet of gold hair tied with a gold threat, three cheap rings, a faded length of watchet-ribbon, a red shoeheel, painted buttons, half the page of a book. She took the paper and carefully studied it. *Comparison of Love to a Stream Falling from the Alps*:

> From these high hills as when a spring does fall,
> It trilleth down with still and subtle course,
> Of this and that it gathers aye, and shall,
> Till it have just downflowed to stream and force,
> Then at the foot it rages over all.
> So fareth love, when it has ta'en a source:
> Rage is his rain, Resistance vaileth none.
> The first eschew is remedy alone.

Some of the words had been underlined in faded ink. She traced them with a pin. *Love . . . vaileth none . . . hew is remedy alone.* 'Love vaileth none: Hugh is remedy alone,' she said aloud. 'Hugh . . . Hugh . . .' Then she gave a low sighing wail.

Something creaked. She hastily bundled all the things back into the box and put it under the bed with trembling fingers. Then she lay back, sighing and shivering at first, but afterwards becoming quieter. A slow smile grew on her face, easing the strained lines. 'Come then, you devil,' she whispered. 'I am not afraid of you as Mary is . . . But you won't come . . . I'm alone without even a devil for company.' She began softly laughing. 'Nothing is hidden, nothing.'

XI

So soon as he was out of the doors and hid himself in a hollybush, immediately came the constables with thirty

persons to search for him, where they pierced the featherbeds,
broke up the chests, and made such havoc that it was wonder-
ful. And ever among as they were searching, the constables
cried, 'I will have Watts, I will have Watts, I tell you, I
will have Watts.' But Watts could not be found.

And when they saw it booted not to search for him, in the
end they took his wife and set her in a pair of stocks, where
she remained two days; and she was very bold in the truth,
and at the last delivered.

XII

Old Fabyan opened the door of the solar very carefully
and stepped into the room. A draught guttered the candle
and spilled a large blob of grease on to the floor. He regarded
it with pleasure and even spilt a little more on purpose. As
he closed the door the draught blew the candle out. He felt
about in his sleeve and found that he had forgotten to bring
the flint-and-tinder case, hesitated, and then slowly hobbled
towards the mantel.

As he was feeling about against the wall, he heard noises
in the yard, and moved along to the window. Getting inside
the curtain and peering hard, he made out a confused movement of forms drowned in the starlight. Someone was close
up against the window—on a ladder. Peering again, he dis-
entangled himself from the curtain with some difficulty,
moved across the room, found the door-latch, and went out.
'Merric,' he muttered, 'Merric.'

He calculated, and then started off up the stairs. 'Merric.'
He found Merric's room and entered. 'Merric.' He stood over
the bed, muttering and feeling for the sleeper. He caught hold
of Merric's arm and tugged. 'Wake up! Robbers!'

Merric sat up. 'Who is it?'

'Me, Fabyan your grandfather. Robbers environ the house.
I saw them in the yard. I went down to get my bottle of
lettuce-water and rub my brows with it; and I heard them.'

Merric was pulling his breeches on. 'What were they doing?'

'Scores of them, climbing a ladder into Kit Jones's room.
If they do no worse than murder him, we shan't complain.

What a mercy I left my bottle of lettuce-water on the mantel. Indeed it's still there.'

'Go and rouse father,' said Merric, 'and then if there is time, go down for Ybel.'

'I'd like to know what'd happen to this house if I didn't keep an eye on things,' chuckled Fabyan.

Merric went out, taking his knife. He went downstairs half-way, then along the passage and up the stairs leading to Jones's room. He listened outside the door and heard low voices, and after a while a muffled screech. Opening the door as quietly as possible, he slipped in. Two men were bent over the bed. One of them turned, and Merric, with a leap, struck the knife deep into his throat under the ear. At the same moment Jones dragged the blanket up and threw it in the second man's face. The man staggered back, yelled, and made for the window. Merric could have caught him, but he stood staring down at the man he had killed.

The house was now in a bustling stir of footsteps and voices. Merric ran to the window. The ladder was being pulled away. It crashed over, and three figures went skurrying to the backgate. Turning, Merric saw his father enter with a drawn sword, lighted by Ybel with a lantern. Old Fabyan stood behind them, dodging from side to side as he peered in. 'What'd you do without me in the house? Is he dead?'

'They came for you,' said William to Jones. 'This is the last disorder I shall suffer from you. Out you go!'

'But how have I deserved it?' pleaded Jones. 'Consider that my words are proved; for if there were no treasure, why should these villains attack me for it?'

'You knew that they were on your trail. That's why you haven't been out of the house for a week.'

'No, my belly has been troubled.'

'I am weary of your pleas. Not another word. Out you go!'

'I am naked. At least allow me to wait till after breakfast.'

'I give you time to dress yourself. Then you must go at once.'

'But what of this dead man here?'

'I can see him as well as you. Dress yourself and go, I say.' William left the room, signing to Merric to follow. Merric gave a doubtful glance at Jones and went out, down to the solar.

'What are we to do with the body?'

'We cannot throw it into the street. There has been too much noise, which the neighbours must have heard. All the more reason for sending the Welshman away. I should have sent him before, but I have been distracted by divers intentions. As soon as he goes, go yourself to his room and cast the dead man through the window. I shall tell the sheriff that he was killed in a thievish attack on the house.'

Nest came in, holding her cloak at her throat. 'Ybel says that someone is killed.'

'It is none of us. Let all womenfolk go back to bed.'

'Where is Kit?'

'In his room, and safe. He is to be left alone.'

She seemed about to protest, but glided from the room. Merric was about to follow; but his father called him back, and, after taking a few paces up and down the room, went uncertainly on:

'If only we could lay this matter at the door of Gregory Hawes. The Clothworkers have been claiming the right of search as well as refusing to grind our shears. Some of them have been threatening to test the matter by action.'

'But we make and prepare no cloth.'

'Yet they might come to search my house to anger me. A man could be found to testify that he saw the dead man in conversation with Hawes.'

'This dead man is a sailor, and it would be hard to daub him as an agent of the Clothworkers.'

'No doubt it is so,' said William reluctantly. 'But, at any rate, I can throw the living villain out. Go and fetch him.'

Merric went up. Jones was settling the collar of his doublet. 'If he will not be quieted,' he said, 'I'll send you word where to meet me. I have not forgotten my promise to make your fortune, and now it is triply deserved. For you gave me back my life when Ben had it on the point of his knife.'

'Help me to cast him from the window.'

They heaved Ben's corpse up and pushed it feet first through the window. Jones leaned out to watch the fall. 'Fare you well, Ben, old companion. You were ever an intemperate and obstinate man; but for the sake of our drinking days I forgive you.'

XIII

The pious kneeled without cushions and wore little deaths-heads among their beads; but most of the people in the church were dozing, talking, paring nails or scratching their heads. If they knelt, they crooked only one knee or had cushions for their elbows. Agnes was at the end of a pew-row in the women's block, and kept looking up at the window dazzled by the crimson sun. Across the passage a devout worshipper was crossing himself, kneeling down heavily on the stone slabs of the floor, and praying: the sort of man who wore under his clothes the robe of the third order of St. Francis and read daily the office of the Blessed Virgin. Some pedlars were peeping in from the porch.

A rustling hush: the priest praying, crossing himself, kissing the altar. The altar was censed in the middle, on the right, on the left, in the middle again. The voices of the *Kyrie* uprose amid the granite heavens. 'She bore twins ten months after the birth of her first child,' said the woman behind; and someone in the pew ahead began sneezing, couldn't stop sneezing. Sanchia had her palm turned up in her lap and was tracing spirals on it, shivering every time she came to the centre. Nest was leaning forward with her wide eyes fixed on the nape of the woman in front. Agnes looked back to the blazing window.

Voices of the *Gloria*. The priest, having kissed the altar, stood with uplifted hands. *Oremus.* The subdeacon went to the priest, made a reverence and kissed his hand, then went up to read the Lessons. The mutter of gossip increased. 'Like the jealous man who cut off the best part of himself so that if his wife got with child he'd be quite sure she'd played him false . . . Better than that is the woman who hanged herself because she saw her husband's shirt hung out on the hedge in her maid's smock.' Agnes put her hand over Sanchia's, to stop the finger-spirals she was still tracing; and Sanchia in surprise closed her hand and caught Agnes's for

a moment. Then she flushed and lowered her head, dropping
her arms at her side. Nest raised her eyes, stared at the
tapestried chancel and then at the rich carpet on the flat
grave-monument to her right.

The Gradual, and cries of *Alleluia.* The procession began.
The deacon held the Gospels aloft, amid scattered incense
and the song of thankfulness. The acolytes set the candles
down, and the .priest recited the Creed. The choir lifted their
voices, and the priest prayed, incensed his hands. He prayed
the secret prayer, amid the chanting, and ended with the
piercing cry: *Per omnia secula seculorum.* Then at last the
eucharistic prayer began, and the choir sang the *Sanctus.*
The priest genuflected. Everyone in the church was straining
to see, craning, standing up, jostling, getting on bench or
tomb.

To see. To see the Elevation.

The Sanctus bell rang. 'I saw it, I saw it,' a woman cried,
and fainted. A deep thrilling sigh of ardent excitement rose
from the crowd.

The Lord Mayor rode in armour, in crimson damask, with
his swordbearer lofty in front. Two sheriffs in red surcoats,
and two pert-nosed pages holding their helmets. The Mayor's
Guards in worsted liveries and part-coloured says. The
sleepily dignified Aldermen.

William came moodily in the rear, with other belatedly
worthy citizens. A tile fell and split open a journeyman's
head. A tall fair girl with a yellow cat on her shoulder stood
on a barrel. Someone pushed a Spaniard down a flight of
stone steps. A mountebank span five golden coins in the air,
and said that if he dropped one the man who picked it up
could keep it. A ballad of monstrous births was sung in back-
alleys. The sky was serenely azure.

Green boughs had been hung on the doors, and sprigs of
fennel or St.-John's-Wort. Posies of orpin and white lilies,
garlands of many flowers. Lamps of glass with wick and oil
ready for lighting were set in niches in the house-fronts; or
boughs of wrought iron, with candles, or little lamps, were
strung from upperwindows, especially in Fish Street and

Thames Street. The boys had been busy from daybreak building bonfires in every street and lane. And now the richer citizens were having large trestle-tables set up before their houses, and stacked with food and drink.

Standing watches in bright harness had been appointed by every ward and street; and a marching watch started off on its progress long before dark. 'Thirty-two hundred yards of assize we traverse,' said the man with the longest pike, a stickler for facts. Two thousand men marching, old soldiers and officers, with wiflers and drummers, with standards and trumpeters on spotted mares, with demi-lances on huge horses and gunners with handguns, archers in coats of white fustian and pikemen in polisht corselets. Also bearded giants and green morris-dancers.

As the bonfires mounted, the boys went running round them and up and down the street. 'Can we light them now?' And the poorer folk in their best clothes gathered near the well-spread tables of their rich neighbours, discreetly waiting for the word of invitation. Lutanists plucked little preluding notes in the doorways, and girls put on their brightest garters, stood on stools, and laughed for no reason.

William came to the door of his house and regarded the table set up near the bonfire of Finkes Lane. Ybel and Edgar carried a bench out. 'Let us set our tables close together,' said William to Richard Ympson, his righthand neighbour, the next most esteemed man of the street, 'and then we together may judge the nagging wives and the quarrelsome companions.'

'With all my heart,' said Ympson, a cheerful redfaced man, and called to his servants. The two tables were brought near, and Nest conferred with Mrs. Ympson, a very small and worried woman who always expected the worst and liked to see it happen. Then William, standing with his hand on Ympson's shoulder, shouted and beckoned to the knots of poorer folk, who came forward, shy at first, and then making a rush for the benches, suddenly loud and unawed.

'As long as nobody chokes himself,' said Mrs. Ympson. 'I don't mind how greedy they are, as long as nobody chokes himself. But you mark my words, there'll be a choker or a spewer among them before an hour's out.'

A couple of huge sirloins were being cut up under the sharp supervision of Old Fabyan. 'An old ape has an old eye,' he said, and chided the carvers. 'Do it lovingly now, do not hack at the meat as though it were your sworn enemy on the field of battle. Lovingly with the carver, I say.'

'As soon as the first appetites are stilled,' said Ympson, 'let us carry on with the reconciliations that befit St. John's Vigil.' The diners shouted agreement, and beat on the table with their knife-hafts.

'Let us lose no time in such a godly matter,' said a flat-nosed pewterer named Wall. 'And for our first family of discord I name Mistress Skete the nagger and Master Skete the nagged.'

Everyone shouted for the Sketes, and they were found at the end of the further table, in the shadow. At first they sat with bowed heads, hoping that the cries would die down; but Ympson went over and offered his hand to Mrs. Skete, who said, 'With all due respects, Master Ympson, I bid you begone and lend the light of your cheer to Mistress Ympson, who needs it more than I.' This roused a slight laugh, but Ympson persisted, and she had to rise. Her husband came slouching behind her, wiping his nose all the while with the back of his hand.

'Who will speak the kindly words?' asked Ympson. 'You accused her,' he said to the pewterer, 'you must placate and emollify her.'

'Mistress Skete,' said the man, leaning back and surveying her. 'Your voice is loud and long, so that we hear in our cellar or attic whatever you whisper in complement to your husband under the bedclothes. We consider then that he, set so much nearer to your tongue, must have his ears pierced and deafened to the pity of all mankind. Yet you are a well-favoured woman with a mouth as trimly made for kissings as those less furiously gifted. Considering then that the eyes of the angels and Finkes Lane are upon you, will you make a good effort of reformation for the coming year, or do you defy our meddling love?'

'If my man is hurt, let him speak for himself,' said Mrs. Skete, bridling. 'Also, if my mouth is kissable, let him kiss it. Maybe then I should have less time to show him charitably his shortcomings. As for you, Master Akins, I know that you have gained mastery in your own household only because you drowned your wife's voice with the hammering of your hammers before your marriage-night was out.'

'Will you then kiss and show an example of amity to our Lane?' asked Ympson to the Sketes.

Skete rubbed his nose, and Mrs. Skete turned towards him. 'I have never forbidden him the use of my mouth; and if his clumsy attempt upon it in public will not deter others from such lip-work, I have no objections to utter.'

Skete kissed her to the best of his ability, amid the cheers of the street. Then they returned rather proudly to their seats, and Ympson asked for further names. The accusation that Mrs. Walls spent all her husband's money on cherries and codlings was not thought worth proceeding on; but after some whisperings Brack the draper with the shop at the corner rose to speak of the quarrels that had been going on between two inmates of the street, to the detriment of their common content and labour. Ympson then called on the men in question, a skinner and a plasterer, to set forth any true matter of argument between them, so that the neighbours could intervene and find a way of salving wounds.

Ybel, going into the house to fetch some more wine, looked back to see if this appeal had any effect, and bumped into Sanchia coming out with a pie. 'Take care, you fool,' she said, angrily pouting. He put his arm round her and tried to kiss her. 'You'll make me drop the pie, let me go.' She averted her face, but he managed to kiss her on the neck.

'Why do you hate me?' he asked miserably.

'I don't hate you,' she said, shrugging up her small brown shoulders to push his face away. 'But that is no reason why I should love you. Must a man take to his bosom every spaniel that falls simpering and whimpering under his feet? Let me go, I tell you.'

He sighed and let her go.

Merric, under the pretext of fetching some custards, slipped away and hurried for Fenchcurch Road. In the boisterous streets movement was difficult. Tables were everywhere set out, in a golden glare from the many lights before the doors,

the crackling bonfires, the hundreds of cressets carried by the
constables and the straw-hatted men with painted badges,
who had been given breakfast and paid by the Companies:
going in pairs, one man holding a bag with the materials of
light-making, and the other bearing the cresset.

Merric pushed through the merry groups, and ran down
the unimpeded spaces, till he reached the corner leading to
Hawes's house. Then, carefully moving down the street, he
neared the table where Hawes sat, with Martin at his side.
Jacint was moving about, helping Lettice and Tace with the
food. Keeping in the shadow of a stall, Merric took out a slip
of paper, read it over, and beckoned to one of the bonfire-boys
who were running about on a quest for more wood. 'Do you
know Mistress Jacint Hawes?' he asked.

The boy nodded, but Merric took the precaution of making
him point her out. Then he gave him a silver penny, and
bade him hand her the note and show her where he stood
by the stall. The boy darted off and made for Jacint, who at
that moment went into the house. The boy hesitated, looked
back to where Merric stood, loitered on the doorstep, and
seemed about to go to Aunt Gertrude. He turned away, then
turned back, shouted to one of his friends running with an
armful of faggots, and then saw Jacint returning. He handed
her the note. She read it by the bonfire-light, and looked
quickly round, saying something to the boy. He pointed to
the stall, and she patted his head, giving him a tart from
the table. Then she went down to where Martin sat, patted
him also on the head, and laughed at something. Her Uncle
Rafe came from his stool under the window and touched her
from behind. She turned sharply and then laughed again,
kissing him on the brow. She gave him a tart, and turned
back to the house.

But she stayed within only for a moment. Coming out, she
went over to the bonfire, helped for a moment with the new
fuel, and then, as she turned back to the table, swerved and
made for the stall.

'Who lurks in the shadows? What banisht man looks with
jealous eyes on a lost world?' she said in a clear voice. Then
came closer. 'It is you, Master Rigeley. I thought someone
had forged your hand; for I know that you are no brave

adventurer to come seeking a bride in the enemy's teeth.'

'I have come,' he said, emerging into the flickering sheeted light of redgold.

'Go back into the shadow.'

'Then come with me.'

She went with him into the shadow of the stall. 'Now I am also in the shadow, prettily mizzled in the head with wine and noise, and as reckless as a virtuous and vainglorious virgin may well be. What comes next, my lurker?'

He took her squarely in his arms and kissed her. 'This.'

'I have been kissed before.' She set her hands on his chest and pushed him away. 'By you and by others. Have you no new offering to make? Take your chance while the bonfires last. I am moonmad in a tumult of light, but in the morning I shall be as dull again as the others, and as cowardly.'

'Marry me.'

'In the mazes of the moon, or the land of whipperjinny?'

'Here and now.'

'Are you a priest that you may marry yourself? Or do you want only a hedge-wife, a greengown tumbler?'

'I'll find a priest if you'll say the word.'

'No, you must find the man I love before you talk to a priest.'

'I am the man.'

'Then prove it, and all is well. But I think you are another person, named Merric Rigeley, a good lad as the world goes, but a grumbling faint-hearted fingering fellow, who wants golden apples to grow on his privy appletree and who lurks in the shadow of a vain anger. If you are another man than this, tell me, and I shall hold you by the ears while I kiss you.'

'What must I do to win you?'

'First, you must never ask me that question; for it will be answered only when you cease asking it.'

He tried to kiss her, but she drew away. 'At this moment I love you, my shadow-lurker, but I despise your friend Merric. Now I must go.' And she ran off.

Martin had risen from the table. 'Where have you been?' he asked as Jacint came running breathless up. She smiled without answering and went to her aunt. He drew back towards the door and watched Lettice go in, hesitated, and

then followed. But she had disappeared. He stood listening
a moment and then went up the stairs to the solar. Opening
the door without warning, he stepped in. Mrs. Pernel Wicke
was sitting on the settle, fixing the golden garter of her
right leg.

'Come here, Prue,' she said without looking up. He stared at
her plump white comely leg, unmoving, till she looked up
and uttered a cry, stricken in surprise. Her mouth opened, but
she didn't speak. Then she pulled her dress down. He went
on staring, and made one step towards her. Then drew back
and hurried from the room.

At the foot of the stairs he met Tace, coming in with a
large empty dish. 'Set that down,' he said harshly. She set
the dish down on a side-table and stood waiting. 'Now come
up with me to your room.' She looked at him with scared eyes
for a moment, then slowly she smiled and her body swayed up
and towards him. 'Come on,' he said harshly. 'Come on, I
tell you.'

'Yes,' she said at last, resigned, and then again, with a
rising note of eagerness, 'Yes.'

XIV

Stephen came white-faced in, clenching his hands. 'Are we
to go?'

Hugh winced. 'No, no . . .'

'I must go, though it kills me.'

'Then I must go too.'

Hugh rose, and they went out into the street with set bleak
faces. After a while Hugh said, 'You know that proclamation
has been made at Newgate that no man or woman shall pray
for the seven martyrs.'

'I know. They may cut out men's tongues, but they cannot
silence the prayer of the heart.'

They went on through the City, and others passed them,
going this way and that, talking and laughing, silent and
haggard, coming and going on multiple purposes, men and
women, with lute-music and whip-crack, and over them all
the sweet sunlight. Stephen and Hugh went on with bleak

set faces, and others went their way, moving towards Smithfield, moving slow and fast, men and women with bleak set
faces.

They came through the gates, and went faster still towards
Smithfield, under the clear blue sky. Sparrows nestled in the
dust, digging small holes with their soft breasts, and a blackbird's call came down the sighing freshness of the air.

The officer was ending the proclamation as they came up.
They heard the last words threatening with arrest anyone
whose lips should move with the words *God help them*. Then
up came the hurdle on which lay the three men, bound,
ragged, bleeding. Jon was there in the middle, thin, pale,
grimed, with a straggling beard. After, came a second hurdle,
holding four men among whom was Polard, Mrs. Hudley's
brother.

Guards cut the ropes and the seven men stood weakly up,
leaning on one another for strength. The press of people
broke through the ring of soldiers, and made towards the
condemned men. More billmen came up from the gallows to
hold the people back. An officer, standing on a block of wood,
called for arrests to be made.

The people pushed the guards back and embraced the
prisoners, wept over them and struggled to touch their hands,
their shrouds, their feet. Stephen pushed through and came
up to Jon, who was standing dazed amid the heaving crowd,
with bowed head, striving to keep his foothold. Stephen
embraced him, weeping; and suddenly Jon realised who it
was. 'We are here,' said Stephen, and Jon smiled, a faint
deathly smile. The people around were singing. The soldiers
had fallen back round the gallows. The officer had taken out
the roll of the proclamation and was reading from it again.

Bentham came up and shoved the officer aside. 'We have
heard you before. Continue with your murder, but spare us
your words.' The officer stared at him but dropped the paper,
and Bentham climbed on the block. The people fell away, leaving an open space between the prisoners and the mound of
burning. A deep hush came over the place, in which the
blithe calling of some children in a near field was clearly
heard.

'We know these men are the people of God,' Bentham cried,

'and we cannot but choose to wish them well and say: God strengthen them.' Then he raised his voice, 'Almighty God, for Christ's sake, strengthen them!'

The people cried, 'Amen, Amen.'

The officer was staring round as if to fix the faces in his mind. The condemned men slowly came forward. 'The moment is ours,' said Stephen. 'The moment is come.' But no one answered. All men and women were watching the seven men slowly, with stiff shambling bodies and faces of calm inflexible dignity, advance towards the stakes and the faggots. No one laid hands on Bentham.

XV

Merric entered the tavern and gave a long look-round. A girl whom he did not know smiled back at him. He returned the smile but shook his head. Then, as he was hesitating, the tapster came up to him. 'What would you like, sir? Angels milk or go-by-the-wall?'

'Huffcap,' said Merric.

'This way,' muttered the tapster. 'He awaits you, sir.'

Merric followed the man out, down a passage into a back-room. Jones was seated there, stirring a cup of claret with a straw and watching the eddies. 'You got my message then?' Merric nodded, and the tapster slid off. 'Sit down. I have smelt out a trail, which may well bring me upon the gold in a few days.'

'I'm sick of the matter,' said Merric, turning from Jones to the rough wall-paintings of devils and monks. 'Whether the treasure exists or not, I am sure that we shall never lay hands on it.'

'Now, now,' said Jones indulgently, 'you are young, and do not yet know what obduracy of heart and hope is needed for the enriching of a man. The gold is assuredly there. Why should it comfort another when we have the better right to it?'

'No one has any right to it.' He went up and traced the faded outline of a monk with his hand on a nun's knee. 'I have lost all my certitudes and know only that I grow angrier every day without knowing what I wish to strike at.'

'Tell me everything,' said Jones with a grin. 'You are still teased with the smell of that Jacint. You are no nephew of mine if you let a smockful of bitchery defeat you.'

'You don't understand.' He sat down at last and looked at Jones. 'She scorns me and I cannot find any way of disproving her scorn.'

'Get the gold and she will dance to its clink.'

'I thought that once, but now I believe otherwise.'

'Can a wellknit lad die of a witless wench's scorn?'

'You don't understand. If she simply disliked me, I could forget her; but she loves me, almost, I am sure. She looks into me and sees a thing which she desires to break; and afterwards, however I rage, I feel that she is right. But what it is that I must break in myself, I cannot tell. I have tried to hate her, but in vain. For in the end I only increased my own pain.'

Jones looked at him sideways. 'Maybe I understand better than you think. Yet for your own sake I counsel you to turn from this woman, who has a subtle devil in her head. Rather, I think a woman with a simple devil in her heels.' He grasped Merric's arm. 'Nevertheless I love you and will save you in your own despite, especially if I can harm your father in the doing of it.' He grinned. 'I trust that my sister has upheld the honour of the Joneses by diverse adulteries and such wifely rebellions.'

'Don't you dare to say such things,' scowled Merric. He stood up to go, but cursed and sat down again.

XVI

In the dusk Stephen came down the street, walking on the side opposite to the Hudley's house. As he neared the house, he walked more slowly; and then he knelt down to untie and tie again a shoelace. Not a sign from the house, not a glimmer of light, not a voice. A red-haired woman, coming up the street with a basket on her head, looked at him curiously, stopped, and then went on, singing a ballad of a millrace. Down a little side-alley two girls lay ungainly in a cellar-

opening, one of them hushing a hungry baby. Stephen took all
the coins from his pocket and went up to them. He tried to
speak, but his voice failed. The younger of the women raised
herself into a crouching position, blew the hair out of her
grey eyes, and took the coins in a cold hand. He stood there,
still trying to speak, and the barefoot girl said in a quivering
voice, 'Will not here serve?' He saw her strained young face,
broad and big-mouthed, with eyes of glittering fear. He made
a hopeless gesture and turned away, hearing her in weak
incredulous tones, say, 'He has given it for nothing . . .'
Weeping, he went down the street.

XVII

The Hall of the Merchant Taylors was loud with bustling
merriment of food and wine. The servants were running up
and down by the trestle-tables with pies and pastries and
small roasted birds, with jug after jug of wine. Dogs cracked
bones under the tables. Gravy was spilt all over the slimy
boards, wiped with napkins and crusts of bread.

Hugh sat quiet at his table, eating little except bread and
apples, taking no notice of the jests of his neighbours. They
had grown tired of trying to draw him out, and were discussing wines. 'Where does this black and bloody wine come
from?'

Borde, a small man with a crumpled face, who prided himself on a knowledge of wines, seized the chance. 'That's
Orleans wine. Myself I prefer the small wine of Rochelle,
though this is an excellent claret.' He smacked his lips. 'It'd
turn a windmill.'

Frazer, large and rollicking, came in with a rhyme: 'Ho,
I'm for the sack of Spain. It wets well and washes the brain.'

And Heber piped up: 'Me for a cup of Rhenish wine. For
it makes a man speak latin fine.'

'The only latin you'll ever speak is that with Bacchus for
the master, and words flowing faster,' retorted Frazer, with
raised eyebrows at his own improvised rhyme. He banged on
the table. 'There, I said that without intent. Where are those
devil Greeks who in Alexander's days were renowned

drinkers? O, the poor goblins are dead. Let us drink deeply and make reverent water thereof on their graves. Aye, let us drink as do the camels in the caravans, drinking for the thirst past, for the thirst present, and the thirst to come.'

Borde broke in, 'Look at that petty drinker, knuckle-deep in goose, who put water in his wine, doing as the London vintners do; for they make two tuns out of one by the addition of riverwater. That is bad enough, yet they do worse still, putting in lime, brimstone, honey and alum, with other things too beastly to be spoken. Nothing is more harmful to men's bodies. Such rogues should be chastised publicly as thieves and murderers; for they cause an infinity of ills, and specially the gouts.'

Hugh went on chewing a small crust, with downcast eyes.

The Master and the four wardens (one of them, William) came forward on the dais and looked down to where the Lord Mayor sat as guest of honour. At the sides the servants waited with the wafers. The Master and wardens then came down and moved about among the tables, asking how the diners did. The waits of the city went jauntily ahead, playing a light merry tune, then came the beadle and the clerk— the one with a silver wand and the other with the names of the brethren in a scroll.

William as the youngest of the wardens went on, garlanded, holding an election cup; and then the other wardens with the Master's cup of hippocras set with flowers. The Master himself, attended by two old masters of the mistery, came after; and they all went to take their stand by the hearth of the hall, before the gilt statue of St. John the Baptist and the red gay hangings painted with pictures of the Saint.

The Master went to the Mayor and offered his garland. The Mayor took it, put it on, and then handed it back. The Master moved on among the guests, offering his garland. The waits, officers and wardens went down by the livery-table on the northern side. Passing from the group of previous masters, the Master set his garland on the head of the Master Elect, took the hippocras-cup and drank from it, then handed it to the other.

Next the waits, officers and wardens went down to the screen at the lower end of the hall. Here the four warden substitutes were waiting to get their cups and bear them high in their hands. The one for Watling Street took the Master Warden's cup, and they all went over to the hearth, making for the Lord Mayor and the livery-table, where the names of the new Master and Wardens would be published.

But the slow staid motions of the ceremony were interrupted by a young man rising at the back of the hall, from a non-livery table. 'I protest against the elections as unjust and tyrannical,' he shouted, pressing down on the table-boards with all his finger-tips. The officers of the Guild, after a moment of stupefaction, began making their way towards him; but the Master raised his capable hand to stay them, and called to ask the young man what he wanted.

Merric rose from his seat against the wall and pushed past some servants towards the place where the interrupter, Peter Larch, was standing. A deep silence had fallen, everyone turning to see Larch and hear his reply. 'We desire to know the authority of the election,' he cried.

'It is the old custom of the Fellowship,' answered the Master. 'Sit down and let this unmannerly display cease.'

'We cannot believe that,' replied Larch, speaking louder. 'We hold that the rights of the commonalty have been usurped, and a secret election by the rich and the mighty set in its place. We the poor artificers who form the yeomanry of the Company, have been set underfoot by the traders who know nothing of our craft and who use us only for their private enrichment. Thus all the common rights of the Fellowship are villainously changed and encroacht upon. Now the election of wardens is constricted to some score of rich men, and the rest of us may go hang.'

'And hang you will!' shouted one of the new wardens, making a slipknot gesture.

The Master commandingly raised his hand. 'I bid you be silent now. If you have any complaint, however farfetched and baseless, it will be sifted at the proper time and place.'

'Now is the proper time and place when all the freemen are gathered,' insisted Larch. 'We demand a direct part in the elections. We demand an accounting of the charitable endowments of the Company. We demand that the common seal be not used and no ordinance made without the commonalty's consent. We demand a full right to use the hall and to have proper oversight on our craft.'

'There is no substance in your protest,' said the Master, 'yet if you submit it respectfully in a paper it will be granted a reply. Now I must bid you to cease from disgracing our Mistery before the worshipful guests who have honoured our dinner.'

Larch continued his protest. At once a score of servants and officers rushed at him. About a dozen of the Yeomanry rose to his support; and Merric, edging nearer, joined in the scrimmage. In a few moments the protesters had been hustled on to the steps outside the Hall; and Peter Larch, turning, saw Merric close by with a cut across his chin. 'What are you doing here?' he asked.

'I have already asked myself that question and found no answer,' said Merric. 'Therefore I now ask you in turn: What are we all doing here?' He laughed. 'And if not here, elsewhere? for a man is a man, I trust, wherever he goes. And if not the worse for him.' He strode off.

CHAPTER EIGHT

July

I

THEY WERE gathered in an upper room overlooking the river. From outside came the river-noises, the rattle of cranes, the rushing of water between the starlings of the bridge-piers, the cries of the playing watermen, *Eastward Ho* and *Westward Ho*. Stephen was standing amid the others who sat on boxes or the floor. 'We could have taken them away,' he said passionately. 'We were blinded by our vision of glory, as though we were angels looking down through a floor of crystal. Did we sacrifice our friends to the pride we took in their suffering for righteousness?'

A weaver from Norwich said, 'No, we had no power to save them. The soldiers would have come out against us. Nine years ago I saw the iron men, the lords of England and their Italian horsemen, trample the commons of my own country.' He flushed and added, 'Not that I counsel fear and despair. But we must be prepared. We must have arms and a design of raising the people.'

Another weaver, a man of Southwark, broke in, 'But how are we to succeed where the others failed? Kett against the landlords and Wiatt against the mass mongers. Did not the lords overthrow the Protector because he had a kind heart? Now the lawyers hurry on with their devices, so that by law the landlords may gain what land they have failed to take by force. The merchants break up all fellowship in craft; and if the drapers fight them, it is only to gain the poor for their own slaves under the bloody beadle.' He ended in a violent fit of coughing.

'What then are we to do?' cried Stephen.

'The end of the world is near,' said a bony-lowering man from the window-nook. 'All signs confess it.' His eyes moved jerkily in fixed slots, from side to side, settling on nothing, and a large vein flickered in his brow.

'If things are grown tangled in a mesh of evil beyond the worst fears of our fathers,' said Stephen slowly, 'we have the greater test put upon us. Perhaps this confusion is the result of our fathers' falling-away, their refusal to stand up in the name of justice; and so, unless we fight now, our children will indeed be the children of darkness, inheriting only the earth of Cain.'

Outside someone was hammering at tub-hoops and chanting a fierce song in time with the blows. 'Then will come the great hour,' said the bony man, 'when the earth will be torn loose from its foundations and all things be turned upside down. We must fast and pray in expectation of the fire from heaven.' He sat with jerking eyes, his large loose hands held dangling breast-high.

'I saw his face in the fire,' cried Stephen. 'I cannot forget it.'

'We all have a burning face in our hearts now,' said Mat Osborne, speaking for the first time. 'There burns the fire that must overwhelm the world.'

Stephen went to the head of the stairs. A lad below put forefinger to nose and pointed to the left, then ran off. 'We had better depart at once,' said Stephen to the others, and went on down the stairs.

II

'You were among those who disgraced our Company before the Lord Mayor.'

'I joined in, yes. I was drunk if you like. But the truth is that I'm weary of the way my life goes, and I don't care what happens—as long as it happens. As well fall into their tussle as sit yawning.'

'Merric,' said William, fidgetting and dropping from his tone of severity into one of something like appeal, 'I have asked you to find a little patience. Well, the time of your

waiting is near its end. But it will have no end if you behave
so ruffianly.'

'Did you get ahead of Kit and cheat the cheater of his gold?'
asked Merric carelessly with a flicker of bitter smiling.

William stood up, with jutting underlip. 'You are insolent.
I have borne much from your tongue and eye, knowing that
you feel a cribbed melancholy. But there are limits to my
kindness, and you have found them.'

'I hazarded a guess,' said Merric with less assurance.

William looked long and hard at him. 'You are too full of
your own small miseries to note the largeness of my cares,
which include your fortunes as well as mine. But now, thanks
to a brother and my own endeavours—and the providence of
God,' he crossed himself, 'I am nearing a happier condition.'
Then, with a fresh kindling of wrath, he struck the table.
'But I'll give all my gains to the poor rather than hand them
on to a son who withholds respect from me and my works.
Consider this well, and leave the room before I become angry.'
Merric bowed and turned to go, but William halted him at
the door. 'Let me add that those young fools with whom you
sought to disgrace me at a difficult moment of my fortunes
are now all markt men. They will get no work from any of
the livery unless they manifestly mend their ways; and jail is
their likeliest lodging. Now go.'

Merric went out. William paced the room for a while, then
stopped, expanded his chest with a deep breath, and returned
to the table. Taking out a new ledger, he studied the notes
which he had written on the first page, and went on trying
to master the system of double-entry, the new-fangled Italian
method which had come over from Amsterdam.

III

*Richard Woodman: 'My lord, I have told my mind plainly
without dissimulation, and you get no more of me unless you
talk with me by the Scriptures; and if you will do so, I will
begin anew with you, and prove it more plainly three or four
manner of ways, that you shall not say nay, to that I have said,
yourself.'*

Then they made a great laughing and said, 'This is a heretic indeed; it is time he were burned': which words moved my spirit, and I said to them, 'Judge not that you be not judged: for as you judge me, you shall be judged yourselves. For that you call heresy, I serve God truly with, as you shall all well know, when you shall be in hell and have blood to drink and are compelled to say for pain: This was the man that we jested on and whose talk we thought foolishness, and his end to be without honour: but now we may see that he is counted among the saints of God, and we are punisht. These words shall you say, being in hell, if you repent not with speed, if you consent to the shedding of my blood: wherefore look to it, I give you counsel.'

Priest: 'What, you be angry, methinks. Now I will say more to you than I thought to have done. You were at Bexhill a twelvemonth agone, and sent for the parson and talked angrily with him in the churchyard, and would not go into the church; for you said it was the idol's temple.'

Woodman: 'That I said, I said; and whereas you said I was angry, I take God for my record, I am not, but am zealous in the truth and speak out of the spirit of God, with cheerfulness.'

Priest: 'The spirit of God! hough, hough, hough! think you that you have the spirit of God?'

Woodman: 'I believe it surely, I praise God therefore: and you be deceivers, mockers, and scorners before God, and be the children of hell, all the sort of you, as far as I can see.'

And therewith came in Dr. Story, pointing at me with his finger, speaking to the Bishop in Latin, saying at the length, 'I can say nothing to him, but he is a heretic. I have heard you talk this hour and a half, and can hear no reasonableness in him.'

Woodman: 'Judge not that you be not judged: for as you judge, so shall you be judged yourself.'

Dr. Story: 'What, be you a preaching? you shall preach at a stake shortly with your fellows. My lord, trouble yourself no more with him.'

IV

Blaise came into the Exchequer and looked quickly round. Then, after nodding to those near the Table, he took his seat on a settle beside a man with a roll of tightly-claspt vouchers. A dim warm light came through the mullioned windows with their flax-curtains and fell on the great table in the middle of the room—a table with raised rims all round and squares markt off in the dark russet cloth. At the table-head sat the Justiciar with his constable and chamberlains, and the Marshal at the end of the bench. Down the left side were the lounging clerks with the tally-counterparts, and opposite them the Treasurer, his scribe with the great roll and the chancellor's scribe with his copy of the roll. Opposite the stiff Justiciar sat the applicants trying to look at ease.

An attendant came up with a bag full of counters. The Treasurer called, 'Are you ready to render your account?' There was a stir among the suitors and sheriffs on the settles and benches round the walls. A hawk-nosed man, with grey streaks in his hair that fitted like a skullcap, came hemming forward, bowed to Justiciar and Treasurer, and took a paper from his belt. At the third item which he read out, the scribe raised a challenging finger, and at once the whole gathering woke from its lethargy. Clerks began turning the membranes of rolls to compare the entries of previous years. The chamberlain's sergeant heaped up on the table rouleaux of silver. The clerks fingered their counter-tallies and warrants representing the applicant's credit in the treasury. The applicant himself moved round the table, to prepare for the demonstration, the exchequer-game.

The scribe of the roll, assuring his importance by waiting till everyone was still again, began reading out items in a clear voice. The Justiciar blinked and closed his jaws on a yawn, and the Marshal leaned forward with his hand on the hilt of his sword. As the scribe announced each entry of the farm of the applicant's county, the chancellor's scribe checked it, the clerks checked it, and the applicants leaned over to arrange counters in the compartments of the table. Then he sorted out the credit before him into heaps in the same column, lower down.

The calling of items, the checking, the movement of counters in the squares on the table, closely watched by everyone, was completed at last. The applicant then subtracted his credits from the sum which he owed the Treasury, pence against pence, shillings against shillings, pounds against pounds. Now the whole room was tense, watching with breathless interest. The Marshal rose a little from his seat, with parted lips. The clerks completed their comparison of the notcht tallies kept by the sheriff's servants with the exchequer-foils. 'There,' said the applicant in triumph, 'not a penny is at fault.' The Treasurer nodded, the counters were swept off the board for the next trial of accounts. The Marshal sat back and the Justiciar yawned without shame.

Blaise rose and went to the door after a few words with one of the clerks. Outside, he waited for the sheriff who had just won the table-game. 'Ah, there you are, Master Rigeley!' cried the man, beaming and bustling. 'This is a pleasant day indeed.' They walked on, and the sheriff said with lowered voice, 'I shall not forget that your informations aided me in many ways.'

'I am honoured if that is so,' said Blaise, 'but you must not exaggerate my small service. Without it you would of course have balanced your accounts with equal certainty.'

'The will was good,' said the sheriff with a benevolent insistence. 'Now, Master Rigeley, I hear that you are becoming a land-owner in my county. We shall see more of one another, I trust, and you may rest assured that I am not a man who forgets a service.' He pressed Blaise's arm and changed the subject. 'Is there clear news of the battle fought at Graveline?'

'Nothing clear as yet.'

They parted at the Gates, and Blaise went on towards Whitehall. Great while clouds lay lazily in the deep blue sky. A carriage rolled past, and Blaise glimpsed a great lady sitting stiff with stomachered dignity and a sharp face of white clay. Passing the palace, he went on up to Charing Cross. An old woman was selling cockles; and a water-carrier lifted three-gallon tankards of conduit-water from a cart. Blaise crossed the road and went into a tavern.

x

In the inner room, by the cloth on which was painted Danae mounted by the Swan, Sir Francis was waiting, with Don Pedro aloofly smiling, and Walter Conyers with his crisped black beard and twinkling eyes. 'Here is our notable friend with the nymph of a wife,' said Conyers with a smirk. 'To lie nightly in such a field of plenty must require a husband of no mean abilities and resources. You are a bold man indeed.' He slapped Blaise on the back. 'Restore your veins with the blood of the grape, my Trojan, and I'll call for oysters and onions.'

Sir Francis laughed loudly and took out a dainty handkerchief embroidered with D, with which he flicked an orris-scent across his nostrils. 'Some men are interested in higher things than you, Walt.' He stood stiffly, afraid to move his head hastily lest he spoil the set of his neckinger.

'By higher things,' said Walt, 'men mean always either God or Gold. Now, most strangely, there is between these two words only the difference of an *ell*: which, aspirated by our labouring breath, becomes *hell*. Therefore between God and Gold is only an ell of difference, yet that ell entails hell.'

'Say that again,' said Don Pedro. 'It is so English a jest.'

Walt repeated his words with pleasure. Then he cried, 'Let us now turn to the oxen, the little bones, and let them speak for us; for their eloquence defeats us all. Tapster, give me the dice.' He looked round at his companions. 'Gresko, hazard, passage?'

'Hazard,' said Don Pedro, 'all is at hazard.'

They began tossing the dice in turn. 'I've won,' said Sir Francis.

'We hadn't started yet, had we?' demurred Blaise.

'I've won it and I'll have it,' said Sir Francis with a jarring laugh.

'I lose by one ace only,' said Don Pedro.

'One ace is enough to lose. One ace only lost St. Martin his cloak.'

Blaise pleaded a headache and went aside by the window-seat; and his place was taken by a tall dank-haired fellow, who won the next three casts to Sir Francis's cost. The tapster brought a fresh round of wine; and the fellow again rattled the dice. But Walt caught his wrist and swore at him. 'You're a cogger of dice. You slipped your own dice in the place of our honest ones. These of yours are horned, they're false, they're full of quicksilver.'

'The man's a rogue,' cried Sir Francis. 'It is unjust to cozen your companions in this manner. Aye, these dice run low.'

'They're highmen,' said Walt, throwing them into the air and scattering them over the floor, 'they're cut by-ace fashion.'

The man went scrabbling on the floor for the dice. Walt kicked him, and the man snarled up at him. 'Go to the gallows, you thief,' screamed Sir Francis, 'or I'll stab you through the hand with my poignard.' The man darted out of the room, amid pursuing howls of derision.

'But now I have let him go with my money,' Sir Francis complained leaning against the wall. He beckoned to Blaise, who came over almost falling as he trod on one of the lost dice. 'I need another fifty pounds by nightfall,' Sir Francis remarked in a drunken whisper.

'You shall have it,' muttered Blaise.

v

Stephen went straight up to the door and knocked. A thin servant girl whom he did not know answered the door. 'I wish to see both Mrs. Hudley and her daughter Mabel,' he said firmly. 'My name is Stephen Rigeley.' The girl stared at him in round-eyed surprise and withdrew one step, calling for her mistress.

'Who is there?' Mrs. Hudley answered from within the house, and then appeared wiping her hands with a hempen clout. 'Who is there?' She peered and came forward. 'Ah, it is you, Master Stephen. I thought perhaps you might come one of these days. Come in. There are matters I wish to inquire into with your help.' She crossed herself and led the way into the parlour, where a new carving in painted wood of the Virgin had been set up by the chimney.

'I shall call no Mabels,' said Mrs. Hudley, folding her arms, 'and it is not best in any manner that she should hear what we say. If that is all you had to propound, be silent and go, Master Stephen Rigeley, apprentice and (I fear) something worse.'

'You force me to speak plainly. Mabel is my wife, and I fear for her.'

Mrs. Hudley raised her hands in horrified amazement. 'O, that I should hear the son of a respected neighbour utter such a falsehood. Mabel is married to no man, least of all to such as you. Further, if there is anything to fear for her, it is only your own lewd and irreligious influences that endanger her, body or soul.' She crossed herself. 'How truly did Father Leo observe that where heresy gets into the head, venery gets into the nether regions, so that damnation is completed.'

'Mistress Hudley,' pleaded Stephen, 'you have heard the sweet words of the truth. How can you utter such vilifyings and forget the comfort of the spirit?'

'Better Christians than I have been misled for a season. But now I warn you, young man. Leave this house and never let me hear you coupling Mabel's name with your own, or I'll inform against you to the monks.' She came closer and almost struck him in the face as she whirled her arms about. 'It was you that kept my poor girl in the fields all a mayday. It was you that lured her out again while I was abroad, so that we feared for her life; and though I beat her till my arm ached, nothing would she say of her deceiver.'

'I feared this,' said Stephen, humbly and miserably.

'Who are you to go fearing, you ravisher?' she shouted. 'You may well fear the spikes of hell-fire, but yesterday you broke the body of my girl as bread is broken for the banquet, you drunken rioter.'

As she stood with her tremulous hands raised over his unresisting face, the door opened and Mabel came in. Mrs. Hudley at once lowered her hands and set them in her broad linen sleeves. 'Go back to the kitchen.'

'I am sorry, mother,' said Mabel in a small voice. 'But my husband is here, and I must obey him rather than you. Therefore, till he bids me go, I must stay.'

'Your husband, say you?' screamed Mrs. Hudley, 'rather the defiler of your soul and the gluttonous consumer of your body! You will bring ruin upon our house, you little whoring fool of heresy.'

'How can you use such words,' asked Stephen, 'remembering your holy brother who died in the Smithfield flames?'

'He was deceived, and such as you have sent his soul to worse fires.' Mrs. Hudley turned again upon him, and again seemed about to beat at his face. But instead she ran over to Mabel, tore her hair down, and hit her on the chest and face. Mabel stood there without a cry, with her arms hanging loose at her sides and her white-gold hair in shining disorder round her calm face. 'You fool, you fool!' Mrs. Hudley sobbed. 'Could you not wait a year till you were married to a better man with the Church's blessing? was there so much hot blood in this face of milk?'

Stephen came up behind and irresolutely caught her arms. She struggled a moment and then collapsed against him, so that he had to hold her with an arm round her waist. 'Villain,' she muttered, 'whoremonger . . . do what you will . . . you have wounded my maiden . . . you have set secret fires in the foundations . . .' She tore herself away and dropped at the feet of the painted Virgin, sobbing and praying. 'We are all lost.'

Mabel paid not the least attention to her mother. She looked with questioning eyes at Stephen. He took her hand: 'What can we do? If you come with me, the priest will send the sergeants after us . . . and my master also will be ruined . . . yet how can you stay here?'

'Let me stay,' she said calmly. 'I am not afraid. She cannot hurt me. I am quite happy.'

He kissed her in a long gentle kiss on the mouth. 'May I be as steadfast in the truth as you, my beloved. Wait for me. The time of our loving will return.'

'I am happy,' she said, with a faint smile. 'We shall meet another time. Am I not your bride?' She let him go without accompanying him to the outer door. But after a cold glance at her sobbing mother she also left the room, returning to the kitchen, where she went on scouring pewter with sand from a bucket, without remembering to draw up her hair again.

VI

The Bishop was sitting by the trellised wall under a canopy with gilt fringes, a long switch in his hand. Before him stood two lads of about seventeen years. 'I detest to see a comely lad with a stiff rebellious mind,' he said, blinking his red-rimmed eyes. 'Have mercy on yourselves, I beg you.'

One lad, short, with brows already furrowed, said bluntly, 'Yet I shall have none of your God-in-a-box, your jackanapes, my lord.' The Bishop lashed him across the throat. 'I'll be rackt under the earth before I kneel to a round-robin,' he went on stubbornly. 'My knees shall be pared off first.'

'Then we shall pare them,' said the Bishop, and flicked his face, 'but you shall acknowledge God.'

'Why, a baker made him. Such an idol is good to toast mutton, but that is all.'

The Bishop stood up and beat him furiously. Dust came out of the ragged clothes, then the clothes tore again, and the weals showed on the flesh. 'Take him away,' said Bonner, falling back in his seat. 'Away with his sodden-headed sheep-face and set him in the dog-kennel under the stairs.'

As the guards came up, the lad pointed to some black beads hanging on a nail in the trellis. 'I think the hangman is not far, my lord, for the halter is here already.' Then he was dragged away.

Bonner turned to the second lad. 'Are you as obstinate? I trust not; for you have a pleasant face.' He spat. 'Ah, I weary of you Arians, you Pelagians, you Herodians, you Sacramentaries, you Anabaptists. The earth is weary of you, and the heavens.' He touched the lad on the chin with the switch. 'Are you a villain, or as honest as you seem?'

'I shall do my best to please your lordship,' he answered blushing.

'That is better speech to hear,' said Bonner heartily. 'Come closer, my good fellow.' He took him under the chin and raised his face. 'No need to redden for a virtuous word. You shall be set free if you promise reformation and confess at once to your parish priest.'

'I promise, my lord.'

Bonner kissed him. 'Report to my house in St. Paul's on Saturday.' He called to the guard. 'Let this worthy young man depart in peace.' Rising, he belched slightly and broke the switch between his hands. Then, followed by his attendants, he went down to the river-bank and boarded his barge. 'To

Lambeth,' he said, with tight lips.

As they neared Lambeth, he saw boys swimming in the Thames and set two of his retainers ashore, who ran to cut the boys off along the banks, beating them with nettles and pulling them naked through nettle-bush and bramble. Some boys, swimming out, were almost drowned. One, who broke through the reeds, came near the barge; and the Bishop called to him, asking if he had learned his lesson. But the boy replied *No,* and scrambled up on the bank.

'Let him be taken and whipt,' cried the Bishop.

A retainer ran after the boy, shouting to a man who leant on the rail of the fence, to catch him. But the man did not stir.

'Let that man be taken and whipt,' cried the Bishop.

Then, as the retainers went towards him, the man ran off as well among the bushes.

VII

'Tell me another story, mistress, said Tabitha, tucking her dress in round her ankles against the slight breeze blowing up from the water. Sailors were unloading kegs from the near boat, and singing, stript to the waist in the bold sunlight.

Dousabel laughed her small laugh, took a pebble and cast it in the water. She watched the ripples break and flow away. 'This then,' she said, and laughed again. 'A certain man went to a priest saying that he wished to confess; and so the priest asked him to set forth his sins. The man then said that he had stolen something from another, but added that this other had stolen more from him. At which the confessor said that one thing cancelled out another, and the two men were quits. Then the man said that he had beaten a certain man with a stick, but added that this other had beaten him back. At which the confessor said that one thing cancelled out another, and the two men were quits. Then the penitent blushed and said he had yet another sin, which he was ashamed to utter. But the confessor urged him to set his shame aside and confess. So the man said: I once lay with your sister. At which the priest replied: And I have lain many times with your mother, therefore one thing cancels out another and we are quits.'

Tabitha laughed a long merry laugh and clapped her hands.

Dousabel added quietly, 'And in some such way I am quits with my man, though I cannot untangle the threads of good and evil in it at all.'

Tabitha thought awhile. 'It was a jest,' she said thoughtfully, 'and then you make it bitter as a friar's sermon.' She stared at the sailors, at the glistening green-brown of the waters, at the little red-sailed boat going by. 'Tell me yet another.'

Dousabel threw a second stone into the river. 'This then.' And she laughed her small tinkling laugh. 'A widow told her neighbour that though she cared little for the things of the world, she would like to find a peaceful man of advanced years to live with her, so that they might comfort one another. For she cared, she said, more for the welfare of the soul than the burden of the flesh. So the other woman promised to find her a man of such a sort, and next day came to the widow, saying that she had already found him, the very man whom the widow desired—for, in fact, he was a eunuch. Then the widow said: No, I won't have him at any price. I said that I wanted to live at peace with my husband, and how can we live at peace if when we quarrel, we have no means of making it up together?'

Again Tabitha laughed, but now she looked at her mistress, waiting for a further explication. 'Is that bitter too?' she asked.

'It is the tale of my own marriage,' said Dousabel in a withdrawn voice. 'Am I not afraid to quarrel with my husband because we should have no means of making it up after?' She shuddered. 'And would not such a ventless heat turn a murderous thing?' She rose. 'Let us go home. For we have nowhere else to go.'

VIII

Stephen heard the uproar and walked towards it down the dusty street. At the corner a man collided with him, and he saw that it was Merric. They eyed one another distrustfully. 'What is the tumult?' said Stephen.

'A Spaniard drew a dagger on a prentice,' replied Merric, 'in a dispute over a wench. And now I think that he and his companions have broken heads or worse.'

They turned and went on walking down the lanterned ways towards Broad Street. 'It is many months,' said Stephen, 'since we spoke together; and now so much has happened that I don't know where to begin.'

'What has happened to you which is so strange?' asked Merric with a slight interest. 'I thought you worked daily, said your prayers, and soundly slept. Can it be that a maid has got between you and your sleep?'

Stephen flushed. 'For your privy ear, Merric, I am married.'

'Married,' cried Merric, 'and to whom?'

'Mabel Hudley.'

Merric roared with laughter. 'My dear good Stephen, you are twice the man I am, and yet I have been jesting at you. But what will father say when he hears? and surely Mistress Hudley has found out?'

Stephen groaned. 'Merric, you understand little of what has happened. This my marriage, in a sense, is but a sign and advancement of deeper issues. We are plighted as far as the stake and the faggot.' He took Merric's arm. 'Do not tell me that you are of the Roman party.'

'I am of no party,' said Merric. 'I have no love of the monks, but I see no reason to die under their hands. I have my life to live.'

'Ah, but speak truly, brother. Do you live it?'

Merric was silent, 'I was told that I lurk in a shadow . . . But speak truly in turn, brother. Have you found the breath of life indeed? have you a sure foot on a tottering world?'

'I suffer,' said Stephen in a muffled voice. 'I suffer. But always I hold to something beyond the suffering, in which is certain fellowship, and I dare not deny it, whatever the cost.'

'It is no use,' said Merric thoughtfully. 'I too suffer in my way; but I suffer in large part because I am cut from my Jacint. What else there is in it I am ready to bear.' He hesitated and was about to say more, but held himself back. 'Yes, I am ready to bear it,' he repeated.

They came to the corner of Finkes Lane, and found Ybel idling there. 'But the world cannot fall thus headlong into

mire and cruelty,' persisted Stephen. Merric frowned, trying
to make Stephen break his discourses in Ybel's presence, and
then, finding that Stephen took no notice, he turned away and
left them.

'What were you saying?' asked Ybel.

'No man may claim the name of manhood in such a world
unless he works against it with all his strength, day and night.'

Ybel considered the proposition. 'You speak as one of the
reformed religion,' he said at length.

'And as an Englishman.'

Ybel looked round. 'You must not speak so openly. Merric
was afraid of your voice, I see. But I'm not easily scared as
he is. I'd like to hear more of what you say.' He whispered,
'There's a friend of mine shut in the coalhouse of the Bishop's
palace at Fulham this very moment.'

IX

Hugh sat writing at his table. 'A Brentford man tells me
that he saw the six faithful burned there on the fourteenth
of this month, all six known to me, having been apprehended
that day at Islington. Of whom I knew Robert Dynes most
well as a good and loving man. And Pikes the tanner: I spoke
once in anger to him, a slow-minded man, and never asked
his forgiveness. May I be forgiven. They had their articles
ministered to them by the bloody bishop's chancellor, a warty
man whose name I forget: every one of them remaining
strong for the truth. Now they are gone in the ravening fire.
I saw them three days before their death, at Pauls, where
they were nagged to deny their love, the good poor lambs:
two of the Queen's officers with baleful eyes stood despitefully
but vainly over them. The man tells me that at the burning a
marvellous cross as white as paper showed in the flames on
the praying face of my Robert Dynes, extending from shoulder
to shoulder, with a compass in every place as broad as a man's
hand.'

He paused with a sudden groan and beat on his head,
muttering an unintelligible name.

'I am afraid,' he said after a while, 'I am afraid and unworthy. It would be worse to fall down and deny the truth before all men's eyes, to the shame of the faithful, than to cry out privily in fear. Make me sure that I could bear the pain and the hours of waiting.' He groaned again. 'Rather clean out this rottenness from my bones. I shall come to it yet. O my child, my poor child . . . how have I sinned against you?' He beat his heart. 'O the barren hypocrite, O the whited sepulchre. My friends have love, but I remain nailed to a rusting fear. Lord, send down your most wrathful angel to hiss against me . . .'

Shuddering, he took up the paper on which he had been writing the memorial of the Brentford martyrs and hastened into the kitchen. There he knelt before the sinking fire and thrust the paper into the pale glow. It burst into flame and he let it go, but still knelt there. Then he cried out in mortal terror as Rosbel came in slippered silence behind him, thrusting her chin upon his shoulder and breathing hotly against his ear.

x

Hawes, in the shop, was talking with two fellow cloth-workers. One, Pryce, was telling of a Venetian inventor who had offered the Company a machine to full broadcloth, but had been sent off with a noise of thanks and twenty shillings as a gift. 'No, I didn't see it,' said Hawes. 'I am not a man drawn by such piddling toys.'

'Rather, devil's devices,' said Hill, who was chewing nutmeg against his face-ache. 'It would cause the decay of the Company if it were used, and throw most of the craftsmen into lack of work. Which reminds me that we must bring up anew the matter of fixing wages at a lower rate.' He winced and touched his swollen face. 'Also, let us petition against the haberdashers who act as middlemen of the crafts, supplying tin to pewterers and yarn to weavers.' His bloodshot eye roved round in quest of something else to protest against. Finding nothing, he groaned.

'We must apply again for searching rights against the Merchant Taylors,' said Hawes. 'They despise us as craftsmen young in incorporation. At the same time we must fight against the new threat to control prices and prevent imports.' Hawes widened his straddle and assumed his most important tones. 'I have seen many such ordinances, and all they did was to cause a lack of the wares that were to be made cheap. Nature will have her course, I say, even if she is expelled with a fork; and never shall you drive her to consent that a pennyworth of new ware is sold for a farthing. For who will keep a cow, that may not sell the milk for as much as the merchant and he can agree together?'

The others nodded hard, and Hill even forgot his face-ache. Hill and Pryce went out, and Hawes hurried up into the solar. 'The king's sheriff is a sick man, and likely to die soon; and then I shall be sheriff, there is no doubt of it.'

Gertrude, whom he hadn't noticed, broke in, 'Will it then be necessary for you to sell your name to a patched-up widow in order to gild yourself with the dung of her money? I pray for your soul's sake that you may shake her off and wipe yourself clean.'

'Are you there?' he asked, confounded. 'How you jump to hasty conclusions.'

'Better than to jump to hasty marriages. Hasty pudding never did anyone good but the bitch under the table. For he that pays no heed to what he sets in his mouth may spit out more than he swallows.'

'We have settled all this before.'

'It is well for you to say that a matter is settled when it unsettles all other matters. For those who think that a bit of straw will hold a mad mare are like to win a fall in the ditch. A curst woman will have her sharp word at midnight though you buttered her mouth at supper. Here indeed is a pestilent and slippery snake, said the man who tried to drown the eel.'

'You have broken your wit with proverbs,' he said and hurried out.

'Better than to break my neck with a marriage-halter,' she called after him. Then she added pityingly to Martin. 'They say that youth will have its swing though it be in a rope; but an aged neck in a gawdy garter is a dirtier death.'

Jacint looked in. 'What has angered father? I suppose it is you, Aunt Gertrude.'

'I?' exclaimed Gertrude with uplifted palms. 'I said nothing to him but the plainest truth, and in the kindest way of morality that I have ever used to an erring soul. No, no, my dear Jacint, do not believe it. I have done nothing to anger him. It is his tormented conscience that sits in all his old wounds.'

Jacint closed the door and ran up to her Uncle Rafe's room. 'You are to take me to St. James's Fair tomorrow. I was going to let you idle free on a holiday inside your books; but when I looked in the solar, Martin had so dark a face, I gave him up. Nowadays we cannot bear one another.' She whispered, 'I'd like to know why Tace looks at him with new eyes since St. John's Vigil.'

'You have quite run from your lessons these last weeks.'

'I can learn more from the missel-thrush than all your Ovids in such a summer.' She went to the window. 'Has it always been like this? A mad world with the swell of burning flesh on the breeze when it blows from Smithfield. Sometimes I lie considering it before I sleep; and then I embrace myself and think of apple-blossom, and the bubble-faces blow away. Tell me, Rafe, are you and I the only ones on the earth who have such thoughts and such dreams? are the others as mad as they seem? above all . . .'

'Above all,' he said, coming up and putting his arm on her shoulder, 'is Merric inside this circle you have traced, or is he outside it among the others?'

'Yes.' She put her head on his shoulder. 'I should rather not die a maid; but I shall take the man of my own choosing or none at all.'

He pointed to a kite hovering over the roofs. 'There it goes, the bird of prey, the carrion-feeder. And below the mongrel dogs gulp and choke among the heaps of offal. Are we kites or mongrel-dogs, Jacint?'

'Rather than say yes, I'd defy the Bishop and go to the stake. Yet I wish to prove myself more than the kites and the dogs, and still not go into the solitude of the fire.'

He gave a sighing laugh. 'Luckily we need not decide the matter here and now. Today you will translate me a rowdy poem of Catullus, and tomorrow we shall go quietly to the Fair.'

The Fair was held at Westminster; and the bright day brought hundreds from the City to get cheese at a penny a pound, shoot at apples with crossbows, or buy milk from the maid who milked a cow with gilt horns into a silver tankard. Merric went early and loitered with Stephen near Charing Cross, watching the people come down the Strand from the City. Ybel joined them; but as he found them taciturn and unconcerned about the possibility of wrestling-matches, he left them.

Dousabel and her maid came up from their side-street, but Merric turned away till they had passed. Then, after a while, Agnes and Sanchia. Agnes stared at Merric, but he made no sign for her to stop, and she went on. Then at last he saw Jacint coming with her stooping withered Uncle Rafe, and loitering at a distance, Lettice. 'Here comes Jacint Hawes,' said Stephen, as if surprised to see her again. 'It must be two years since I spoke with her. You once told me that you meant to marry her.'

'I still say it. Now let them go by without seeing us.'

They went into the shadow of a pent-roof till Jacint and her uncle had passed, then followed after. 'What are you going to do?' asked Stephen.

'I don't know. Perhaps we shall go straight to them and speak.'

By the time they had come into the first way between booths, they were close behind; and then a sudden press of people from a sideway pushed Jacint back. Merric elbowed forward till he could touch her shoulder. 'Goodday, Mistress Jacint.'

Without looking round, she answered, 'Goodday, Master Merric.'

Rafe glanced back and said, 'We are well met, my friend.'

'We are in no way well met,' said Jacint, 'for in this noisy confluence we are like to be compressed into one flesh: which is a sin before holy matrimony gives the unholy word.'

But at that moment the crowding eased, and Merric drew Stephen up. 'I am glad to see you, Stephen,' said Rafe. 'I think you and I are more solemn-minded than our companions, and I have many things I should like to broach with you. Let us find a lair on the edges, among the pegs of the booths, where we may distil afresh the deadly truth out of apple-juice.' He took Stephen's arm, and turned to let Merric and Jacint slip away.

They slipped away to the river bank; but no sooner were they seated by an old pier than a dozen young boys came running up to throw off their clothes and plunge into the water. 'Let them splash us,' said Jacint. 'We are none of us so clean that a sprinkling of river water will mar our faces.' She leaned forward to watch the boys. 'Now you have your will and we are alone.' She laughed her gurgling laugh. 'For these young divers might as well be silver river-birds. Tell me what you have wanted so long to tell.'

'I love you.'

'Your voice comes from far away, a voice from across the waters. If you were at my side, I might answer.' He tried to take her in his arms, but she pushed him away. 'That isn't what I meant.'

'You have been kindlier of late,' he said weakly. 'I hoped you had come to love me.'

'I have come to love others less. Sometimes it seems that that has made me love you more—or rather, love you a little. But then I grow unsure. Perhaps I feel like that because there is no one but you who keeps plaguing me with words of love. I know hardly anything of you; and what I know is not much to my liking. You have changed much over the last year.'

'Yet at moments it has seemed that we know one another to the very quick. That time you came to me in the shadow on the Eve of St. John.'

'Did you also feel it? I am glad. Now for the first time I begin to think there may be a true love between us. Tell me more of yourself. How have you felt since then?'

He hesitated. 'I have longed for you . . .' He felt her eyes searching him, and he went on, 'Yes, and I hated myself. I felt that I wished to pull down the roof of the world; but the feeling grew dim and ugly, as evil a thing as the evil it abhorred.'

'Go on. I know that man of whom you speak.'

His face was set in an extreme effort of thought. 'I spoke with Stephen and was drawn for a while to join him and his friends.' He paused. 'In telling you this, I show my entire faith in my love for you and the love it should gain as answer from your soul. For I am putting Stephen in your hands; and though I have my wickedness, I should die rather than betray my brother. Therefore if you betrayed him through what I tell you, I should kill you . . . No, I should go to the stake with him and die there in simple bitterness, as the sole atonement I could make.' He put his hands over his face. 'It grows tangled and more tangled. What was I saying?'

'That you spoke with Stephen and thought to join him.'

'Yes.' He sat up. 'But I cannot hear the voice that he hears in his soul. I am so torn from my old bonds that if men were to rise against the Spaniards, I should join them; but I cannot take on myself to claim a guidance of grace against the Bishops.' He paused. 'There again I have put myself at your mercy.'

'Is it necessary to tell me so?' she asked coldly.

'No, I was at your mercy before I said any of these things.'

'Yet you want me to swear my secrecy.'

'No.'

'You still want it, but you are trying hard to feel otherwise.' They were silent awhile, and the boys splashed and dived beside them. Then she said, 'Now you are beginning to hate me a little. And that is right. You have spoken with much truth, and I have given you nothing in return.' She cut him short. 'No, don't speak yet. I am beginning to know you and to love you; and if I decide at last that I love you in wholeness, I shall come to you whatever my father may say or do.'

They sat unspeaking again. 'I seem to have no place in the world, except here at your side,' he said at length.

'Your brother Stephen is a good man,' she said, plucking at the grass, 'though he is not one whom I could love save in a sisterly way. You must cherish him; for you are not so good, though you are one whom I can love in a way not at all sisterly.'

'Are you asking me to go to the stake with him?'

'No, no, but I am none the less asking you to learn from him.'

'How do you know so much about Stephen?'

'I have known him as a lad, and I had only to look into his face this afternoon to know the rest, to know the man who has grown from the lad.'

'He is married to Mabel Hudley, in secret.'

She furrowed her brows. 'That indeed surprises me; but I am still sure of his goodness. As for her, I know her only as a slight slip of a white thing.' Then she turned again to watch the boys, scattering the grass-blades she had torn up. 'How cleanly are they alive. How nobler they look unclothed. But they are still young.' She smiled. 'Younger than Eve and Adam at the Fall.'

'And what was the age of those two when they fell.'

'The age of you and me.' She laughed. 'Now you may kiss me.'

He gave her a long tender kiss, and then she stood up, saying that her Uncle would be expecting her. Merric tossed a silver coin into the river and bade the boys dive for it.

Rafe and Stephen were waiting up towards the Cross. 'I think we agree more than you fancy,' said Rafe. 'But I use different names for the purposes of men and mother nature than you do. I see in all things a mystery and yet at the end I desire to set the things on the table of my senses for no ignoble banquet.' He mused. 'Perhaps I differ in this, that I touch compassion at the heart of the living. I cannot take sides in your dispute because I pity both the judge and the condemned, the oppressor and the oppressed.'

'Did not our martyrs know a deeper compassion when they cried for forgiveness on their murderers, yet died still in their faithful love?'

Rafe shook his head. 'I make no claims. I take no sides, and yet I am on your side. And then again I am alone in a mystery.'

Stephen shaded his eyes. 'I see them coming now.' He went on eagerly, 'Let us talk again, I beg you.'

'It is more to my good than yours that it should be so.'

They stood silent till Merric and Jacint came up. Jacint said, 'I have been telling Merric about my father's white-leaded widow.' She looked round, 'O, I have quite forgotten Lettice.'

'I saw her with a tall young man,' said Rafe, 'buying pins from a pedlar. Leave her to come home at her own pace; for she has pins enough to mend any tears in her dress.'

As they went off, she asked Rafe, 'Did you see Martin at the Fair?'

'No,' he said, thinking of something else.

XII

A servant of one of the bailiffs threw a faggot at his face, so that the blood gushed out in divers places: for the which fact the sheriff reviled him, calling him cruel tormentor, and with his walking-staff brake his head, so that the blood likewise ran about his ears. When the fire was kindled and began to take hold upon their bodies, they lifted up their hands towards heaven, and quietly and cheerily, as though they felt no smart, they cried, 'Lord Jesus strengthen us.' And so they continued without any struggling, holding up their hands and knocking their hearts, and calling upon Jesus until they had ended their mortal lives.

Among other things this is also to be noted, that after their three heads, by the force of the raging and devouring flames of fire, were fallen together in a plump or cluster, which was marvellous to behold, and that they all were judged already to have given up the ghost, suddenly Palmer, as a man waked out of sleep, moved his tongue and jaws, and was heard to pronounce the word 'Jesus.'

XIII

The attendant told him that the Treasurer was in the Garden by the Pond. Blaise went on, and looked about among the shining heraldic beasts who guarded the flowers inside their rails of white and green. A page told him the Treasurer had gone in only a few minutes before. Blaise hurried back into the palace, to an arrased waiting-room, with perfumed cloths of diaper on the table and diamond-leaded window-panes. An official looked in, scowled, failed to answer Blaise's question, and went off. Somewhere a girl was laughing a sweet long laugh. Blaise made some calculation on his fingers, then went to the window and stared through one of the clearer panes, rubbing it with his sleeve.

The Queen and Cardinal Pole went strolling by, and he put his eye close against the glass to see them as long as possible. The Queen's hands were folded over her bulging girdle. The Cardinal was slowly waving the beads in his hand as he talked. They went out of sight round a tall hedge.

Sallow and shrunken-faced, Mary tightened her lips yet tighter. She was dresst in a sort of man's gown with a long trailing underpetticoat. A gold chain glittered round her cap, and sewn gems on her gowns. She walked slowly, mastering something stiff and painful in her body. Pole, lean and taciturn, looked down on her slight sick frame, himself hollow-eyed and uncertain in his movements, holding his gown up towards his throat.

'You have had news of Rome from Carne?' he asked at length.

'Yes,' she answered in a deep gruff voice, 'but nothing to the purpose. Only what he has said before, that the friar's death has quieted the debate and there seems no likely movement to revoke your legations again.'

He sighed. 'God will decide. He knows the weariness of my heart. Yet He knows also, unless I am much deceived, that I shrink from no burden if it is useful to His Church.'

Mary looked at him a moment and paused. 'My lord, you must not ail. With my beloved husband away, I need your loyal voice, being as I am blest with child.' She crossed herself. 'Ah, what hammers can break these hard hearts? What engines can open these closed ears?' She stiffened. 'Yet they shall be broken, for God is the hammer. They shall hear, for God speaks in His Church.'

They came to a sunny seat half-shaded by a rose-bower; and she slowly seated herself, motioning him to sit at her side. 'Tell me what is in your thoughts, my sweet lord?'

Whether it is the old story, or a new turn of malice against me, tell it.'

'There is nothing new. I have sought again to lessen the charges on the Crown, and they murmur that the dismissals increase the number of the poor.' He sighed. 'I have done what I must do, under God's will. Having seen in Italy so clearly how a pestilence reigning in the body politics dissevers the parts, I have mourned to see the fate come upon my England, where no man or condition of men keeps to an appointed course. This is the ground of all ruin of policy.'

'Yet you foresee it and act against it.'

'Have I not sought to knit all together in a unity?' he went on meditatively. 'So that by common law and authority every part may exercise its office and duty—that is, every man in his craft and faculty may meddle only with such things as pertain to it. For nothing causes so great malice, envy and debate in city and town as one man meddling in the craft and mistery of another. Then one man is not content with his own profession and manner of living; but ever when he sees another more richer than himself, he despises his own faculty and runs to the other . . .' He sighed. 'And of such evil meddling is heresy the worst of all, a cancer more pernicious to the commonwealth than any thieves, murderers or adulterers. No kinds of treason are to be compared with theirs who undermine the chief foundation of a realm, which is religion, and so give an entry to all vices and confusions, all greeds and covetings. Therefore the briars must go to the fire.'

'Aye,' she said distractedly, 'the world is ungrateful . . .' Her mouth set in a yet tighter line, and she looked heavily around. 'They grudged me my marriage though I entered into it with no thoughts of bodily comfort, but only for my people's good. They cried out against it, and in their carnality came between me and God's will.' Her voice weakened and her eyes closed. 'What has darkened the way when all was so clear? What has made crooked the way that ran so straight? How have we failed?'

Pole was still staring ahead. 'If the fault is mine, if I have shed one drop of unrequired blood, may I pay for it through all the eternities of God; but let the work not fail . . .' He turned in time to see her swaying. 'O my dear mistress . . .'

He caught her by the shoulder as she was slipping from the seat. 'Where are your women?' He raised his voice: 'Where are the Queen's women?'

XIV

'Let us look at yonder bank,' said Nest. 'That seems a likely place.' Sanchia ran on ahead over the grass. Then before Nest had crossed half the ground she had run back with a handful of little white flowers, eagerly asking if they were eyebright. 'No, no,' said Nest, with a knowledgeable puckering of the lips, 'these are not sprinkled and powdered on the inner side with yellow and purple specks. The time is a trifle early, but the summer has been dry, and I'll forswear malmsey for a month but we go home with a handful.'

Sanchia ran off again, but stopped and called back, 'What did you say the edges of the leaves were like?'

'Snipt and saw-edged are the leaves,' said Nest. She saw a woman coming down from the thicket on the left, and shaded her eyes to watch. The woman came with a steady plodding gait, with eyes on the grass and folded hands holding a small basket in front of her. As she came near, Nest said, 'So it's you, Tace Kemp. I thought I knew your manner of going.' Tace looked up with contracted brows, and made a slight backward movement. 'Run away then if you must bear your master's enmities on your head as well as your own privy troubles.'

'I am sorry, Mistress Rigeley,' Tace said. 'It is long since we met and had a pleasant word together.' She tossed her dark head. 'It's the way of the world. Some mount higher, and others sink to the muck.'

'I heard that your master was marrying again,' said Nest, vigorously nodding. 'He who takes a corpse to bed may wake in the grave.'

'And so he shall, if wishes may do it,' said Tace with a high wild laugh. 'I have gone so far, and may go no farther. I have eaten my bellyful of shame, and now comes the vomit. But some may vomit toads, I am told, and toads are noisome things.'

Sanchia came running over with some more small white flowers. 'Are these eyebright?'

'No, child, I told you that eyebright had small hairy roots, not these long and dingle-dangling things.' She turned to Tace. 'I seek eyebright to distill with mace, for an old man's eyes, though I shall myself be glad enough to take some of the water in white wine of a morning. For all the gates of my sense are closing up, yet death will thereby find an entry all the easier.'

'Yellow and purple specks?' asked Sanchia, and then, at Nest's nod, sped away again.

'Ah, that I had my young legs back,' said Nest. 'How I would run. How I would run to many things that are now lost to me. How I would clap my legs and bid them run.'

'I'll be going on,' said Tace after a moment. 'You were ever a kind woman, Mistress, with a pleasant word for those of lesser condition. I pray that the years have a purse of pleasure yet to open in your lap . . .' Her mouth quivered. 'I had meant to go without a word to any living soul; but you have revived old gentleness, and I ask you to set a flower on my dead body and a prayer on my lost soul.'

'Fie on such talk,' said Nest. 'What have you there in your basket, Tace Kemp?'

She lifted the canvas flap before Tace had time to draw back. 'Nothing,' Tace said thickly. 'There's a cat I'd set free from a life of mange and hunger, but I cannot catch her to wring her neck.' She faltered to a·stop, with hanging jaw.

'You mustn't do it,' whispered Nest.

'You have seen nothing,' muttered Tace, setting her mottled hand over the flap. 'You have seen nothing. You took me unawares, speaking with such a kindness . . . Whatever I do, I do as I am driven. You have seen nothing.'

Nest crinkled up her face and narrowed her eyes. 'My heart is clear and I have warned you, Tace Kemp. But I have seen nothing.' She licked her lips and smiled. 'I too have suffered, as all women must suffer for the Eve they carry under the navel; I still weep in the darkness for the unstaunched wound of the snake. But I am unconsoled, and therefore rebellious . . .' She looked round. 'This is a hidden matter, easier to meditate than mouth. But I heard a friar once say that woman has had a great wrong and that the righting of it would be a joyous restoration of delights undreamed . . .' She pressed Tace's hand. 'Go your way with a careful tread, but I have seen nothing.'

As Tace moved away, Sanchia came running up with yet another wildflower. 'Is this it?'

'No,' said Nest. 'Now I shall show you how to find it.'

xv

William let Blaise in. He looked with an obsequious fear, smiling, but said nothing. 'You are a fortunate man,' said Blaise, clinking some coins.

'You have raised the money then?'

'Yes, though the terms are a little harder than I thought.'

. 'How is that?' William put his trembling hands behind his back and spoke with a flat voice.

'You will have to add your house as security, and the houses you rent in Southwark. Also the Wapping tenements.'

William bowed his head. 'Yes.'

'Also a clause binds you to share, in certain proportions, any merchandising ventures into which you may enter.'

'Am I to tie myself for life,' cried William, 'to an unknown usurer?'

'First, he is known to me, though he has exacted my solemn promise to hide his name. Second, he ties you for ten years only.'

William gave a bitter laugh. 'Ten years only.'

'Thirdly,' said Blaise, unabashed, uncrossing his legs, 'he tells me that he sets this clause about ventures in the paper, not through greed, but through a wish to draw you from rash projects, which for some reasons he considers you addicted to. And in return for certain aids you can give him, he is ready to advance you a share in ventures of his own.'

'And where do you stand, brother, in this tangle of taking and giving, giving and taking?' asked William with angry sarcasm.

'I desire your good,' said Blaise, ignoring his tone of voice, 'that it may be my own; and if all goes well, my good shall be yours also. For many years you have kept me at a distance, moving among the great men of the city and looking upon me as a clerk who might hear much gold clink, but never in his own pocket.' He slid from unctuous protestation into a triumphant note not without menace. 'Is it strange then that I am pleased to show a knowledge of golden mines closed from your sight? We meet henceforth as equal fellows, or not at all.'

'This is indeed a new voice,' said William with answering haughtiness. But at that moment the door swung open and old Fabyan stumbled in. 'I am busy, father,' William began, but was silenced by a shout.

'Busy! Indeed you are busy, you are too busy, let me tell you, but not busy enough in the right matters.' Fabyan turned to Blaise. 'I am glad you are here, and I have sought this moment for telling Will my anger and my plain intention. You are the only one of my sons who has shown a proper regard for my dignity, and I wish you to hear all I have to say to my eldest villain before I smite him to the ground.'

'Father,' Willliam demanded in a loud voice, 'tell me in what I have offended.'

'I'll tell you that,' said Fabyan, nodding and grinning, 'I'll tell you that soon enough. I'll tell you that in a voice reaching from Flete to Tower and Moorgate to Bermondsey, till no one in the whole world has failed to hear. You are the lowest thing in all London, William. You are a bankrupt and therefore a damned man.'

'Where have you heard such tales?'

'Where have I heard them? Where should I hear them but in the streets and the shops, the taverns and the churches? Yet if you will know the place and time as sharp as a document of the law, I'll tell you. It was at the house of Hugh Wokins, my poor old friend. I had gone once again to commiserate with him on the hard way that time has treated his liver and spleen. Then a tall huffling fellow comes in, who hears my name and declares for all to hear: Are you related to that bankrupt cheat William Rigeley, whose bills are now not worth the paper they have blotted?'

William flushed darkly; and Blaise glanced with a malicious

smile of grief at his crestfallen state. 'It is all lies, father,' William began.

But Fabyan still had some breath left. 'In all my days and nights I never had such lies spread of me. Let me tell you, William, when such lies are told about a tradesman, he is lost.'

'I tell you there was some mistake, or the fellow was a scandalmonger hired by my enemies.'

'Only a falling man can breed such bold-tongued enemies,' replied Fabyan. 'Yet I would not deny you your right to fall into the bottomless pit, if only your own credit was concerned. But if you are a broken man, what is to come of the covenant you have signed to keep me in a fitting dignity? Are you to pull me down among your pitiful devils in rags of fustian and a sup of barley-gruel? Are you to take my Edgar from me and set me in a leaky shed? Are you to ensure my damnation in the world-to-come because I shall be ashamed to step inside my parish church among my old companions? O, but you may grin at the trick you have played me, yet I'll have my revenge, both here in our Mistery and hereafter at the Judgment Day. God Himself is a father, don't forget, and though you may scorn my words, He'll give you a flea in the ear to your consternation.'

'There is no danger whatever of my breaking,' said William, 'and all your words are a mere fluster of chaff in the wind.'

'You shall come with me at once to the Master,' said old Fabyan, 'to be shamed before the Livery. That at least I can do. And what is yet to be saved from the fire of your fortunes is mine. In that I am sure the Master will vindicate me.' He turned to Blaise. 'And you, Blaise, my one obedient son, are to come beside me, as a sign that the Rigeleys are not wholly graceless.'

Blaise bowed his head. William, breathing hard, looked at him in turn. 'If our father will not listen to me, will you please tell him that there is no fear of my falling. Tell him that at the very moment of his coming we were discussing an agreement which sets my fortunes on a higher rock than before. Tell him that our credits are now one.'

'It is true, father,' said Blaise, 'and I will give you any satisfactions you desire. William has indeed suffered some reverses, but they are now turned to his advantage, and never was our house in happier condition.'

Old Fabyan regarded him closely as he spoke. 'This is better news,' he said calmly. 'Let me know more of it.'

Blaise glanced slyly at William. 'We are in entire accord on the course to be followed?'

William nodded. 'In all ways we agree.' He bowed his head.

XVI

As she neared Charing Cross, Dousabel laid her hand on Tabitha's arm, and they halted. Dousabel turned and waited till Christopher Jones came up with a sly grin. 'Why are you following me?'

'You don't recognise me, kinswoman? Yet I am the brother of Mistress Nest Rigeley, and thus in a good sense your brother, since the sacrament of holy matrimony has made her your sister.'

'I recognise you well enough,' she said calmly. 'But whether you are brother or no-brother, there is still no reason why you should follow me all about the City and then down the Strand.'

'I met you by chance, mistress, but followed by design.'

'And that design?'

'To speak with you.'

'Yet now you speak, and say nothing. Come, Tabitha.'

'May I go with you, for what I wish to say needs a quieter place and more than a dozen words?'

'However quiet the place and many the words, we should still be as far from an understanding.' She turned to go.

'No, mistress, you shall not so easily leave me and my unspoken words.' He walked on beside her.

'I have read your face. Leave me.'

'You are not so disobliging with many others. You receive them into a busy quiet, eh?' He grinned into her face.

'I like to oblige my friends.'

'You are a house with many frequented entrances,' he began, but she cut him short.

'Master Jones, the house is my own and it has no door for

you. I know you better than you think, and I tell you that there is nothing to be gained by your baiting of me.'

'You have a pretty jewel on your finger,' he said with another grin. 'May I see it?'

'As the world may see it, but no nearer.'

'You may regret this hasty dismissal on a later day.'

She shook her head. 'No, whatever came, I should never regret it.'

With a mock-bow he let her go.

CHAPTER NINE

August

I

A THRUSH WAS singing lustily from the cherrytree. Agnes stood beside the broken statue of some saint, with grass growing in the stone hand. Behind her stood Sanchia with a parcel in her disdainful hand, and before her stood Sister Orabilis, scratching one leg with the toes of the other. 'She's gone.' She looked round as if suspecting that Mary might still be hiding nearby, under one of the bushes. 'She's gone.' She lowered her voice. 'And the porter lost his shirt and breeches at the same time. She must have taken them.'

'Did she show by any signs beforehand what she had in thought?'

'She told me that she had a great thing laid on her, to astonish the profane world, and that all would be duly revealed. Also, that everything would be reversed in the world, as we reverse a cloak when it is worn out, finding a new life for it through the lining turned to the world's eyes, so she would turn all things inside out and show an exalted providence. But she had said many such things at divers times, so that I paid no special heed. Afterwards, however, I remembered and wept.'

'Can you interpret her words?'

'Darkly I took them to mean that she intended a work for the faith and a peculiar revelation of virtue. There is much holy and edifying rivalry in this place.' The nun became sad. 'Therefore her words were not unusual. Though I myself am never visited by angels or led by the spirit into an endurance of whips and fasts beyond the others. I do in humbleness what I can, and that is all. When she spoke to me, I thought it meant no more than ordinary in the way of miraculous events; but now I fear for her.'

Agnes considered, then she said, 'I brought her some cheesecakes.'

The small nun's eyes glistened but, she said nothing. The thrush burst in a yet-gayer song, and a sparrow alighted on the grass in the broken saint's open hand.

'You were her best friend here,' said Agnes. 'Will you take them?'

'To waste is a sin,' said the nun and took the cakes from Sanchia, who yawned and stared up to find the singer in the treetop. The nun put the cakes in the bosom of her dress.

'Send me word if any news comes of her,' said Agnes, turning away.

II

'The men have brought the plate on loan from the Company,' said Martin to his father, who nodded importantly.

'I shall be late for the service at Paul's,' he grumbled. 'Have the women finished with my cap? Where are the new laces that I set out?' He bustled from the solar.

'He has grown three inches since he became the King's Sheriff,' said Jacint from her window-corner, setting down her samplar. 'When he becomes alderman we shall have to rebuild our doors.' She smiled, 'Unless the widow brings his pride down and teaches him the gap between will and act.'

'You talk too easily of such matters,' said Martin thickly, without looking at her.

'Passion of my heart, I shall cease talking about them when I am a married woman, because I shall have larger opportunity for their enactment. It is a maid's privilege to talk lewdery, as it is a wife's to turn words into deeds.'

'Some do not wait . . .' He blurted the question out, 'Tell me, were you with Merric at St. James's Fair?'

'Ask Merric himself if you wish to know. Who has told you these tales?'

Tace came in, and, seeing Martin, stood with half-open mouth and pleading eyes. But he frowned at her. She turned away, then looked back, muttering, 'Why are you become so unkind?'

He shrugged. 'I am neither kind nor unkind.'

'You spoke differently once . . .'

He frowned again, 'I am talking with my Jacint and have no time for these other matters.' He turned aside, and after one more glance of disregarded appeal she went out.

'Some do not wait,' said Jacint. 'Those were your words. Of whom did you speak?'

'Of you and Merric!' he shouted. 'Let me tell you once for all that if you play with that villain to anger me, I shall indeed be angered. Do you dare to smile?' He advanced towards her.

'I dare to smile.'

Aunt Gertrude looked in. 'Where is Tace gone? O, Jacint, your father is in a trampling fury. Someone has mislaid his cap, and he swears that I did it to annoy him.' She withdrew and could be heard calling, 'Tace, Tace . . .'

'The world is mad, and I am still smiling,' said Jacint.

'If you speak with him again, I shall kill him, do you hear?'

'Yes, sweet brother, I hear you.'

A heavy thump somewhere in the house shook the floor. Hawes was yelling in the backyard. Lettice came screaming up to the solar door and beat upon it. Then the door opened and she entered, followed by Rafe. 'Tace has hanged herself over the master's bed,' she howled.

'She isn't dead,' said Rafe. 'There is no need for such noises. I cut her down and Gertrude is seeing to her.'

'What are you all doing here?' shouted Hawes, stamping in. 'Where is my new cap? What cross-eyed devil of hell has hidden it?'

'Tace has tried to hang herself over your bed,' said Jacint.

Hawes scowled, then he said, 'Manifestly she is the person who had my cap. Can she speak? I'll teach her to set her malice against my new dignities.'

He was about to leave the room when Gertrude came in. She caught his last words. 'For shame, Gregory,' she said. 'If you want that tawdry cap, it lies in the cypress chest over there. But it would befit you better to think of the sin that lies on your soul if Tace dies.'

'She won't die,' said Hawes, going to the chest. 'But if my cap is too crumpled for wearing, I shall be angrier than you have yet seen me.'

III

'How can you live without opposing yourself to such a world?' said Stephen to Merric as they walked down Chepe.

'I have no liking for the world,' said Merric, 'but what use is there in dashing my head against the unregarding stones.'

'The stones will give way.'

'Many heads have been broken but the stones are still there.' He paused, and then said, 'Yet Jacint, whom I love, told me to listen to you.'

'Is she one of ours?' cried Stephen joyfully. 'The Lord be praised.'

'No, she is no more with you than I am, and no more against you. But I think that I know her meaning. I feel a hardness here.' He touched his chest. 'I want to break it, yet I cannot. I feel it as a sort of fear that drives me into doing things I despise.'

'It is the old man, the death in your soul. Turn as we have turned, to the only source of love, and wash the bitterness away.'

They walked on, turning into a sidestreet. 'I shall make myself a better man,' said Merric suddenly. 'That at least I can do.'

'Not alone,' protested Stephen, 'not without grace and fellowship. Else you will backslide into the old deceits by new ways.'

They passed some tenements, where a fat woman sat on a doorstep suckling a babe at each breast. At her side sat a young woman with parched yellow face shivering with fever. 'Tell me what you hope to do?' said Merric. 'Perhaps I may be able to help without sharing all your creed.' He looked back at the woman in the doorway. 'There is so much that a man dares not think or know.' Then with sudden resolution, he added, 'No matter, I am with you, for mere manhood's sake. I can live no longer as I have lived. Anything is better.'

IV

John Boswell, the Bishop's Scribe to Bonner, Bishop of London:

It may please your good lordship to be advertised, that I do see by experience that the sworn inquest for heresies do most commonly indict the simple, ignorant and wretched heretics, and do let the arch-heretics go; which is one great cause that moves the rude multitude to murmur, when they see the simple wretches (not knowing what heresy is) to burn. I wish, if it may be, that this common disease might be cured among the jurats of Essex; but, I fear me, it will not be, so long as some of them be, as they are, infected with the like disease.

From Maldon. Your lordship's poor officer and daily beadman, John Boswell.

V

A slight tap on the door, and Jones came in. William rose in anger from his chair. 'I told you never to enter this house again. Who let you in?' He clenched his fist and moved forward.

'Nest let me in,' said Jones quickly and pleadingly. 'For I have news deeply touching your life and fortune.' He retreated, but went on speaking, 'You are betrayed. You are betrayed. I know who has the gold.'

William halted and lowered his hand. 'Tell me then in one word.'

There was a pause. Jones rubbed his nose. 'I can't tell you in such a flockmell way. Give me time to set the matter duly forth.'

'A name needs little breath. Say it, and then I may listen to more.'

'First let me explain how I came to the knowledge.'

'The name, the name, or out you go.'

Jones scratched his beard, cocked his head on one side, and said with a slight leer, 'Blaise.'

William swayed and took a deep breath. 'How do you know?'

'I found I'd been on the wrong trail in suspecting Ben. So I thought again. I drank night and day for a week, to clear my brain and find new threads of suspicion to unravel. I saw the world without its faces, a forest of beasts, and on the seventh day I woke and beheld Blaise transfixed on the ceiling in the shape of a white bat. In the night someone in a dream had bitten me on the throat, and now I knew it all.'

'You are still drunken,' said William distrustfully. 'Stand back from me.'

'No, no, that was weeks ago. I have thoroughly searched the matter since then. There is no doubt of it. He has the treasure and has already disposed of divers items. How he learned where the chest lay I cannot yet tell. His ears are long, and he may have pieced word to word and composed the secret. Or maybe he gained a clue from sources beyond my knowledge; for the fellow who first had the paper was once a servant to the Master of the Star Chamber, and later a spy for the Council, among other guisings. But all this is a conjecture. What is certain is that I distrusted Blaise from the outset; and when you thought I was hiding matters from you, I was hiding them from him.'

'Your proof, man, your proof.'

'I am coming to that. As soon as I grew sure of his double-dealing, I followed him in many places with my head in a cloak, till at last I saw him going to a goldsmith near the Chepe Cross.'

'He may have been arranging a loan.'

'I thought of that. I waylaid one of the shop's apprentices in a tavern, and by scattered words I learned what I sought: that Blaise had sold a notable piece of goldwork to the master. And I learned certainly that this goldwork was the kind of thing plundered out of the abbeys.'

'It seems that you may be right,' said William thoughtfully. 'Yet a single piece of church-stuff might have come into his hands by other means.'

L

'I thought of that,' said Jones with a chuckle, 'but yesterday he sold another piece to the master; and there is no doubt any longer.'

He has the gold then,' said William, with a frowning sigh. 'What can we do at this late hour?'

'Take it from him, as he took it from us.'

'But then it lay out in a broken chapel. Now he has it secure in some privy place of his own.'

'Yet we can take it. Shall I find some stout fellows to break into his rooms? Or shall I have him taken one night and carried off to undergo the question?'

'Do nothing yet. I must think the matter out.'

'That is what I came to request.'

William gave him a helpless and hunted look. 'Do nothing without my agreement, do you hear? First I shall sound him carefully myself, and consider what had best be done.'

'Don't let him see into your mind, or he will hide the gold away with double surety.'

'I shall do nothing unconsidered or intemperate.'

Jones grinned and nodded. 'You see then that I have been a much wronged man.'

'It seems so,' said William reluctantly; then he went on with more confidence. 'But there must be no apparent sign of concord between us, or he will be warned.'

'Surely I may visit my dear sister?'

'Discreetly then, and after dark,' said William, frowning.

VI

The flap-eared friar hemmed and looked out over the people gathered below. In the front sat the well-clad city-merchants; behind them stood the poorer tradesmen and prentices, sprinkled with priests who had ended their services before nine o'clock and come to hear the preaching at Paul's Cross. Over by one of the buttresses boys were playing with a mastiff-dog. The friar pointed at them and called to one of the beadles, who ran over with his staff, knock-kneed.

William, who had come a little late, was seated in the second row of the benches, and glared at Hawes who sat in

the middle of the front row, straight under the preacher.
'. . . Who are these simple men caught in the nets of men
even simpler than themselves and yet foul and beastly sots
of Satan? Who was this Cranmer of whom they made much?
A creeping fellow, the son of an ostler. One day in the far
north, about Scarborough, a priest, sitting among his neighbours outside the alehouse, listened to some others commend-
ing the man. What (said he) make you so much of him? He
was but an ostler and has as much learning as the goslings
of the green that go yonder.' He paused, and the listeners
broke into laughter. 'For which words the priest was cast
into the Fleet by the lord Crumwell. So much for crooked
Cranmer, who smacked of the stable till in the end he stank
of Satan. And who was that Lord Crumwell? He perished
criminally on the scaffold as a traitor, and with him died Lord
Hungerford, who dealt with conjuring devils and sodomiti-
cally depraved his own daughter. Such were the brocks who
strove to lead you all astray into backslidings and be-
devilments.'

A boy, trying to climb a buttress, slipped down with a yell.
Overhead a crow cawed rudely. Martin slipped away from
the group standing on the left, and walked on through the
churchyard. A stubble-bearded man moping on an old gravestone looked up. 'A sad world, master.' He held out a coin in
his grimy palm. 'My very last, and I wish to spend it on a
gallon of beer; but who can be trusted in this lousy London?
The last man I asked to fetch me a tankardful skipped off
with the money.'

'You are a felon in sanctuary,' said Martin.

'I am hunted by villains,' replied the man with a wink.

'Still, I am no errand-boy,' said Martin, and walked on.
He came into Chepeside. A child was singing for bread in
the quiet street, and a man stood with his ears nailed to the
pillory. Wives in their best clothes looked down from the
firstfloor windows. An idiot girl sat dribbling on a doorstep,
putting her forefinger in and out of a holed stone she held. A
group of monks went chanting by. Then, as he sauntered,
Martin saw Merric ahead turning down a side-street. He
hastened; but a family-party coming out of one of the houses,
all ready for a walk in the fields, impeded him, and by the

time he reached the corner he could see Merric nowhere. Only an old fellow, clearly risen from a sick bed, girded in a long nightgown with a double kerchief tied about his head and a large hat set on the kerchief.

VII

With their caps in their hands, the three young men stood before the carved table in the Company's Parlour. The Master turned over some old pieces of parchment and whispered with the Clerk, then he turned his heavy-browed face to the young men. 'We have examined your complaint, even though we knew that it arose from graceless rebellion and not from any zeal for our customs. We can find no support for your contestations, and therefore we dismiss your suit with all the weight of our authority. Seeing your youth, we are ready to to overlook this act of malice, made worse by the wicked way in which you presented your complaint before our worshipful guests; but if there is any repetition of the offence, we shall handle you without mercy.'

The wardens at his side murmured loudly their assent.

'You have given us no grounds for your decision,' said Peter Larch, 'except that tyrannical will against which we protest—'

'Enough,' said the Master. He signed to the beadle, who seized Peter from behind. Other officers laid hold of his companions. 'You are under arrest for this contempt,' the Master went on. He nodded to the beadle. 'Clap them in jail till they sue in obedience.'

'This is the argument that betrays your lack of all right,' said Peter; then he was dragged off.

'We will now consider the matter of the rents in Aldgate, and that of the lease of the Mora Field,' said the Master mildly, as soon as the journeymen were removed. 'We must gain the field from the Merchant Taylors, as it would serve well for racks and tenters of cloth, and therefore I have been speaking with the Prebend of Paul's . . .' He folded his hands, and his pale eyes roved over the painted panel on which was depicted Susanna in a stiff sort of armoured nakedness under the small green snake-eyes of the Elders.

VIII

Merric and Ybel came out of the tavern and walked down Fenchurch Street. 'If we could annoy this Mrs. Wicke,' said Merric, 'it would please my Jacint. We'll look at the house and then go on to the place by the river.' He loosened his doublet-collar. 'The heat comes out of the plaster with a sickly smell.'

'Sanchia let me comb her hair in the sun yesterday,' said Ybel with a piping pride, and then flushed. 'If man is made the master of woman, how is it fitting that he should be laughed-at and tormented by her?'

'Wiser men than you have asked that question, and found no answer.'

'I dreamed last night that the Virgin came and gave me an apple from under her gown; yet when I bit, I found a scaly worm,' said Ybel. 'And seeing my tears she took from the same place a sweetmeat shaped like a candle and bade me console myself and wiped the tears from my cheeks. So there is good in women as well as bitterness.'

'If you dream enough, you will end as a wise man.'

Merric pulled down his cap and they went past the Hawes house. He glanced up at the windows, but saw no one. The door was closed. At the bottom of the street Ybel said hopefully, 'Then we may now go on to the meeting-place?' And Merric nodded.

Martin came out as they were turning the corner, and set off after them. They were making southward, to the river, and he kept them in sight, lessening the distance between. But when they neared the bank, they hurried down an alley, and he had to run to keep them in sight. He just glimpsed them going round the back of a small decaying warehouse, with broken breastsummer. Walking slowly past, he found himself overtaken by a lad in a prentice-cloak, who passed round the warehouse just as Merric and Ybel had done.

He went to the end of the alley, and found a broken stall to sit on. A wisp-haired slattern came up out of a cellar and began talking huskily and without pause. He answered her, with his head turned to see if more persons came down the alley for the warehouse.

'. . . while they were dancing to the beat of devil-drums, the whole house came down on their heads . . . when they pulled her out, both her legs were broken. Five sailors were crusht to death, but in a hollow under the main-beam there lay a baby unhurt . . . So that's why there's no ale-house nearer than Wimp Lane, and that's kept by a miserly fellow who'd cut your throat for the change out of a farthing.'

A man, and then two prentices, came down the alley and went round the warehouse. 'What's that place there?' asked Martin. 'It seems to have many visitors. Is it a bawdy-house?'

'No, no, it's a warehouse, but I've seen no wares go into it all the year I've lodged here. Is it a bawdy-house you're wanting?' She blew her nose between her fingers, whistled, and a girl of about fifteen years, with yellow hair stringy over her face, came yawning up the cellar-steps, wearing no more than a dirty shift kept open to the navel. When she saw Martin, she blinked, pulled the hair back from her round snub-nosed face, and tried to smile. But as she swayed there, still half asleep, she couldn't manage the smile and merely screwed up her face, unable to bear the light.

'What's a clock?' she asked hoarsely, and answered herself. 'Drinking time, swinking time . . . and the year of the great itch.' She stared at Martin. 'Haven't seen you before, have I? Come on down.'

'Wait a moment.' He asked the slattern: 'Why are there so many men going into that house? I've counted about a dozen.'

'Thieves or heretics.' She spat. 'Heretics or thieves. There's nothing else nowadays.'

'I hate those heretics,' said the girl. 'I like to see them burn. They don't swear, they don't drink, and they hate bawdry worse than ratsbane. What a world we'd have if they made the laws. Why, they even detest the sweet Virgin Mary and want to throw her out of the churches. They'd put us all in treadmills and chain our legs together.' She yawned. 'Who bit me in the knee, mother?'

'Heretics?' said Martin. He watched the warehouse with a new interest. Hugh Rigeley and Stephen came down the alley and made for the warehouse-rear. Martin smote his thigh.

'Here you are.' He tossed a groat to the woman. 'Buy your daughter a ribband for her hair, and let her send her shift to the washing-women if she has no time to spare for washing herself.'

'Give me one too,' the girl called, and added, 'Yah, you jotter-headed gawpsheet, I wouldn't be seen at a hen-race with you.'

But he was moving off. Then he paused, unbuckled and buckled again his belt. Across the space ahead a lad was hurrying to the warehouse. Martin gave him a hard look and then lowered his head, turning sideways.

Inside the warehouse over a score of journeymen with a few prentices and small-masters were gathered. Tom Hinshaw was holding forth. 'Now as to his plea that he is Peter's successor, it cannot be found in Scripture that Peter ever came to Rome, for he dwelt in Antioch, preaching there all the days of his life. So the Bishop of Antioch should rather be Peter's successor than the Bishop of Rome; and the keys appear by the Gospel to be given to no successor, but to Peter only, who had no less of the Holy Spirit than the Pope has of the unholy devil. And what effect those keys have may well be seen if we consider our own miserable sins. If I never sin, how can the Pope bind me? And if I sin, I bind myself. If the Lord pardons me my sins, what devil can annoy me? And if the Lord refuses to forgive me, what creature can bring me into heaven. So, unless you say that the Pope is greater than God, binding or loosing him at will, you must confess his authority to be vain and superstitious.'

They chimed agreement as Hugh, with Stephen close behind, came in, and then Will Yarp, a clothworker's apprentice. The newcomers found seats among the straw as Mat Osborne took up the argument.

'Let me tell you how the keys came to Peter, companions. When the gates of heaven were bolted and barred on the inward side, Peter was bidden hold the keys safe till the day of judgment. Until that day no man was to enter the gate corporally, but was to fly in spirit over the wall. For a lively faith and not a carnal superstition would save a man, and so Peter taught, hiding the keys in his house at Antioch, where

they lay unknown for many years. At last, in the time of
Phocas, the Emperor of Constantinople, a simple priest found
them, marvelling at the curious workmanship, and took them
to the Court. But the Emperor did not know what to do with
them, and gave them to Pockyface, by whom I mean Boniface
the Third; and thus they were first brought into the Roman
church. Then this Boniface, seeking the gates of heaven after
death, failed of his way and strayed on the gates of hell,
where unwittingly he put those keys into use. Thereupon the
gates of hell opened wide, because the gates of hell itself shall
not prevail against the truth, and all the devils got out. By
plain force they drew Boniface in and kept the gates so wide
open that all who have since followed Boniface on the papis-
tical path, thinking to climb to heaven, have fallen
another way.'

No one laughed, but a smile lightened the faces of most,
in the dim shafts coming through the square holes high up,
roped with cobweb and edged with rain-rotted planks.

Bennett the plasterer rose. 'The time is come for the drawn
sword. We must each of us take a pledge to find three good
men and confirm them in resistance to Antichrist. Then when
those three are secure in the whole armour of the Spirit, let
each of them find three more . . .'

'Where are we to gain arms?'

'When will we know the time is come to strike? . . .'

The river ran with a gentle tumult beyond the wall.
Stephen spoke of those who say peace when there is no peace,
the men of painted terms, between whose actions and pro-
fessions is no agreement, those turncoats and changelings
who go with the golden wind. Hugh sat with closed eyes
near the door, now and then starting and uttering a groan.
'The time is come . . .'

IX

John Cornet, being a prentice with a minstrel, was sent to
a wedding in a town near Colchester, called Rough-hedge,
where he being requested by a company of good men, the
constables also of the parish, being present thereat, to sing

some songs of the Scripture, chanced to sing a song called News Out of London, which tended against the mass and against the Queen's misproceedings.

Whereupon the next day he was accused by the parson of Rough-hedge, called Yackalay; and so committed, first to the constable, where both his master gave him over and his mother forsook and cursed him. From thence he was sent to the next justice, named Master Cannall, and then to the Earl of Oxford, where he was first put in irons and chains, and after that so manacled that the blood spirted out of his fingers' ends, because he would not confess the names of them that allured him to sing.

X

'I don't know,' said Agnes, 'but I feel indeed as though I were being tempted all the while to a sin which is unknown and impossible; and as I lie in bed, I think that I have risen and dressed myself, yet then I wake and find myself still naked under the sheet. And as I walk the street, I seem to step out of my body and go ahead round the corner, while in effect I lag behind and seem dwindling into a hole in the earth. But this is a small matter next to the great convulsions you speak of.'

'Yet akin to them,' said Stephen eagerly. 'A token that you cannot rest in your own flesh as a thing apart, and that you must either rise from the bed of death into a new life or pace ahead of the world's slow ignorance into a quickening embrace.'

'It may be,' she said vaguely. 'Where is my Uncle Hugh?'

'He is away, calling on a friend, but will soon be back.'

Rosbel came out of the kitchen with two blue cups, which she carried very carefully. 'A sip of ippocras,' she said, keeping her eyes on the cups as she spoke. 'There's little enough to drink in this sad house but small beer, yet I found this for a rare visitor.' She tripped on a cobble in the yard and blurted out a curse. 'As well the master didn't hear that. Here you are, Mistress Agnes.' She handed the cups to the pair seated on the bench against the workshop, rubbed her blotchy nose with the end of her apron, and retired.

'Have you noticed that our father and mother never speak to one another,' said Agnes suddenly. 'I mean that they do not speak directly. They never say: *Nest,* or *William,* or *my beloved.* They do not look one another in the eyes.'

'I have never noticed it,' said Stephen with a frown.

'What can they say when they are alone together?' she said musingly. 'How I would like to know. When they are alone with a candle at night and the door closed. I have listened at the door; but I heard nothing.' Stephen went on frowning, but made no reply. She touched his hand. 'Can you hear me? Can you hear me?'

'Why should I not hear you?' he asked, startled.

'Sometimes my voice seems a ghostly voice, and I am sure that no one can hear me. I seem falling far away.'

'Beloved sister,' he said and stopped with a sob. He took her hands between his. 'How we go seeking for love and fail to see it by our side. O the poor hungry hearts of men . . .'

'Do you not feel as if you were changed at birth?' she asked with kindling voice. 'Perhaps you are no more my brother than Mary is my sister.'

But he was carried away by his own thoughts. 'Mabel is waiting for me, and I do not know if I wrong her more by staying away than I would by going to her. Every morning at Terce I pass her house, and she sits at her window that I may see her, and that is all.'

'Take her away,' said Agnes in a dry whisper.

'I cannot. I have another command laid upon me.'

Before he could say more, Rosbel appeared at the backdoor wiping her hands on her apron. 'A friend to see you.' And Rafe Heygate appeared.

'Agnes,' he said, coming up to kiss her. 'I think I have given you a farthing or two in the lost years, and now you pay me back with a kiss of the womanhood you have bought from life.' He lifted her chin. 'There are tears in your eyes. There is a spirit in your eyes, my child no longer a child.' He ran his finger round her face. 'I can see your mother here, your mother in her youth.' He sighed. 'She had a wildwood beauty in those days.'

'Tell me about her, please, please . . .'

'I have told you all. She was young and now she is weary.'

Stephen broke in, 'Have you brought the book?'

Rafe nodded, 'In entrusting it to you I make you my spiritual son, for this book is as dear to me as my life, seeing that I was reborn through it and for the first time perceived the earth on which I dwelt. Here you will read the history of Gargantua, Pantagruel, and Panurge, and you will discover the earth.'

Stephen frowned. 'But I know little French.'

'You will learn more.' He took out from his doublet a small book. 'Here is the first volume. More will follow when you deserve it. But guard it for me as your own soul.'

Stephen touched the book and shuddered all over. 'I am afraid of it.'

'You are afraid of the earth on which you live,' said Rafe, 'so are we all. Yet we are also dowered with the need of the truth. We fear, yet we confront our fear, and then our fear becomes the strength of our courage.'

'The beginning of wisdom is in the fear of the Lord,' said Stephen in a troubled voice.

'You may put it that way,' said Rafe, stroking his chin and watching Agnes. 'Only, let wisdom truly begin.' He put the book in Stephen's hand. This time Stephen controlled himself and slowly turned the pages, and Rafe went on, 'And though men must always suffer for his wisdom, let the pangs come from their own flesh and spirit. Let there be an end of racks and faggots. Do you hear?' Stephen went on turning over the pages of the book without reading anything. 'Did not the Queen come to her throne with a general goodwill?' said Rafe, now half-speaking to himself, 'and is she now not hated by the commons?' He sighed. 'Give me the book back. What a fool am I, what a gross and gravel-blind fool, to go meddling in another man's soul. I had as soon ravish a half-witted girl as tell the truth to a frightened man. It breeds maggots in his brain.'

He tried to take the book back, but Stephen clung to it. 'No, now I have it in my hands, I must look into it.'

'You kissed my mother when she was my age,' said Agnes.

Rafe turned to her, but Hugh came out into the yard. Agnes at once rose 'I must go.' She hastened over to where Hugh stood near the door. 'Your daughter is lost,' she said in a low voice. 'Your daughter is wholly lost.' Then before he could recover from his surprise she turned and ran into the house, with her hand over her breasts.

XI

'If you are indeed a faithful son of the church,' said the monk, 'there is no need to fear anything. We shall cherish you as a mother her baby. Only, you must tell us the truth.' He twined his fingers together and set them under his chin, looking over the table at the lad with a benign smile. Then he changed his tone. 'But if you are obdurate, we shall break your bones in the rack.' He took a pen from the table and snapped it. 'Like that.' Then he smiled again. 'It is for you to choose. We in our longsuffering love can do no more than hope for the best.'

'I was drawn into it by Peter Larch,' said Will Yarp in a thin voice. 'I knew little of its purpose. I thought it had to do with the demands of the yeomen in the Company. Then I found it was conspiracy of heretics, and I was sorely troubled.'

'A sign of grace,' said the monk. 'Yet if you had confessed without being arrested, it would have been a better sign.'

'I meant to do it tomorrow,' pleaded Yarp. 'I was going to the parish priest, I swear to you.'

'There is no need of oaths,' said the monk. 'We ask only the truth and a contrite heart. Now you will tell us why these heretics meet and what they plot together.'

Yarp jerked his head about as if loosening a pressure round his neck, stared for a moment at the dank vaulting of the low stone ceiling, and began speaking in a thick hurried voice.

XII

Tabitha went to answer the knock. When she saw Jones, she tried to close the door, but he put his foot inside. Dousabel appeared at the inner door and motioned Tabitha to stand back. Jones came into the room. 'You know what I am going to say,' said Dousabel, in her loose watchet-gown and slippers, with ribboned hair and red wine wet on her heavy mouth.

He nodded. 'Yet I hope you will listen to me.'

'It will make no difference.'

'If you bid me stay awhile, I have many things to say which will surprise you and which you will find very useful.'

She slowly shook her head. 'Though you are a liar, all that is doubtless true enough. But I still do not wish to hear you.'

'Why? You listen to many others.'

'I have no reason, except that I will not.'

'If we worked together, it would be to the profit of us both. Your Blaise is not so securely seated in the saddle of his hopes as he thinks. I can tell you strange things.'

'Who of us cannot tell strange things?' she asked. 'Between now and tomorrow morning I shall fancy more wicked and lewd things than even you could act out in a lifetime; and yet I am indifferently chaste and virtuous.' She smiled. 'You are a simple goatish villain, Christopher. You are a hermit in your own small wickedness and have forgotten that there are always spies upon the spies.'

'What a work we could do together,' he cried, chuckling and coming nearer.

'I am no morsel for your mouth,' she replied without moving. 'I should lie like a poison on your belly, and you on mine.'

'There are pitfalls all round you.'

'I am one who falls easily and lightly.' She waved him off. 'You waste your breath. Go at once.'

'How can you give yourself to such as that zany Francis and my dull-witted Merric, the Spaniard and many others, and yet withhold yourself from me, the only one who sees with admiration the woman you are?' asked Jones with a note of hurt bewilderment. 'For the last time, throw in your fortunes with mine, and I swear you shall never regret it.'

'For the last time, no.'

He stared at her in a puzzled way, then snorted and went to the outer door. 'One day you will shed tears because of those words.' She made no reply and he went out.

'Bring me my pomander-ball,' said Dousabel to Tabitha. 'I

hate that fellow as a devil's mirror in which I see too much of myself. He smells of river-mud and burnt bones.'

XIII

'The youth William Yarp has confessed,' said Hawes to Martin. 'I had a word with the Bishop's scribe, who says that his Lordship ·is highly pleased with our part in the matter.'

'What then is to happen?'

'He said nothing more, and I thought it safest to ask no questions.' Hawes clapped his son on the back. 'You did well in piercing through the devices of the villains with so daggering an eye.'

They went up into the solar. Hawes called for Lettice and bade her bring them some of the new pie that Tace had mentioned. 'We have no time to wait for the others,' he said. 'We must go at once to the Guildhall.' And they sat at the table. Jacint came in, but said that she would eat later, and sat at her samplar by the window. Lettice came with the pie, and Hawes cut two large slices from it. Martin poured some beer, and they drank and ate. 'The pie tastes bitter,' said Hawes, drinking beer, 'and Tace said that it was a new sort that she wished especially to make for Mrs. Wickes's delectation. But I cannot recommend it. The deer of this venison must have browsed upon sharp herbs.'

Martin set down the piece that he was lifting at knife-end. 'Aye, a man would need a great hunger to relish this stuff.'

'Send up Tace,' said Hawes, 'that she may explain the matter.'

Jacint went out. Martin laid down his knife, and poured out more beer. 'It's a foul pie. No kinder word would well serve.'

Hawes beat on the table and Lettice came running up. 'Where's Tace?' he shouted. 'Bring us something fitter for eating.'

'We can't find her,' said Lettice, stooping more than usual, with pale blue eyes of flurried fear.

Martin stood up with his hands to his stomach. 'I ate more than you,' he muttered. 'What did she put in the stinking pie?'

Jacint came running up. 'Tace has gone. She isn't in her room or the kitchen. She's taken her best dress from the chest in her room. What's wrong?'

Martin staggered over to the window and vomited out, groaning. Hawes sat rubbing his stomach with flickering grimaces on his face. 'She's poisoned us . . .' He leaned back too far and fell off his stool.

Gertrude entered. 'What's this noise?' She looked at the fallen Hawes, sprawling weakly on his back, and Martin leaning out of the window with low retching sounds. 'Drunk at this time of the day? Isn't is enough that you disgrace the house with a marriage of lecherous greed? Must you also let the neighbours know that you reel boozing at broad noon? I can bear the shame no longer, and tomorrow I shall depart for Dunmow.'

'They are poisoned,' said Jacint, trying to get her father to his feet. 'Help me lay him on the settle.'

'O poor man,' cried Gertrude, 'has he been visited at last by a heavenly judgment? Then I forgive him all his enormities and trust that he may die in peace.' She helped Jacint to draw Hawes to the settle. 'I shall brew a potion of nuts, rue and figs without delay.'

She rushed down to the kitchen, while Jacint called men from the workshop. In a few minutes the sickly groaning pair were carried to their beds, undressed, and given emetics.

'I shall send at once for Doctor Higson,' said Gertrude, coming out of the kitchen.

'No, no,' said Rafe, drawn at last from his attic-study. 'He is a doctor *in nomine domini,* admitted by a bishop's licence. Let us send rather for Doctor Bowry, who comes from the College of Physicians—even though he lives one more street away.'

And so, since Jacint agreed, Dr. Bowry was fetched, a man with a long curly beard, which he stroked reassuringly. 'I remember a similar case at Padua,' he said. 'Mithridate is sovran against it.' He fingered the hyacinth stone which he wore on a string round his neck as a protection against the plague. 'Kindly indeed is nature which provides such preservatives; for mithridate will cure consumptions and ptisicks as well as old rheums running down into the stomach, a dull appetite as well as excessive wind, pain-fulness in the making of water as well as gatherings of melan-choly. For sudden poisoning, take it with a few Grains of Paradise, as the unlearned call the seeds of the greater Carda-momum. Have no fear, my dear young mistress.' He patted Jacint on the cheek. 'Every ill has its counter-good, if only the signs of correspondence can be read.'

Gertrude came in with a squawking fowl in her hand. She plucked the remnants of its tailfeathers. 'I mean to lay this against his suffering stomach,' she said defiantly.

'It will do no harm, it will do no harm,' said the doctor, playing with his hyacinth stone.

'Is he dead yet?' cried Mrs. Wicke entering in a fluster.

'Not yet,' said Gertrude darkly, 'but it will be no thanks to you if he plucks up heart and lives.'

'To think that I was saved from a like fate through a broken lace in my stomacher,' said Mrs. Wicke. 'For I was all ready to come, and then I bended to pick up a ball for my spaniel, so that the lace broke with a loud twang.' She smelt the golden phial hanging from her bracelet. 'Thus I had to undress again till the lace could be got at and another set in its place. O never again shall I cry out at the fashions which tie a woman up like a bale of spices; for all things have a purpose if we look closely enough. Tell me.' She sniffed and stared round with her thin pale eyes. 'Tell me which one of them poisoned the other for my sake and then in despair sought his own damnation?' She delicately sobbed. 'I never thought to have two goodly men killing one another for my love.'

'Fiddlesticks,' said Gertrude, 'they ate some bad pie that Tace made. And let me tell you that for years, at no worse price than her own tears, she gained what you are buying with a great weight of gold. Also, I am sick to the heart with the shames you insist on bringing thick upon this house like a crowd of crows on the rooftops. Tomorrow I shall depart for Dunmow.'

XIV

The journeyman knocked three times and the door opened. At once the spy whistled, and the sergeants came running with their men across the street. With his sword-hilt an officer knocked on the door. By his side stood a man with a wheel-lock pistol, carefully bringing up the cock that held the pyrites on the pan-cover. One of the men behind pushed against his elbow, and he pressed too hard on the trigger. The wheelgrooves caught the pyrites, struck out a spark, and fired the priming. The shot rattled on the door, and the echoes of the blast held everyone unmoving for a moment in the quiet dusk. Then three of the men ran against the door and it fell in.

Mat Osborne was waiting on the other side. He heaved up a block of wood and dropped it on the officer's head. The officer fell back with a broken skull and knocked a sergeant over. Mat struck out again, this time with a dagger, and caught the nearest man in the cheek. From the other side a soldier slashed with his sword, hitting Mat on the shoulder. The next moment the soldiers were inside the dim room.

Stephen saw a soldier with drawn sword coming straight his way. He stood for a moment motionless, then, snatching up an old pulley that lay on the floor, he flung it in the soldier's face. Turning, he made for the upper storey on the rickety stairs, came out into the room overlooking the river, and after listening for a few seconds to the noise below, leaped into the dark water. The tide was near the turn, and the water was deep; but as he came up, he knocked against a pile. Then, with blood running from his temple, he swam out and round a barge. Once on the further side, he drifted quietly downstream.

He had swum a couple of hundred yards when he paused and shook the water out of his eyes, looking for somewhere to land. A rope trailing from a boat at anchor drew him on, and he grasped it, taking deep breaths. Then, looking up, he saw a sailor watching over the side. Without a word the man reached out his arm and helped him up on board. 'Lie there,' he said, pointing to a heap of sailcloth; and when Stephen lay shivering down, he drew another length of cloth over him.

XV

Nest stared into the deepening dusk. 'Who's that?' she asked suspiciously.

'Me, mistress,' came a heavy whisper. 'I did it.'

'You shouldn't have done it,' said Nest, also whispering. Then she added, 'I don't know what you're talking about.'

'Hide me,' pleaded Tace, coming closer out of the gloom of the yard. 'Hide me.'

'How can I hide you?' Nest replied. 'I've nowhere to hide you. You'd be found; and then you'd be no better off but I'd be ruined. No, you must go away at once.' Tace shuddered, and Nest asked with a note of complicity, 'Which of them died? Was it he or she, or both of them?'

'I don't know,' whimpered Tace. 'I meant it for her; but he asked for food earlier than expected, being called to the Guildhall, and so I ran away. I don't know what happened. I have been waiting for dusk, so I might come to you.'

'But why to me?' asked Nest. 'Why to me?'

'Why?' William's voice echoed from behind. He put his hand on Nest's shoulder and drew her aside. 'Who are you?' he asked Tace.

'I am Tace Kemp, so please you. Till noon today I served Master Gregory Hawes, but now . . .' She began weeping.

'I want none of Gregory Hawes's offscourings here,' he said roughly. 'Away with you.'

'So please you, I killed him,' said Tace weakly.

'What is that? You killed him. How could you do that?'

'With a poisoned pie,' she said humbly. 'Egg and venison it was, but the name of the poison I cannot say, for I only know the colour of its flowers.'

'Why have you come to me?'

'I thought you would be glad to hear of his death, master.' She whined and burst into tears.

He crossed himself. 'The servant who thus seeks the death of her master is doomed by the law to a cruel death. You will be boiled alive.'

She beat herself in the face. 'Save me, master, save me. He treated me worse than a dog. I was a maid when I went to his house; and when I tried to keep him off, he almost choked me to death. He took our child away and would never tell me where it went; and after that my blood was venomed. Then this year he wooed his puling widow without even a word of kindness to me, without a farewell kiss. And yet he still came to me in the night.'

'He shall answer to God,' said William. 'I am neither his judge nor yours. But there is a law on earth to which you are forfeit.'

'You should not have told us what you did,' said Nest from the background. 'If we had not known, we could have sent you down tomorrow to Colchester with a waggonload of wool, and you could have served Master Hobbs there; for he wrote last month that he desired some willing servants, man or woman.'

'Send me, and I'll be utterly yours till my last breath,' sobbed Tace.

William lifted her face to the faint starlight. 'I remember you now. You were once a comely maid . . . But I cannot help you.' He stood back. 'Remember: I know nothing.' Suddenly his voice was hoarse with fear. 'If it was found I had helped you, everyone would believe I instigated you against your master, who is my known enemy.' He fumbled in his purse and handed her a crown. 'Go away at once.'

He hurried back into the front of the house. 'Wait a moment,' said Nest softly to Tace. She retired into the still-room a moment and then came out with a hood and a handful of coins. 'Take these, and go to Colchester. Find out Master Hobbs and say that I sent you. If you get as far as that in safety, you are not likely to be caught; and there will be no harm in saying what I have said. And now, go, before you are seen.'

Tace still wept. 'I weep for a thing lost,' she said between her teeth. 'Not for my deed, which was just, but for something else, as though I were dead and weeping over myself in another place.' She turned away. 'The Virgin bless you. You are a good woman.'

As Nest went back into the kitchen, Edgar came dashing in, 'Master wants to know if you've been breaking up the crabs' eyes and carpbones into powder for him? He says it must be done overnight.'

'I haven't done it yet,' said Nest, 'but I will. Tell him I will.'

'He's sure he's got a stone in his bladder,' said Edgar cheerfully. 'He's promised to give it to me if it comes out after he's had the buttered toast and nutmeg tomorrow afternoon. He says he'll void it then for sure.'

'As sure as most things in this world of ours,' said Nest, 'but not as sure as sorrow or death. Tell him to have no fear.' And she added to herself, 'But it's not so easy to be sure of what comes out of you as it is of what you put in. That's my secret and certain opinion.' Then, seeing that Edgar was still listening, she waved him away. 'That wasn't said for you, do you hear? I didn't say it.'

No sooner had William lighted the candles in his room than he heard a knock on the front door. 'Ybel!' he called, then frowned and went himself to answer. 'Who is there?' He heard the low voice and opened. 'What more have you to tell me? This is a bad moment. I am busy, and Merric is gone with Ybel to fetch some wares I bought. What is it?' Still grumbling, he let Jones in, bolted the door again, and led the way back into his room.

'He has taken another piece of the treasure to be broken up and sold,' said Jones, with a grin. 'He needs ready money to supply one of his snared victims, Sir Francis Ascow.' He plucked at his beard and grinned yet more broadly. 'Indeed he has intricate devices for netting a gull. The gold that he lends out to this knight is in large part brought back into the family by gifts which the knight makes to the painted whore Dousabel.'

William stood back. 'You go too far. No brother of mine would act so basely. You have maliciously made this invention—'

'Ask your own son, Merric, and see what he tells you. He has been one of the scores who know her nakedness.'

'Merric?' said William, stepping back so hastily that he knocked his head against the edge of the cupboard.

'And as for the besotted knight, let me tell you that out of his latest loan from your brother he bought his Dousabel a diamond ring engraved with a loving posy, and that the shop from which he bought it was that of Master Herrick in Chepe.'

William sat down at the table and took his head between his hands. 'All this goes too deep for me. I begin to think the world in very truth is falling apart.'

'Let me waylay this Blaise of yours,' begged Jones. 'Thus, when next he posts down to the manor where the steward already counts him master. I warrant that if he is hanged by his wrists from a bough and tickled with a daggerpoint under his feet, he will soon tell us all we desire to know.'

'No, too many things may go awry in such a matter. Remember that he has many lawyers to friend, and if you make one slip with him you are lost.' He pondered. 'And Dousabel, you say . . . Well, it's not to the point.'

Jones chuckled. 'Ask Merric.' He paused and hit himself on the brow. 'I see it now at last. She learned from Merric where the gold lay, and told her lousy fellow-thief—for I cannot call him her husband. Ah, she's a deep one; but when we are put to it, we can be yet deeper, eh, brother Will?'

'Yes,' said William distractedly.

XVI

'Come from that window,' said Mrs. Hudley. 'You shame-less slut, I know what you're looking for. But you'll never come to it while I'm alive.'

Mabel slid from her stool and went to the door.

'Don't think you can hide from me in your room,' Mrs. Hudley called after her, and went to the door. 'Don't go up-stairs. Go down to the kitchen, scour the pewter and scrape the platters. And you'll have nothing to eat till you say an *Ave Maria.*'

Mabel did not reply, but turned and went downstairs.

XVII

As William Saxton, weaver, went to the fire, he sang psalms. The sheriff, John Griffith, had prepared green wood to burn him; but one master John Pikes, pitying the man, caused

*divers to go with him to Ridland, half a mile off, who brought
good store of haulme-sheaves, which indeed make good dis-
patch with little pain in comparison to that he should have
suffered with the green wood. In the mean space, whilst they
went for the sheaves, Saxton made many good exhortations
to the people.*

XVIII

There came a crashing noise on the door, and Hugh went
out to see what it was. A sergeant, Bearde the informer, and
constables stood there. Bearde, a short heavy man nicknamed
the Shelt-toad, took off his broad hat and struck Hugh in the
face with it; and one of the constables pushed him back with
a staff. They all came in crowding in. 'You have been this
evening at a house near the Three Cranes,' said Bearde. 'I saw
you go in.'

'I have been here at home since noon.'

Rosbel appeared with a gridiron in her hand. 'It's true,'
she shouted, and brandished the gridiron.

'Quiet, you whore,' said Bearde, and one of the constables
drove her back into the kitchen. The others began searching
the rooms, throwing things on the floor or breaking them to
find hidden papers. One searcher looked for loose boards and
tore them up. 'Where is your prentice Stephen?' asked Bearde.

'He went out after None.'

'He is a traitor, and so are you. We have proof of it. We
have your words written down against you. For months we
have watched, using you as a decoy duck for the others. Your
only hope is to confess everything.'

They bound his hands and took him out down the street.
He held his head high, till a constable pushed him from
behind and jarred his spine. And so, with a bill pressed
against his back, he came at last to the Fleet, where he was
delivered to a drunken turnkey, who, after smiting him a few
times on the head with a large key, shoved him into a small
cell with half a dozen ragged men. 'There you are now in
Cappadocia,' he shouted, 'you must sing here among the
canary-birds.' And slammed the door.

But after half an hour the jailer himself came, and drew

him out. 'You look clean enough to pay for your dinner,' he said, and took him to an upper room. Here there was only one other man, a tall fellow with wild elfed hair and with a rebeck in his hand.

'I am Bristo,' he said as soon as they were alone, and plucked a tune from the strings. 'The batchelor most joyfully in pleasant plight does pass his days. And who are you? are you a hot gospeller?'

'That is not the name I choose, but I suffer for Christ's sake.'

'Then suffer in quiet, and hide it from the jailer. Even more, hide it from his wife, who loves all honest sinners but detests a godly reformer of religion.'

'I shall hide nothing.'

Bristo made a wry face, and sang, 'Wherefore should I hang up my horn upon the greenwood tree?' He laughed. 'Though the priests have no wives, yet the wives will have the priests. And though the ploughman has fennel-soup, the lords will have their peacock-pie, ho jolly ruttekin!'

'I desire no kindness from Belial.'

'And if you sleep, the cock will crow. If you are rich enough you will gain kindness from Belial, whatever you say. As for myself I am poor, yet they bear with me; and I know them through to the marrow, for I am an old sojourner in these rat-climes. The jailer and the jailer's wife love music very well, and thus with my rebeck I please them. Now if you would only take a lute to yourself, we should ravish them out of their wits. For he loves drinking to a merry tune; and she, being lousy as everyone must needs be in a jail, likes scratching herself to a good tune after the day's work.'

'I cannot play the lute.'

'Yet if you will bestow on them a quart of wine at dinner, I shall play my rebeck and you shall be their white son.' He plucked at his rebeck and sang. 'Welcome be you when you go, and farewell when you come!'

Hugh settled quietly in one corner. Across the passage a roomful of prisoners were shouting as they diced. And Bristo, seeing that Hugh listened to the noise, gave him an explanation, walking up and down the bare room, and plucking now and then at the strings:

'These prisons of correction are the dens and schools of un-
thriftiness. Yet we should be glad that we do not lie in Newgate, under that devil Alexander who cannot bear to have
poor men unprofitably in his rooms. He goes daily to Bonner,
saying: Rid my prison, I am pestered by packs of heretics.
For he hates equally a poor man who cannot give him money,
and a heretic who will not. And though the Lord Mayor
has spoken of his cruelties, yet he boasts that he cannot be
turned out, since the prison is his own property.'

The door opened, and a buxom woman with sleek black hair
and short upper lip looked in. 'I see you have company, Bristo.
Can he help you in making music?' She pointed at Hugh,
slightly squinting. The little-finger was missing from her hand.

'He can blow on the horn of wine and arouse a response of
belly-gurgles,' said Bristo. 'And if you will not pledge, you
shall bear the blame!' He jangled on his rebeck. 'She would
have no man that was made of mould, unless he kissed her at
her will with a mouth of gold, so dangerous she was.' He
kissed his fingers at the woman. 'So it all fell out just as Joan's
buttocks on the close stool. All good men were satisfied, and
the others went home by devious ways. For if soil be better
for thick dunging, shall not a wife be sweeter for a daily
adultery? Who shall be so bold as to separate bawdry from
beauty or declare that even the most ill-favoured of women
may not be bettered by a fortnightly fit of fornication.'

The woman looked doubtfully at Hugh! 'He smells to me
of a filthy lollard.' She scratched herself in the armpit and
sniffed. 'I hate all sad dogs that snarl at women and lift a leg
only in way of insult.'

'Give her a crown,' pleaded Bristo. 'Give her a crown, I
beg you.'

Hugh started and raised his eyes as if out of a deep sleep.
He took a crown from his pocket and handed it to Bristo.

XIX

*Otherwhile I went privily, otherwhile openly, otherwhile I
went from home a fortnight or three weeks, otherwhile I was
at home a month or five weeks together, living there most*

commonly and openly, doing such works as I had to do; and yet all mine enemies could lay no hands on me, till the hour was full come: and then by the voice of the country, and by manifest proofs, mine own brother (as concerning the flesh) delivered me into their hands.

For my father and he had as much of my goods in their hands as I might have £56 for by the year, clear. It was a lordship and an honour, and half an honour, that I had delivered into their hands to pay my debts, and the rest to remain to my wife and children. But they reported that it would not pay my debts, which grieved me sore; for it was £200 better than the debts came to: which caused me to speak to some of my friends, that they would speak to them to come to some reckoning with me, and to take all such money again of me as they were charged with, and to deliver me such writings and writs as they had of mine again, or to whom I would appoint them.

So it was agreed betwixt my father and me, and the day was appointed; my brother supposing that I should have put him out of most of all his occupying that he was in; for it was all mine, in a manner, that he occupied, as all the country know. Whereon he told one Cardinnar (my next neighbour) and he told some of master Gage's men or Master Gage himself. And so Gage sent to his brother, and his brother sent twelve of his men (he being sheriff) in the night, who lay in the bushes not far from my house, till about nine of the clock, even the hour that was appointed amongst themselves.

CHAPTER TEN

September

I

'IT'S SAFE TO go now.' The rough voice spoke out of the darkness. The rough hand shook him. He drew himself slowly up, with signs of pain, and went to the boat's side. The sailor helped him down into the wherry, 'Drop him on the other side, at a quiet place.' The wherryman grunted, and the wherry slid away into the glimmering.

'I forgot to thank you,' said Stephen belatedly, turning back towards the boat.

'He can do without your thanks,' said the wherryman.

After a while Stephen asked, 'Did you speak to me? or did I hear my own thought?' And then he added, 'Now goodness is as strange as evil.'

The man grunted, and rowed steadily on, with the water whirled in little coils of glinting foam at his oar-ends. They came to the southern bank, running on to mud and reeds. 'God be with you,' said the man. Stephen stepped out, sinking footdeep in the mud, and the boat slid away into the closing night.

He stood watching the wavering spot where it had faded out, then sighed, shivered, and climbed squelching up on to the grassy bank. He sat there for some minutes, staring at the reeds and the wall of flowering darkness. Then rose and felt his way through some bushes. Reaching the edge of a stubble-field, he walked across and came to a track. Then in a few moments he was stumbling into a slightly sunken lane, and starlight lay on the earth like an evanescent silver dew.

Through the **warm** smell of earth he walked for hours, doggedly, now and then nodding his head with closed eyes, but still keeping on, at an unchanging pace. A baying dog made him pause and then move more carefully, and he saw the dim roofs of a hamlet. He felt the few coins in his pocket, and then went aside into the cavernous dark of a copse, where he lay on dry leaves and crumbling earth. At once he slept.

He jerked his head awake at the singing of birds. After a short while he rose and looked round. At copse-edge he found some berries and ate. Then after leaning with closed eyes against a tree until the thrush ceased calling, he returned to the road, below the hamlet, and walked on. He passed a labourer with a rake, who turned and looked long at him with hardening eyes.

When he had passed round the corner of oaks, he ran for a few hundred yards, then hurried across a field, and, coming to a young hedge, crawled along beneath it. Looking back, he saw a horseman cantering down the road he had left. This horseman stopped near the oaks, stood in his stirrup, and scanned the countryside.

He lay breathing in the dust and then went on. A tethered cow was rubbing against a tree, and a woman with a brace of buckets was drawing water from a well. Village-smoke curled above the elms. He hid in some bushes, then came boldly out. Brushing the dust from his coat, he walked into the village. A dog sniffed at his legs with cringing hostility, then sheered off and barked. He said, 'Good day, mother,' to an old woman making quills in a doorway. Then he saw someone moving in a small side-shed, and heard a level voice with a deadness of accent in it. He went closer and heard the words.

'. . . but now we are delivered from the law, that being dead wherein we were held, that we should serve in newness of spirit, and not in the oldness of the letter. What shall we say then? . . .'

He stepped from the grass patch to the cobbles, and the voice stopped. He went on to the door and saw a girl twisting rope. 'What do you want?' she asked after a moment of silence.

'I heard you speaking.' Then with a note of surprise, 'You are blind.' He put his hands over his own eyes. 'I am sorry.'

A countryman in kersey stockings and russet doublet came

up to the side of the shed; but before he spoke, the girl said, 'Here is a stranger, brother, needing our help.'

'You are not of this parish,' said the man heavily, looking on the ground. 'Have you a licence to beg? are you a poor scholar?'

Stephen did not answer, and the girl said, 'Take him in, brother. He is tired.'

'Are you in flight then for the truth's sake?' asked the man, looking up into Stephen's face.

Stephen nodded, and the girl repeated, 'Take him in, brother.'

'The constable is over at Lighe Farm,' said the man, and beckoned to Stephen. They went on round the shed to the cottage's backdoor, and the girl put down her work and followed. 'We too are of the faith. How much longer we shall be unmolested, I cannot tell. The farmer, Grice, has had his eye on us.' His sister came up and linked her arm with his. They went into the cottage: into a kitchen with open fireplace. A fire was burning on a stone against an iron fireback; and as there was no chimney, the room was fusty with smoke.

The girl fetched out a stool from under the table for Stephen, and asked eagerly, 'Can you read in a book? I have no eyes and my brother knows no letters. Can you read us a holy chapter? We have our Bible thrust in a hole of the thatch.'

'I'll fetch it,' said the brother, and went out.

'There was a good old man,' said the girl in her small withdrawn voice, 'who read to us for a penny, but he went away to Guildford. From his reading I know many chapters by heart, so that I have only to open the book and lay my hand inside it, and then the words come out of me like a spring from the earth.' She reached out, and her hand, cold despite the warmth of the day, touched his cheek. 'You are a good man. I know it from your voice. I am sad for you.' He shivered and seemed about to fall from the stool.

The brother came in with the book in one hand and a turnip in the other. 'You are hungry,' he said in soft self-reproach, 'and we have not given you to eat.' He set the turnip in the hot ashes.

II

The Mayor in scarlets, with gold chain round his neck, led his aldermen out of the reeking dinner-hall to the Guildhall Chapel. Then after prayers they all came in their gawdy lined gowns and climbed a little unsteadily on their horses and made for Newgate. Sceptre, cap, and sword were borne before the Mayor, as he made his way into the Cloth Fair in the wide space on the north side of the Church of St. Bartholomew and its churchyard. Here the rows of tents were pitched, and here the Mayor, amid the cheers of the crowd, drank ale from a sliver flagon. The proclamation droned on. 'And that no person sell any bread, but it keep the assize, and that it be good and wholesome for man's body, upon pain that will fail thereof. And that no manner of person buy or sell, but with true weights and measures, sealed according to the statute . . .' After the Mayor had drunk, the wrestling matches began on the ground levelled with eighteen cartloads of sand; people behind pushing in to see, and people in front pushing back to save themselves from falling on to the wrestlers. Except for the lucky ones crawling over the house-roofs. And the big brawny wrestlers heaved and grunted with sweat-shining bodies and mad eyes. More and more people bunched round the gates to pay their penny entrance-toll, and the officers were making their last rounds to see if anyone with a stall had escaped paying stallage.

A parcel of live rabbits were turned loose in the crowd, with boys diving and scrambling after them among the legs. Long Lane was already filled with cloth-chafferers skilfully fingering the bales and bolts of woollen cloth. A woman on stilts sang with a baby in her arms and a jug on her head near the pig-market. A bear was gloomily dancing to a drum by pasty-nook or pie-corner. 'Sack and sugar out of Spain! Who said they were the only good things that the Spaniards brought?' (The officer glared round.) A fool with a cap of hare's ears was shaking a rattle. Someone threw down a basket of refuse; and many of the bystanders bent down to see if there was anything worth picking up. While they bent, the

man who had thrown down the basket plucked off several hats
and cloaks, and ran away round a booth.

'Sir Robert Rich has given back the Church,' said a dealer,
feeling some kersey linen, 'but he keeps the land and its tolls.'

A marmoset danced the Cheshire Rounds. A tooth-drawer
stood with pincers ready at the door of his tent under a gilt
bowl. Hobby-horses neighed. A hoop-tumbler tumbled, and a
giant looked over the tent-tops at two lovers huggled in a
cart. Flies thickened above the pig-sauce. A pearl-faced girl
sold nuts and apples in an arbour of green boughs. 'I'll no
more, the ale's too mighty,' said a northcountry clothier, setting down his stoneware jug with a bearded face on it. The
Clerk of the Market prowled by with sidelong eyes, looking
for evasion of tolls. In a cautious corner an ape sat on his
tail at the name of the Pope and jumped over a stick for
England. 'My head's full of bees.' Come, said someone, to a
banquet of gingerbread. Come to a dish of neats tongues and
black-puddings. The wise hare beat the tabour. Come to the
pie of larks and cherry crackers. The girl had a long straw-
berry-birthmark on her left calf.

They jostled, monsters and pocketgods, nuns of venus and
men with bagpipes, dragons and jackpuddings. The duck-
arsed blinker in Shoemaker's Row and Peter the Dutchman
walking on a rope. 'Before I'll endure it, I'll be drawn with
a gibcat through the great pond at home as my uncle Hidge
was.' Rufflers and uprightmen, hoopmen and anglers, progmen
and fraters, swaddlers and peddlers. Whipjacks and other
freshwater-seamen whining of storms that cracked the moon
in half. Deadmens of glimmer, bawdry-baskets, doxies and
dells with breasts bursting through their stained seams.
Clattering tinkers and an old man who swore pillows were
fit only for women in childbirth. 'As for him whom I need not
mention,' said the merchant, 'he's not so much as master of
an old urinal-case or a candle-box.' A madman with a sprig
of rosemary stuck in his bare arm broke into sheep-laughter.

Merric peered into the booth and saw a woman standing on
her head on a green cushion.

The girl at the toy-stall wiped her nose and coaxed him,
'But a Bartholomew baby in a box. Buy a dollpoll, buy a
proper poppet, buy a merry mammet.'

'Nor are we so miserable as to make a great repast on a cocks-comb,' said the red-nosed man dressed in gooseturd green and pease-porridge tawny, soberly swallowing Spanish figs.

'Give me a dish of dragon's milk,' said Merric angrily, stopping at an ale-stall.

Buy a fairing, see a wild child with hair all over his body, see a cock with two egg-vents, buy a sucket. This rapier, sir, is lineally descended from half a dozen Dukes. Buy a ballad of godly garters.

Merric moved on, hurrying to a stall of twopenny halberds and wooden backswords. Hocuspocus bawled with three yards of ribbon on his hat. 'Saffron is so plentiful in Essex,' said the dealer, 'the folk are beggared at Waldron and say that God shits saffron.'

Cozeners and palmsters, fortune-tellers and criers, trulls and tomboys. A girl bought carraway-seed comfits to eat with an apple. Sir Francis Ascow in popinjay blue and a dress of jags went giggling by, and his gold earrings glinted; the long seams of his hose were set by a plumbline. A clapperdudgeon, showing wounds made by unslaked lime and iron rust, wailed at him; and the cook waved a dripping spit from a booth-door, yelling, 'A delicate show-pig and crackling, and a glass washt with Hoxton water.'

Merric went on to the Horse Fair, to the coursers with their mane-ribboned horses, the lads with stable-breath, the knights of the knife and children of the hornthumb, the vapourers who stole little penny-dogs. Someone was whispering, 'Aye, for reliable false-dice go to Bird's shop in Holborn.' The horse-cheapening had begun. 'That's an Irish Hobby.' No, an English Hackney, starting and stumbling at every foot, a poor lean jade, nothing but bones and blind of an eye, lame of a leg and all the hooves of his feet spoiled. 'No, look how he frounces his neck and tramples bravely with all his members.' The bargainer spat, a man with side-paunch and Croydon complexion that wouldn't let him blush any more than the Black Dog of Bungay.

Merric moved away again, and stood for a while listening to a barber, who kept on speechifying though the customers waited:

'Will you be cleanslaven like a Turk or wear a beard as
round as a rubbing-brush? Or will you be fashionable with a
pique-de-vent? I tell you, sir, that we barbers are the moulders
of men's faces. For if a customer have a lean and straight face,
we give him a short cut and make him broad and large. If he
be platter-faced, we give him a long slender beard which
narrows him down. If he is weasel-beaked, yet by leaving hair
on his cheeks we make him look big as a bowdled hen or
grim as a goose . . .'

Merric passed on. Searchers, led by a knock-kneed constable, ran past him. He found himself tangled with three
arm-in-arm girls, who would not let him go till he kissed
them.

'Let the cottagers do the spinning and weaving,' said the
small wizened dealer. 'Then we have no charge of them and
they may work all day and night if they so wish. By such
means we may get the wares cheaper.' He looked round
warily and spat. 'Much cheaper.'

A screeching pick-pocket was being carried off to the court-
of-pie-powder for summary judgment.

'Credit? No, no, sir. Trusting engenders the fever.'

At last he found her, at the stall where the bald man was
shouting, 'Almond-butter and puffpaste for pretty ladies!'
She beckoned him over. 'Here, Lettice, is my secret lover, so
secret indeed that I can never find him when I want him.'

'Yet I am here.'

'Who said that this was one of the moments when I want
you? But quickly, if you desire me to stay, give me a good lie.
For I am thought to be visiting my father's widow.' She put
on a scarlet loo, a half-mask with a band coming under the
chin. 'Am I not more handsome with this vizor? You see, my
eyes are still hidden, but my mouth is all the more free for
kissing.' She took his arm. 'Carry me somewhere, into the
heart of the trumpets or an absolute silence. For I am tired
of half-measures. And you, Lettice, keep close to my rump;
for if you must bring an unneeded baby into our house, let
it be one whose father you can name.'

They walked on. Merric said nothing, and Jacint touched
his mouth. 'Why are you so silent, my lover? Surely you have

long prayed for this day when sugared sack and bacon would quarrel under my girdle. Yet now that it has happened and I feel no chaster than a church-sparrow, you are silent and afraid.' She turned and called to Lettice. 'Come closer, fool, and kiss him, to show our mettle.'

They paused between two booths. Lettice tittered, and her long smooth face was flusht under her faint curls. Jacint pushed her against Merric and repeated her order. Lettice tittered again, then flung her arms round Merric's neck and kissed him. Jacint held their heads together.

'He is too stiff and scared,' she said, letting them go. 'But we will teach him better before the day is done. Within seven days my father is taking his widow to bed, so that they may talk over mortgages at midnight; and now I am thirsty.' She grasped his arm again. 'Never was an elephant more fearful of the silly sheep than you are of my laughter.' She laughed and pointed to a fat woman before a cookshop. 'If I had such a wife, I'd present her tallowface to the devil for a candle; but you men have no courage or clarity.'

'We'll find a perrywater stall.'

'I want more wine, Merric. Do you hear? wine of the earth and sun, *sanguis Bacchi* as my belovèd uncle declares. Passion of my heart, you must see me exactly as I am. Take me to more wine, *pocula solis et seminis deorum*. There, I'll talk Latin to baffle you. *Vinum veneris defututae*. Give me wine.'

They wandered down between booths to a quieter part of the Fair, where business-deals were being discussed, and at last found a sleepy wine-booth. A drunken man lay asleep on a bench, and two clothiers were talking apart in a corner. Merric fetched a flagon from the lad who was catching flies and putting them into a box through a small hole. 'The master's dead,' said the boy. 'He bent down to pick up a pin and he fell on his face. He's in the back there under a piece of cloth. The mistress told me not to tell anyone or I'd spoil custom. She's gone off to the Court of Pie Powder. But I'll let you have a look at him for a penny.'

Merric shook his head and carried the wine over to the girls, who were whispering together. 'You think that I am on trial,' said Jacinth, taking off her half-mask, 'because I have drunk more wine than you; but I warn you, my lover, that you

are the one awaiting judgment. For I am myself from foot to
crown, but you are only half yourself, and half a dubiety. Put
your entire spirit into your eyes or I shall find you a stranger.'

Merric frowned. 'I wish only you'd leave off mocking me.
I am enough bewildered without it.'

'Sit on his knee, Lettice,' said Jacint, drinking. 'I want to
see how you appear in his arms. For I have no other mirror
here to show me myself; and though I sound noisy with
wine, I am in truth as sad and uncertain as a newly-caught
starling in a wicker-cage.' She pushed Lettice, who sat on
Merric's knee. 'Kiss him.'

'But it's you I want to kiss.'

'All things in their proper order. I'll not be taken in an unsanctified tumble. No, I'll be led to church between two
sweet boys with bridelaces and rosemary tied about their
silken sleeves; and one of them shall carry a bridecup of silver
gilt with a rosemary-bough of ribbons. And with them shall
go a noise of musicians and a merriment of maidens weaving
garlands of gilded wheat. O, what a day that will be!'

'Jacint, have I asked you for anything else?'

She waved him silent. 'But with Lettice it is different. She
hasn't been a maid for three years, and I have commanded
her to do whatever she desires as long as she tells me all
about it. For I want to know everything. I want to know what
is in books and what has never yet been put inside a book.'
She laughed. 'Only last week Lettice encountered the next-
door prentice in the backlane after dusk, and came home with
gravelled knees and palms, but she told me the tale obediently
in the still-room, where I tended her with rosewater. For at
such a moment she was certainly queened and I her true hand-
maid of lower condition, a vessel without wine and a bush
without flower, whereas she brimmed with wine and burst
with a red flower.'

Lettice wriggled and got off Merric's knees. 'O mistress,
how could you say such a thing?'

'I dare say anything that's true, to the devil's shame. What
is there in men and women that makes them think they are
hidden in the darkness, though they walk abroad in a net?
They are blind geese, all of them, coming to the fox's sermon.'

Lettice gave Merric a wild look and lowered her face. 'Be

kinder to the girl and to yourself,' he said.

'That is no way to win me over.' Jacint drank again. 'If you are not careful, I'll bid you both to a snug place behind the booth, where you may clip under my eyes. For I am both angry against the ways of the world and mad for knowledge as a childing wife for rotten fruit.' She took Merric's hand. 'Let me feel the throbbing of our pulse, my lover. Can it go calmly when you sit so near to our lustful flesh and your brother goes hunted through the gallows-world?' She turned to Lettice. 'Yes, there is scarcely a quickening of his blood.' She threw his hand off, drank, and laughed scornfully. 'Yet we are a good pair, he and I. He cowers under my eyes, while his brother enjoys his wench and then defies the villainies of the law. I talk of my bravery, and yet lack the heart of the little curd-faced wench who went under the obvious bush with Stephen. Should we not smuggle our cowardices together and grow shrill-tongued in a shared contempt?' She laughed. 'The curd-faced child with a secret cat in her lap . . .'

'What must I do?'

She considered his strained face. 'I had half a mind to bid you join your brother. But what use would that be?'

'I spoke with him,' said Merric eagerly. 'I went to the house where they met. I was ready to fight with them when the time came. But by a good chance I was away when the attack came . . .' He frowned. 'Or was it indeed a good chance? You would like me better if I had fought and been killed. If I lay this moment in prison, you would wholly love me.'

'Is it true?' she asked herself. 'Am I as cruel as all that?'

'No, no.' He tried to take her hands.

'Yes, it is true. For I am the fool of words. I am cruel because in a dream it is strong to be cruel and yet nothing happens to stain the red hands. But in life it is different, and I am quite unfit for living.' Two tears welled out from her open eyes and ran down her cheeks. He took her hands, but she wrenched herself free. 'Now I must drink yet more wine, or go home with limp wrists and burning eyes. Which shall it be?'

'Let it be neither,' he said, rising.

She took his hand quietly, saying, 'Please let me be proud of you, Merric, or I am lost.'

III

Before daybreak he left the cottage of the blind girl. He now had a cap, and his clothes had been cleaned and brushed; and he knew the way to the next township. Meeting a labourer in the grey light, he said, 'Good day,' and got no answer. The man trudged on with his heavy hob-nailed boots, and Stephen began hurrying. He passed a sturdy-beggar and his hare-lipt wife croucht, bleary and tattered by a small smouldering fire in a ditch, and then a hairy madman, who called and leered out of a bush. Two women, gathering stubble for thatch or oven-fuel, showed him a short way over the fields to Roger Matthew's house. Skirting a meadow where several more women were cutting branches of madder, he reached Matthew's house in a sheltered close, and knocked.

A girl with nutbrown face answered, and he told her who had sent him. At once she let him in, and took him to the parlour. There Matthew, a square-jawed man with hairy ears and nostrils, bade him welcome, but said that things had been growing ever more difficult in the last few weeks. 'There's a man Drainer, whom the people call Justice Nine-holes, for he has bored nine holes in the roodloft through which to spy on the people in the church, noting which ones hold aloft their hands in adoration of the Baker's God, when the bread is lifted up. Though some say he spends most of the time looking on the women, and the parson bored five holes to his four. However that may be, it is certain that informations have been sent to the bishop.'

'I'll go straight on,' said Stephen.

'No, no, not till you've eaten. I know no danger yet to make me send one of the faithful away without succour.'

At dusk he went on, and lay that night in a wood, waking in the chill of the stars and talking to himself, with a leaf-echo. 'I must do more than I have done. I must rouse men to strike against Belial. What other use is my hunted life? Give me the words that will break the stone of their heart . . . O my beloved in the green of the year . . . Why did I not read more of Rafe's book while I had the time, despite its hard French?' Then he slept again, and at dawn ate some of the bread and cheese put by the nutbrown girl into a scrip for him, and soon, with joyous and tearful face, went down the road.

Within an hour he met a Franciscan Friar coming out of a side-track, and tried to hasten on. But the friar was not to be left behind. He padded along at Stephen's side, and said that he was an Englishman, happily back in England at last after ten years in Italy. His accent was foreign, but he spoke anxiously, with a pleading in his voice and eyes. 'Are you of the faith?' he asked at last. Stephen nodded, and the friar went on, ' The Catholic faith?'

'Aye, even that faith and church which received the whole-some sound, uttered by Isaiah, David, Malachi, and Paul with many others. The sound that has gone throughout the world, in every place, as it was written, and to the ends of the earth.'

'That is very true,' said the friar, wiping his round uneasy face with his loose sleeve. 'And he who doesn't believe the sound of the holy church, as Saint Cyprian says, must err, since whosoever is out of the church is like to them who were out of Noah's ark when the flood came upon all the world. Therefore the ark is likened to the church.'

'And now the flood is here.'

'Yet the church is not only in Germany,' the friar went on, glancing swiftly at Stephen, 'nor was only here in the time of the late schisms, as the heretics affirm. For if the church should be only there, then was Christ a liar, since he promised that the holy ghost should come to us, lead us to the truth, yes, and remain with us to the ends of the world. So now, if we take him for a true sayer, we must needs affirm that the way which is taught in France, Spain, Italy, Denmark, and all Christendom over, is that of the true catholic church.'

'Ah, but I spoke of all the world,' said Stephen, raising his voice 'and not of all Christendom only; and I speak as the word speaks in the Bible. For I am sure that the gospel has been preached, and has been persecuted in all lands. First in Jewry by the scribes and pharisees, and since that time by Nero, Diocletian, and their kingly like, and now here in our own days by men whom I need not name. For that church you term catholic is none otherwise catholic than is figured in Cain, observed by Jeroboam, Ahab, and innumerable others, and set forth in Herod; and as both Daniel and Esdras say in a plain prophecy, which is now fulfilled, and which Christ and his apostles affirmed: There shall come grievous wolves to devour the faithful flock.'

'Are you then so guiltless?' asked the friar gently, 'and have no men died for the catholic faith under the ravening wolves of your apostacy? Also, if you attain to wisdom, you will learn that the prophecies are more plain, and yet less plain, than you now rashly surmise.' They were passing some fields where men sowed in the furrows, and the friar paused to point at their work, 'Yet the grain is sowed and brings forth the bread of life in all fields save those where the darnel chokes it.'

'You know now,' said Stephen, as they moved on, 'that I am one of those whom your bloody bishops call a heretic?'

The friar gave a low laugh. 'I knew it at the first moment.'

'What then are you going to do about it?'

'Nothing. I am too humble a man to judge another. Also, I have no great liking for bishops.'

'I think you have been sent by the devil to break my constancy. For what you say is quite another thing than that which the Bishop of Rome says, or your Cardinal Pole.'

'Yet I say it, and I declare that I am of the catholic faith.'

'If you say it louder, you will be burned like me.'

'I shall keep on saying it, neither whispering nor shouting.'

'You admit then that there are evil courses in your church,' Stephen asked stubbornly.

'It is of the world worldly, and of God godly. In it is the whole truth of man daily set forth, both the murder and the resurrection.'

'Yet it should be wholly of the new life.'

'So we strive to make it. But you strike at the roof of unity; and though your aim is good, your blow is deadly.'

'We seek another sort of unity.'

'You seek to sell Christ another way.'

'In the fire? A strange place for market-bargains.'

'Your particular soul may be saved by your love. I do not

know. But I know where my bond lies and where lies that of the sellers of souls. Pope Gregory the Seventh in Council promulgated canons of which the fifth declares that soldiers and merchants may not carry on their trade without sin, and that unless they turn to other occupations they cannot look for salvation. And the Canonists agree that all profit is *turpe lucrum,* a vile gain.'

'Yet you know well that all these words have been blotted out. If the present Bishop of Rome repeats what your Gregory says, and acts upon his words, I shall listen. Do your leaders say what you say?'

'My leader is my Lord. He says it every hour of the day and night.'

'To me also he says it.' After a while he added, 'I see we shall never agree.'

'We agree more than you think.'

They walked into a village. There, by a great oak, the blacksmith hailed the friar, 'Come and let me feed you, father. It is never merry in England since the Bible was brought in by the heretics.'

'We must part for the moment,' said the friar to Stephen. 'The peace of God go with you.' He turned aside to the blacksmith and Stephen walked on.

IV

Jones was twirling the wine round in his cup, while William walked up and down the room. Then at last came the knock on the outer-door, and Ybel admitted Blaise. William, who had peered through the half-opened door of his room, stood back. 'Where is mistress Dousabel?' he asked as Blaise entered. 'You promised to bring her.'

Blaise sat and crossed his legs. 'At the last moment she had to visit a friend outside London. She swore six months ago to be with her when the pangs of birth began.' He smiled. 'But I understood that you wanted to broach a business-matter. Surely a matter of great profit could alone unite two men whom I thought to be sharply at daggers drawn.'

Jones plucked his chin. 'Yes, a matter of great profit, we believe.'

Blaise looked at William. 'Yet you did not warn me I should find Master Christopher here.' Then, as William stared frowningly, he went on, 'However, why should you? And I am glad to see amity rather than anger in our family. What can I do to help you both?'

William sat heavily down, with face half turned away. After a pause Jones said very suavely, 'To be brief, we ask from you a gift of four hundred pounds each.'

Blaise set his fingertips together, smiled, and answered in undisturbed tones. 'I lack the sums; and even if I had them, I should hold it unfair to my wife and posterity to give away so large a fortune on so light a form of request.'

'The sums are not so large,' said Jones, 'and the request not so light, as you shall find.'

Blaise turned to William. 'Brother, have you any reason to complain against me? Have I not helped you to the best of my ability when you were like to sink in deep waters? I smell here an ingratitude.'

William cleared his throat, but Jones spoke first. 'Here is no matter of gratitudes or beatitudes, but of plain justice. For you owe us the money.'

'Show me the bond and my hand set to it.'

'I cannot show you the document, but I have here a memorandum of our treasures in your custody. Thus, two collets of gold in which stand three coarse emeralds. Fourteen knots of pearls. A chalice of gold . . .' He waved a paper. 'Shall I add up the sums? There are many more items.'

Blaise gripped his chair. 'First, you will explain why you have compiled a list of articles I sold on behalf of a friend of mine, spoils of an old abbey that had come into his hands.'

'You did it with much secrecy.'

'It was a secret matter.'

William spoke at last. 'We know that these things came from the chest in the chapel. We know that you learned where the chapel lay, and slipped in ahead of us.'

'We know how you learned it,' said Jones gleefully. 'We know that you set the painted poppaea your wife to pull down Merric into her riggish snares. We know all your trickeries.'

Blaise sat tautly silent for a while, then he said in a low toneless voice, 'You meant to cheat me of my share, and in defence of my rights I sought to defeat your plot. But you overestimate what I found. Also, you forget that I have been using this gold to supply the needs of my brother Will.'

'At a price,' said William harshly. 'At a price that ties me down to your will for many years to come.'

'Only for your own further profit. I tell you that you have set too high the value of what I got from the chest.'

'Shall I read the list all through?' said Jones. 'And shall I add that you told the buyer of many more such valuables, which would be his if he kept silence and paid a good price.'

'It was said to gain his interest. You have no proof that any of these things came from the chest. I have many dealings with plate and land of which you know nothing.'

'Show us the chest and how much yet remains within it.'

'I know nothing of your chest.'

'But you admitted that you cheated us.'

'I admitted nothing. True, I went first to the chapel, but I found only an empty hole. Even so, I borrowed money to save Will from a bankruptcy. Now you all turn on me with your jealousies.'

'You have lied,' said William, 'and still you lie.' He took up a cup and smashed it on the floor. 'I have been too easy-hearted. I have let you tyrannise upon me, younger brother though you are. But now I shall set you in your place.' He moved threateningly towards Blaise.

Blaise curled up in his chair. 'Stand back. I have no ready money. I have lent it all to you and paid it out against an estate that I seek for our family's good.'

Jones grasped William's arm. 'What you will now do, my friend, is nothing much,' he said to Blaise in silky tones. 'You will write a short note to your Dousabel, telling her to hand over all her jewels and show us where the other things are kept.'

'Her own jewels she will hand over at no man's signature,' said Blaise, with a small mean laugh. 'And she knows nothing of the place where I keep my own savings.'

'Then you must tell her in your letter, and I will go with her to get the treasure, making sure that nothing golden is lost under her greedy skirts.'

Blaise put his hand to his ear. 'There is None ringing, and the monks are going to the frater for a bellyful of beer.' He looked quickly round. 'If I am not returned home within the hour, there will be a sergeant knocking at your door.'

'How is that?' asked William.

Blaise gave a snickering laugh. 'Do you think I came here so unprepared? I knew that your Welshman had been asking questions about me where he had no right. Therefore I bade my wife go straight to my good friend, Mr. Popham, with a letter, if I should fail to return within a certain time. Do you truly think I am such a great fool as to be taken by your raw baits? And while I speak, Will, let me tell you that if I had not spoken up on your behalf you'd be this moment in the Fleet with Hugh, and Merric would lie with you. The Bishop was in a great anger at Stephen, who was reported to be a ringleader in rebellion; but I had divers friends intervene for you. Thus you and Merric have escaped for the moment. I told you nothing at the time, yet I can still undo what I have done.'

William paced up and down the room a moment, deep in thought. Then he said weakly, 'Blaise, I lent my countenance to this matter against my will and judgment. But I have now changed my mind. You can go as you wish.'

Blaise rose slowly, shaking himself. 'It is easy for a man like the Welshman to act against the law, since he can flee at a warning. But you, Will, are a man of family and fortune, and no fit friend for such a fly-by-night.'

'You are right,' said William humbly. 'I beg you not to hold my imprudence against me.'

'Not if you rid yourself of this halter from round your neck,' said Blaise, going to the door.

'And you will continue with your loans?'

'I may have to reconsider the terms.'

Blaise went out. Jones drew a knife, but William grabbed his arm. 'It was a lie!' cried Jones.

'I cannot take such chances,' said William. 'He was right in what he said. Let the knife go.'

The knife dropped to the floor. 'Then I shall get the gold myself alone. You have renounced your share.'

'I don't want a quarrel, but you must go.'

'Then give me five pounds for all the expenses met on your behalf.'

William considered. 'I will give you two pounds, but not a farthing more, now or any other time, do you hear?' He paused. 'Go and get your case. I'll give you the money when you come down.'

Jones watched his face, then without a word went out. William bent to pick up the knife, which had fallen with its point down. For a moment it resisted and then came out of the timber, and he staggered back against the table. Nest opened the door, stared at him, and then shut the door with a bang.

Nest went upstairs to Agnes's room. She paused for a moment, listening with her ear against the door; then she drew a bolt and looked in. 'You still haven't eaten anything?' she said, and went into the room. 'You'll die.' She went over to the window. 'It is better to be alive with a rat in your belly than dead in a golden grave. Anything is better than death . . .' Her voice trailed away. Then, still speaking out of the window, she went on 'There are some mothers who beat their children night and day. There are some mothers who'd beat their daughters for refusing to eat good christian food . . . I have never beaten my children. I have spoken kindly words always, and so they despise me.'

'Once you hit me in the face with a boot and almost blinded me,' said Agnes from the bed, in slow accusing tones. 'Once you pulled a hank of my hair out. so that my scalp bled . . . Once . . .' She wept.

'But I did all that in a moment of anger,' said Nest, 'meaning nothing . . . if I did it at all; for indeed I begin to think you have made it up against me in your mind, knowing that my memory is weak.'

'Why did you say you were going to Chepe last Wednesday,' said Agnes in the same tones, 'and yet you went to Paul's?'

'How should I know?' asked Nest in surprise. 'Do you know why you go to one place rather than another?' Then she tiptoed over to the bed. 'You must get married at once, do you hear?' She whispered. 'It would be better to sin with a man than lie here with such thoughts.'

Agnes gave a wild laugh. 'First you must prove to me that I am a woman.'

v

Stephen sat on the edge of the bed, making shoelaces with the sick man, Woodman. The child Debora came running in below. 'Mother, mother, there's a score of men coming!' At once Woodman thrust his leg from under the bedclothes, and Stephen helped him into his hose. The woman below was barring the door. Stephen and Woodman went down. Staggering slightly and holding his hose up with one hand, Woodman ran to bar the other door, while Stephen helped him. Someone began banging on the front door: 'Open, or we'll break in.'

Debora stood aside with the fingers of one hand in her wide mouth. Her pale stringy hair fell over her face. Mrs. Woodman was pulling the table towards the door. Stephen ran to help her. She climbed up on to the table and lifted out a part of the panelling over the lintel. Stephen got Woodman onto the table. Then he and Mrs. Woodman managed to raise him up into the cavity. 'There's room for two,' she muttered, and with an effort he clambered up after Woodman. She put the panel back.

The oblong space was dark except for a dim shaft of light through a little grating. Down in the room the woman was moving the table away. The crashes on the door were growing louder. Then the door gave way.

'Why did you bar us out, mistress?'

'I thought you were thieves. The child came running in afraid, to say that thieves were upon us.'

'A born heretic,' cried someone with a high-pitched voice.

Sounds of stamping feet and cracking wood.

'Why didn't you look through an upper window and see for yourself?'

'Alas, they say that whoever takes my husband will hang and burn him, and so I fear for my own fate, being flesh of his flesh.'

'We know he's in the house, with another runaway traitor. And so we must search you, for we are sheriff's men. Give me a candle, to see into your dark places. A neighbour has told us that there are many lurking-holes in this house of yours.'

'And it is written,' cried the high-pitched voice, 'that the candle of the Lord shall search the backward places and very bowels of the sinner. There is tit for tat, citation for citation, eh?'

'I think you must be a turncoat christian, with a conscience that stings you,' said Mrs. Woodman and then cried out at a blow.

Feet tramping, more cracking of wood, shouts: then the noises retreated. 'They are going into the churchyard,' whispered Woodman. 'Pray that they think I went that way despite all their watchings.'

Footsteps. The high-pitched voice. 'Come here, my sweet child, what is your name?'

'Debora.'

'Tell me where your father lies, and I'll give you some comfits.'

'He told me to shut my eyes so that I shouldn't see which way he went.'

Footsteps going. Then a trouble of voices coming nearer. Woodman whispered. 'Ah, that is my old father they've brought in. But they'll get nothing out of him.'

VI

'I'm staying at the fifth house past the new tavern in Kent Street,' said Jones. 'Make a note of it, lad.' He drank and banged the mug down on the tavern-table. Then scratched his front teeth. 'I must go to a barber and be unscaled.' He gave a harsh laugh. 'I never give up, lad. No matter how many times I'm beaten, I never give up.'

Merric sat sprawling. 'You're beaten this time. And so am I.'

'I'll get the gold, and you'll get the girl. Come on, let's go and eat a salmon stuck with cloves.'

'In a moment. First I'd like some more ale, and a plate of those saffron cakes with raisins.' He belched.

'He was lying, lying. I learned afterwards that his Blousabel was in Chepe all the while, buying buckram. He'd written no letter for Popham.'

Merric gave a drunken grin. 'You're beaten, Kit, and so am I. Think of it. She was plump as a berry with wine, and I took her home in the dusk with no more payment than a corner-kiss. She taunts me when I'm with her, and makes me want to be a better man than I'll ever be. But I'm sick of virtue. What's the use? If I married her, I'd feel all the while that she despised me for not being other than I am. She wants a man as steadfast as Stephen and as merry as a fiddler on Twelfth Night.' He belched again. 'I don't know what she wants me to do. That's what breaks me down.' He muttered, 'Let's set fire to the Guildhall.'

'Aw, go and pick a daisy,' said Kit. 'No profit in that.'

'Who was the man for whom you and Ben carried cloth to Flanders?' demanded Merric with a rising voice.

'Sssh, it's not safe to say it aloud. He's a sea-captain, lad, who'll tear your tongue out as soon as spit in your eye. This year I hear he's been harrying the French coast under an English flag.'

'If the worst comes, we'll go and join him. Do you know how to find him at need?'

'Aye, through a man at Southampton.' Jones beckoned to the tapster. 'But I haven't given up Master Blaise yet, O no.'

VII

The sergeant gave Hugh a shove through the doorway, and Bishop Bonner turned sharply from the bay window in the great chamber of St. Mary Overy's. 'Come here, sirrah.' Hugh went slowly over and stood with downcast eyes. The Bishop hemmed and tossed onto a chair his silver-ouched gloves 'You are a member of a worshipful company. I am surprised to find you in the gospel-gossips.' He said in a smiling voice, 'Look up, man. There is no need to study my gilt slippers. Are you indeed one of the desperate dicks?'

'The light is in my eyes if I look up,' murmured Hugh.

'It is understandable that the simple people should run out

of their wits by reading of deep matters; but the part of a good citizen is to offset such violence with gravity and good sense.'

'I trust I have not offended,' said Hugh, louder.

The monk who had come behind him spoke. 'One of his apprentices has been burnt as a heretic, and the other is hunted by the law at this moment.'

'Still it is not shown in what I have offended,' said Hugh, with more confidence.

'We shall soon clear that matter,' said Bonner, now sharply.

The monk consulted a piece of paper. 'It is credibly reported that he has called the blessed host a slice of bread and not the natural body of Christ who was born of the Virgin.'

'I believe that the soul of man does not feed on natural things as the body does,' said Hugh, with a note of warmth.

'How then does it feed?' demanded Bonner.

'Through faith.'

'Yet the body must feed on natural things, or the soul cannot continue with the body. Therefore the body must feed on natural things that both may live together.'

'Yes, but man does not live by bread alone. I pray you, what did Judas receive at the supper?'

'Why, he received the very body,' said Bonner impatiently, 'but to his damnation.'

'What then, the devil had already entered into him, so that he had both Christ and devil in his flesh?'

'No, no, the devil entered him after,' said the monk.

Bonner chafed. He put his cap off, and ran his finger to and fro over the forepart of his head where a lock of hair was always standing up: which lock many men used to call his Grace. 'After, after,' he repeated. 'The devil entered him after. Now are you satisfied?'

'But also before,' Hugh persisted. 'I think he had a legion of devils at the latter end.'

'Well,' said the monk, 'but case it is so: what say you to that?'

'I ask how the devil and Christ, if both in him at the same time, did agree together?'

The monk replied with drawling condescension, 'We grant

they were both in Judas at that time. For Christ may be where the devil is, if he will; but the devil cannot be where Christ is, if Christ wills him away.'

'Surely Christ would not be in an unclean place with the devil?' asked Hugh in eager argument. But then his face changed, and a bleak look of suffering came into his eyes. He touched his brow.

'Was he not in hell?' crowed the monk. 'And yet you will grant that the devil is there of all places.'

'He did not suffer Mary Magdalen to touch him, when she sought him at the grave,' said Hugh with faltering voice. He passed his hand over his face and groaned. 'O, O . . .' He stared at the monk. 'What was I saying?'

'Little enough to the point. Was not Christ in hell? I ask you.'

'It is true,' said Hugh meekly.

'Then what of the other things? Is he not in the bread when it becomes his body? Is he not in the church of God?'

'Yes, it is true.'

Bonner came back from the window where he had been fuming. 'This is a better speech.'

Hugh lowered his head. 'I trust I have not offended.'

'Let me try him again,' said the monk.

'If he speaks to the point and agrees with mother church, there is no need to torment him.' Bonner turned to Hugh. 'My good man, do you agree with the church that Christ is bodily present in the sacrament?'

'Yes, my lord.' Without raising his head he spoke louder. 'Yes, my lord.'

'Let him go,' said Bonner. 'Let him go, and bring in the next man. See that you keep to your good counsel, Master Rigeley, or you shall hear from me again. Fetch us here a paper saying that you have confessed and received communion within the week.'

The monk went out with Hugh. 'See that you wear the faggot-badge when you stir from your house,' he said fiercely, 'or you will be considered a relapsed heretic, do you hear?'

VIII

On the outskirts of the village he met a small girl, about eight years of age, and stood for a moment, swaying with fatigue. 'Tell me,' he asked, 'are there any heretics in this place?'

'O, yes, indeed,' she said with a smile, and went on mending an osier-basket.

'Where are they?'

'At the Anchor Inn.'

He went on about twenty paces and then halted again. He stood swaying and after a while returned to the girl. 'How do you know that this innkeeper is a heretic?'

'O, well enough,' she said, screwing up her eyes against the sunlight and lifting her head so that the yellow hair fell down her back among the leaves of a hollybush. 'And his wife too.'

'But how do you know? I beg you.'

'How do I know? Why, because they go to the church. And those who will not hold up their hands there, they present them before the justices. And Master Rigson himself goes from house to house, to compel everyone else to come to the church.'

Stephen stood with closed eyes a moment, then went up into the pinetrees on the left. The girl continued demurely plaiting the osiers.

IX

Agnes walked slowly down the stairs and into the solar. Nest came running up from below and thrust a book into her daughter's hand. 'It is a book I bought in Paul's for you. Since you needs must read, here is something, but I forget what it is.' She began peering anxiously. 'Tell me what it is. It is no heretical book, I hope.'

'*The Castle of Knowledge*,' said Agnes, opening the book. 'By Robert Recorde, printed last year.'

'Well, there is no harm in a castle,' said Nest; 'and as for knowledge it's been a rotten apple these many years, but digestible by those who know how to spit out the pips in time.'

She hurried from the room, and Agnes idly turned the pages, then began reading with interest. Ybel entered the solar and stood waiting for her to look up. At last he coughed, but she still read on. Then he coughed again, and she started. 'What is it, Ybel?'

He came nearer. 'How sick you look, mistress.' He blinked and said softly, 'May I ask you what Sanchia has been saying about me?'

'Nothing as far as I know. Why do you ask?'

'I tried to kiss her yesterday,' he faltered. 'Well, a trifle more than that; and she said she'd complain to the master about me. She said she'd get him to send me away.'

'I'm sure she hasn't said anything.'

Ybel brightened. 'He's always very kind to her, as indeed it is only right he should be.' He came closer. 'Merric advised me to use roughness. He said a girl wouldn't respect me for looking sad and beggarly. But neither way seems any use.'

Agnes smiled wanly. 'Merric is sure to be wrong about women.'

'He told me to make her jealous too. But I don't see how I can do that.'

Agnes considered him for a while. 'Poor Ybel, why can't you?'

'It wouldn't make her jealous if I kissed Gladus, would it?' He wiped his mouth at the thought.

'Gladus isn't the only other woman in the house or the neighbourhood.'

'I tried to talk with Alice next door, but she wouldn't wait.'

Agnes smiled and sat up. 'What about me?' she said, leaning her head on one side. 'Why haven't you asked my loving help before?'

'Will you help me to deceive her?' he asked in surprise. 'But how?'

'You shall pretend a love for me, and I'll be kind in return. Perhaps that will make her look at you with new eyes and warmer heart.' She held out her hand. 'You might as well begin at once. Kiss me here.' She pointed to her cheek.

'You don't mind?' asked Ybel, wide-eyed.
She pointed to her cheek.

x

'She came here dressed as a drunken man, and went up-stairs with Cicely. But Cicely cried out after a while, and I ran to her room. There she sat with a cut on the palm of her hand, and the stranger lay on the floor in a swoon. So we put her to bed, till she woke and called with milk and pease-pudding. But who she was, she didn't tell us, except that she'd never had a father. I've been sent to suffer all things, she said again and again. So we named her Suffering-all-things, till Cecily shortened it to Sophie. Will you abide by the custom of the house? I asked her. That is the very thing I desire, she answered, drinking milk out of a long jug. And that's the way it is. Not once has she been out of doors except to the jakes in the backyard, and she cannot bear even to look out of the windows. Not that she gains any visitors except among those too drunk to care how strangely a woman may talk.'

'I'd like to see her,' said Jones.

They went upstairs and the woman opened a door. Jones looked in. A tall emaciated girl was lying naked on the rumpled bed, holding a mirror above her face at arms-length. Hearing the noise, she rolled over and stared at Jones. 'I know you,' she said at last, 'despite the mask you wear over your face. You have been sent by my father. But it is no use. I am nightly visited by the Angel Gabriel.'

'What shall I say to the world?'

'That it has come to pass, as the prophet Jeremiah said, and all shall be well except for you and the myriads who wear your face.' She gave a shrill laugh. 'Why do you keep so mis-fitting a mask? Cannot you pay for one that has the likely features of a man? Or if that is too costly, cannot you buy the vizard of a viper or a lion?' She laughed again. 'Are masks then so rare that you must botch up a painted thing like that and set it upon your shoulders? Alas for my pretty devils with faces round as eggs . . .'

'Farewell, Sophie,' he said and closed the door. Something that she threw after him hit on the wood.

XI

The poor were feasting at the trestle-tables set before the garlanded doors of Hawes's house. Minstrels were playing and children were dancing for nuts. Every now and then Hawes came out to see how things were going, and the feasters gave him a cheer. Up in the solar the marriage-feast proper was being celebrated, with Mrs. Pernel Hawes simpering through her enamelled face. 'Sir, you come looked for in good time!' shouted Hawes to a late-comer.

'I have played the villain,' said Walls the draper, 'for I was bidden to dinner and not to make you stay for me.'

'You are all welcome,' repeated Hawes. 'You are all welcome.'

'Yes, indeed,' said Pernel. 'That is easy to say, sirs, you are all welcome.'

'Heartily welcome,' said Hawes.

'That is to say, sirs, most heartily welcome,' said Pernel.

'Master, do not push me,' said Mrs. Fiscont, with her hair already sweaty on her brow, 'for I am with child.'

'Take them a basin of water and a towel,' called Hawes, 'let them all wash together, for good manners' sake. Come to table, everyone of you. Aye, sit down, my magnificent masters, for there remains nothing now but to eat and drink, and all will be well.'

'Let my little boy Harry say grace, I beg you,' said Mrs. Fiscont. 'He will cry for an hour otherwise. For he dotes on saying grace.'

'Come, little Harry,' cried Hawes, 'say us grace.'

'There is a fat man still eating plums,' said Harry pointing. The fat man choked and spluttered, and had at last to be led out by a servant. Then Harry, appeased, recited in a high piping voice, 'God send us of his grace, and in his Paradise a place.'

'Draw your knives,' said Hawes, drawing his own from the case in which he carried it. 'Help that gentlewoman. See there

the venison pasty. And there is one of stag's flesh. Begin
where it pleases you. You see our cheer. Welcome all. Bring
in the roast. Fie, this piece of beef is raw, take it out. Help
yourself, sirs, in the meanwhile. Cut up this hare and open
the lid of that pigeonpie. Slice up that shoulder of mutton,
dismember that capon, be doing with those rabbits. Assault
that bulwark-pie and make prisoner its valiant kidneys. Set
in order on the table the hens, conies, pheasants and wood-
cocks.'

'What sauce shall we have for these dishes?' asked Mrs.
Fiscont, with watering mouth. 'For I yearn most strangely
for sharp sauces.'

'There is citron sauce,' said Hawes, 'and olives kept in
pickle.'

'O, reach me hither the dish of olives,' she cried. 'I once
saw a man who swallowed down olivestones, as an estridge
swallows iron.'

'Now I drink to you all,' said Hawes, 'and you are all very
well welcome. Where are our crystal glasses? Will you drink
after the Greek fashion in this great goblet? Let us drink
together by good accord in charity. I drink to you all; for
you seem to me true christians, I drink nothing to those dogs
the devil Turks, Mohometans, I deny and renounce them for
villains who are accursed never to drink a drop of wine. If
no other mischief were in the Alcoran, yet would I never be
of their law. We are happily met here, my friends, for you
know that this day I change for the better. Therefore in
conclusion of my oration I will merely say to you that as for
myself I think I am descended of some rich king in olden
time. For you never saw a man who had greater desire to be
a king, and rich, than myself, to the end to make good cheer,
to take no pains at all, to care for nothing and to enrich
my honest friends. And now, go to, make a long arm, and
fear not the Lombards' bit.' He sat down suddenly.

'You speak so much, cousin, you eat nothing,' said Mrs.
Fiscont, spilling mint-sauce. 'O, how my belly wambles.'

'He has already drunken well,' said Walls behind his hand
to the man at his side, 'for I never heard a man speak more
out of character.'

'He will eat his words with the cheese,' said the other.

Mrs. Fiscont squealed, 'Something is crawling up my leg.'

'Cousin Jacint, may I press you to a little pretty eel in a milky sauce?' asked Lionel Wicke, come pallid from his mother's country-house to attend her wedding. 'Not that you are my cousin neither,' he added with a snivelling laugh. 'For this marriage makes you sister, and yet not sister neither, since we are still free to marry, I trust, if the will unreasonably took us.'

'No eel please,' said Jacint, 'and no marriage neither. For a man and woman who are free to marry are also free to go another way, I trust. So take up your eel and depart with all your compliments upon a plate, well-soused with a milky sauce.'

'I said it only in the way of wit, cousin,' said Lionel, draping his long pale finger round a tall kinecup, 'and not as a tendering of legal contract. For if a man were to be held religiously to every gay word that passes his lips in wine, it were a monstrous injustice.' He leaned over to his mother and pressed her arm. 'Don't forget that I agreed to this occasion only after you promised to spend the daisy-months of the year in the country with me.' He returned to Jacint, 'Alas, that the children must beweep the follies of their parents, who cannot learn that a pleasure repeated once too often becomes a sorrow, as the sweetest musk is sour when tasted and the finest pills are bitter when chewed.'

'I use no musk, but am a woman unadorned,' said Jacint, 'and since I take no pills, my health is good. Please do not tempt me, dainty cousin, from my city-simplicities into your country-confections.' She smiled across the table at dark-browed Martin.

'I am returning tomorrow,' Lionel petulantly answered, 'and I know that I shall fall ill at the thought of what I leave behind.'

'Please, Lionel, be good,' pleaded his mother. 'Please, please do not write me a cruel letter again. You know that I will do anything for your solace.'

'Ha, false fever, will you not pack hence?' cried Hawes, drinking. He turned to Pernel. 'You are a-cold, my love. Let's speak of drinking. As for myself, I drink only at my hours, like the Pope's mule. I have a great thirst.' Then to

Rafe, 'Which was first, thirst or drinking?'

'Drinking,' said Rafe. 'For *privatio presupponit habitum*.'

'I drink only by letter of attorney,' said Walls.

'Do you wet to dry or dry to wet?' asked Hawes, glancing at Pernel for applause.

'I do not understand the rhetoric,' said Brack. 'With the pratique I help myself a little.'

'Courage,' said the small dark man, 'I wet, I moisten, I drink, and all for fear of dying.' He fondled Mrs. Fiscont's knee under the table, and this time she did not cry out.

'Drink always and you'll never die,' said Rafe.

'If I stop drinking, I am dead,' said the small man and spilt a cupful of red wine into Mrs. Fiscont's lap.

'You are all welcome, you are all very well welcome,' said Hawes.

Jacint stole up the stairs after Rafe, stepping quietly, and touched him from behind as he paused before his door. 'I thought it was Mrs. Fiscont's mouse after me.'

'Let us hide from the mad voices for a moment.'

He opened the door and they went in. She went to the window while he lighted his candle. 'It is no use,' he said as he fumbled about. 'It's no use at all . . . Yet the earth is a sweet place, more sweet than bitter, and love is a lovely thing, more lovely than brutish. Cease kicking against the pricks, and find your place under a summer-tree.'

The candle-flame wavered and burnt up, and they were enclosed in a cavern of faint gold. 'Beside a certain cloth-worker and his widow-wife?' she asked sharply. 'I prefer this rotting tower among the stars.'

He went to the window and stared out. 'Somewhere in this night young Stephen is hunted by the bloody-hounds. I begin to find my patience wearing thin after all. But as for you, niece, if you cannot love your parents, at least laugh at them, and so get free another way; but do not hate them. For hatred is the worst bond of all.'

'Then I shall laugh at them,' she said coldly.

'There is no laughter in your voice.' He turned. 'What do you want of this Merric of yours?'

'What do I want of myself?' she laughed angrily. 'I have

no desire to see him hunted to a foul death like Stephen. I
have no desire to see him cheating his way into fortune and
good-name . . .' She went to the door. 'You cannot help me,
Rafe,' she said sadly. 'No one can help another.'

'Of course we can help one another,' he replied. 'That is a
better truth than yours, the only truth in the end.'

But she was gone. At the foot of the stairs she bumped
against someone, and found it was Martin. He muttered
thickly. 'Drunk as an ape,' she said in distaste. 'Let me go.'

'You admit you were seen at the Fair with Merric,' he said
heavily. 'You only do it to make me angry . . . Well, now I
am angry. Either you give him up or I'll beat you.'

'One more word from you, Martin, and I'll go straight to
him, do you hear?'

'I hear.'

He tried to twist her arm, but she slipped away and opened
the door into the solar. 'You are all very well welcome,'
Hawes was saying. 'Eat some of that gammon, and you will
drink more courageously. Fear not that wine and victuals
will fail here. For though the heavens should be of brass
and the earth iron, yet wine would not fail us, a longer time
than the famine lasted in Egypt, I swear.' She closed the door.

XI

For three days he hid in a wood, eking out his bread and
cheese with berries and a turnip. Sleeping under sprays of
barberry tasseled with crimson fruit. Creeping to the edge nearest to the village: hearing the sound of the flail on the granary
floor. Low rumble of the cider-mill and (nearer still in the
night) the scent of crusht apples heavy on the air. From
stubble-fields the creaking of the plough. Apples on lichened
boughs: wasps and starlings at work. Crossbill cutting fruit
in two at one stroke of the bill, one bill writhing over the
other, to get at the pips. Spikes of agrimony against the sky,
and convolvulus hanging white bells on the hedgerow with
browning leaves. Ringdove grey-feathered under the oak at
the acorns, chiffchaff's cheery note, O sweet earth, earth-
pulse, nuthatch's tapping bill.

He muttered to himself under the bushes. 'Lost for ever. In vain, in vain. Go back, go back . . . to life, to death: which is which? life, death . . . Mabel in the May of the year . . . in vain, in vain. How may the heart of man be opened? . . .'

Then he started in fear at the echo of his muttering, and lay still in a ditch, while the mute and hasty lovers went past. A woman riding pillion on the highway, a man lashing at a post-horse, a four-wheeled carriage lumbering with six horses. And back again to the place where the gallows showed stark against the sky on the hilltop, dangling the thief that the provost-marshal hanged last week. A man with a dog.

He climbed into a tree. The dog sniffed at the tree-foot, but went on at a whistle.

'Go back, go back . . .'

He went into a village and found a small crowd near the Cross. A Bible was being burnt. No one noticed him, but he saw a man who clenched his fists. Afterwards he followed the man down a lane.

'Are you one who rejoices in the burning of the truth?'

The man looked at him narrowly, then said, 'No.'

'I am hungry, and hunted for the truth's sake.'

They went on down the lane, and all the while he talked in a low rambling voice. 'I was bidden to go back. I tossed two twigs in the air and they fell in the shape of a cross pointing this way . . . I lie at the pool's brink and every man goes in before me. But have no fear. I have overcome death. I have dared the eyes of the enemy again and again, but they never see me. The angel of the Lord pitches his tent round those who fear him. Yet now I am fearless once more . . . I am afraid . . .' Then he said nothing for a while, till they turned in through an old stone gate; and then he asked quietly, 'How are the hearts of the people?'

'They are not bound in malice,' said the man mildly, 'but they are fallen in dismay. For the priest is a heavy man, who lacks wit, learning, and honesty. It seems that they all await a token of the Lord's will . . .'

'We are ourselves the tokens,' said Stephen, as they came to the door of the timbered house. 'We are ourselves the signs. I have seen miraculous deaths and lives of men stricken lower than the worm or the blind things of the sea. For life changes before our eyes like the rack of clouds in a tumbling wind . . .'

They went in, and were served with food by a silent heavy-browed woman. The man began an argument on the interpretation of Daniel, growing hotter and louder in his words, till suddenly Stephen, who had been tracing with his fingernail a knot in the wood, started up and said, 'I must go back to London.'

XIII

He sat listening in the dark room. A faintly creaking house, a door closing, a distant voice like the voice of a drowning man, and feet padding on the stairs. At last he called, 'Rosbel!'

She entered with a candle, and came up close, staring into his face and saying nothing.

'What are we to do, Rosbel? what are we to do in such a world?'

'What we have always done.'

'Sit down,' he said, and she sat with the candlestick on her lap, coughing now and then, licking up over her upperlip, sniffling, and all the while staring at him. He went on in a hurried voice, 'There are men writing abroad who loose us from all obedience. Knox declares that the Queen is not to be obeyed since it is monstrous in nature for a woman to bear empire, since she is a traitoress and a bastard, and since she is a cruel Jezebel. Therefore are we loosed. Also, Goodman says that when the laws fall into evil it is lawful for the common people to enforce the true laws against the transgressing magistrates. What is your answer to all that?'

'That a woman should bear empire is strange, I admit. But it is a thing seen in more households than are called upon to fill the ducking-stool. For the rest, I know nothing, and the less said the better.'

He groaned. 'I have done evil, Rosbel. I have denied the truth, and now I shall be haunted by informers and spies. I have even forfeited my life to the law by telling you the words of Knox and Goodman.'

'I have already forgotten what you said.'

'Therefore I needed no courage to say it. But if I went out into the street with such a declaration, I should horribly die. So I sit here.'

'The less fool you. And now tell me what you desire for supper.'

'Nothing. All that I eat tastes of blood and burnt flesh.' He groaned. 'O, I stood before him, Rosbel, and I spoke in all meekness. But my soul cried out: You bloody Bonner, you limb of Leviathan and working-tool of Satan! What is your idolatrous mass and lousy latin service but the draff of anti-christ and dregs of the devil, you sosbelly swillbowl! Turn in shame on your doing, you beastly bellygod all ringed with golden pillows! So my soul cried out, but my tongue was afraid.'

'Such harsh words were indeed better left unsaid.'

He held his head in his hands for a while, then said, 'Some bread, please, and some cabbage-broth. But don't yet go. I am afraid of death when I sit alone.'

'They say it is good to think upon our death.'

'But not all the while, Rosbel.' He raised his head and looked curiously at her. 'Once you were a neat and smiling girl. I remember you fifteen years ago.' He paused and said with a gulp, 'In the days when my sweet wife was still alive.'

'I laid her out with my own hands.' She lifted her hands towards him, swollen and darkened hands.

'What has happened to you, Rosbel? What has happened to us all?'

'Ah, you were a handsome man in those days, and now you're a withered stock. Time meddles sadly with all flesh!'

'How old are you?'

'Thirty-three, I think. I make a nick every Mayday at the side of my bed. Else I'd forget.'

'You have long given up hope,' he said sadly, watching her. 'When did you first despair? I have taken too little thought of those about me.'

'You mean that I give no considerations to my clothes or the manner of my hair?' she asked, tightening her brow. 'I forget . . . Maybe it was fifteen years ago, maybe it was last year. But whenever it was, you never noticed. And I have forgotten.' She rose. 'Shall I fetch you wine or beer?' She added musingly, 'It's easy holding down the latch when nobody pulls the string.'

'Stay and talk with me.'

'You mean: listen.'

'No, talk . . . I want to hear another voice.'

'I've nothing to talk about. I sleep and I wake. I eat and I drink. I have no complaints.'

'Has no man ever loved you, Rosbel?' he asked tenderly.

'I don't know.' She sat again. 'Years ago there was someone, but it's all confused in my mind. And then another, but he went away, I think. It all happened for the best. Doubtless they were men as good as the next, and yet they would have broken my heart if given time enough. I am thankful after all that I live with no child to make me afraid of its father's cruelty. Now my life is my own concern, and my death also, nothing to be grudged me, if I like it best.'

'I seem to remember you had a sister . . .'

'Ah, Marian. She was maidservant to a farmer near Chelmsford, and one day she was leading a pair of horses with a harrow, walking in front. Her master was ploughing in the next field and thought she went too slowly. Which is like enough, for she was given to musing. So he stole up behind her horses and belaboured them of a sudden; and they passed with the harrow over her fallen body.'

'She was killed?'

'They brought him up at the sessions; but he pleaded her laziness, and was found not-guilty. Still, when my mother wanted me to take her place so that I might again live at home, I refused.'

'You never told me.'

'You never asked before. Besides, I am glad that I stayed with you.'

'Why?'

She rose with a sigh, 'The blind eat many a fly, and I have swallowed a peck. Yet I am as well fed as many who have roamed far, to die in an unfriendly ditch.' She sighed again, 'Well then, for the moment I must love you and leave you.'

As she reached the door, he cried out, 'O, I have acted badly in all things. I drove my child out into the darkness, and I drove the truth from my mouth. Lord, send me no comfort, but overwhelm me with your tempest!'

XIV

'You may take my hands and kiss them,' said Agnes. Ybel gave a shy grin and took them. 'She will come into the room soon,' Agnes went on. 'Now you may kiss me on the mouth.' She laughed. 'No, you kiss without kissing. You move your lips upon me like a cow feeling at the grass before she munches.'

'I don't want to show any disrespect,' said Ybel.

'Then close your eyes and imagine I am Sanchia.'

He closed his eyes and kissed her on the ear. 'But now I cannot see you.'

'You mouth will learn its way in the darkness. Now call me Sanchia, and maybe I shall indeed become her under your hands. For what is there different between us two? Can you now swear upon your salvation that I am Agnes and not Sanchia in warm truth? Already that is better. It is the daylight which limits our differences and cuts us apart; but in the night, though we are afraid, we come out beyond our fears into an embrace of angelic liberty. Therefore I think, at times that night, despite its goblins and succubating sirens, has a starlight of Eden . . .'

The door opened, and Sanchia gave a little scream. Ybel at once started guiltily up, blushing; but Agnes lay back smiling among the cushions. 'Wood to chop,' muttered Ybel, hurrying to the door.

'Don't go,' said Agnes to Sanchia.

'You should have told me,' said Sanchia. 'I'm surprised . . .' She flushed and her voice faltered. 'I mean, I didn't think . . .' She turned away. 'I'm wanted in the still-room.'

'No, come here,' said Agnes. Sanchia came unwillingly over; and Agnes, reaching out, took her hands. 'He's a pretty lad, and he told me so often how much he loved you that we came to another sort of love-talk.' She pressed one of Sanchia's against her cheek. 'For I knew that you had no will to him.'

Sanchia drew her hand away. 'Indeed it's all one to me. But even so, I cannot help being surprised . . .' Her small chin trembled, and her greenish eyes glinted.

'Why?'

Sanchia went to the door. 'It proves only what liars are men; for he swore that nothing could snatch him from loving me, however cruel I was. I am glad to find him untrue. For now I know . . . I know that men are as I thought them to be. And so . . .' She went out.

xv

'The constable's coming,' said the ale-wife; and Stephen went out to the backdoor. He ran behind an outshed, then doubled over to some old appletrees. Half way across the field beyond the trees, he looked back, and saw that three or four men were running after him.

He threw them off the trail in a stretch of woodland, and by nightfall he came into Southwark. For a while he roamed about the approaches to the Bridge, then he turned aside and took a wherry across to Limehouse.

In a tavern he talked with some sailors and learned where to find the next boat sailing for Colchester. 'I'll show you the way,' said a halfdrunken sailor with a beard-fringe and a broken nose. 'I'm going to a near wharf.' The fresh night-air made the man blink and stagger, and Stephen took his arm. Turning a corner, they came right upon the watch and were told to halt. 'Stand from our way!' roared the sailor, 'or we'll pitch you in the river.'

One of the watch drew sword, but the others bade him stand away. 'There's nothing to be gained but cuts and bruises from such sea-fools,' said one of them. 'And nobody thanks us at the Counter for penniless fish.'

'If I want to be arrested, I'll be arrested!' shouted the sailor. 'I'll not have seamen insulted. One word more, and I'll bring the whole crew to pluck your watch-house down over your cuckolded ears.'

The watch passed on with as good a show of unconcern as they could muster; and Stephen went with the sailor to the wharf where lay a boat sailing at dawn for Colchester. The captain, after first making sure he had the fare in his pocket, received him into a hold stinking of fish, and told him to find his own sleeping-quarters. And so he lay down between a salt-cask and a fevered teeth-chattering passenger who clutched a buckram-bag to his chest; and fell heavily asleep.

XVI

'I remember the days when there were only tenements,' said Rafe, waving his hand across Throgmorton Street. 'Here indeed you may see a good example of the ways in which a great man increases his land. My friend John Stow has told me how his father had a house here; but one day Lord Crumwell gave orders for his own walls to be extended twenty-two feet in all directions. Which was done before nightfall. And as for Master Stow's house, which stood against the south wall, they loosed it from the ground with spades and bars, and set it upon rollers, rolling it back twenty-two feet. And so when Master Stow, who was away, came home, he found his house had moved as though it were some great snail, and the surveyor would say nothing except that he had opened his lord's orders. Yet Master Stow paid the same rent for a halved estate.'

'I like that talk of the walking house,' said Jacint. 'I shall dream of it, I know. For in my dreams I forever enter a house and then find myself outside it by the door through which I entered. Or else whenever I go out, I come in.'

They walked on towards Paul's Yard, where they loitered among the bookshops and Rafe tried to beat down the prices of books with fine types and woodcuts from Italy and France. 'Here are some beasts for your cage,' said a bald-headed seller who knew him. 'The Butterfly of Ballavius, the Fly of Lucian, the Flea of Ovid, and the Wasp of someone I forget ---all neat books of an even height, bound in calf's leather.'

'Ah, but has the price a wasp-sting?' asked Rafe. 'Myself I am sick of love for that Petrarch. Let me handle it again.'

'Honest man, what book do you lack?' asked the shopkeeper to a thin longnosed man who had knocked a pile of books over.

'I desire a certain book,' said the man, scratching his head. 'But I cannot hit on the name of it.'

'Is it in verse or prose?'

'Neither,' said the man with brightening eye, 'it is a history. Yet if you cannot find it, give me a little pretty book to read in the chimney corner.'

At long last Rafe bought a small book with cuts of the Roman gods and goddesses, and went with Jacint to sit on a bench in the Yard while he looked through it. 'How strange,' he mused, 'that men should burn one another over a name for the Mass, and yet they leave these earthly gods alive in words and stones. Yet till Venus is branded and Mercury has his wings clipt, they shall never seduce men from their laughters and their lovers. Not till Pallas has her tongue cut out and Bacchus is cut in another place. O sweet gods who trod upon the earth. They lay in the down of the clouds, Jacint, but thought it sad stuff beside your whiter bosom. Are not they indeed the deathless ones, who have been slaughtered, yet are never dead?'

'Hush,' said Jacint. 'Whatever powers they own, they are no aid against the rack and the stake, and the most dull-witted of monks can argue you down with a whip.'

'Now I shall die without ever having seen Rome and its ancient stones,' said Rafe, suddenly cast down. 'At moments I seem to understand, my dear goddess-child, and then it all goes, and the riddle of this darkness is too much for my wits. Why must man turn away from the breasts of milk and the meadow-songs? Why is a burst rose more terrible in his nights than a lion's breath? For a fear in the depths of sleep is what governs the words of noon, and all things go awry. Only the loins of youth are indomitable and blest beyond all words or thought. Find your joy, Jacint, my brat of Venus, and cling to it.' He caressed the book. 'Ah, my poor mutilated gods, twisted into strange forms by the gibbet-dance.' Jacint's grip on his arm tightened, and he fell silent. But when the strollers had past, he said in a low voice, 'It is all quite simple. While the grass grows, the horse starves. But there are some men who do not starve. Three hungry make the fourth a glutton.'

XVII

'One of the creditors we have found to be unsound in religion,' said Popham, straightening his cap and knocking it off by mistake. 'Thank you, Master Rigeley. My joints are a little stiff, and I prefer to bend as seldom as possible.' He dusted the cap. 'So I have persuaded him for his own good to let the three hundred pounds go.'

'Thank you, thank you,' murmured Blaise. 'I am infinitely in your debt.'

'Not infinitely, for we omit infinities from our ledgers,' chuckled Popham. 'But reasonably, I trust, reasonably, as one good man to another. There is more, however. The matter of the copyholders is going well. I might say very well.'

'I pray to heaven I may soon have a chance of serving you as well as you have served me.'

'Heaven will hear you,' said Popham, still in high spirits. 'The time will come. You are a man of many interests, Master Rigeley.'

'I am in a position to hear various things that may be of value to my friends,' said Blaise modestly.

Popham raised his eyes into the trees. 'The leaves are falling, they remind us of our mortality. Let us lose no time in hastening the good work, for no man knows what the morrow will bring.'

'Ah, yes,' said Blaise with a rapid glance round the garden, 'we are surrounded with emblems and characters of decay. Vertumnus, the changeable god, is here to be seen. Yet there are certain things that defy the rusting tooth, such as gold and a good name. We labour as we may, Master Popham.'

'And reap as we deserve.' Popham failed to observe a low bough and again lost his cap, which Blaise picked up from the gravel. 'Thank you indeed. Now we knew all along that the Court of Requests would not serve, yet it was necessary to begin the suit there, that they might think themselves safe. Accordingly, as they are lulled and assured that the case has been adjourned till Easter, I have raised the matter afresh in Chancery. I have served them with notice to put in a new answer within three days. However, as a friend of mine in

N

the Court has dated the notices back by two days, they cannot possibly make any answer in time.' He laughed in a crackling laugh. 'Therefore they are left at the mercy of the Court. That is, they are in your hands.'

He laughed so heartily that he lost his balance, and Blaise had to catch hold of him. 'I am indeed raised into a new life by your kindness.'

'By next spring the whole estate will be yours,' said Popham, puffing and coughing. 'You will be a great man.'

'No, I seek only a sufficiency: that I may do my country as much service as possible in my bettered condition.'

'You will agree then that the law has proved its worth?' asked Popham with a dry chuckle, arranging his collar.

Blaise made a humble bow. 'I trust this is only the beginning of our connection.' A thrush burst into belated song, blithe and loud over the muttering swell of the monks chanting in the chapel.

XVIII

He hung round the taverns by the ships, where men were likely to talk about sailings and arrivals. At last he ventured to chat with a bluff-faced sailor. 'Is there a ship soon departing for Flanders?'

'The weather's foul,' said the man, carefully spitting. 'No master wants to sail if he can help it. But sooner or later a sailor's got to go to sea, despite all the weeping of wenches and the warring of waves.'

Stephen looked around and saw a cold-eyed man watching him. He walked away and went into an alehouse round the corner. Two men were talking about Lord Darcy who had come with soldiers in search of a rebel heretic named Trudge-the-world-over. 'The wives say he can hide in a horse's ear.'

'No doubt they know best, for they are well skilled at hiding a man in a taffeta placket or a navel of naughtiness.'

'If I were seeking heretics, I'd look for them in Elmstead,' said the first man, and then stopped, noticing Stephen.

Taking his bread and cheese, Stephen went out, and inquired of an old woman the way to Elmstead. She showed him the road and told him that he'd have a four-mile walk.

About dusk he arrived. Halting by a tall elm, he knelt on the earth for a while, then rose and went to the first cottage. A young woman with unbound hair and cornflower-eyes came to his knock. 'I am a man hunted for the truth's sake,' he said at once in a clear voice.

She stared at him, then drew him in. 'If you had gone to the next house, you would have found a Roman informer. But you come in an evil hour. Search is being made. The soldiers are at the other end of the town. You must go at once.'

'I am happy,' said Stephen, 'having seen your face.'

She knelt before him and kissed his hands. 'How sweet is this love we share, that we have not met till this moment and yet are at once united in its power.' He saw her oval smooth-browed face misted through his glistening tears. She rose and led him to the kitchen-door.

'Isaac,' she called, and an old man came from a shed. 'Here is one of the faithful. Lead him without delay to Dedham Heath and set him in safety there.'

The old man went back into the shed, came out again with a billhook, and beckoned to Stephen. Stephen bade the woman farewell and went off across the fields with the old man. After about half an hour they came to a wooded hollow in some slight hills, where the old man cut down boughs for him with the billhook and made a bed in a nook by a ring of brambles.

He stayed there all next day, sometimes talking to himself or singing in a low voice. Then at dusk the old man came to him with food, and they went on over the hills to a small farm where the farmer received them with a hearty clasp. 'I hear you've come a long way to see us,' he said to Stephen. 'Take a seat in the chimney and let the fires of God warm you.' He brought some cider. 'Every dog has his day, they say, and every cat two Sundays. And the chosen will yet possess the earth and its fullness. Nor shall we need to wait till there are two moons in the lift or apples grow on oak-trees.'

'Friends in Kent gave me the money for a passage to Flanders,' said Stephen, 'but when I came to Colchester, I found the wharfs were closely watched; and now the country is filled with soldiers.'

'It's a sad day when the soldiers come,' said the farmer. 'It's a sad day when the soldier eats the ploughman's porridge.'

Stephen drowsed in his chimney-seat. Then he woke to find another man in the room and listened to his words.

'Aye, your servant came and informed against you.'

'So much the worse for his own soul,' said the farmer. 'Also, it would do no harm if he broke his neck.'

'I asked him how he knew, and bade him take heed what he said, for his master was an honest man.'

'I thank you for the good word,' said the farmer.

'More, I bade him consider what a troublesome hour it was, and the punishment he would get for slandering his master if we searched the house and found nothing at his report.'

'What did he say to that, the snotty-nosed traitor?'

'He said that he was sure of his matter, since the house was never without some heretic or other—and most of all when there was a fire in the parlour. Therefore he said I should know by the smoke whether there was a fire of heresy within your house. So I told him to go about his business and we would prove the thing before midnight.'

'Thank you, George, thank you,' said the farmer. 'Why the earth should breed such traitors and clash-bags I cannot tell, except that I know no way of growing wheat without darnel and thistles.'

'Look then for a search about an hour before midnight,' said the man, 'and henceforth light no fires in your parlour chimney.' He looked over at the seat where Stephen sat. 'There are men who would think you had visitors, but my sight is not good nowadays and I see only a bundle of shadows.'

The farmer saw him out and then hastened back. 'You heard his words,' he said to Stephen. 'He is the parish constable, yet a good fellow. You must be far before midnight. Aye, in half a dozen cracks of cobbler's thumb, you must be off upon your journey up atop of down yonder miles-endy-ways.'

XIX

Jones stepped quietly up the stairs, and then, with one look back, knocked on the door. He set his ear against the door, and at once signed to the two men lurking in the dusky courtyard. As the door opened, he thrust it violently open and went in. The two cloakt men came running up to join him. Tabitha stood facing his drawn dagger with scornful eyes. 'Are you not tired of being thrown from this house?'

'I am an obstinate man, and I know your master is out of London. Where is your mistress?'

'Beyond your reach.'

Don Pedro entered in shirt and breeches, with naked sword. 'Who the great devil are you? Leave the place at once.'

Jones turned to glance at his cloaked bravos, but they were already half out of the door. 'If you call for aid,' he said to the Spaniard, 'you will shame your mistress.'

'And if you call, you will die. I rather hope you'll call.'

Dousabel came in behind the Spaniard, dressed in a light yellow wrap. 'The fox that breaks into a lion's cage after pullen has a sad sense of smell. Kill him, sweetheart, and have no fear of the scandal.'

'No, let him go, I think,' said the Spaniard. 'Remember that I bear an honourable sword.'

'For the last time then,' she said, tossing her hair back. 'But consider, Welshman. I shall tomorrow lay informations about you that will make your sojourn in London inadvisable, do you hear? I am not afraid of your paltry villainies, but they are a nuisance.'

'I should have guessed you would be attended,' said Jones, backing. 'You are one of a fitchew family. Last week I found your niece Mary in a bordel of Turnbull Street. She left Sion House for a nunnery of better service. Yet she does less well than you in your rooms without a street-sign.'

'Heaven save her from such offal-dogs as you,' said Dousabel. She took a jug from a table at her side and threw it, hitting him in the chest. The Spaniard advanced; and Jones went rapidly out with a curse on to the stair-head. 'Poor rogue,' said Dousabel, and burst into tinkling laughter.

In the small solar over a draper's shop in Colchester, Stephen listened to the draper and a sailor discussing the situation. Browne, a J.P., who lived in Bornt Wood, had come raging with his lawyer, Gilbart, into Colchester, to insist on stricter proceedings against the heretics. Men had been brought in during the last twenty-four hours from all around the town, and were being examined. Orders had been issued for close search of all houses after strangers. 'This town is a harbour for heretics,' Browne had said, 'and ever was.'

So it was decided that Stephen had no hope of a passage to Flanders from Colchester. He must return to London.

The sailor took him down to a fishing-boat, where he was stowed away after dark under some empty barrels. And dreamed groaningly.

Next day they sailed for London, and he sat dazed in the strong breeze and stinging spray, heavy with lack of sleep, under a driven sky of small clouds.

The sailors moved respectfully about him, and he gazed at the endless coil of waters.

After nightfall, when the ship had tied up at some posts near Somers Quay, he slipped into a wherry and went across to Southwark. At first he walked about the streets; but then he came upon the watch, and turned into a tenement where lodgings for the night could be hired in a cellar. Paying a farthing to a toothless old woman who sat at the entry on an up-ended wooden bucket, he went down into the large sunken room where twisted lengths of lime hung from the damp walls in the light of two dim lanterns of horn and oiled linen.

About fifty people, men, women and children, were gathered there, trying to find sleeping-places. The fortunate ones had secured the corners or lay with heads to the walls. As a late-comer, Stephen had to look round for a space nearer the middle of the room. He lay down near a family of man, woman, boy and two girls, in muddy straw, fishbones, rags, ammoniac filth. After a while the girl near him, who seemed about fifteen years, rolled over a little and looked at him with a faint sickly smile. 'Lie close,' squawked the old woman, who had come hobbling up to put out the larger lantern hung at the inner end of the room. 'It's warmer, and it leaves more space for late-birds.' She took the lantern down, blew into it, and hobbled back to her bucket.

Stephen moved closer in, and the girl's small hot hand moved over his face, till he kissed it. Shivering, she pressed against him, moving till they lay face to face, on their sides. She clasped him in her slight arms and her small hot mouth strayed hungrily over his face. He lay there motionless, making neither resistance or response. But at last he said, 'What do you want, child? How can I help you?' Then she lay still, and her breath came in little husht sobs. He felt in his belt-pouch and took out a piece of cheese, which he set between her lips. She drew back in surprise, and then chewed the cheese slowly and carefully. When she ceased, he touched her face and found it wet with tears.

He held her close, and she seemed to sleep. All round them, in the gloom the lodgers were tossing about, groaning, crying out in fevers or nightmares, rolling at moments in a furious embrace, then falling away in dull misery, groaning again, spitting, crying out. Someone screamed, 'She's dead.'

But the old woman shouted back in a wheezing voice, 'Don't disturb the sleepers. We'll see to it in the morning.'

Someone was sobbing aloud, inconsolably. Others began protesting. 'Shut up or go out.' And then, 'Throw him out.' Blows were exchanged, and the old woman hobbled over with her small lantern. The girl in Stephen's arm had thrust her small hot fist inside his shirt, against his heart. 'O my people,' he muttered, 'my people . . .' Shadows flickered on the wall. 'What have they done to you?'

'What did you say?' the girl murmured, half-asleep. Then she woke. 'Who are you?' She shivered again. 'Hold me fast and I can sleep . . .' She trembled all over and couldn't stop trembling. 'Hold me faster . . . faster . . .' He held her against him with all his strength, and slowly she relaxed with a soft sigh which travelled down her body. 'O . . .' her sigh was ecstatic, and she slept again.

He lay awake all night, holding her fast. But with the first light before the dawn he gently let her go. The arm which had lain under her was stiff with cramp, and he found difficulty in getting to his feet. Rubbing the stiff arm, he went over to the steps, where the old woman was nodding on her bucket, with a spider running over her hair. He looked back at the room where now the lodgers had all sunk into an uneasy slumber broken only by snores and grunts. He reached out his hands, and tried to utter a blessing. 'My people, awake, awake in time . . .' His voice failed him, and the old woman woke with a snort. He hastened up the steps, into the slushy street.

Slipping into an early tavern, he bought a breakfast of ale and stockfish, washed his face, brushed his clothes with a fox's-brush that the tapster brought, and then went to the wharf where he had been told a ship was sailing for Antwerp. No questions were asked as soon as he produced the passage-money; and an hour later they set sail down the river for Gravesend. Anchor was cast, and everyone went ashore but he, the boatswain, and the boy. Looking in his purse, he found three pistolets left, and gave one to the boatswain, asking him to go after the shipmaster and speak on his behalf. For he had heard the boy say that the searchers would soon be coming aboard.

The boatswain slipped ashore, and in a few moments the searchers came. The officers asked Stephen his name, and he answered, 'Stephen Rigeley, going on business to the Antwerp Bourse.' The officer looked him over and saw him neatly dressed; then sought in his doublet for a paper with names, but found it left ashore.

'No matter,' he said. 'I have no wish to molest true travellers. I know your father by name and good report.'

The searchers went ashore, but the boatswain came up to Stephen and whispered that he should beware of one of the passengers, a promoter and informer: Mr. Beard, a merchant-tailor of Fleet Street. Stephen nodded. 'I know him.' The boatswain slid away as the other passengers began coming aboard. Stephen went aside into the bows, but Beard had seen him and came after.

'Sir, what do you do here?' He scanned his face. 'I know your face. I have a sharp memory of faces.'

'I am of the same mind as you,' said Stephen.

The man flushed darkly, 'You do not know my mind, so how can you say that?'

'I mean to go to Antwerp, and I think you mean the same.'

'But you are no merchant as I am. A few months ago you were still an apprentice, and things have indeed moved fast if you have taken out your mastership and got your finger in the Antwerp-pie. Still, I have been ill these last three months, and know little that has happened.'

Stephen smiled at him, 'Master Beard, no man is bound to open his business to another, as you will agree. But when we meet in the English Bourse, you shall see what cheer I can make you. In the meanwhile, let us be friends, I beg you.'

'I know your father, William Rigeley, as a good and trustable man,' said Beard, nodding, 'so I shall not press you now for your purpose abroad. But I am sorry that we did not meet ashore in Gravesend, for I should have entertained you as your father's son, believe me.'

Another of the merchants had been listening. 'William Rigeley, did you say? Aye, he is a good man, but his son Stephen is a rank heretic. Are you that Stephen?' Stephen gave no answer, but the man read his face. 'I'll never sail in the same ship as such a damned rogue, for I am assured it would sink with such a burden.' He turned and called to the others. 'Gentlemen, I warn you, I'd rather lose my velvet coat than sail with such a whoreson heretic as we have amongst us.'

The shipmaster was giving his last orders, and the sailors were already hauling up the anchor. But Beard shouted to them to stop, and then brought the searchers back to the landing-place with a halloo. Stephen stood with a gentle smile on his face, a smile of weary relief. Behind Beard's back the boatswain made a thumb-gesture of contempt.

CHAPTER ELEVEN

October

I

'I DON'T WANT to hear anything more about it,' said Merric,
but Jones still hung at his side, sneering.

'Has your father then taken you to his bosom at last and
set you up with his enemy's daughter as your bride?'

'That's my concern,' said Merric, with a scowl.

'Is it your concern or mine,' asked Jones with his snickering laugh, 'that your aunt Dousabel has taken a new lover,
a Spaniard? Or that your cousin Mary now lives in a bordel
of Turnbull Street.'

'I don't believe it. I don't believe anything you say.' Merric
stopped and faced Jones with hand on knife in his belt.

'It's true. Go to the second house on the left and ask for
Sophie Suffer-all-things.' He paused and said sadly, shaking
his head, 'Also it is true that your brother Stephen lies in
the Marshalsea.'

Merric leaned back against the shutters of the shop. 'You
are glad of that news too. I see it in your eyes. Go away, or
I'll stab you.'

II

The three young men in the wherry were speaking earnestly
together. 'Here at least we are free from spies,' said Peter,
looking at the grey waters of the wind-chopt Thames.

'It is resolved then,' said Mat, fingering the hole which a

beadle had burnt in his ear gristle. 'This time we shall meet only for action. We must decide whether we kill the Queen or burn the palace down, whether we arm for rebellion or print proclamation-sheets against the Bishops. All that is to the point, and nothing else.'

'I know a printer who will print for us,' said Tom. 'That is what we shall first do. Print papers against them. They are afraid of such papers more than God or devils.'

'Let us have no waverers in our ranks,' said Mat. 'Only those with angry and bleeding hearts.'

'Now make for the wharf below the bridge,' said Peter. 'I have three companions in Bermondsey who will rejoice your spirits. They have new books from Amsterdam.'

'But no arguments,' insisted Mat, 'except how best to tear the heart from her devilish body.' And as a wherryman was nearing, he struck up a song: 'Then say maidens *Farewell Jack,* you bear your love behind your back . . .' He winced as the wound in his shoulder hurt him; and he said in a low voice, 'How I swam away that day from the soldiers with only one arm, I don't know; but I did it, and here we are.' He began singing again, this time from mere high-spirits.

III

'Don't go yet,' said Agnes. 'I am glad that you have laughed in her face, Ybel, but we must drive her yet further to a love-sadness.'

Merric came in, and Ybel took the opportunity to slip away. 'You spend much time talking with that fool nowadays,' said Merric moodily, and tried to catch a drowsy fly in his hand.

'You show little enough desire to take his place and give me a loving word,' said Agnes. She picked up her book. 'Listen, Merric. In this book the Master declares that the sun is likely to stand still and the earth to go roundabout.'

'It is heretical prophecy,' said Merric. 'I cannot bear such stuff.'

'No, no,' she protested. 'He speaks in all soberness.'

'Then he must be out of his wits.'

'Listen.' She held the book up and read in a high excited voice. 'The scholar says: Nay, sir, in good faith, I desire not to hear such vain fantasies, so far against common reason and repugnant to the consent of the learned multitude of writers, and therefore let it pass for ever, and a day longer.'

'He speaks as I would speak,' said Merric, sitting on a stool.

'Then the Master replies to him thus,' she said eagerly. 'You are too young to be a good judge in so great a matter: it passes far your learning, and theirs also that are much better learned than you, to disprove this supposition by good arguments, and therefore you were best to consider nothing which you do not well understand: but another time, as I said, I will declare this supposition, that you will not only wonder to hear it but also peradventure be as earnest to credit it as you are now to condemn it.'

'No wonder that they burn books nowadays,' said Merric dully, 'when such idiocies and wickedness are set forth. Burn it yourself, before it earns you trouble.'

'You must read it all,' said Agnes, offering him the book.

He waved it away. 'No, no, I do not wish to touch such lies even with my fingertips.' He rose and went out.

She read a few more lines with her head on one side, then put the book away under a cushion. A slow smile spread over her face, sly and childish, and then suddenly, wincing, she sat stiffly, with widening eyes. She touched her knees gently, opened them wide, and shivered all over. Rising rapidly, she took a knife from the table and went straight from the solar up to her mother's room.

Nest was sorting out some coloured threads. Agnes shut the door and said breathlessly, 'You must tell me the truth or I shall kill you.' She went straight at the bed, raising the knife.

'You are mad,' said Nest, cowering. 'Can you take a knife to your loving mother? You are mad.'

'Call out if you wish,' said Agnes in a low hard voice. 'And I shall tell them all why I am here. I cannot bear the pain any longer. You must speak the truth.'

'But what truth?' moaned Nest.

'Tell me who my father is.'

Nest quivered. 'Who but your father? Who else?'

'That is what I need to know.' She took the knife and

set its point against Nest's bodice, under her left breast.

'Who has told you lies?' asked Nest faintly.

'No one but you. You have never told me anything but lies. I know the truth, but it is no use to me unless I hear it on your lips.'

'What do you know? It was so long ago you can know nothing. Unless someone has told you lies.'

'It wasn't long ago,' cried Agnes fiercely, 'it is happening here, it is happening now. That is why I must know.'

Nest screamed as the point entered her flesh. 'You will kill me,' she moaned in astonishment.

'Tell me the truth.'

'But you say you know it. Tell me then, for I have forgotten. You know how bad is my memory. I have forgotten, I tell you.' She screamed again. 'You are hurting me.'

'Tell me then.'

'What am I to tell you? Say it first, and I'll repeat it.'

'You know . . .'

Nest began to cry. 'O you cruel child. You all but killed me once before, and now you come with a knife . . . There is no such thing as the truth you ask.'

'Yet I ask it.'

Nest began stammering, speaking slowly, as if each word was dragged out of her. 'Your father, in a way, was Hugh.' Then she put her hand over her face. Agnes stared at her, wailed and dropped the knife. She sank on her knees and set her face against her mother's thigh.

'My poor mother . . .'

Nest stroked her head. 'You understand so little, my daughter. I am always sorry for you, and now you understand even less. I cannot tell you how it happened, except that your father was away and I had stayed at home from church to take a bath.' She shuddered. 'I cannot remember it clearly at all. Yet he must have begotten Mary the same day or near to it. O what a darkening maze is memory, and yet the light at its heart burns clearer with the years, until that which was evil becomes good and that which was good becomes evil. And at last only the light remains. A woman's lot is difficult and entangled, my dear, and when she strives to understand it as you do, she is lost.'

'I won't believe it,' said Agnes, muffled with tears and the cloth of Nest's skirt.

'Now it seems that everything happened to someone else, so that I spoke truly in saying I had forgotten. And though I sought to atone with all proper penances, it now seems that they did not matter at all, and I have been forgiven for quite other reasons. I bid you cleave to cleanness, Agnes, and yet I know that the life of the world is sustained in strange ways which are sinful in a churchman's eyes, yet seen another way by Mary Virgin. And the time may come when only a distant sin sweetens a woman's life and ripens her for heaven. Yet never take pleasure in deceit, or all will be defiled.'

'But surely you wanted to go to Hugh,' murmured Agnes peaceably.

'At times I did, as at times I hankered after Stephen's father—O what have I said?' She held Agnes's head down on her lap. 'But it was an easier matter with him, and now you know so much you had better know all. His father was a smiling and godly priest who died more than ten years ago, the kindliest man that ever I knew, with a love of lilies above all mortal things.' Suddenly she wailed, 'My poor Stephen, they are murdering you, and no one cares.'

Agnes sat up with staring eyes. 'But what am I to do? Must I go to my father who needs me?'

Nest felt the knife against her hip and took it up. 'No one needs you.' She clenched the knife and struck at Agnes, but lost her balance, falling sideways. 'No one . . .' She wept into her hair.

Agnes sat watching her. 'Yes, mother, you need me.'

IV

Stephen was taken to Blackfriars, before the Bishop of Chichester and two examiners, Dr. Story and Dr. Cooke, attended by a chuff-headed priest. The Bishop yawned and said, 'I am sorry to see a young man from a worthy family here. Do you consider yourself wiser than all the realm?'

' If it please you,' said Stephen quietly, 'I cannot do other than I do.'

'So might a sheep speak, but not a man.'

'I am indeed a sheep of the shepherd, and maybe set aside for the slaughter. If you can find any fault in me deserving to be reformed by gospel truth, I stand to be reformed; and likely if my blood is shed unrighteously, it will be required at your hands, since you have taken upon yourself to be the physician of our country.'

Dr. Story beat on the table. 'Is not this a perverse fellow, to lay at your charge that his blood will be required. Fellow, do you think to be put to death unjustly? No, not if the lord bishop should condemn a hundred such heretics. I have helped to get rid of a goodly number of you, and I promise to do my best to send you the same way.'

'Tell me, sir,' said Stephen, 'since you would give me spiritual counsel, are you sure that you possess the spirit of God?'

'No, I am not sure of that.'

'Then you are indeed like the waves of the sea, as James says, that are tosst about with the wind, and you can look to no good thing out of your confusion. Yes, you are neither hot nor cold, and so you will be spewed forth.'

'He has the devil within him and is mad,' said Dr. Story. 'O, it is worse than the devil.'

'He asks me to teach him,' remarked the bishop, 'and at once sets out to teach me instead. Do you yourself, young man, believe that you possess the spirit?'

'I believe it.'

'You boast more than ever Paul did, or any of the apostles: which is a great presumption.'

Dr. Cooke coughed, 'Away with him to the Lollards Tower.'

The bishop smiled, 'I think he is afraid of prison.'

'I praise the living God,' said Stephen.

'Here is a heretic indeed,' cried Dr. Story. 'He has the right terms of all heretics. The living God! I pray you, are there dead gods that you say the living God?'

'I speak the words of the gospel.'

'Bibble-babble, there are no such words,' said the bishop.

'I do not deny that it is written,' said Dr. Story, 'but such is the speech of all heretics.' He turned to the bishop. 'I say this, my lord, so that you may know a heretic by his words; for I have been more with them than you, by your leave. They forever say: *The Lord, We praise God,* and *the Living God.* By these words you may know them.'

The bishop said with a mild interest to Stephen, 'Cannot you say with us: Our Lord and Our God?'

'When I speak of the sentences where it is so written.'

'If you must use such words, you should turn to the Church, in which is the life of Christ. Thus your own words confound you.'

'I am so linked with Christ in a chain of faith that it is not in the power of man to unloose it,' said Stephen.

The bishop yawned and took a comfit. 'Take him away, he wearies me. Take him back to prison.'

v

William stood irritably at the door. 'What is it now? Have you come to ask for fresh help? I cannot give it. My own children are in sore straits, Agnes is ill and Stephen is in prison. And as for Merric, I no longer know what he thinks or desires . . . But this is no concern of yours. What do you want?'

'I want to waken your soul, brother,' said Hugh.

William took his arm and drew him further down the yard. 'Do you want to drive me mad? Do you think I haven't been trying to do what I can for poor Stephen? But I must act carefully, or I shall ruin everything.' His grip tightened. 'You are the one to blame, if penances are to be allotted. It was you who drew him astray.'

'Brother, brother,' said Hugh in a long-suffering voice, 'how could you turn your religion so easily? You were among the foremost to greet the changes under King Edward, and yet at a word you veiled the truth in your soul and conformed to an evil thing.'

'I must obey the laws,' said William with stifled anger. 'I cannot destroy my family for a whim. If there is any sin it lies on the souls of those who compelled me.'

'The soul is uncompelled. The soul knows good and evil.'

'Go away at once.' William's voice quavered with suppressed fury. 'Must you bring further disgrace on the family? Go before I strike you.' He turned and strode into the house, disregarding his father who had come out to call in querulous tones, 'Where is that Edgar of mine? He'd be a good one to send on an errand to Sorrow, so much he lags.'

Agnes was standing at the solar-window. 'I must go to him,' she muttered. 'He needs me after all.'

Nest came swiftly behind her and caught her round the waist. 'No, no, you must not go. There was no truth in what I told you. I said it only because I was afraid.'

Merric rose from the chest of papers where he had been looking for a lease at his father's request. 'What is this?'

'My father—' said Agnes, but Nest put a hand over her mouth.

Merric ran to the window. 'It's Uncle Hugh,' he said and stared at Agnes's tormented face. 'I have something to tell him . . .' He went out of the room.

'What is he going to say?' sobbed Agnes.

'A business matter,' said Nest soothingly. 'You mustn't leave me now, my daughter . . .'

'Why am I not happy,' asked Agnes in a small plaintive voice, 'if I know the truth?'

Merric caught Hugh up at the rear-gate. 'There is something I must tell you. It may be lies . . . Is your daughter Mary still in Sion House?'

Hugh lowered his head. 'No, I don't know where she is.'

'Then perhaps I know. I'll go with you . . .' They went down the backlane, and Merric continued, 'I have wanted to speak with you also about Stephen. I feel that I have somehow betrayed him . . . We have a goodly distance to go: so let us talk of these other matters.'

They walked towards Clerkenwell, talking in quiet voices. When they reached Turnbull Street, Hugh drew back. 'Surely not here,' he said. A painted girl went by, lavishly rounded, arm-in-arm with a man in a cloak of tawdry goldwork. A shrill chattering, a stink of stale scents came from the street.

A thin raw-elbowed woman, naked except for her red stock-ings, ran across from one house to another, followed by a drunken man who slipped on the cobbles with a scream of jeering laughter from the windows. A small boy with a tray of empty beer-mugs came whistling out of the nearest door.

Merric took Hugh's arm and led him to the second house on the left. The door was open, and they went in. A blotchy slattern was pouring the dregs of many cups into one. 'What d'you want?' she asked. A snoring woman lay on her face under the table.

'We wish to see Sophie,' said Merric.

'Back room, top floor,' said the slattern and hiccoughed.

They went up. Merric opened the door. Mary lay on her back in a shift staring at the ceiling-boards. 'Mary,' he said, 'your father is here.'

She looked unseeingly at him. 'I know. He never leaves me.'

Hugh came in. 'O my poor girl . . .'

'Go away. You want to take me from him.' She kicked out. 'Go away, you killed me once before.' She screamed. 'Help, help!'

'No rough play there,' said a fat woman with hairy upper-lip in the doorway. 'She may be mad, but she's well-behaved and respectful. Leave her alone.'

Mary kicked again with her long lean legs. 'Go away. I'll tell my father.'

Hugh picked her up in his arms, and Merric found a ragged cloak hanging from a peg, which he threw over her. 'Take her away,' he said. 'I'll deal with the woman.'

VI

When he had seen them back to Hugh's house, Merric went down the street with clouded face, striking every now and then on the wall. As he neared Paul's, he saw a crowd gathering before a printer's shop. A sergeant stood outside the door, bidding the people stand back. A struggle was going on in an upper room, and suddenly an iron chase fell through the window, scattering the pieces of type all over the roadway.

'Down with the Spaniards!' Merric shouted. 'Down with the Roman tyranny!'

Nobody near him moved or looked his way. The sergeant ran over, and stared at the faces, seeking some sign that would give the shouter away. His eyes slid across the strained unmoving faces. 'Who cried out? Who cried out?'

No one answered. The sergeant gave up and went back scowling to the door.

Merric strode off round the corner, making for Paul's churchyard. There, he sat on a gravestone and looked round. After a while Tom Hinshaw came out of a shop with another young man, and walked into the yard. Merric waited till he was close at hand, and said in a quiet steady voice, 'Tom . . .'

Tom turned sharply, and hesitated. Then he came over with his companion.

'Do you hesitate?' asked Merric. 'Do you know that my brother Stephen lies in the Marshalsea? What base thing do you take me for?'

'Your brother was carried before the Bishop of Chichester this morning,' said the young man with Tom.

'Give me a chance to strike against his tormenters,' said Merric passionately.

Tom and the other exchanged glances. 'We shall give you your chance,' said Tom.

VII

George Eagles, after he had hanged a small time, having a great check with the halter, immediately one of the bailiffs cut the halter asunder, and he fell to the ground still alive, though much amazed with the check he had off the ladder. Then one William Swallow of Chelmsford, a bailiff, drew him on the sled that had drawn him thither, and laid his neck thereon, and with a cleaver (such as is occupied in many men's kitchens, and blunt) hacked off his head, and sometimes hit his neck, and sometimes his chin, and did foully mangle him, and so opened him. Notwithstanding the blessed martyr abode steadfast till such time as the tormenter Swallow plucked the heart out of his body.

*The body being divided in four parts, and his bowels burnt,
was brought to the foresaid Swallow's door, and there laid out
on the fishstalls before the door, till they made ready a horse
to carry his quarters, one to Colchester, and the rest to
Harwich, Chelmsford, and St. Osyths. His head was set up
at Chelmsford on the market-cross, on a long pole, and there
stood till the wind blew it down; and lying certain days in
the street tumbled about, someone caused it to be buried in
the churchyard in the night.*

VIII

Tabitha set the dish down and stood back against the wall
with an air of pride. 'There was some powdered parsley put
with the boiled bacon in the chicken-pot?' asked Popham
anxiously. 'Assure me on this point, or I am afraid for my
stomach. It is the queasiest stomach that ever a man had,
with its likes and its mislikes, its whims and its whams. I
might as well lie with the longest-tongued wife in Christendom as with my fickle stomach.'

'I assure you that your belly-fancies have been remembered in all things,' said Dousabel.

'Only a small supper-dish,' repeated Blaise, tearing at his
fingernails. 'A small relish among good friends. Yet the claret
is good, I believe.'

'You are too modest,' said Stoddard, beaming round with
reddish face. 'I know no more modest man than my friend
Blaise.'

The moss-haired clerk Yardly, somewhat tipsy, was helping
Tabitha with the service. Blaise leant against the chimney-
piece, while Popham sprawled on the settle, with Dousabel
in a lace-collar seated on a stool at his side. In a corner Will
Sonders sat in a leather-chair, watching with respectful
interest the movements of the others and every now and then
looking back at the chickens with a lick of the lip. Stoddard,
in the guise of a jovial harrier of servants, was pinching
Tabitha on her taffeta-behind and giving a wink-smile at
Dousabel.

'Seldom it is,' said Blaise, 'that a man has the excellent fortune to see so many of his peculiar friends gathered under one roof. I think I may say that in some sort I deserve this honour; for I have laboured to gain it with much love and humility.'

Popham reached out for a cup of wine and knocked against Dousabel. She slid from the stool and Stoddard leaped to her aid, falling on one knee and catching her round the waist. Popham tried to rise and kicked out with his right foot, damaging a small table. Blaise hurried to his rescue, setting the distracted foot on the carpet and managing to get the cup into the straying hand. Will Sonders gave a dry chuckle. 'That which won't go one way,' said Yardly, 'will go another way. But it takes a shrewd man to find the way after all, in a given confusion. Forgive me, masters, for the adage, but I speak in the merest admiration of Master Rigeley.'

'I'll have a wing and a leg,' said Will Sonders, 'and some bacon on a slab of mutton.'

'It's the rheumatics,' said Popham, 'and the proximities of beauty.'

Dousabel stood up, steadying herself on Stoddard's lowered shoulder. 'Sirs, you are all too sober,' she said. 'In an unsteady world there is need of wine to keep a man's motions in sympathy with the tottering floor of things. Therefore, drink and again drink.'

'The Queen's ladies-in-waiting have no such discourse,' said Stoddard. 'I often listen to them behind the traverse; and they talk only of sickness, clothes, and bawdry. Mistress Rigeley among them would be a witty Dido among clodpated Cleopatras; and in saying so I speak of matters in which I may claim long acquaintance.'

'He has listened twenty years to the babblery of unmaidenly maids,' said Yardly, 'and has a right to his own opinion, if I may add my unneeded testimony to his unmistakeable self-praise. For a fool who listens to foolery becomes thrice a fool; but a wise man behind the traverse is confirmed in his wisdom.'

'Serve yourself with some bacon,' said Blaise, 'and champ into silence; for we are all friends together here and take the nimble intention of your wit in place of its lame performance.'

'I cannot be eloquent,' said Yardly, ducking, 'but I can be the cause of eloquence in others. *Verbum sapienti.* Drink, Dickon, and be quiet.'

'Two legs will serve,' said Sonders in tones of agonised anticipation.

'You have forgotten Master Sonders,' said Dousabel, giving Tabitha a push.

'And now I come to the reason of our meeting,' declared Blaise. 'At the advice of a good and beloved friend whom I shall not name—' Popham almost fell off the settle in disclaiming the attribution to himself— 'At the advice, I repeat, of a good and beloved friend,' Blaise repeated firmly (and the others applauded, except Popham, who knocked his wine over), 'I have made a certain investment. I have bought the wardship of an heiress to an estate in the very county where I myself have been increasingly interested of late months. I owe to other good friends the information that this wardship was coming due.' Sonders choked with the chicken-legs which he was devouring with all possible speed. 'And to others a number of points about the relations and connections of the said heiress.' Stoddard cleared his throat, and Blaise went on, 'Indeed small is my own merit in the matter; for the mentioned friends help me abroad and the dear wife of my bosom helps me at home.'

'Yet a shrewd man is a shrewd man,' observed Yardly, drinking. 'Rebuked as I am, and conscious of my own blushes, I yet hold fast to the belief that it takes a shrewd man to make up the market-bundle, though anyone may cut the faggots in the highway hedge.' He drank again, muttering, 'Drink, Dickon, drink . . .'

'Wife,' said Blaise, 'fetch us the ward whom I have happily bought.'

Dousabel went out, and the others drank in silence. With her departure they seemed to grow dull and self-absorbed. Only Yardly, who had drunk too much, went on muttering to himself, and Stoddard, moving into a position where he might pinch Tabitha, gave out a dim smile. Then Dousabel came back with a young girl of about seven, with small shining face, shrinking in a heavy dress of red brocade.

'Here she is,' said Blaise, 'worth more than her weight in

gold. Worth more acres than she could well pace out in a summer's afternoon.'

'Fortunate girl,' said Popham, trying to sit up, 'opportunely orphaned . . .' He slid sideways, and Yardly went to his aid. Stoddard withdrew from Tabitha's taffeta-folds and lurched courteously over to where Dousabel stood.

'Bow in maidenly courtesy,' said Blaise coldly to the girl. 'Bow, I bid you, Julia Compton, heiress of Compton Wold and Mintern Unford.'

'Show me the painted hangings in the next room,' said Stoddard hoarsely, and took Dousabel's arm. They went out.

Julia Compton, heiress, stood with a face of whitening fear, rigid, as Popham clawed out amiably at her. 'A good young girl . . . a good young girl . . .'

In the next room Dousabel pushed Stoddard away as he leaned to kiss her. 'Tomorrow at eleven. You shouldn't have brought me here. We're going back at once. At once, I said.'

She returned into the supper-room in time to see the ward fall on the floor in a faint. 'Why has she done that?' asked Popham testily. 'Why has she done that? She must have a bad nature. You will have to mortify her, friend Blaise, mortify her, mortify her.'

'I shall do all that is requisite and decent,' said Blaise, drawing aside to let Tabitha get at the fainted child.

'Carry her in to bed,' said Dousabel, 'and rub vinegar on her brow.' She turned back to the men. 'As for you, sirs, drink on, I beg you. There is nothing else for it, whatever you say.' She left the room with Tabitha, holding up the brocade train, 'Gently now.'

IX

'You are my children as though I had borne you in my own body,' said Pernel. 'Why is that Prue of mine so long away?' She yawned.

'Drink another cup of wine if you love me,' said Jacint.

Pernel giggled. 'I have drunk one too many already.'

'No matter. Father won't be home till after nightfall, and you can sleep till then if you wish it.' Jacint poured out another cupful of wine. 'Drink that, and I'll call Martin up, to hear your loving words. For I am sure they include him as well as myself.'

Pernel giggled. 'Yes, but I cannot speak so plainly to a handsome man, even though the thought is pious enough in all truthfulness. Besides, I am confused with the wine and my hair is untidy.'

'He's not so handsome as all that,' said Jacint, 'nor is· your hair so untidy. As for the confusion, it becomes you.' She went to the solar-window and called. 'Martin, come up.'

Pernel giggled. 'Are you sure he'll desire it? I am so frightened of him when he looks fiercely at me.'

Martin came in and glanced inquiringly at Jacint. 'Our mother is graciously inclined,' she said. 'Drink to our amity together. She is afraid of you because you are stern and handsome, and also because her hair is untidy. That she is confused she does not mind so much, because it becomes her.' She handed Martin a cup of wine.

He drank and bowed to Pernel. She simpered. 'You mustn't believe a word Jacint says. She only says it because . . . she says it.' She simpered again.

Jacint poured her out another cupful. 'Then you don't believe him a handsome fellow.'

'O yes,' said Pernel, and drank. 'What am I saying? You are pouring out the cups so fast I have lost count. What will Martin think of me?'

Jacint winked at him over Pernel's shoulder. 'He thinks you are far too young and beautiful to be his mother.'

Pernel giggled and put her hand over her mouth. 'I don't believe it. O dear me, something has gone wrong, but I can't think what it is. Let us all love one another. That is virtuous surely.'

'Drink to it,' said Jacint, and pressed another cupful upon her. A lock of hair fell forward over Pernel's face as she went to drink, and she giggled. Jacint held the cup to her mouth and made her drink. The wine ran at the cup-edges over face and throat, and down into her corsage.

'Why?' asked Martin in a whisper, frowning down at Pernel.

'She desired a cup of loving-kindness,' said Jacint with a

wink, 'and we liked it so well that we have gone on being kind to one another. Now we are drowned in love.' She poured out another cup and held it to Pernel's feebly-resisting mouth. Pernel drank, gasped, and sat back with her hand twitching in her lap.

'O, I feel so sleepy,' said Pernel, yawning. 'I wish my Lionel was here, he likes tying my laces and untying them. Poor boy, he won't look at another woman.' She giggled, 'And now I'm so wet. What happened? I'm so wet . . .' She looked at Jacint and Martin 'Now we're all loving together, as it should be. I feared you hated me, but now it's different.' She pouted her lips shapelessly at Jacint. 'To show there's no ill-feeling . . .'

Jacint kissed her and then pushed Martin forward. 'You must be dutiful and obey her.'

'O, you're too strong for me,' said Pernel, fluttering. 'I was wrong to be afraid . . . I have sat too long at windows, but you'd never guess all the things I thought.' She began crying. 'Why do I weep when I am so happy? Open all the windows . . . open everything . . . all the backdoors. For love, they say, comes in through the postern . . . and I am so sad without love, so sad. There are always so many laces to tie and untie . . . tie and untie . . . open all the windows.' She waved her hands helplessly and then lay back, staring with one eye at Martin.

'It's a foolish trick,' he murmured.

'Not so foolish neither,' said Jacint. She stood back and surveyed the weakly smiling and gasping Pernel. 'Behold this beautiful woman.' She streaked the paint on Pernel's cheeks with her finger. Pernel simpered dimly, struggling to keep her eyes open. 'What shall we do with her now?' asked Jacint. She loosened some of Pernel's hair and smeared the paint with it, and set at a ridiculous angle the cap with delicate needle-work cuts.

'He'll be angry.'

'He won't be home for hours,' said Jacint. 'Go on, drink some more wine yourself.'

Martin drank and then laughed. 'You're indeed a wicked wench, Jacint. What shall we do with her now?'

'We'd better put her to bed, I suppose,' said Jacint. 'Aunt Gertrude might come in from church. She's gone to confession.' She caught hold of Pernel from one side. 'You take the other.'

Together they lifted her from her chair. She giggled faintly and lolled her head, and her fine-linen apron came half-off. They got her through the door without much trouble, then considered the stair-ascent. 'Take her on your back,' suggested Jacint. 'It's the only safe way.' So he knelt down and Jacint draped Pernel on his back, holding her by her belt while Martin caught her round the knees.

In the bedroom he turned round and dropped her on to the bed. Pernel fell with a dim gurgle and lay there. Jacint went and unlaced her boddice. 'Take her shoes and stockings off.' In a few moments they had rolled her over and back again, undone all her laces and points, and cleared her of her many heavy clothes. 'She looks like a pretty poppet after all,' said Jacint. 'One that has been left in the rain, with a smudged face.' She stood back. 'I am almost sorry for her, now that I see her small hands and feet laid so helpless on the sheet. And the paint so draggled on her nose. And her hair all clotted with sweat.' Then she saw Martin's face and gave a small cry.

He took her arm and pushed her from the room. She went down slowly to the solar, and sat with her palms to her brow. After a while Martin also came down.

'Don't look at me like that,' he said, 'You dragged me into it. Don't lie. You meant it all the while.' He poured out a cupful of wine, drank it straight down, and then belched. Hurrying unsteadily to the window, he retched out into the yard.

x

The man with the handbell struck it slowly and solemnly twelve times outside Newgate. When he finished, everyone began talking again, and the prisoners renewed their hubbub, crying for food. Merric walked on, making for Scalding Alley.

Hugh let him in. 'She is now calm, and knows me,' he said. 'I cannot utter my gratitude. Rosbel has made her milk-broth, and she has taken it without being ill this time.'

'I am glad to hear it. But I have come to speak of another thing. After I left you the other day, I went to Paul's Churchyard and met Tom Hinshaw.'

They went out into the backyard, and walked to and fro. 'When I went to see Will that day,' said Hugh, 'I had made up my mind I couldn't bear the badge of recantation any longer. I meant to make a last effort to awaken his conscience and afterwards go straight to the bishop. I meant to throw my badge of cowardice in his face and demand a faithful death. Then you took me to Mary, and now I have forgotten what I felt. Surely my duty is to her after all she has suffered at my hands?'

'Listen first to what I have to say,' said Merric gently, 'and then judge.'

He frowned. 'How did it all happen? I can scarcely remember how and why I first joined with Stephen. Perhaps I thought that Jacint would praise me. But however that was, I found I could bear no longer to be shouldered aside and treated as a thing without a face. I am no saint like Stephen, but I have my pride, and I know in my heart how a man should live.' He pressed his brow. 'Yet how did I find the strength to come back to the hidden strife? I can hardly tell, I was sorely afraid after the arrests and waited every moment for the sergeant's mace on my shoulder. Then I slowly lost my fear and returned to anger. And by chance it seems, looking into Agnes's face, I saw something that brought back to mind what Kit told me. Then, after I came back with you and Mary, I went to Tom. I knew I'd meet him if I sat long enough in Paul's Yard, for he works under a printer nearby. Thus it appears that I took over into my spirit the command you'd felt; and now I come back to you with it. In my own way I have come to a full resolve. I will fight as best I can against the tyranny that rules us. And I am afraid, yet content.'

Hugh meditated. 'Yes, I will join you all again. I had become so lost in my own thoughts I forgot there were others.' He looked at Merric. 'How happy Stephen would be to hear you.'

Merric reddened. 'I am not fit to untie his shoelace. I can love and hate in my own way, but that is all. Now I think

I have found the way to my honesty. I claim no more than that.'

'Would that all men could claim as much.'

Rosbel put her head through the backdoor. 'Is Master Merric staying to the meal?'

XI

'I don't mind the fine,' said Hawes for the third time to Walls the draper. 'I am angry at the false accusation.'

'It's the way of the world.'

'Let it be the way of the world for others. I shall never accept it for myself. I kneeled in the shrine at least a yard away from him, yet he said I pressed too close. Lord Mayor though he is, I'll have no man falsely accuse me. He dared to say I almost pushed his face against the stone. Now he swears he'll charge me before the Court of Aldermen.'

'It's not the fine,' said Walls, trying to hide his grin. 'It's the injustice of the charge.'

'Aye,' grunted Hawes and went on.

In the solar he found his wife Pernel sitting weakly in a chair by the window, in a train gown stuck full of silver pins, with watering eyes that blurred her cheek cosmetics. 'Don't come too close, Gregory,' she begged in a whimpering tone. 'I still feel so sick.'

'What's come over the world?' he roared. 'Have I swollen to twice my size that everyone from the Lord Mayor to my own wife accuses me of pressing in against them?'

'I didn't accuse you of anything,' she murmured. 'I can't help being sick. It was something I ate the other day. I think I must have been poisoned. I've never felt so dreadful . . .'

He nodded. 'There may be something in that.' He hammered on the floor with his stick till Gertrude came up. 'Have you been trying to follow the foul example of that witch Tace, who has faded unpunisht through our hands? Did you try to poison my wife the other day?'

'If I tried to poison her, I'd succeed, I can assure you,' said Gertrude. 'I am no half-hearted poisoner like Tace, when I once start. Who knows that I may not be driven to it? But the day has not yet dawned, though you are doubtless right, Gregory Hawes, in deciding my patience is tried to breaking-point.'

'Please don't speak so loudly,' cried Pernel tearfully with her hands to her head. 'It goes clean through me.'

'So my voice is insulted now,' said Gertrude with tight-lipt satisfaction. 'I expected it. I said so to Jacint only this morning. There's not much left about me that isn't insulted, I said. But they haven't insulted my voice. Still, it won't be long, I said. For I know them now and all their envious ways.'

Jacint came in quietly, looking away from her mother-in-law. 'What is it now?'

'They lack the courage to tell me to go,' said Gertrude, 'and so they charge me with disgraceful things, such as failing to poison the poor decrepit creature in the chair over there. Indeed it would be a mercy to put her out of her sufferings. For though they may blame the cooking for her state, I have other views on the matter. A man of such a crooked lust as one whom I refuse to mention is capable of violence as well as miserly greed. I can well understand why his poor wife wishes to have the truth hidden; but it's no use—'

'I have stood more than mortal man can bear,' said Hawes, grinding his teeth. 'Now you shall go at last, no matter what your excuses.'

'If you had ears in your head, Gregory Hawes,' she observed firmly, 'you'd have heard that I mean to go tomorrow from your stricken house.'

'Then go.'

'Meanwhile I wish to observe only that there is a carter at the backgate asking for sixteen pence in payment of carriage for twelve pigeonpies. But since you have told me to go, I leave you to manage your own household.'

Jacint began laughing. She put her hand to her mouth, but couldn't stop. Hawes turned on her in fury. 'Leave the room at once.'

She abruptly stopped laughing, but did not move. 'Gregory,' said Pernel in frail pleading tones.

He made a gesture of brushing a fly away, but did not look at her. Jacint began laughing again. 'Leave the room,' he

shouted, 'and leave the house with your aunt if you cannot
behave yourself better.'

'Come, my poor child,' said Gertrude, and they went out
together.

'Gregory,' repeated Pernel with fluttering eyelids. Then
Martin came in and she uttered a little squeak.

'What has happened?' asked Martin, lowering. He looked
round, but neither of the others answered him.

Then Hawes started. 'I forgot the carter.' He went out.

'How are you feeling?' asked Martin with voice suddenly
tender.

She fluttered her eyelids. 'A little weak, but very happy.'
She smiled at him, and put her hand over mouth. Martin
moved involuntarily towards her, then drew back.

'We shall see,' he said.

XII

Merric and Ybel were already there. Hugh looked round the
faces in the room. Tom nodded to him, and Peter. 'We can
get away over the roof there,' said Merric, pointing through
the back window of the attic room. Hugh looked out, and saw
the river with a carack of a thousand-ton sailing downstream.
'See the boy with the flag in his hand,' said someone at his
side. 'If he falls he'll be drowned . . .'

Another man, a sailor, laughed. 'Now he's sliding down the
tackling. That's a good thick mast. It looks as though it grew
in the West Indies.'

'Have you been there with the Spaniards?' asked Tom.

'A man can know something of a country without having
been there.'

Across the river crows were circling Paul's steeple. Hugh
went to the seat beside Merric. They smiled without a word at
one another. 'We have the papers ready for throwing into
houses and churches,' said Tom, pulling some ink-smeared
papers out of his shirt. Then, as the proofs were being passed
round, Mat the weaver of Lambeth, came stumbling up the
stairs. He stared round, nodding his head, and then cried in
an excited voice:

'Count Peria is coming over from the Spanish King with a physician. They are whispering in the palace-kitchen that the King fears she is dying at last. And so indeed she may, with all this mad blowing-up of herself that she hopes to cheat God into thinking a pregnancy. What he most fears is that the Lady Elizabeth will marry an enemy of Spain.'

Hugh spoke. 'It is true. I have read a letter from Amsterdam, with much secret matter in it. The Spaniards aim at humbling all Europe under their yoke, and they are burning their own people as well as ours. Already they have gone far to split Germany with their plots; for they desire above all things to leave nobody at peace. Yet unless they can hold England, they will fail. For France, though under a Catholic king, cannot approve their hopes of dominion; and the Netherlands are hot with revolt.'

'Aye, but is the Queen truly dying?' asked Tom. 'We hoped that before, but it turned out otherwise. Maybe the Cardinal has put the story round to weaken the growing rebellion against the devil-bitch. Even if she lives long enough for the King to marry the Lady Elizabeth to one of his Catholic princes, we are lost.'

'The Lady Elizabeth will never do it,' said Merric.

'They may compel her to it,' said Peter.

Merric shook his head, but Tom went on, 'We cannot be sure. The Earl of Westmoreland or Arundel would suit the Spaniards well enough. Aye, and others. The Spaniards have their hirelings among us.'

Mat chuckled. 'If I understand the matter aright, the Queen is indeed in a cleft stick. All these years she has held her sister a bastard and fought against a Spanish husband for her, since she wishes to see her unwedded and unacknowledged. Yet now she is being urged to take her as heir and hasten a marriage of high rank. Which choice is the less bitter for her? If she holds Elizabeth still a bastard she leaves the throne vacant and knows that Elizabeth will get it. If she weds Elizabeth to a Catholic, she must call her the true heir and admit Anne Bullen an honest woman truly married. No wonder that she is torn by devils and gets herself with child by wind.'

'We may hope for her death,' said Tom, 'yet we must plan

as though she will live till we pluck her down.'

John Lithall of Southwark stood up. 'I must carry the news
at once to our friends in Surrey and Kent; but I lack the
fee for the horse-ferry at Fulham.'

Tom passed a cap round, and five-pence was collected.

'Arms,' said Peter, 'bid them above all things gather what
arms they may. Arms will decide this matter.'

XIII

The gunners stuck wool in their ears, waiting for the command to begin the firing of blank shot. In the streets below
the Tower lads in jacks of green and woodmen with clubs
were leaping about, letting off squibs amid the squeals of
pleased wenches. Then the first cannon sounded: from the
battlements of the Tower, from Paul's Wharf, from Westminster Wharf.

Sanchia was coming down the stairs in her new taffeta
dress, refusing to notice Ybel at the foot; but she stepped so
daintily that the boom of the cannon startled her into a fall.
She clutched the bannisters, yet slid down into Ybel's arms.

'Let me go,' she said hotly. 'You keep your arms for someone else nowadays.'

'If I do,' he replied, still holding her, 'it's only because you
won't come between them.'

'I don't believe it.'

'Yet here you are, and I won't let you go.'

She pulled away, but not very strongly. 'Go to her, I say.
How could such as I take you from her?'

'If you were to try, you'd find how soon you could do it.'

'I don't believe it,' she said uncertainly.

'The proof of the pudding is in the smacking of lips.'

She resisted his kiss for a moment, and then weakened.
'Do you truly like me better than her?' she asked in a wondering whisper.

Banners and streamers rustled in the light wind, and the
flutes rippled with them. The marching had begun. Traders in
welted velvet, with doublets of sober damask and black hose;

bachelors of the companies in scarlet hoods; the poor in new blue woollen caps. And the booms went on, two hundred chambers of shot, at the cost of ten pounds.

The shields of notabilities, and then the trumpeters. Figures and painted sheets with allegories about the new Lord Mayor Legh. The children of Westminster School singing in white led by their master; men carrying javelins from the Tower; and girls sprinkling rose-water. A merchant knocked against an overhanging pent-roof and fell from his horse. A child burst out crying, a pick-pocket nipped a purse, and a kite killed a sparrow. Two lovers coupled on a roof, a woman brought forth a child in Chepe, and a man with a fishbone in his throat coughed till he broke a blood vessel and died. And the aldermen ate till they belched.

A gentleman trod on an apprentice's foot in Paul's Yard and told him to keep clear of his betters. The apprentice tripped the gentleman up. The gentleman drew his sword, the apprentice called 'Clubs!' By the time the greasy watch came up, the gentleman was trampled, a tavern-bully had lost part of an ear, and an apprentice was wounded in the hand, etcetera.

'That's right,' said Old Fabyan to Edgar, 'your face is as clean as if the cat had lickt it.' He stumped over to William's counting-room and looked in without entering. 'You're following Blaise's advice still, I trust? Don't forget I've got my eye on you.' William answered something gruff. Fabyan chuckled, 'You don't catch an old bird with chaff.' He closed the door and returned to Edgar. 'Bear it in mind, boy, that age and wedlock tame man and beast, and no man can evade both of them.'

Edgar gave a superior smile. 'Yes, master.'

'Now we can safely go and enjoy ourselves,' said Fabyan, straightening Edgar's collar, while Edgar tried to pull away. 'But first let me see if that boil has come up on the nape of your neck.' He felt about on Edgar's neck, to the neck-owner's indignant grumbles. 'Ah, it's doing well. Now we can go and see the sights of London and I'll tell you of all the noble burials I've seen in the churches. And we'll call and find how poor old Hugh Wokins is getting on, poor fellow, he's not long for this world, I fear. It's sad how some men cannot bear their years.'

'I am sure that we shall meet Merric,' said Jacint to Lettice. 'We always meet him on a holiday so crowded that meeting would seem impossible.' They turned into Chepe and made their way slowly towards the Cross. Then as they neared, Jacint exclaimed in surprise. 'There indeed he is, waiting for us instead of Rafe. There is more than magic in this: there is some simple villainy.'

Merric bowed as they came up. 'I hoped we should meet.'

'But why are you here?'

He handed her a note. 'Read that rhyming. I know it now well by heart.' He recited: 'Go at None to the Cross of Chepe, and you will find no cause to weep: rather with laughter will you leap, seeing the harvest you must reap.'

'The hand is Rafe's,' said Jacint. 'He told me to meet him here.'

'My endless gratitude to him.' He looked round. 'Where shall we go then, in obedience to his rhymes?'

She considered. 'I ask for the fields and a sillabub. Give me the earth and the sky, and maybe I shall give you my mouth in return.'

They turned and walked northward, soon moving into less flocking streets, then pushed through the frequented gates and saw the open grounds, with some boys at archery-practice and a windmill against a silver cloud.

'I shall be leaving London tomorrow,' she said, and pressed his hand against her breast as they walked on, with Lettice at a discreetly distracted distance. 'No, don't ask any questions. Nor grow excited. I shall tell you all in a few words. My Aunt Gertrude is finally going to her sister at Dunmow, and I said I'd go with her for a while. My father said he'd be glad of it, and hoped I'd have a better mind on my return. But I own no intention of returning, if I can help it. Someday I may tell you all about it; but there are many reasons why I cannot bear the house any longer. I have quarrelled with my brother—'

She stopped abruptly, and they walked on in silence. At last he said, 'I am further than ever from a place in the world.'

She cut him short. 'Yet I liked you better this morning, the moment I saw your eyes. You have made me happy.'

'Something will come of it,' he said, 'as we desire. I cannot yet see what it is; but I am certain now that we shall meet in marriage.'

She laughed merrily. 'I too have felt it since we came together today. I feel that we have entered into a different world, and the birds have welcomed us.' She shivered. 'But let it be soon, Merric. I know my father plans to marry me off next spring to a pitiful fellow, Will Lupset, who owns a goodly estate. I overheard him discoursing morally on the matter with his widow-wife—I call her that, for, though he married her ten times over, I should still think of her as a widow. But enough of her painted sepulchre, where only the dead lie down. I think I am strong enough to defy my father for a hundred years, but I may have overestimated the length of time.'

'Give me three months, and I'll manage something. If need be, I'll cut my father's throat.'

'No gallows work. We shall find a way.' She turned and sat on a stile. 'You are thoughtful this morning. Don't deny it, for I like you with this sadder face. If I were brave, I should ask you now under a shadow to get me with child, so that we might be tied in a snare past ravelling. And truly, when we first came out of the Gate and looked upon the dying green of the year, I decided to do it. But I have changed my mind once more, out of respect for your gentler eyes. We have no need of a snare. We shall command life another way, and be tied without knots.'

He kissed her hands. 'I think only of two people, you and Stephen.'

XIV

Light straggled through the heavily-grated window, falling on the monk's warty face. 'Remember who were the beginners of your doctrine,' he said in a slow deep voice, 'a few fleeing apostates, who ran out of Germany for fear of the faggot. Remember what they were who have set forth your doctrine in this realm, flingbrains and light-heads, never constant in one thing, as might be seen by their turning the table one day west, one day east, this man that way, and that man this way, even like a sort of apes that could not tell which way to turn their tails.' He laughed jovially. 'Repent, my good man, and we shall laugh this matter over with a tankard of quickening beer.'

Stephen turned over in the straw, and the prisoner against the wall clanked his fetters. 'Thus we chime against your bell-clappering.'

Unperturbed, the monk went cheerily on. 'These leaders of yours, they say that they'll be like the apostles and have no churches. A hovel is good enough for them and their God. They take a mug, and one of them says: I drink and am thankful! And another: Here's joy of you! Aye, a runagate Scot has even made the heresy that Christ is not God at all, and has matched it in the last communion-book. You see what company you have fallen into.'

'We are content that it should be so,' said the man who never left the corner under the window.

The monk said, 'May the Spirit give you better wisdom in your dreams, that you may wake up as sensible men.' And went out.

The man in the corner resumed his story, 'And so they set me in the stocks all night, and then in the morning, at terce, they whipped me about the market with a three-corded dog-whip.'

'I can forgive them everything but one thing,' said Stephen. He tried to go on, but broke down sobbing. The man beside him took his hand.

'It does not matter,' said the one hunched up in the corner. 'Are we not the chosen generation, the kingly priesthood, the holy nation, the peculiar people? How then should we expect mercy from cathedralisters and minister-men, from abbey-lubbers and hell-hirelings?'

A jailer opened the door, with a wild-haired woman leaning open-mouthed over his shoulder. 'Anyone here want six-pennorth of harlotry?'

'Bah,' said the woman, spitting, 'come away. These are not men, but eunuchs of the fire. I know them by the death in their eyes.'

XV

Hugh stared hard at Rafe, then closed his eyes and stood back. 'I thought you were another. Come in.' He took him upstairs to the small solar where a guttering fire had been lighted. 'You know of Stephen?' he asked, bending to stir and blow upon the fire.

'It grieved me more than I can say,' replied Rafe, sitting on a stool beside him. 'And my errand is connected with his flight. I lent him a book that was very precious to me, and I'd like to know its fate if I may.'

'I remember,' said Hugh, pulling the hair back from his brow. 'It was in French, and he asked me many words, which I mostly did not know. He guarded it with care. But in so many fears and doubts I had forgotten it.' He went to the door, and called, 'Rosbel!'

She came shuffling up. 'What is it now? don't tell me that the fire has gone out again.'

'Do you recall a small book in French that Stephen was reading? A book he kept with much care.'

'I do,' said Rosbel with a triumphant sniff and head-shake. 'You all forgot it in the search, but not I. I put it away, and it's still safe. If you must know, I thrust it between the garter and my thigh, for though I seldom wear stockings, I find a garter comes in handy more often than you'd think for such storage and the like.' She sniffed. 'I guessed there was much power of heresy in that book by the way it made Stephen wrinkle his brow and stare hard.'

'It is my book,' said Rafe. 'Can I have it back?'

She looked at Hugh, who nodded, and went out. 'I am glad, I am very glad,' said Rafe, warming his hands at the crackling fire. 'Let it be an omen that Stephen will escape by some devious way, though I hope he finds a sweeter hiding-place.' He smiled and frowned. 'Ah, how our tongues run away with us. We darken the very sun for a dirty jest. There could be no sweeter place than a faithful body and loving soul, and such, I dare swear, is this woman we have heard.'

'Your words are true,' said Hugh.

Some one entered, and they turned. 'Mary wants you,' said Agnes, and then hesitated before she added, 'Uncle.'

Hugh at once went out. 'You are the sister of Stephen and Merric,' said Rafe, with a smiling scrutiny, 'and we met after many years when I brought my golden book to Stephen. Now we meet again when I reclaim it from Rosbel's suitable lair.'

'Lend me the book,' she said eagerly, 'or at least tell me what is in it.'

'I have sworn to Pallas Athene not to lend it again,' he said gently, 'and what is in it is no more and no less than man and his earth.'

'But that is what I want to know.' She came closer and said in a low voice. 'Is there then no heaven and no hell in this book of yours?'

'What is earth,' he asked sadly, 'but heaven and hell at once in the heart of man? Only, when he knows it quite simply, all things will be changed. He will look at his hands and find them bloody. He will look in the eyes of his fellows and find them loving. He will wash himself in the seas and be clean. Do what you will: that will be the whole of the law.'

'Do you indeed believe it?'

'Why not?' He shrugged. 'If one man can make peace with his own heart, so can all men. But for the moment we must keep this love of ours a bitter secret, or we shall be torn by the bloody hands.' He smiled wryly. 'There is much matter there for laughter and jest.'

'Much matter for tears.'

He took her hand. 'You are Stephen's sister, and that is why I speak so lovingly and dangerously to you. Truly I begin to believe that the golden days will come upon us before we think; for within this year I have spoken in truth and without fear to three persons. At this rate, within a hundred years, a man will be able to say a dozen words of the free truth in open street without being torn by the bloody hands.' He sighed. 'Don't tempt me to say more or I shall not sleep for a week.'

Rosbel came in, rubbing the small book with the edge of her skirt. 'Here is your book, master, not much the worse for wear and tear. If it smells fishy, that is because I hid it afterwards under the fish-barrel.'

Rafe took the book. 'I thank you for its preservation, mistress, and now I will go.'

'I did it for Stephen's sake,' said Rosbel, standing back.

He turned the pages. 'I was afraid I had written my name on one of the pages, to test a new quill. But it seems I was mistaken.' He kissed Agnes, and turned to go.

'I must yet have a word with my uncle,' she said.

XVI

Agnes unclasped her cloak and threw it on a chair, then she sank wearily among the cushions of the settle. 'I have been to our cousin Mary,' she said to Merric without looking up. 'She is mending fast.' She paused, then went on quickly. 'She told me that she was with child, and I told . . . her father. He didn't know.' She bent her head lower still and her voice could hardly be heard. 'I think he was glad to hear it. She is much clearer in the head . . . He loves her . . .'

'Why are you so unhappy about it?' He sat down beside her and took her hand. 'Once we were very close, but for months now we have scarcely exchanged a word. Why is it?'

'You had better answer your own questions.' Then she added anxiously, 'but I am not blaming you, brother. Also, I feel once again close to you.'

'I am sorry for your grief, for I am myself caught up in a high happiness. I am sure now that Jacint loves me.' He laughed, 'And only an hour ago I saw Ybel and Sanchia climb into the loft, taking the utmost care that no one should see them.' To his astonishment she burst into tears and put her face against his shoulder. 'I thought you would laugh too. Do you grudge them their contentment?'

'No, no, indeed I do not. It was I who brought them together.' She went on crying and laughing together. 'I bade him make love to me, so that she might feel jealous and find him less despicable. And so it happened.' Now she only laughed. 'How foolish I am, Merric. I never truly wanted him, but I did my best to make him turn his semblance of love for me into a fact. Only from vanity, or almost only, I did it; and I failed. The apple was there for his plucking, but he merely breathed on it and rubbed it delicately into a more shining red. Poor fools, both of us. Yet it all happened for the best . . .'

'We must find you a likelier husband,' he said, stroking her face.

'No, leave me to myself. I am woken now. For months I have been in a slow dream, as though I lived under water. But now I am woken, and my hands can touch things before they fade. This silly matter of Ybel has been the last morning-phantom before I look out on broad day. I am happy to have come up out of the deep night . . .' Her lips began to quiver again, but she controlled them. 'Mary is so sadly broken that I seem quite strong at her side, and must become stronger, for everyone's sake. All things yet seem so pitiful . . .' Again she controlled herself. 'Tell me of your own happiness, Merric, for I feel now that I need the happiness of others to make me strong.'

'It is nothing to talk of,' he said, partly to himself. 'While Stephen is jailed, I am half shut out of my own soul.'

'Yes, Stephen, Stephen,' she cried, 'Heaven forgive me!'

Someone called Merric from the yard. Merric untwined her fingers and went to the window. 'Go away,' he said, seeing Jones. But Jones continued gesticulating and opening his mouth, grimacing and jumping about, till Merric nodded, hastily kissed Agnes's mouth, and went downstairs. Out in the yard Jones greeted him with a dumbshow of excitement, grasped his sleeve, and drew him down towards the back gate. 'What is it?' demanded Merric. 'Be brief.'

'I have found at last where the treasure lies.'

Merric frowned impatiently, 'I told you that I never wanted to hear another word of it. Off before my father comes back and finds you here.'

'Dousabel the Blousabel has carried it away,' cried Jones, cock-a-whoop. 'She's sent her maid Tabitha ahead with a lad and a pack-horse of baggage; but she herself and the Spaniard have left only an hour or two ago, with the treasure on his saddlebow. I've had my men spying on them for weeks, and I know everything. They're riding for Dover.'

'Let her go. The gold's got a curse on it.'

'All gold's got a curse on it, and a blessing too. Think

again, my bold boy. There's a fortune waiting for us on the Dover Road. Shall a pert-faced Spaniard get away with the woman and the treasure as well? No, not if you're as English as I'm Welsh.'

'Let me think,' said Merric angrily, but added, as Jones stood back, 'Right then, let us go. I find I have a better use for this money than any Spaniard of them all.' He laughed loud.

They went out down the lane, making for the nearest inn where mounts could be hired. Then, with a brown mare for Merric and a dun horse for Jones, they rode across the Bridge and took the Dover Road. Jones had a sword and two pistols, one of which he gave to Merric.

About ten miles out they saw a man riding ahead, clumsily urging his horse up a small hill. Spurring, they overtook him. 'It's Blaise,' cried Jones, and rode abreast. 'Stop, or it's the end of you!'

Blaise reined up with grinning teeth of rage and tried belatedly to get his pistol out. Kit knocked it out of his hand with a whipblow. Merric dismounted and picked it up.

'Shall we kill him now, my boy?' asked Jones in panting glee. 'I've long waited for this moment.'

'If you kill me,' cried Blaise in a crackt voice, 'you set yourself outside the law, and the gold will bring you down. But if you join with me now in a proper contract, you keep within the law and share my own right in pursuing a thievish and adulterous wife.'

'It's true,' said Merric, and looked threateningly at Jones.

'Then let him live,' said Jones. 'But we need more than his word as contract.' He pointed to the leathern inkhorn at Blaise's belt. 'Get out your pen, and write what I bid you.' Blaise took a sheet of paper from a book in his pocket, and wrote as Jones dictated, 'I Blaise Rigeley of two Nicols Chambers, Westminster, freely and in full possession of my faculties do hereby offer my brother-in-law C. Jones and my nephew Merric Rigeley an equal share of all goods, moneys, jewels and other precious wares to be found on or about my wife Dousabel in recompense for their aid in seeking and finding her . . .' He added with a wink at Merric, 'Always state the reason for a payment. It helps to prevent legal arguments after.' He turned back to Blaise, 'Now add the date and other such rigmaroles.'

'Here you are,' said Blaise. 'Now I expect your swiftest aid in this matter.'

'How did you find out in time?' said Jones, putting the paper inside his shirt. 'I thought you had gone down into the country.'

'I had my suspicions,' said Blaise sullenly.

They caught them up about twenty miles further on, turning a corner and coming full upon them. Merric and Jones at once spurred ahead; and Jones fired at the Spaniard as he was drawing his sword. The shot struck him in the throat, and he fell bloody from his saddle into the dust of the road, with one foot still gripped in the stirrup. Blaise rode up and caught his wife's reins. She looked him contemptuously in the face.

'Give me that pistol!' he called in a screech to Merric. 'Let me shoot the bitch.'

Merric laughed, and Jones said, 'Kill the pretty lady with your bare hands. That would be the most fitting way.'

Dousabel climbed down from her horse. She was wearing fawn-coloured riding-breeches and a hat with a curving feather. 'He tried it once before,' she said, 'But this time I am more prepared.'

Jones was rummaging in the capcase strapt to the Spaniard's saddle. 'It's here,' he said in a high voice that broke on a bird-scream. He went over and began undoing the case on Dousabel's saddle. 'Ah, yes, we have it at last. At last.'

Merric stood watching Blaise and Dousabel. 'Come on, my notable husband,' she said, straddling the way, with arms on hips. 'You have spider-threads in many lives, and I thought too easily to break the one which held me down. I was careless after all, but at least the filthy thread is broken. Look at him,' she cried to Merric, 'look at this man whose hands twitch with a murder that he dares not commit. You think that they twitch now for the first time, but I know better. I know they have been twitching for years, and I could bear no longer to feel them all about me.'

'Close your mouth!' he screamed, but came no nearer.

'He has stolen the land from a poor vain fool, and then he has used the law to break the copyholders. He draws money as a brothel-landlord that goes to grease courtly palms. He has entrapped his brother Will because he wants to share in merchant-venturers without a risk. He gains the sheriffs of the county and the lawyers of Chancery with informations stolen out of the Exchequer. And yet with all this secret work of power he remains a mere starved radish of a man, less than any yeoman he drives into a ditchdeath. Ah, to think that my nights will no longer be haunted by this withered ghost who mumbles on the edge of the living world . . .' She laughed a mad taunting laugh. 'Kill me with your bare hands? Try it, now that I am free of you.'

He approached her, shaking with fury, and sprang with his hands at her throat. But she struck him aside in contempt, and he fell over on the road. She kicked at him, and then stood with all her weight on his back, while he coughed and yelled.

'Give me my pistol,' he cried. 'Please, Merric, give me back my pistol. Ten pounds for a knife or a pistol. Fifty pounds . . .'

'It's all here,' said Jones, who had transferred the cases to his own and Merric's saddles. Rubbing his hands, he watched Dousabel with admiration. 'Every ounce a woman.'

'Then come with me across the seas,' she said, stepping from Blaise's back after a last dig with her heels.

'No, it is too late. I gave you your chance, but you wouldn't take it.'

'You too were entangled in his snares, and I couldn't see you apart from them. Now I fear you no longer.'

'No, you can't tempt me now,' he said with a snort of laughter. 'Or not so far as all that.' He went closer and laid his hand on her shoulder. 'Yet I love you for the way you kicked and trampled that man of yours.'

'Then give me at least my horse and a share of the gold.'

'You can have the horse, but none of the gold. I have no doubt you've tucked a few jewels and angels among the baggage that Tabitha's taken to Dover; and you'll soon add to them.'

She held out her hand. 'Cross my palm with gold for both our lucks.'

'You're a woman after my own heart, and I'm glad I lost you.' He snorted with laughter. 'Better that we go our own ways.'

Blaise had scrambled up from the road and stood back, dusting his clothes. Merric took the Spaniard by the feet and lugged him into a ditch of nettles. When he looked round, Jones and Dousabel were out of sight behind some bushes, but Dousabel's tinkling laugh rose up.

'Give me the pistol,' whispered Blaise. 'I'll pay you a hundred pounds for it.' Merric smiled and shook his head.

They climbed on to their horses. Jones came out from the bushes with a dog-grin fixed on his face. Taking a handful of gold coins from the capcase on his saddle, he leaped into his saddle; and as Dousabel appeared, pushing a green bough aside and smoothing her hair down, he tossed the coins to her. She held out her hands, but the coins fell in the dust. Then they rode off.

'Soon or late,' said Jones to Merric, 'I always get what I seek.'

After a while Merric replied, half to himself, 'It depends on what a man seeks.'

CHAPTER TWELVE

November

I

BLAISE RAN UP the steps ahead of Jones. 'The door has a spring-lock,' he explained with pride, opened and went in. 'Julia!' he shouted, 'Julia!' No answer came. 'Can she have turned the child adrift to spite me?' he muttered to himself, disregarding Jones's inquiries; and ran on through the rooms, looking under tables and beds, till at last, in a cupboard of soiled linen, he found the girl.

'I never thought you a father,' said Jones, grinning behind him.

'I am no father in the sense you mean,' replied Blaise. 'But in the legal sense I am fully father of this wicked woman-child.' He shook her. 'Do you so early learn to hide away in coverts and alcoves? are you so soon going the way of all womanflesh in deceit and lust? are you rehearsing the day when you will tryst in privy places with some beastly horned creature?' He shook her again. 'Why did you hide and give no answer?'

'She was afraid,' said Jones. 'Let her be.'

'What could she be afraid of?' cried Blaise angrily. 'Of me, her legal father, she has no right to be afraid; and there has been no one else here except my good friends. No, I tell you, it is the stirrings of her womanly nature, which is a dung of all evils and which re-enacts in all rooms the whoredoms of our first mother.' He shook the speechless child. 'Strip that I may beat you the better for your salvation.'

'Let her be,' said Jones. 'At least while I'm in the house.'

'I'll beat her into obedience,' said Blaise, shaking her. 'It may be that I cannot beat the evil thing out of her, since that would mean the beating of life out of her loins. But I can at least beat it down into the dust where it will fear to raise its slimy head.' He gave her a last shake and threw her down. She lay on the floor, staring up at him with wide eyes.

The men went back into the parlour where some wine stood on a sidetable.

'Now that my grosser evil is gone,' said Blaise, as they sat down, 'I must consider whether I shall not marry this female for her land when she reaches the age of twelve or thirteen, or whether I shall sell her at a profitable rate . . .' He blinked and took the wine that Jones handed him. 'Ah, busy mind, let the world go for a moment. All that can wait.' He turned to Jones. 'I detest waiting beyond all things. I must press hard and harder upon my stratagems, till they conclude in an open issue. I must always have the whole labyrinth clear in my head or it torments me with a sense of lost ways. But what am I saying?' He pressed his palms to his eyes. 'I am not myself, I am not myself. Yet I am glad that my grosser evil is gone, with all her many smells of treachery . . .' He lay back exhausted.

Jones drank slowly. 'We returned here for a serious conversation, Blaise. I think we know one another now, and no longer do we need to pull at cross-purposes. We have many interests in common . . .'

Blaise stirred. 'That is so, Kit . . . I am ever one who holds that men of goodwill can profit better in combination than by a lonely accounting.' He sat up, fully in possession of his faculties again. 'If then in sad truth you wish to join with me in various ventures, explain a few matters which I still find dark.'

Jones spread his hands out. 'Ask anything. I wish to prove my entire trust in your discretion.'

'Tell me why you killed Faxy, that man of many names.'

Jones wrinkled up his nose. 'I didn't do it alone. Ben Long was with me in it. Faxy was a greasy coward and yet an obstinate stammering man.'

Blaise cut him short. 'What part had a certain captain, recently in Dublin and more recently in the Narrow Seas, in the killing?'

Jones's face stiffened. 'You know of that too. Then I'll tell you all. He it was who instructed Ben and me to kill Faxy. For Faxy, as you know, was a man of many masters, working both for the abbot and the Privy Council as well as for himself. Also he was a spy in the service of the captain you mention.' He laughed. 'Here we need not change the colour of words. The Captain is called by the world a Pirate, but in fact he has long been also a trader in woollens—only that he dislikes paying the taxes and tolls on the export of cloths. Faxy had played him false, as he played all his employers, including himself; and the Captain is no man to stand such tricks. He bid Ben and me rid the world of an unnecessary fool, and we did it. But when we drew the fool into our confidence as a preparation for his death, we found other matters.'

'You found that he had this gold.'

'Yes, he wanted to get across to Flanders. Fool and lazy rogue as he was, he knew that his treacheries were catching up with him; but the danger he smelt was from the Council, not from us.'

'And where did the gold come from?'

'That you can guess as well as another. Maybe it had truly been the abbot's, hidden away during the days of Dissolution. Maybe it had been stolen from the Exchequer by Throgmorton. Maybe it had been filched from spoils of the Captain. Maybe it had come from some nobleman's treasure-room when Faxy was doing spy-work for the Council. Maybe it even came from an alchemic furnace. I do not know.' He paused and then chuckled. 'Do you know that Will visited a scrier, a friend of mine, and gained little for his pains?'

Blaise chuckled too. 'Yes, we had better join forces, Kit. I am of a mind that this Captain of yours, who is pirate, merchant and defender of the realm, may be very useful to men who desire a wider reach for our trade. And it is clear that he is not a man to be carelessly approached.' He considered. 'Will must be reconciled to all this. And we must find worthy men who have the right sort of interest in cloth-making. But all that is simple and can wait.' He lay back again exhausted. 'If only I had been able to wound that woman with a knife.'

'Give me your hand,' said Jones, 'and let us swear a proper oath of brotherhood. I have never broken such an oath, unless it has been first broken by the other man.' They clasped hands, and then Jones, hearing a slight noise in the next room, cocked his head on one side and asked, 'What are you going to do with that ward of yours?'

'Tonight I shall beat her for her soul's sake,' said Blaise harshly, 'and tomorrow I'll send her down to my estate in the country. For now I think I may boldly call it my own.'

'Someday I too will buy a notable house in the country,' said Jones in a muse. 'But I am yet doubtful whether I shall marry or whether I shall stock the place with half a dozen bid-able wenches, all of them small and plump and golden-haired. And blue-eyed,' he added, nodding with pleasure. 'All of exactly the same height, and all dressed in red shoes and stockings and in watchet gowns. I have even thought out the names for them: Agatha, Alice, Agnes, Anna, Audry, and Amy. If they were born with other names, I should re-christen them with yellow wine out of a gilt chamber-pot, and keep them all in a great garden with a high wall. I have even at times drawn up the by-laws for this garden of goldilocks, and I know at least where Agatha and Alice live.'

In a sudden rage Blaise ground his teeth and lay back panting. 'If only I had thrust a knife into her . . .'

II

The spy Cox with another named John Launce informer of the Greyhound came to the house of William Living in Shoe-lane, who made buttons. They asked for buttons, but he had none: so they said that they would come back. Then they came back with the constable and the beadle of the ward, and searched the house. Looking through the books, they found De Spaaero, a work of astronomy by Johaanes de Sacro Bosco, with figures to show the movements of the heavens. This book, being gilt, seemed the chief book to the spies, and they carried it out open into the street, saying, 'We have found him out at length. It is no marvel that the Queen is sick, seeing that there are such conjurers in privy corners. But now I trust he will conjure no more.'

So they took Will Living and his wife Juliana through Fleet Street into Paul's Churchyard, to Darbyshire's house, where Bonner's chancellor lay, who bade them set Will in the stocks till suppertime, when a cousin of his came and gave the constable 40 pence to let him out of the stocks while he ate, and then they set him back in the stocks.

'They didn't find anything,' said Tom to Hugh. 'Pass the word on to Merric.'

And they took Juliana and questioned her, and Dale, a spy, said to her: 'Ah, you hope and you hope, but your hope shall be a-slope. For though the Queen fail, she whom you hope for will never come at it; for there is my lord cardinal's grace and many more between her and it.'

'Will they come between me and my God?' she asked.

Then the chancellor asked the constable of St. Bride if he would be bound for her appearance between that day and Christmas, and he said yes. Then the chancellor said, 'You are a constable and should give her good counsel.'

And the simple man said, 'That I do, for I bid her go to mass and say as you say. For by the mass, if you say the crow is white, I will say so too.'

'Warn John Lithall,' said Hugh. 'For I know that Will Living had passed on to him certain lists of persons and weapons; and I think also a box of pistols.'

And then, as some of Will Living's books were in the custody of John Lithall, the constable of Southwark with others of the Queen's sergeants went and broke open the doors to get them, and took away also Lithall's books, writings, and bills of debt. But not Lithall, for he was not at home.

'Lithall has now gone down into Kent, to see some stout fellows at Tunbridge,' said Merric to Ybel. 'You must come with me this afternoon, for there are arms to be buried in a brewery-yard.'

But next Saturday, the spy John Avales, who had set careful watch, caught Lithall as he was returning home, and said, 'Sirrah, you are a pretty traitorly fellow indeed, we have had somewhat to do to get you.' And when Lithall tried to speak, he shouted, 'Come on you villain, you must go to the Council.'

III

Old Fabyan groaned. 'There has been a whoreson witch-craft in the year. I cannot recall such a heavy heat and griping cold. Now I have a grudging of ague in my bones.' He groaned again, loudly. 'The humming in my ears is begun.'

'Then you'd better go to bed,' said Nest.

'The humming gets worse if I lie down. What I require is a good blistering fire in the chimney-place. Where is Edgar? Let him bring me my ear-trumpet.'

'I shall give you a glister at midnight,' said Nest with gleaming eyes. 'I have bought a new one, made from as tender a sheep's bladder as you'd hope to see, which I have wanted to use for weeks.'

William came into the solar. 'Where is Merric?'

'In his room, I think,' said Old Fabyan. 'He was carving a piece of boxwood into a devil's face with a monk's hood over it.'

William went out, and up to Merric's room. Merric was sitting on a stool by the window, fitting new laces to some shoes. He looked up without speaking. 'I met your uncle Jones in Threadneedle Street,' said William. 'He mocked at me and pressed me against the wall, saying into my ear that you and he had run the treasure to earth after all.'

'It is true.'

'Why have you hidden it from me? Tell me where it is, or you'll find me angry at last.'

'Kit has a third, Blaise has another, and the third third has come to me.'

'Hand it over at once.'

'No, it is not mine to give.'

'Enough of such lying words. Come to the point. Where is the gold?'

'Where you won't find it.'

Merric stood up, leaning against the wall. William regarded him with a furious malevolence. 'Do you know what you are saying? . . . Do you understand all that your defiance brings in its train? . . . If you give me that gold, I may yet be able to clear myself and stand on my own feet. Without it I have no course but to borrow from Blaise and become his creature. I have spoken this plainly enough, that you may judge the urgency of my case and not think I demand the money in mere assertion of fatherly right. I take you thus far into my confidence—though I know few fathers who'd say as much, considering it rather a derogation of their authority and power, which draw their strength not from arguments and appeals but from God's own innermost purpose . . . If now you still gainsay me, what can I do but curse you?'

'The money is not mine to give.'

William darkened with rage. He looked round the room. 'Is it hidden here? I'll have your bed torn to shreds . . . Tell me before it's too late.'

'It isn't here. I can't tell you more.'

'What a luckless father am I. One son doomed for the stake as a traitor, and the other defying me to my face. For the last time, give me that gold, or leave this house for ever.'

Merric moved towards the door, still keeping close against the wall. 'More than a year ago I asked you to set me up, and you gave me only a mouthful of pithless words. Now I have found my own way in the world, and you curse me for it.'

William struck him in the face. Merric fell on one knee, and William struck at him again. Merric rose and tore at the latch, still beaten by his father, then he opened the door and ran out.

On the ground floor, at the foot of the stairs, he met Agnes. 'What has happened?' she asked, holding her breasts and bright-eyed with fear.

'We have parted, once for all,' said Merric, in a harsh voice that he tried to make sound casual. 'Don't beg me to make my peace. I tell you it can't be done. You'll never see me again in this house.' Then, seeing her pain, he took her in his arms and kissed her. 'My poor sister, have no fear. We shall meet again and smile together.' He let her go, and went out into the street.

IV

'Come away from that window,' cried Mrs. Hudley. 'I
know why you're sitting there. I'll beat you again. You're a
shameless slut.'

Mabel got down from the tall stool, and went straight out
of the room.

'And don't think you can hide in the attic, neither,' said
her mother. 'Go down to the kitchen and roll some dough.
I'll break your spirit if it takes me a hundred years.'

V

Hugh came out of his workshop, his hands dripping with
dye. 'I have left my father's house for ever,' said Merric, 'and
now I feel happy in all my soul.'

'Let it be no devil's glee of hatred,' said Hugh, wiping his
hands. 'Let it be a pure happiness of suffering for the spirit's
sake, for that liberty of love without which the world travails
in endless throes of despair.'

Merric laughed lightly. 'No, Hugh, there is no suffering
in it, and hatred is not its heart. I am simply happy because
I stand on my own feet and can find my own way without
being hindered and pulled to and fro against my will. I am
happy because my mind is made up.'

'After many wanderings, to come home to the centre.'

'That is nearer to what I feel.' He paused. 'I have left in
your room a capcase filled with gold and jewels, several
hundred pounds in worth. Don't ask me how I got it. You
know a little of the story.'

'It is Christopher Jones's gold,' Hugh interrupted.

Merric nodded. 'A part of it. It came into my hands
through violence and bitterness, for which I have little regret.
Violent matters must have violent ends. But my conscience
is exercised on the use that must be made of this treasure.
Myself I need it sharply; and if I had gained it a few months
ago, I should have set it aside for my own comfort. But now

I feel differently. I wish to cleanse it of the smell of blood by yielding it up to a good cause. All last night I wrestled with this matter. I have been sorely tempted to keep it for my own ends; but I know that she to whom those ends belong will approve of my resolution, though she may not understand it. All the night I heard her voice and saw the face of Stephen. Now I am calm and happy, for I know I made the right choice. We need money for the buying of weapons. It may be this gold that will win our success.'

Hugh pondered. 'I am so new to this thought of bloodshed that I cannot think clearly about it. I have accepted the thought that we must submit no longer, but my hands shudder from the sword.'

'I have brought the capcase here for you to guard. My movements are uncertain for the moment, and I cannot carry it about with me. Hide it well.'

Hugh bowed his head, and muttered, 'Yes.'

'How is Mary?' Merric asked as he turned away.

'She mends daily,' said Hugh with a sigh. 'How grave is the wrong we may do a soul without ever having broken one clause of the world's law. Go your way, Merric. Weak as I am, I have set my hand to the plough, and now I shall not fail the Spirit.'

VI

The two cloakt men darted out of the side-street, grasped hold of Blaise, pulled his cloak over his face, and lifted him off his feet. One of them bundled him over a shoulder, and they ran down the side-street, turned into a lane, and then passed through the backgate of a tavern. Blaise was dumped down and the cloak pulled roughly off his face. In the firelight Sir Francis sat on a chair with outthrust legs, grinning with ugly pleasure. 'Hit him across the face for me, Simon,' he bade one of the men. 'I don't want to feel the touch of the cur's flesh.' Simon smote Blaise across the face with all his strength.

Blaise staggered back. 'You'll pay for this. You know you will. You know you will . . .'

'Where's your wife?' shouted Sir Francis. 'She left you and she left me.' He turned to Simon. 'Look at him well, Simon. He grubs for money in a dunghill, but his wife would be a virgin still if she'd had to rely on his devices.' He spat. Simon gave a neighing laugh. 'Tell everyone about it,' said Sir Francis with satisfaction. 'Tell them how he let out his wife to all persons on whom he sponged. Say that I told you so.' He took out a paper. 'She wrote to me before she ran away. I'd been beginning to grow suspicious, but I never knew how strong a net he'd knotted about me.'

'I have done nothing to which you did not assent,' said Blaise. Then he fell silent.

Sir Francis looked round at his two bravos. 'What shall we do with him? Slash his face? But he could scarcely look uglier. Castrate him? But he's castrated already.'

'It's not true!' screamed Blaise.

'Pull his breeches off,' said Sir Francis with a snigger.

Simon and the other tore off Blaise's belt, then wrenched his breeches off. Blaise stood there shivering with his knees together, while Simon shore away his shirt with a dagger, to make his nether nakedness complete. 'Now cut the gristle of his nose,' said Sir Francis. 'His big nose is always before him, and I want it marked, so he may thrust a badge of shame into the faces of all men hereafter.'

Blaise screamed. The second man grabbed his arms behind him, and Simon, drawing a knife, gave him a savage nick on either side of the nose. Blaise howled with pain, and when he was released he fell to the floor, still howling.

'Now thrust him out into the open street,' said Sir Francis, 'and let him find his way home to hell as best he can.'

VII

He arrived at Dunmow about three of the afternoon and asked at an inn for the house of Jacint's aunt. Then, riding at once to the door, he rapped on an upper window from the saddle; and she came to the window as though she'd been waiting there. 'Wait, wait,' she said, as though he might ride off before she came down. Then she ran from the window, and came to him in the street. He bent down to kiss her, and then caught her round the waist, swung her up on the saddlebow before him, and rode down the road.

An hour later they came back, and this time she sat behind on the horse's rump, with her arms clasped about him. They went into the house, where Gertrude was waiting to catch them; but Merric spoke first. 'Within the last week I have gained a fortune and given it away, and now we are married.'

'Beyond a doubt,' said Jacint. 'We have broken a ring in two halves and smelted our two lives into a single round.'

'This is strange news for a loving aunt on a windy morning,' said Gertrude. 'I wonder you found a spot dry enough for such games; but when two wilful youngsters come to it, they'll converse through a hole in the wall, or under the very bed in which a father snores, as in draughty truth happened to a headstrong wench I knew. But what am I saying? I don't know whether to scold or bless, though I am sure it makes no difference which it is, and after the way your father has treated me, Jacint, I'm in no mood to enact the watchdog of his properties. If you two have played the wanton honestly, I cannot find it in my heart to rebuke you; for there are some sins with more virtue in them than all the sermons heard in a Christendom of Sundays. Besides, you make such a sweet pair as you stand hand-in-hand together that I cannot blame you. The end of the world is close upon us, and it's as well that the young folk should make the most of their kissing-time.' She burst into tears. 'Come and embrace me, Jacint. For I'm the nearest thing to a mother you've known for many years; and a mother feels her girl's wedding-hour in her own divided flesh. Indeed, before they told me you'd been carried off by Merric, I felt a weakness in my limbs and had to lie for a moment on my bed to end the giddiness; and I make no doubt that was the moment when the bells of this new dignity rang in your blood. Ah, what a thing it is to be young and eat honeycomb without a cloying mouth.' She kissed Jacint again. 'Now take her, young man, and use her lovingly and kindly.'

Then her widowed sister Matilda came bustling in, slightly deaf, with a face like Gertrude's, only smaller; and everyone had to shout the morning's story into her excited ear. Then

she smiled and said that nothing had been heard like it since
the Danes invaded the country and ravished everyone; but
that was a long time ago, and so it would be best for Master
Merric to sit down to a supper of cold beef and vinegar, with
a shoulder of mutton and two chickens with sauce, sops and
parsley, and beer.

Then they ate in the parlour: while every now and then
Gertrude turned to weep and kiss Jacint and give her advice
about her first baby, and Aunt Matilda said it was a pity
they'd eaten the best ham last week, for she wanted Merric
to have as good an opinion of Dunmow as possible, where
the cows had the biggest udders in all England and no
adultery had been known since the time of the Danish invasion. As for the foreigners of Halstead or Bishop's Stortford,
they were liars if they claimed to grow as fat-eared wheat
as the Dunmow fields, and their wives were known to be so
loose that no harlot had prospered there for at least a
thousand-and-one years.

In came a friend, a rosy-faced member of the town council,
who said that he'd already supped, and then ate half a
chicken and a mutton-pasty. Learning that Merric was son
of William Rigeley, Merchant Taylor, and bethrothed of
Jacint, Clothworker's daughter, he proposed that the married
pair should settle in Dunmow. 'We need some new men,' he
said. 'If you come as a master-weaver, I'll see that you get
a certain broken-down church and its yard at a small rent.
Which is more than any young man could get among the
great traders of London.'

'And I'll add an orchard-close to the bride's dowry,' said
Matilda.

'And I'll lend the bridegroom a hundred pounds,' said
Gertrude. 'For I do so long to see Jacint's children growing
up in the honeyed air of Dunmow. Also, I'd like to spite
a person whom I need not name.'

'We'll think on it,' said Merric. 'You tempt me more than
I can say.'

Later, he and Jacint sat in the parlour alone, by the fire.
'How strange this quiet seems,' he said, 'this scent of
orchards, after the angers and fears I left behind in the
London streets. I cannot believe it true.'

'I desire most whole-heartedly to stay,' said Jacint. 'And even though you have given the money away, it seems we could find a place here.'

'The councillor did not know I'd quarreled with my father,' said Merric. 'He thinks to build a London connection. He'd not have spoken so warmly if he'd known where I stand in many matters.'

'Still, it is surely possible.'

He took her hands and kissed them. 'I am no dreamer of the ending of the world, as Stephen is. Yet now that I am in the toils of something stronger than my own will, I cannot rest my thoughts on this or that, on a scheme for London trade or Dunmow crafts. Even this moment crumbles in my mind. There is an evil thing which must be pluckt down, and now my hands have strength only when they work at the plucking.'

'Have I dwindled to a ghost then in your mind?'

'No, no. You know that you are the fire which has burnt all other things to ashes and compelled me into this starkness. Yet you have burnt me and must abide by the consequences. I am yours by this token of fear and courage. No other way leads to your mouth.'

She said very softly, 'Yet for all your brave words, Merric, I think you would forget those demands if I leaned long enough in your breast and said: Come away.'

After a while he replied, 'It is true. What then do you say?'

'I bid you go back to London tomorrow morning, and return to me only when there is no longer any division in the voices.'

'But tonight we are man and wife.'

'Tonight and always.'

He stood up. 'Then I have no fear of the ending.'

VIII

Men speaking with their heads together in a hood. Whispers at the carters' inns, a network of whispers from all over England. Cottagers pausing at lane-end, journeymen coming up out of cellars. Listen.

At Ipswich Master Noone, that bloody J.P., has hunted down Gouch of Woodridge. Aye, Gouch, weaver of shredding-coverlets; and Mrs. Driver of Grundisburgh. When the soldiers came after them, the pair hid in a haystack. So a constable took a pitchfork and probed till he found them out. 'Ah,' he said, 'the lechers lie well shrouded in the heat of hay.' Then they took them wounded to Melton Jail. ... .

Aye, but what came next? Listen. *Mrs. Driver, a yeoman's wife, with honey-coloured hair and thirty years, called the Queen a Jezebel. So the chief judge, Sir Clement Higham, ordered her to have her ears cut off at once, there in the court, and a beadle cut them off with some garden-shears, first lopping at her hair to clear a space. Then she stood there, with her hair all in a tousle, and the blood ran down from where her ears had been, over her shoulders and breasts; and she cried out for joy in being chosen to testify for the truth.*

Who heard her speak?

I heard her speak. *'Have you no more to say?' she cried. 'God be honoured. You are not able to resist the spirit of God in me, a poor woman. I was an honest poor man's daughter, never brought up in the University, as you have been, but I have driven the plough before my father many a time (I thank God), yet notwithstanding, in the defence of God's truth, I will set my foot against the foot of you all, in the maintenance and defence of the same, and if I had a thousand lives, they should all go for payment thereof.'*

So the chancellor rose up and read the sentence in Latin and committed her to the secular power, and so she went again to prison as joyful as the bird of day.

Who was there? Tell us.

Tell us. We are mightily comforted in the example of the saints. Tell us how they died.

At seven o'clock in the morning they were burnt, after praying on the broom-faggots. 'Nail them to the stake,' said the bailiff, Dick Smart, 'make an end of it.' So they were tied, and an iron chain was set around Alice Driver's neck.

'O,' she said, 'here is a goodly handkerchief.' Then many came up and grasped her and Gouch by the hands.

So the sheriff cried, 'Lay hold of them, lay hold of them.'

But at that many more yet ran up, till there was such a press about the stake that the sheriff was afraid and said nothing more. But one of the informers, a barber named Bate, who had handled them as he pushed them to the stake, took off his frieze-gown and sold it before he left the place, saying that it stank of heretics.

IX

'They grow daily more afraid,' said Tom, 'and that is why their cruelty breaks all bonds. The Queen is dying. Yet we must not slacken in our work.'

Count Feria has come at last,' said Peter, 'with a large-spectacled doctor to look into her womb. But he will find no hope there.'

'They are burning us in Essex and Norfolk,' said Mat. 'They are burning us in Kent, but we rise again from the flames, clapping our hands. A collier from Deal has told me of the burnings at Canterbury. There was John Cornford of Wrotham—'

'I knew him,' said Tom. 'As blithe a man as ever saw the dawn come up.'

'And the men of Maidstone and Ashford. And two women, one of them very old, and the other a young and white maid, who called for her godparents. But at first they were afraid. Then a second messenger went with a promise of safety from arrest, and they came. Then all of the prisoners, men and women, were burned, but not before the old woman, Kate Tylney, cried out: I will pour out my spirit upon all flesh, and your sons and daughters shall prophesy, your old men shall dream dreams, and your young men shall see visions.'

'She has laid it upon us as a command,' said Tom.

Then they began discussing the weapons that were gathered in Kent and Essex.

Merric entered, and tossed his cap in the air. 'The Master of the Rolls has gone to Hatfield to see the Princess Elizabeth. It is whispered in the streets.'

'In the palace men say that the Cardinal is as sick as the Queen,' said Peter.

'It may all turn out as we hope,' said Merric, 'but for the moment the spies and informers are more busily at work than ever before. I saw John Avales at the top of Scalding Alley an hour ago, and I fear an attack is to be made on my Uncle Hugh's house. Yesterday another spy was observed in the alley.'

'I must go back at once,' said Hugh rising.

'No,' said Merric. 'How would that help? You would be torn away to prison. And have no fear for Mary. I have sent a message through Ybel to Agnes, and she will go at once.'

Hugh sat down with his hands over his face. 'O, I was afraid of this.'

'The money is safe?' said Merric to Tom.

'Yes, it lies in good hands in Kent.'

There was a pause. 'Are we ready?' asked Merric. 'Are we armed enough to rise when the Queen dies, if the Cardinal or the Bishops try to hold their power?'

After a while Tom said, 'Near enough.'

Ybel came in. He nodded to Merric, 'I have taken your message. And as I passed this way I saw them setting in the pillory an old woman, who had spread a tale of the Queen's death. The monks are walking in procession with sprinkling of water and chants, around the cloisters and back again.'

'Parliament is still in session,' said Peter. 'But we cannot trust the gentlemen and the justices. If it suits them, they will maintain the Cardinal. If it suits them, they will turn to the Lady Elizabeth. We must be ready to strike for England and the truth.'

Everyone murmured an assent.

x

Rosbel answered the crash on the door. 'My master is away. What thieves or traitors are you?'

They pushed her aside and went in. 'Search everything,' shouted John Avales, and the men tore open chests and cupboards, flung jugs to the floor, and ripped down all hangings. One of the beadles, passing Rosbel, handed her a paper which he had taken from the table. 'Good luck, mistress,' he muttered. 'Hide this in case it deserves hiding.' Then he pushed her aside and went shouting and tearing with the others.

Upstairs, Agnes went to the door and listened to the noise below, holding the hair back from her ears. 'What is it?' asked Mary from the bed. 'Is it my devil come back again? Is he breaking up the house because he can no longer get inside my body?'

'It is a band of evil men,' said Agnes, 'who are the best devils I know.' She went back to the bed and sat by the pillow, taking Mary's head in her lap. 'Yet there is nothing to fear. There is nothing ever to fear. The noise comes and goes. The rats gnaw and are silent again. Always it passes away.'

'As long as you don't leave me.'

'I am with you.'

Mary pressed her face down in Agnes's lap. 'Mother . . .'

The door opened and John Avales came in with narrow brown face, with tiny bright bird-eyes. 'Out of bed, mistress. We know too well how your sheets are used for hiding more than whoremongers. Out, I say.'

Agnes stood up and helped Mary out, drawing a wrap round her. 'These are your devils, Mary,' she said gently. 'Look well upon them, and forget to fear.'

Mary stood in her arms, staring at John Avales and the two men who had entered after him. Then she laughed a small child-laugh. 'They are only men,' she said. 'Who would have thought it? They are only men.' She put her hand on her belly and laughed again.

XI

Blaise spoke very slowly as though he feared to crack the huge plaster held by a linen bandage over his nose. 'You must listen to me, Will. It is all for your own good. You will rejoice in a year's time that you listened to me.' Behind him, with pale peaked face stood Dick, the boy aged about four-teen whom he had taken a week ago into his service. 'Give me a comfit for my throat,' he said over his shoulder, and

Dick hurried forward. 'I am afraid of coughing,' Blaise
explained to William, 'for it opens the wounds in my nose
again.' He patted Dick's cheek and tweaked his ear. 'I shall
never again have a woman close to my body. I'd as soon wed
with the pest in a charnel.'

'You ask too much when you ask me to take Kit's hand,'
said William stiffly. 'I'd rather swear friendship with a bearded
goat of the hills. He led my son Merric astray and did his
best to turn my wife against me. He is no better than an
incestuous ape.'

'Brother, brother,' said Blaise with sad patience, 'this life
we have in the world is short, and, even for the happiest,
somewhat troublous. To ease the life of man, though nothing
can make it justly pleasant, I find that friends work much
therein. Then do not throw aside those who wish you best.
The Welshman is wild and rank, yet he has a shrewd mind
and many valuable acquaintances.'

'What then do you want me to do?' asked William irritably.
'Invite him to share my bed and board, and watch him laugh
in my very nose?'

'No, no,' said Blaise, 'but receive him as business-
companion.'

'I'll at least hear what he has to say,' said William with
bitter resignation.

'Go and call him in, Dick,' said Blaise, 'and come straight
back.' Dick went and Blaise added, 'He is a good boy, but
sometimes he is seduced into forgetfulness by others of his
age who play with balls. For he dearly loves a ball-game.'

William grunted. Then Dick returned with Jones noisily
obsequious at his side. 'How is your nose, my dear Blaise?
I told you that you had a loose step in those outer-stairs of
yours, and that one day or another you'd fall through.' He
turned to William. 'You see, Will, I have been proved no
liar in this matter of gold.'

'Lies or truth,' said William gruffly, 'I have gained nothing
out of your tales.'

'That was no fault of mine,' said Jones. 'If you failed in
faith, you must blame yourself.'

'Yet you gave a third to that villainous son of mine.'

'I had covenanted to give it, and no man living can accuse

ne of failure in my covenants,' said Jones, striking himself on the chest.

'Sirs,' said Blaise, 'let us cease from all words over the past. What concerns us now is time-to-come. You have lost a few hundred pounds, Will, but by this time next year you'll have gained twice the profit if you will only listen to me. Within a few days there will be big changes in England, and in a time of changes a quick-witted man can turn many things to advantage. But what we each of us can gain apart is little to what we can gain in combination.'

'I could kiss your hands for such wise and pious words,' said Jones.

'Dick, another comfit,' said Blaise, and coughed delicately behind his hand. 'The wounds are beginning to pain me again, so I shall speak as briefly as may be. There are going to be many new companies formed for trade. We must have a finger in their pies. The hand of Spain will be lifted from our trade, and our adventurers will find their way to the East, by Russia or India it matters not. This is a larger thing than Channel piracy, yet there are such pirates who may well look to richer prey henceforth. That is where Kit can help us; for he knows many captains, and above all one whom I need not yet mention. You yourself, Will, will be sheriff next year and advancing to the seat of the aldermen. I have many friends in the law-courts and the Parliament, as well as among the officers of the Crown, and I shall be master of many sheepwalks when I have turned the copyholders out of the land I now hold . . . Need I go further. Between us we hold a maze of threads in our hands. Why should we quarrel, when we may profit so well out of friendship?'

Blaise and Jones both looked at William, who growled, 'Agreed then, I am with you.'

A loud hammering on the outer door began, and Ybel looked into the room. 'Sir, Master Hawes stands in the street with constables. He demands to see you. What shall I say?'

'I'll send him about his business—'

'No, brother,' said Blaise, 'no brawling in the street. Ask him in, and I'll speak with him for you.'

William held himself back with an effort. 'Ask him to come

to me here,' he told Ybel, adding to Blaise, 'But I shall set no locks on my tongue.'

They sat silent while Ybel gave the message. Hawes was answering in a loud hectoring voice. Someone shouted. Then came a hush of low argument. 'Sit down, brother,' said Blaise quietly.

With tramping feet, Hawes came in. 'I sent for you, Master Rigeley.' He saw Blaise and Jones, and paused. 'I am glad you are here,' he said to Blaise, 'for though you are a Rigeley, I've heard good reports of you, and therefore I ask you to witness closely what is said between your brother and me.' He turned on William. 'Your son Merric has been meddling with my daughter at Dunmow, I know you set him to it, and I am resolved to exact recompense.'

'If my son has caused you displeasure,' said William haughtily, 'I feel a little less angry with him. But the truth is that he left this house over a week ago with my curse on his head.' He added hastily, 'Do not think, however, that these words are in any sense an appeal against your threats. If my son has harmed you, I accept the responsibility with gladness.'

Blaise interposed. 'Forgive me, Master Hawes, if I speak slowly and softly, but a fall on the stairs has injured my nose. You have heard my brother, and I know he speaks the truth. He has dismissed his rebellious son Merric from this house, and it would be hard that you should blame him for what that son has lewdly done to your daughter. How could he more throughly dissociate himself from his misdemeanours?'

'He has done it in guile to escape my anger,' said Hawes without conviction.

'You have flattered me with some words of esteem, and I may therefore ask you to accept my assurance in this matter. I know that my brother has cast his son Merric out in the direst truth.'

'Yet I shall exact an answer from him,' said Hawes with a sneer. 'Unless he will so far forswear his son as to accuse him of bastardy in the womb.'

William started up in rage, but Blaise waved him down. 'Enough of hard words. Master Hawes, you are a man of discretion and gravity. I beg you to set aside old matters of stale anger. Just before you came I said that we stand on the edge of great changes, and it is fitting that men of goodwill and money-weight should agree together. You know Master Popham, I think.'

'He is an honoured and trusted friend,' said Hawes.

'You know him also to be such a friend of mine.'

'Indeed, that is why I spoke to you civilly, Master Rigeley.'

There was a pause. Both Hawes and William stared moodily at the floor. Jones hugged his chair and looked with admiration at Blaise. 'Give me another comfit, Dick,' said Blaise, 'and offer one to each of the good gentlemen.' Hawes waved the little box aside, then, after Jones had taken one, he changed his mind. William stared at the box for half a minute, and then also took one. 'If we may agree on so small a matter as a comfit,' said Blaise, 'surely we may agree on greater things. Master Hawes, I know that my brother William is sorry for the enmity which lies between you—' He motioned William into silence. 'I pray you in all charity to show an equal magnitude of mind and heart. Let posterity praise you as one who forgave in the face of much provocation. Set an example to our whole age, Master Hawes, of a man who put aside petty grievances for the sake of nobler ends, such as the encouragement of our trade in woollens.'

Hawes cleared his throat, looked at his hands, then looked at William. William sat stonily staring at Blaise. Neither man would make the first overture, and in their eyes was seen a flurry of bitter memories.

'Anger has an unrelenting hand on the throat,' said Jones. 'May I propose that we drink together to the new trading-ventures we have in mind. For nothing better than good wine is known for loosening the throat and the heart of man.'

Blaise nodded to Dick, who slipped out. 'To show my own trusts in all here present,' he said, 'let me mention that there is a project for a society of royal mines under consideration. You have heard of it, I think, Master Hawes?'

'Yes.'

'Why should we be at odds, when our interests manifestly lie in the same places?'

Dick returned with a tray of wine-cups. 'Here come the loving cups,' said Jones. 'Let us simply say this: With the drinking of our toast to the coming year we set behind us all

past differences and angers, so that there is no longer any
need of disputation. Each man forgives and is forgiven. Each
man makes the first approaches, and each man answers in
Christian love.'

For a moment it looked as if both Hawes and William were
going to burst out in rage, but instead they each took a cup
after the others; and at a sign from Blaise all four men drank
together.

XII

Merric stared out of the high window at the thin drift of
faintly luminous clouds. Below, on a roof of crackt and
mossy tiles, a weathercock creaked and rattled, reluctantly
turning, heeling a little over. A spray of sparrows came hurt-
ling up in a brief brawl, then dived away again. The weathercock lifted and turned. Merric closed the window and came
back into the room. 'The streets are quiet. If only we knew
for certain that the Queen is dying, and the Cardinal with her.'

'Will Bonner let his power go without calling on the nobles
of the north and west?' asked Tom. Nobody answered.

Mat called from below, 'Merric . . . Merric . . .'

Merric went to the door. 'What is it?'

'A woman calling herself your sister.'

Merric hurried down, and saw Agnes below on the further
flight, whitefaced in a hood of brown fustian. 'What is it?'
He clenched his fists. 'Has anything happened to Stephen?
How did you know I was here?'

She came up swiftly with her hands over her breasts. 'You
are in danger, brother. You are in danger.'

'That is no news, to come so disturbingly to tell me.' He
took her cold hand and drew her up, with Mat coming behind.
In the room he said to the others, 'This is my sister. Now tell
us why you came, Agnes.'

She looked slowly round at them all in turn, and then said
in a lowered voice, 'You are ensnared. Your enemies know
where you meet and are round you at this moment. Within
half an hour they will attack you.'

'How do you know?' asked Merric harshly. No one else
stirred or spoke.

'I heard our father talking with Master Hawes,' she said wide-eyed. 'And two others. They have arrested some of the Company, among them Master Dove. They are coming to take you.'

'Then he set them on my track,' said Merric fiercely, and she bowed her head. 'Let us go at once to our covert-places,' he went on to the others. 'Let us call on our friends to rise without delay; for our hearts die with this deathbed chill of waiting.'

Mat went over to the front-window and opened the shutters with slow care. 'It is too late. They are coming down the street.'

'It is too late for talking,' said Tom, 'but soon enough for swords to come out of the darkness.'

'We must get the word to our friends in Kent and Essex,' said Merric. 'If that is done in time, we can live or die as best our swords allow, but we shall know that our avengers are sure.'

'You have said it,' answered Mat. 'Go across the roofs with Tom, and take your sister with you. We others shall keep the soldiers engaged below.'

'Let us at least draw lots,' Merric began, but Mat broke loudly in.

'There is no time for games. Do as I tell you.'

The noise of a banging on the street-door reached the attic room, shaking the walls slightly. A wisp of plaster fell on to Mat's face, but he showed no sign of noticing it. With a sign to the others, he went out, down the stairs. Merric looked at Tom, who nodded, and then went to the back-window. 'Come, my dear one,' said Merric, turning to Agnes, who stood unmoving in the middle of the room, with staring eyes.

'If only I were a man, to die with a sword, in a cause of great words,' she said.

Merric made a movement towards her, then paused. 'Bring her along, Tom,' he said gently, and climbed out of the window on to the narrow leads. The weathercock of the smaller next-door house was groaning and dipping to one side, and the clouds were thinner. 'Keep low,' he said without looking back, and began wriggling across the flat ledge. Agnes came down behind him, but he kept his eyes straight ahead.

At the end of the leads he had to slide down some nine feet of sloping tiles, with nothing to hold and only a wooden gutter to stop him falling into the backyard. Lowering himself down, he clung to the leads as long as possible, and then felt his heels meeting the gutter, which held firm. Now at last he turned and looked up. Agnes had reached the end of the leads above him. She leaned down with parted lips and bright eyes, unhooded in a flurry of bright curls, and then sat on the edge, slowly beginning to lower herself. He caught her ankle to halt her.

'We are together after all,' she murmured.

Tom crept up beside her. 'Only one at a time on the gutter,' he said, and caught her belt. 'We mustn't try its strength too far.'

'I should like to stay here for ever,' she said.

'At all costs we must get through to Kent and Essex,' said Merric. 'Only when the forces from the counties attack will it be useful to call on the Londoners . . .'

'Move along to the window,' said Tom. 'You have rested long enough.'

Still holding Agnes's ankles to steady himself, he got half-way up on the slightly-raised roof of the further house, making for the attic-window. Then he let Agnes go. A crossbow-bolt rattled through the air and smashed a tile about six yards off. But at that moment the bells began to ring. First one, then another, then another. Bells on bells, ringing in the sky and in the earth, shaking the roof-timbers and the hearts of men. Ringing out of the clouds, out of the deep of the earth. Agnes gave a little cry and slid down on her back beside Merric, who caught her with his free arm. The gutter held, and they lay side by side on the tiles.

'The Queen is dead,' shouted Tom, set against the glistening grey sky.

'Hold me fast, or I am dead,' murmured Agnes.

'Now there is nothing to fear,' said Tom, shouting through the noise. 'Let us go back the way we came.'

'No, let us go on,' replied Merric.

'Now Stephen will be free,' said Agnes close to his ear, with tickling curls. 'How sweet are these bells of salvation,

like a rain of kindly golden fire on the earth. O that I might
lie here for ever, without a name.'

XIII

On the 17th November, Mass was said from five to seven
o'clock in the morning in the Queen's chamber. When the
priest came to the words *Agnus dei qui tollis peccata mundi,*
she answered in her deep bass voice, *Miserere nobis . . . dona
nobis poenam . . .* Then she sank back into a hidden meditation. When the priest took the host, to consume it in his
mouth, she adored it yearningly with her eyes; and at the
moment when the host went into his mouth, she died.

Her women wailed. The cries went down the corridors. The
bells began ringing. The word went whispered down the
streets.

Parliament was called to the Bar of the Lords.

Through London went the word: Dead, dead.

'Is it true this time?'

'Yes, yes, and again yes.'

Wait, wait, and make sure.

Between eleven and twelve o'clock the heralds-at-arms were
announcing that the Lady Elizabeth was Queen of England,
France, and Ireland, and Defender of the Faith. The trumpets
sang, and a crowd of nobles clustered round the heralds. Look,
the Duke of Norfolk and the Earl of Shrewsbury!

This time it is true. Listen to the bells.

XIV

Stephen came slowly and awkwardly down the street,
watching the noisy people. In every street a bonfire was being
heaped. People were dancing and singing. People were
laughing.

He turned down the alley and came to Hugh's door. Hugh
answered his knock, stared a moment, and then folded him
in his arms. 'What has happened?' asked Stephen, reluctant
to go inside the house.

'The Queen is dead.'

'Yes, I knew that. But what has happened? Have you seen the people? I had forgotten the faces of people . . . And how could the death of one woman change the world like this? Now I doubt everything. I am more afraid than when I stood before the men of blood. What is to come of it all?'

'Have we not worked for it?' asked Hugh, drawing him in.

'We worked . . . and we died. But was it for this? What has happened? That is what I cannot understand.'

'Cardinal Pole is dying in Lambeth. The Pope's rule is ended in England.'

Stephen passed his hand over his brow. 'I still do not know what has happened. Perhaps I was one of those marked for the dying, and I cannot return to life. What are we to do now that we are saved? What are we to do if we are to be worthy of the gift of life?'

They went through into the yard. 'I know something of what you feel,' said Hugh slowly. 'We have been resisting evil, till the bar against which we pressed has grown into our flesh; and now it has fallen away and we stagger giddily forward. So long we have thought only of the breaking of that bar, we have failed to see what lies ahead.'

'Ah, yes,' said Stephen, 'but there is more than that. How are we to keep faith with our dead? Can we offer them anything but a brotherly earth in which the people have regained their birthright? For the people are themselves the birthright. The fellowship and unity of the people: nothing less can we give to our dead on an earth without hedges and divisions. I saw the shopkeepers and the merchants rejoicing, but how can Christ reign in a world where profit lives? How can man come home to his own heart?'

'You trouble me,' said Hugh. 'I know what you say is true; but I had hoped for some peace at last.'

'Not I trouble you,' said Stephen sadly, 'but the voices of our dead.'

They turned as Merric came running out. 'Rosbel said you were here.' He seized Stephen's hands, 'Now I am happy, now I am freed into my own life.'

Stephen regarded his face. 'You have come a long way

since I saw you; and now for the first time I feel a lightening of my soul.'

'You are coming with me into Essex,' said Merric. 'I have now a large sum of money under my hand, and I mean to settle with Jacint at Dunmow. Rafe Heygate is coming with us, and you also.'

Stephen stood in a confused state. 'Is it as easy as all that?' he asked. 'Can we ride back into life, with no questions asked?' He shivered. 'My Mabel . . . I have been afraid most of all that I dreamed her love for me. How can I take her hand and lead her into this strange place that is called the world? We were married elsewhere.'

'Go to her,' said Merric, 'and bring her here. Tomorrow morning we'll all start off together.' He turned to Hugh. 'You still say that you won't come?'

'I must stay here,' said Hugh with a shake of the head. 'Here it was that my beloved wife died . . . here it was . . .' He broke down and turned away. 'Here is my life and my death, my sin and my hope of redemption.'

'Go and fetch Mabel,' said Merric to Stephen, 'while I go for Rafe. We shall start a new life in Essex and possess our souls in strength and charity.' He kicked at a stone in the yard. 'I hate this London and its muddy sins.'

'I shall go to her and hear what she says,' said Stephen. The two brothers went out by the backgate.

Hugh watched them go, and then returned into the house. Rosbel, in a neat dress, with her hair glistening and combed, stood aside to let him pass, and then followed him a few paces. But he did not seem aware of her. He went up to Mary's room, knocked, and entered. Agnes was still there. 'I am going now,' she said.

'I cannot thank you,' he answered humbly.

'We are almost of an age to a day,' said Agnes, looking at Mary, who lay asleep on her back. 'And sometimes I feel that we came from the same womb. When she was rent in the convent, I felt as if she was saving me from a terrible attack; and I am glad that I have had the chance to repay a little of what I owe her.'

After a while Hugh said, 'There is nothing I can do for you, nothing.'

'Except love me.'

He made a hopeless gesture. 'There is no merit in that.'

She said musingly, 'You took the words from my mouth. There is nothing I can do for you.'

He smiled wanly. 'And when you say that, I find your answer on my lips. Nothing except love me.'

'It is best like this,' she said at last. 'I must go back to my mother.'

She hurried out, and he stood lost for a moment. Then he saw that Mary was awake and watching. 'I thought you were asleep,' he said.

'I pass from one dream to another,' she said, 'but sometimes I think I never sleep.'

He gave a troubled look at her eyes, but they were clear. He approached and knelt at her side. 'My dear one . . .'

She laid her head on his hand. 'You are still afraid of me, and sometimes I cannot tell fear from hatred. Is that right or wrong? Do you hate me because I killed my mother when I was born? Or is it some other thing? . . . That is one of the questions that have always lain between us. Agnes also fears and hates me, so that I feel you both are alike . . . closer than I can ever be to either of you . . . Why is that? From now on I must ask all the questions that come into my mind, even if I get no answers . . .'

He kneeled there silent for a long time, then spoke in a strangled voice. 'What is repentance? . . . It is a mere retching of the soul unless it leads at once to a new life . . . I want to tear my body to shreds before you like a rotten rag . . . but that would avail nothing . . . The deepest pang and punishment of sin, my daughter, begins when the sinner realises that he does not know his sin. To cry out: I have killed, I have stolen, I have fornicated. That is easy. But when the sinner finds that the murder and the theft and the fornication hold a secret he cannot grasp, a secret which slays him with its hidden daggers, then he is indeed in the hands of the living God. Woe, woe, woe to such a man! For such a man am I.'

She caressed his hair. 'I shall be a good daughter. I shall make you happy despite God.'

Stephen paused outside the door, then knocked. The frail

startled girl answered; but without waiting for her denials he pushed in, and shouted 'Mabel! Where are you, Mabel?' Mrs. Hudley came out of the kitchen, smelling of cloves.

'Mabel has gone away. You cannot see her.'

But Stephen was sure that he had heard a distant cry. Pushing Mrs. Hudley aside, he went on upstairs, still crying out Mabel's name; and as he neared her room, he heard her answer. Unbolting the door, he went in. She was already out of bed, barefooted, doing up her sleek whitegold hair, swaying a little with dizziness. She looked thinner and her eyes were strangely large, but otherwise she was unchanged. When she saw him, a slow flush spread over her pale face and her full mouth half-opened.

'Beloved,' he said, with open hands, unable to touch her.

'I am coming with you,' she said. 'I have lain listening to the bells all day, and I knew that you would come.'

'You want to come?' he asked clumsily. 'The Queen is dead, and the Pope and the Spaniards no longer rule England. Will you come with me as my wife?'

'But I am already your wife,' she said in surprise. 'I am bearing your child. With whom else should I go?'

He fell at her feet and kissed the hem of her gown.

Mrs. Hudley appeared outside the door, hovering haggard-eyed. 'I won't have a jailbird for my son, even if the Queen is dead. The world may fall apart, but a parent still has her rights if she's a widow.'

'Put my shoes on,' said Mabel to Stephen. 'They're under the bed at the end.'

He found the shoes and buckled them on, while Mrs. Hudley still threatened in a rambling scared way. Then he took Mabel up in his arms, brushed past Mrs. Hudley, and walked downstairs. Near the frontdoor the thin maid sidled up and whispered, 'She's got a priest in the green bedroom.'

Stephen carried Mabel out into the street, where a bonfire was being lighted. 'How did you get out of the jail?' she asked.

'As soon as the Queen was known to be dying, they treated us well and swore they had no liking for the monks. Then one of them privily let me out after the proclamation of Elizabeth.' They walked on, and he asked her, 'Don't you want to know where we're going?'

'It's all one to me if I am with you,' she said. Then she laughed. 'It wasn't the first time you got me with child. It was the second time.'

'We are going into the country,' he said. 'Into Essex.'

'I am glad of it.'

They were surrounded suddenly by a shouting group of round-dancers, and found themselves at the heart of the dancing. 'Kiss her!' one of the girls cried out; and there, while the others danced and sang round them, he held her at last in his arms.

XV

Next day they were riding out of London, the four of them, Merric and Rafe, Stephen and Mabel, when they were caught in a press of people near the gates. Moving with them into West Smithfield, they saw a procession coming out of the fields towards Lord North's Place, the Charterhouse. Lords and ladies, knights and gentlewomen, with many banners and with much music.

The people were climbing all over the waterconduit and the trees, on to the roofs of the scattered houses near. So many got on to a thatched cottage that a patch gave way and a man fell through. Merric and his party stood in their stirrups to see.

The Lady Elizabeth was coming to London. For a moment they saw the glint of her reddish hair and sharp blue eyes, and then she was past, in a tumult of cheering. The crowd laughed and sang, waiting with happy interest till the last knight had ridden by, and then rushing to get a glimpse through the charterhouse-gates.

'We can ride on now,' said Merric; and so they rode on away from London, between the furrowed fields where the seed was lying in rich darkness. Towards the bright lines of delicate elm-tracery and the smoky hills of winter.

THE END

The following pages contain a list of titles which have been reprinted in this series

PORTWAY & NEW PORTWAY

NON-FICTION

Anderson, Verily	Beware of children
Anderson, Verily	Daughters of divinity
Armstrong, Martin	Lady Hester Stanhope
Arnothy, Christine	It's not so easy to live
Asquith, Margot	The autobiography of Margot Asquith
Barke, James	The green hills far away
Bentley, Phyllis	The Pennine weaver
Bishop, W.A.	Winged warfare
Blain, William	Home is the sailor
Brittain, Vera	Testament of experience
Brittain, Vera	Testament of friendship
Brittain, Vera	Testament of youth
Buchan, John	The clearing house
Cobbett, William	Cottage economy
Crozier, F.P.	Ireland for ever
Day, J. Wentworth	Ghosts and witches
Dunnett, Alastair M.	It's too late in the year
Edmonds, Charles	A subaltern's war
Evans, A.J.	The escaping club
Falk, Bernard	Old Q's daughter
Fields, Gracie	Sing as we go
Firbank, Thomas	A country of memorable honour
Gandy, Ida	A Wiltshire childhood
Gary, Romain	Promise at dawn
Gibbons, Floyd	Red knight of Germany
Gibbs, Philip	Realities of war
Gough, General Sir Hubert	The fifth army
Grant, I.F.	Economic history of Scotland
Hart, B.H. Liddell	Great captains unveiled
Hart, B.H. Liddell	A history of the world war 1914—18
Hart, B.H. Liddell	The letters of private Wheeler
Hart, B.H. Liddell	The other side of the hill
Hecht, Hans	Robert Burns: the man and his work
Holtby, Winifred	Letters to a friend
Huggett, Renee & Berry, Paul	Daughters of Cain
Jones, Ira	King of air fighters
Jones, Jack	Give me back my heart
Jones, Jack	Me and mine

PORTWAY & NEW PORTWAY

FICTION

Albert, Edward	Herrin' Jennie
Aldington, Richard	All men are enemies
Aldington, Richard	Death of a hero
Anand, Mulk Raj	Seven summers
Andersch, Alfred	Flight to afar
Anderson, Verily	Our square
Anderson, Verily	Spam tomorrow
Anthony, Evelyn	Imperial highness
Anthony, Evelyn	Victoria
Arlen, Michael	Men dislike women
Arnim, Elizabeth von	Elizabeth and her German garden
Arnim, Elizabeth von	Mr. Skeffington
Ashton, Helen	Doctor Serocold
Ashton, Helen	Family cruise
Ashton, Helen	Footman in powder
Ashton, Helen	The half-crown house
Ashton, Helen	Letty Landon
Ashton, Helen	Swan of Usk
Barke, James	Bonnie Jean
Barke, James	The land of the leal
Barke, James	Major operation
Barke, James	The song of the green thorn tree
Barke, James	The well of the silent harp
Basso, Hamilton	Pompey's head
Bates, H.E.	The purple plain
Baum, Vicki	Berlin hotel
Benson, R.H.	Come rack come rope
Benson, R.H.	Lord of the world
Bentley, Phyllis	Love and money
Bentley, Phyllis	A modern tragedy
Bentley, Phyllis	The partnership
Bentley, Phyllis	Sleep in peace
Bentley, Phyllis	Take courage
Bentley, Phyllis	Trio
Birmingham, George A.	General John Regan
Birmingham, George A.	The inviolable sanctuary
Blackmore, R.D.	Mary Anerley
Blain, William	Witch's blood

iii

Blaker, Richard	The needle watcher
Bottome, Phyllis	Murder in the bud
Bromfield, Louis	Early autumn
Bromfield, Louis	A good woman
Bromfield, Louis	The green bay tree
Bromfield, Louis	The rains came
Bromfield, Louis	Wild is the river
Brophy, John	Gentleman of Stratford
Brophy, John	Rocky road
Brophy, John	Waterfront
Broster, D.K.	Child royal
Broster, D.K.	A fire of driftwood
Broster, D.K.	Sea without a haven
Broster, D.K.	Ships in the bay
Broster, D.K. & Taylor, G.W.	Chantemerle
Broster, D.K. & Forester, G.	World under snow
Buchan, John	Grey weather
Buchan, John	The Runagates club
Buck, Pearl S. *(Trans.)*	All men are brothers (2 vols.)
Buck, Pearl S.	Fighting angel
Buck, Pearl S.	The hidden flower
Buck, Pearl S.	A house divided
Buck, Pearl S.	Imperial woman
Caldwell, Erskine	Place called Estherville
Caldwell, Taylor	The arm and the darkness
Caldwell, Taylor	The beautiful is vanished
Caldwell, Taylor	The final hour
Caldwell, Taylor	Let love come last
Caldwell, Taylor	Melissa
Caldwell, Taylor	Tender victory
Callow, Philip	Common people
Chandos, Dane	Abbie
Chapman, Hester W.	To be a king
Church, Richard	The dangerous years
Collins, Wilkie	Armadale
Collins, Wilkie	The dead secret
Collins, Wilkie	The haunted hotel
Collins, Wilkie	Poor miss Finch
Common, Jack	Kiddar's luck
Comyns, Barbara	Our spoons came from Woolworths
Cookson, Catherine	Maggie Rowan
Cookson, Catherine	Mary Ann's angels

v

Riley, William	Laycock of Lonedale
Roberts, Kenneth	Arundel
Roberts, Kenneth	Oliver Wiswell
Roche, Mazo de la	Delight
Roche, Mazo de la	Growth of a man
Roche, Mazo de la	The two saplings
Sandstrom, Flora	The midwife of Pont Clery
Sandstrom, Flora	The virtuous women of Pont Clery
Seton, Anya	The mistletoe and sword
Seymour, Beatrice K.	Maids and mistresses
Shellabarger, Samuel	Captain from Castile
Sherriff, R.C.	The Hopkins manuscript
Shiel, M.P.	Prince Zaleski
Sienkiewicz, Henryk	The deluge (2 vols.)
Sienkiewicz, Henryk	With fire and sword
Sinclair, Upton	Boston
Sinclair, Upton	The flivver king
Sinclair, Upton	The jungle
Sinclair, Upton	Oil!
Sinclair, Upton	They call me carpenter

WORLD'S END SERIES

Sinclair, Upton	World's end
Sinclair, Upton	Between two worlds
Sinclair, Upton	Dragon's teeth
Sinclair, Upton	Wide is the gate
Sinclair, Upton	Presidential agent
Sinclair, Upton	Dragon harvest
Sinclair, Upton	A world to win
Sinclair, Upton	Presidential mission
Sinclair, Upton	One clear call
Sinclair, Upton	O shepherds speak
Sinclair, Upton	The return of Lanny Budd
Smith, Betty	A tree grows in Brooklyn
Smith, Eleanor	Caravan
Smith, Sheila Kaye-	The children's summer
Stone, Irving	Love is eternal
Stone, Irving	Lust for life
Sue, Eugene	The wandering Jew (2 vols.)

PORTWAY JUNIOR

Armstrong, Martin	Said the cat to the dog
Armstrong, Martin	Said the dog to the cat
Atkinson, M.E.	August adventure
Atkinson, M.E.	Going gangster
Atkinson, M.E.	The compass points north
Aymé, Marcel	The wonderful farm
Bacon, Peggy	The good American witch
Baker, Margaret J.	A castle and sixpence
Blackwood, Algernon	Dudley and Gilderoy
Coatsworth, Elizabeth	Cricket and the emperor's son
Edwards, Monica	Killer dog
Edwards, Monica	Operation seabird
Fenner, Phyllis R.	Fun, fun, fun
Haldane, J.B.S.	My friend mr. Leakey
Hill, Lorna	A dream of Sadler's Wells
Hoke, Helen	Jokes, jokes, jokes
Hoke, Helen	Love, love, love
Hoke, Helen	More jokes, jokes, jokes
Hoke, Helen & Randolph, Boris	Puns, puns, puns
Hourihane, Ursula	Christina and the apple woman
Lemming, Joseph	Riddles, riddles, riddles
Lyon, Elinor	Run away home
Parker, Richard	The sword of Ganelon
Pudney, John	Friday adventure
Pullein-Thompson, Christine	Ride by night
Pullein-Thompson, Diana	The secret dog
Pullein-Thompson, Josephine	Janet must ride
Pullein-Thompson, Josephine	One day event
Pullein-Thompson, Josephine	Show jumping secret
Manning-Sanders, Ruth	Children by the sea
Manning-Sanders, Ruth	Elephant
Saville, Malcolm	All summer through
Saville, Malcolm	Christmas at Nettleford
Severn, David	Burglars and bandicoots
Severn, David	Dream gold
Severn, David	The future took us
Sperry, Armstrong	Frozen fire
Sperry, Armstrong	Hull-down for action
Sperry, Armstrong	Thunder country
Stucley, Elizabeth	Springfield home

PORTWAY EDUCATIONAL & ACADEMIC

Abbott, W.C.	Colonel Thomas Blood
Abrams, Mark	The condition of the British people 1911–45
Adams, Francis	History of the elementary school contest in England
Andrews, Kevin	The flight of Ikaros
Balzac, Honoré de	The curé de Tours
Bazeley, E.T.	Homer Lane and the little common-wealth
Bowen, H.C.	Froebel and education by self-activity
Braithwaite, William J.	Lloyd George's ambulance wagon
Brittain, Vera & Taylor, G. Handley	Selected letters of Winifred Holtby and Vera Brittain
Cameron, A.	Chemistry in relation to fire risk and extinction
Clarke, Fred	Education and the social change
Clarke, Fred	Freedom in the educative society
Caldwell-Cook, H.	Play way (1 map, 14 illustrations)
Crozier, F.P.	A brass hat in no man's-land
Crozier, F.P.	Angels on horseback
Crozier, F.P.	The men I killed
Dewey, John	Educational essays
Dewey, John	Interest and effort in education
Duncan, John	The education of the ordinary child
Fearnsides, W.G. & Bulman, O.M.B.	Geology in the service of man
Ferrier, Susan	Destiny. (2 vols.)
Galt, John	The provost
Gates, H.L.	The auction of souls
Gilbert, Edmund W.	Brighton old ocean's bauble
Glass, David V.	The town — and a changing civilization
Gronlund, Norman E.	Sociometry in the classroom
Geological survey	The geology of Manchester and the south-east Lancashire coalfield (H.M.S.O.)
Hadow report 1933	Report of the consultative committee on infant and nursery schools (H.M.S.O.)
Harrison, G.B.	The life & death of Robert Devereux Earl of Essex